THE TIGER'S WIFE

THE TIGER'S WIFE

Téa Obreht

WINDSOR
PARAGON

First published 2011
by Weidenfeld & Nicolson
This Large Print edition published 2011
by AudioGO Ltd
by arrangement with
The Orion Publishing Group Ltd

Hardcover   ISBN: 978 1 445 86946 9
Softcover   ISBN: 978 1 445 86947 6

British Library Cataloguing in Publication Data available

Printed and bound in Great Britain by
MPG Books Group Limited

For Štefan Obrecht

In my earliest memory, my grandfather is bald as a stone and he takes me to see the tigers. He puts on his hat, his big-buttoned raincoat, and I wear my lacquered shoes and velvet dress. It is autumn, and I am four years old. The certainty of this process: my grandfather's hand, the bright hiss of the trolley, the dampness of the morning, the crowded walk up the hill to the citadel park. Always in my grandfather's breast pocket: *The Jungle Book,* with its gold-leaf cover and old yellow pages. I am not allowed to hold it, but it will stay open on his knee all afternoon while he recites the passages to me. Even though my grandfather is not wearing his stethoscope or white coat, the lady at the ticket counter in the entrance shed calls him 'Doctor.'

Then there is the popcorn cart, the umbrella stand, a small kiosk with postcards and pictures. Down the stairs and past the aviary where the sharp-eared owls sleep, through the garden that runs the length of the citadel wall, framed with cages. Once there was a king here, a sultan, his Janissaries. Now the cannon windows facing the street hold blocked-off troughs filled with tepid water. The cage bars curve out, rusted orange. In his free hand, my grandfather is carrying the blue bag my grandma has prepared for us. In it: six-day-old cabbage heads for the hippopotamus, carrots and celery for the sheep and deer and the bull moose, who is a kind of phenomenon. In his pocket, my grandfather has hidden some sugar cubes for the pony that pulls the park carriage. I will not remember this as sentimentality, but as greatness.

1

The tigers live in the outer moat of the fortress. We climb the castle stairs, past the waterbirds and the sweating windows of the monkey house, past the wolf growing his winter coat. We pass the bearded vultures and then the bears, asleep all day, smelling of damp earth and the death of something. My grandfather picks me up and props my feet against the handrail so I can look down and see the tigers in the moat.

My grandfather never refers to the tiger's wife by name. His arm is around me and my feet are on the handrail, and my grandfather might say, 'I once knew a girl who loved tigers so much she almost became one herself.' Because I am little, and my love of tigers comes directly from him, I believe he is talking about me, offering me a fairy tale in which I can imagine myself—and will, for years and years.

The cages face a courtyard, and we go down the stairs and walk slowly from cage to cage. There is a panther, too, ghost spots paling his oil-slick coat; a sleepy, bloated lion from Africa. But the tigers are awake and livid, bright with rancor. Stripe-lashed shoulders rolling, they flank one another up and down the narrow causeway of rock, and the smell of them is sour and warm and fills everything. It will stay with me the whole day, even after I have had my bath and gone to bed, and will return at random times: at school, at a friend's birthday party, even years later, at the pathology lab, or on the drive home from Galina.

I remember this, too: an altercation. A small group of people stand clustered around the tigers' cage. Among them: a boy with a parrot-shaped balloon, a woman in a purple coat, and a bearded

2

man who is wearing the brown uniform of a zookeeper. The man has a broom and a dustpan on a long handle, and he is sweeping the area between the cage and the outer railing. He walks up and down, sweeping up juice boxes and candy wrappers, bits of popcorn people have tried to throw at the tigers. The tigers walk up and down with him. The woman in purple is saying something and smiling, and he smiles back at her. She has brown hair. The dustpan keeper stops and leans against the handle of his broom, and as he does so, the big tiger sweeps by, rubbing against the bars of the cage, rumbling, and the keeper puts a hand through the bars and touches its flank. For a moment, nothing. And then pandemonium.

The tiger rounds on him and the woman shrieks, and suddenly the dustpan keeper's shoulder is between the bars, and he is twisting, twisting his head away and trying to reach for the outer railing so that he has something to hold on to. The tiger has the dustpan keeper's arm the way a dog holds a large bone: upright between his paws, gnawing on the top. Two men who have been standing by with children jump over the railing and grab the dustpan keeper's waist and flailing arm and try to pull him away. A third man jams his umbrella through the bars and pushes it over and over again into the tiger's ribs. An outraged scream from the tiger, and then it stands up on its hind legs and hugs the dustpan keeper's arm and shakes its head from side to side, like it's pulling on rope. Its ears are flattened, and it is making a noise like a locomotive. The dustpan keeper's face is white, and this entire time he hasn't made a sound.

Then suddenly, it's no longer worth it, and the

3

tiger lets go. The three men fall away, and there is a splatter of blood. The tiger is lashing its tail, and the dustpan keeper is crawling under the outer railing and standing up. The woman in purple has vanished. My grandfather has not turned away. I am four years old, but he has not turned me away, either. I see it all, and, later, there is the fact that he wants me to have seen.

Then the dustpan keeper is hurrying our way, winding a piece of torn shirt across his arm. He is red-faced and angry, on his way to the infirmary. At the time, I believe this is fear, but later I will know it as embarrassment, as shame. The tigers, agitated, are lunging back and forth across the grate. The keeper is leaving a dark trail on the gravel behind him. As he passes us, my grandfather says: 'My God, you're a fool, aren't you?' and the man says something in reply, something I know not to repeat.

Instead, shrill and self-righteous in my lacquered boots, brave because my grandfather is holding my hand, I say: 'He's a fool, isn't he, Grandpa?'

But my grandfather is already walking after the dustpan keeper, pulling me along, calling for the man to stop so he can help him.

1

THE COAST

The forty days of the soul begin on the morning after death. That first night, before its forty days begin, the soul lies still against sweated-on pillows and watches the living fold the hands and close the eyes, choke the room with smoke and silence to keep the new soul from the doors and the windows and the cracks in the floor so that it does not run out of the house like a river. The living know that, at daybreak, the soul will leave them and make its way to the places of its past—the schools and dormitories of its youth, army barracks and tenements, houses razed to the ground and rebuilt, places that recall love and guilt, difficulties and unbridled happiness, optimism and ecstasy, memories of grace meaningless to anyone else— and sometimes this journey will carry it so far for so long that it will forget to come back. For this reason, the living bring their own rituals to a standstill: to welcome the newly loosed spirit, the living will not clean, will not wash or tidy, will not remove the soul's belongings for forty days, hoping that sentiment and longing will bring it home again, encourage it to return with a message, with a sign, or with forgiveness.

If it is properly enticed, the soul will return as the days go by, to rummage through drawers, peer inside cupboards, seek the tactile comfort of its living identity by reassessing the dish rack and the doorbell and the telephone, reminding itself of

5

functionality, all the time touching things that produce sound and make its presence known to the inhabitants of the house.

Speaking quietly into the phone, my grandma reminded me of this after she told me of my grandfather's death. For her, the forty days were fact and common sense, knowledge left over from burying two parents and an older sister, assorted cousins and strangers from her hometown, a formula she had recited to comfort my grandfather whenever he lost a patient in whom he was particularly invested—a superstition, according to him, but something in which he had indulged her with less and less protest as old age had hardened her beliefs.

My grandma was shocked, angry because we had been robbed of my grandfather's forty days, reduced now to thirty-seven or thirty-eight by the circumstances of his death. He had died alone, on a trip away from home; she hadn't known that he was already dead when she ironed his clothes the day before, or washed the dishes that morning, and she couldn't account for the spiritual consequences of her ignorance. He had died in a clinic in an obscure town called Zdrevkov on the other side of the border; no one my grandma had spoken to knew where Zdrevkov was, and when she asked me, I told her the truth: I had no idea what he had been doing there.

'You're lying,' she said.

'Bako, I'm not.'

'He told us he was on his way to meet you.'

'That can't be right,' I said.

He had lied to her, I realized, and lied to me. He had taken advantage of my own cross-country trip

6

to slip away—a week ago, she was saying, by bus, right after I had set out myself—and had gone off for some reason unknown to either of us. It had taken the Zdrevkov clinic staff three whole days to track my grandma down after he died, to tell her and my mother that he was dead, arrange to send his body. It had arrived at the City morgue that morning, but by then, I was already four hundred miles from home, standing in the public bathroom at the last service station before the border, the pay phone against my ear, my pant legs rolled up, sandals in hand, bare feet slipping on the green tiles under the broken sink.

Somebody had fastened a bent hose onto the faucet, and it hung, nozzle down, from the boiler pipes, coughing thin streams of water onto the floor. It must have been going for hours: water was everywhere, flooding the tile grooves and pooling around the rims of the squat toilets, dripping over the doorstep and into the dried-up garden behind the shack. None of this fazed the bathroom attendant, a middle-aged woman with an orange scarf tied around her hair, whom I had found dozing in a corner chair and dismissed from the room with a handful of bills, afraid of what those seven missed beeper pages from my grandma meant before I even picked up the receiver.

I was furious with her for not having told me that my grandfather had left home. He had told her and my mother that he was worried about my goodwill mission, about the inoculations at the Brejevina orphanage, and that he was coming down to help. But I couldn't berate my grandma without giving myself away, because she would have told me if she had known about his illness,

7

which my grandfather and I had hidden from her. So I let her talk, and said nothing about how I had been with him at the Military Academy of Medicine three months before when he had found out, or how the oncologist, a lifelong colleague of my grandfather's, had shown him the scans and my grandfather had put his hat down on his knee and said, 'Fuck. You go looking for a gnat and you find a donkey.'

I put two more coins into the slot, and the phone whirred. Sparrows were diving from the brick ledges of the bathroom walls, dropping into the puddles at my feet, shivering water over their backs. The sun outside had baked the early afternoon into stillness, and the hot, wet air stood in the room with me, shining in the doorway that led out to the road, where the cars at border control were packed in a tight line along the glazed tarmac. I could see our car, left side dented from a recent run-in with a tractor, and Zóra sitting in the driver's seat, door propped open, one long leg dragging along the ground, glances darting back toward the bathroom more and more often as she drew closer to the customs booth.

'They called last night,' my grandma was saying, her voice louder. 'And I thought, *they've made a mistake.* I didn't want to call you until we were sure, to worry you in case it wasn't him. But your mother went down to the morgue this morning.' She was quiet, and then: 'I don't understand, I don't understand any of it.'

'I don't either, Bako,' I said.

'He was going to meet you.'

'I didn't know about it.'

Then the tone of her voice changed. She was

suspicious, my grandma, of why I wasn't crying, why I wasn't hysterical. For the first ten minutes of our conversation, she had probably allowed herself to believe that my calm was the result of my being in a foreign hospital, on assignment, surrounded, perhaps, by colleagues. She would have challenged me a lot sooner if she had known that I was hiding in the border-stop bathroom so that Zóra wouldn't overhear.

She said, 'Haven't you got anything to say?'

'I just don't know, Bako. Why would he lie about coming to see me?'

'You haven't asked if it was an accident,' she said. 'Why haven't you asked that? Why haven't you asked how he died?'

'I didn't even know he had left home,' I said. 'I didn't know any of this was going on.'

'You're not crying,' she said.

'Neither are you.'

'Your mother is heartbroken,' she said to me. 'He must have known. They said he was very ill— so he must have known, he must have told someone. Was it you?'

'If he had known, he wouldn't have gone anywhere,' I said, with what I hoped was conviction. 'He would have known better.' There were white towels stacked neatly on a metal shelf above the mirror, and I wiped my face and neck with one, and then another, and the skin of my face and neck left gray smears on towel after towel until I had used up five. There was no laundry basket to put them in, so I left them in the sink. 'Where is this place where they found him?' I said. 'How far did he go?'

'I don't know,' she said. 'They didn't tell us.

9

Somewhere on the other side.'

'Maybe it was a specialty clinic,' I said.

'He was on his way to see you.'

'Did he leave a letter?'

He hadn't. My mother and grandma, I realized, had both probably seen his departure as part of his unwillingness to retire, like his relationship with a new housebound patient outside the City—a patient we had made up as a cover for his visits to the oncologist friend from the weekly doctors' luncheon, a man who gave injections of some formulas that were supposed to help with the pain. Colorful formulas, my grandfather said when he came home, as if he knew the whole time that the formulas were just water laced with food coloring, as if it didn't matter anymore. He had, at first, more or less retained his healthy cast, which made hiding his illness easier; but after seeing him come out of these sessions just once, I had threatened to tell my mother, and he said: 'Don't you dare.' And that was that.

My grandma was asking me: 'Are you already in Brejevina?'

'We're at the border,' I said. 'We just came over on the ferry.'

Outside, the line of cars was beginning to move again. I saw Zóra put her cigarette out on the ground, pull her leg back in and slam the door. A flurry of people who had assembled on the gravel shoulder to stretch and smoke, to check their tires and fill water bottles at the fountain, to look impatiently down the line, or dispose of pastries and sandwiches they had been attempting to smuggle, or urinate against the side of the bathroom, scrambled to get back to their vehicles.

10

My grandma was silent for a few moments. I could hear the line clicking, and then she said: 'Your mother wants to have the funeral in the next few days. Couldn't Zóra go on to Brejevina by herself?'

If I had told Zóra about it, she would have made me go home immediately. She would have given me the car, taken the vaccine coolers, and hitchhiked across the border to make the University's good-faith delivery to the orphanage at Brejevina up the coast. But I said: 'We're almost there, Bako, and a lot of kids are waiting on these shots.'

She didn't ask me again. My grandma just gave me the date of the funeral, the time, the place, even though I already knew where it would be, up on Strmina, the hill overlooking the City, where Mother Vera, my great-great-grandmother, was buried. After she hung up, I ran the faucet with my elbow and filled the water bottles I had brought as my pretext for getting out of the car. On the gravel outside, I rinsed off my feet before putting my shoes back on; Zóra left the engine running and jumped out to take her turn while I climbed into the driver's seat, pulled it forward to compensate for my height, and made sure our licenses and medication import documents were lined up in the correct order on the dashboard. Two cars in front of us, a customs official, green shirt clinging to his chest, was opening the hatchback of an elderly couple's car, leaning carefully into it, unzipping suitcases with a gloved hand.

When Zóra got back, I didn't tell her anything about my grandfather. It had already been a bleak year for us both. I had made the mistake of

11

walking out with the nurses during the strike in January; rewarded for my efforts with an indefinite suspension from the Vojvodja clinic, I had been housebound for months—a blessing, in a way, because it meant I was around for my grandfather when the diagnosis came in. He was glad of it at first, but never passed up the opportunity to call me a gullible jackass for getting suspended. And then, as his illness wore on, he began spending less and less time at home, and suggested I do the same; he didn't want me hanging around, looking morose, scaring the hell out of him when he woke up without his glasses on to find me hovering over his bed in the middle of the night. My behavior, he said, was tipping my grandma off about his illness, making her suspicious of our silences and exchanges, and of the fact that my grandfather and I were busier than ever now that we were respectively retired and suspended. He wanted me to think about my specialization, too, about what I would do with myself once the suspension was lifted—he was not surprised that Srdjan, a professor of biochemical engineering with whom I had, according to my grandfather, 'been tangling,' had failed to put in a good word for me with the suspension committee. At my grandfather's suggestion, I had gone back to volunteering with the University's United Clinics program, something I hadn't done since the end of the war.

Zóra was using this volunteering mission as an excuse to get away from a blowup at the Military Academy of Medicine. Four years after getting her medical degree, she was still at the trauma center, hoping that exposure to a variety of surgical procedures would help her decide on a specialization. Unfortunately, she had spent the bulk of that time under a trauma director known throughout the City as Ironglove—a name he had earned during his days as chief of obstetrics, when he had failed to remove the silver bracelets he kept stacked on his wrist during pelvic examinations. Zóra was a woman of principle, an open atheist. At the age of thirteen, a priest had told her that animals had no souls, and she had said, 'Well then, fuck you, Pops,' and walked out of church; four years of butting heads with Ironglove had culminated in an incident that Zóra, under the direction of the state prosecutor, was prohibited from discussing. Zóra's silence on the subject extended even to me, but the scraps I had heard around hospital hallways centered around a railway worker, an accident, and a digital amputation during which Ironglove, who may or may not have been inebriated, had said something like: 'Don't worry, sir—it's a lot easier to watch the second finger come off if you're biting down on the first.'

Naturally, a lawsuit was in the works, and Zóra had been summoned back to testify against Ironglove. Despite his reputation, he was still well connected in the medical community, and now Zóra was torn between sticking it to a man she had despised for years, and risking a career and reputation she was just beginning to build for herself; for the first time no one—not me, not her father, not her latest boyfriend—could point her in the right direction. After setting out, we had spent a week at the United Clinics headquarters for our briefing and training, and all this time she had met both my curiosity and the state prosecutor's

13

incessant phone calls with the same determined silence. Then yesterday, against all odds, she had admitted to wanting my grandfather's advice as soon as we got back to the City. She hadn't seen him around the hospital for the past month, hadn't seen his graying face, the way his skin was starting to loosen around his bones.

We watched the customs officer confiscate two jars of beach pebbles from the elderly couple, and wave the next car through; when he got to us, he spent twenty minutes looking over our passports and identity cards, our letters of certification from the University. He opened the medicine coolers and lined them up on the tarmac while Zóra towered over him, arms crossed, and then said, 'You realize, of course, that the fact that it's in a cooler means it's temperature-sensitive—or don't they teach you about refrigeration at the village schoolhouse?' knowing that everything was in order, knowing that, realistically, he couldn't touch us. This challenge, however, prompted him to search the car for weapons, stowaways, shellfish, and uncertified pets for a further thirty minutes.

Twelve years ago, before the war, the people of Brejevina had been our people. The border had been a joke, an occasional formality, and you used to drive or fly or walk across as you pleased, by woodland, by water, by open plain. You used to offer the customs officials sandwiches or jars of pickled peppers as you went through. Nobody asked you your name—although, as it turned out, everyone had apparently been anxious about it all along, about how your name started and ended. Our assignment in Brejevina was intended to rebuild something. Our University wanted to

14

collaborate with the local government in getting several orphanages on their feet, and to begin attracting young people from across the border back to the City. That was the long-term diplomatic objective of our journey—but in layman's terms Zóra and I were there to sanitize children orphaned by our own soldiers, to examine them for pneumonia and tuberculosis and lice, to inoculate them against measles, mumps, rubella, and other assorted diseases to which they had been subjected during the war and the years of destitution that followed it. Our contact in Brejevina, a Franciscan monk named Fra Antun, had been enthusiastic and hospitable, paging us to make sure our journey was unencumbered, and to assure us that his parents, conveniently enough, were looking forward to hosting us. His voice was always cheerful, especially for a man who had spent the last three years fighting to fund the establishment and construction of the first official orphanage on the coast, and who was, in the meantime, housing sixty orphaned children at a monastery intended to accommodate twenty monks.

Zóra and I were joining up for this charitable trip before our lives took us apart for the first time in the twenty-some-odd years we had known each other. We would wear our white doctors' coats even off duty in order to appear simultaneously trustworthy and disconcerting. We were formidable with our four supplies coolers loaded with vials of MMR-II and IPV, with boxes of candy we were bringing to stave off the crying and screaming we felt certain would ensue once the inoculation got going. We had an old map, which we kept in the car years after it had become completely inaccurate. We had used the map on every road trip we had ever taken, and it showed in the marker scribbling all over it: the crossed-out areas we were supposed to avoid on our way to some medical conference or other, the stick man holding crudely drawn skis on a mountain resort we had loved that was no longer a part of our country.

I couldn't find Zdrevkov, the place where my grandfather died, on that map. I couldn't find Brejevina either, but I had known in advance that it was missing, so we had drawn it in. It was a small seaside village forty kilometers east of the new border. We drove through red-roofed villages that clung to the lip of the sea, past churches and horse pastures, past steep plains bright with purple bellflowers, past sunlit waterfalls that thrust out of the sheer rock-face above the road. Every so often we entered woodland, high pine forests dotted with olives and cypresses, the sea flashing like a knife where the forest fell away down the slope. Parts of the road were well paved, but there were places where it ripped up into ruts and stretches of gravel that hadn't been fixed in years.

The car was pitching up and down through the ruts on the shoulder, and I could hear the glass vials in the cooler shivering. Thirty kilometers out of Brejevina, we started to see more signs for pensions and restaurants, tourist places that were slowly beginning to rely on the offshore islands for business again. We started seeing fruit and specialty food stands, signs for homemade pepper cookies and grape-leaf *rakija,* local honey, sour cherry and fig preserves. I had three missed pages from my grandmother, but Zóra had the mobile, and there was no way to call my grandma back with Zóra in the car. We pulled over at the next rest-stop with a pay phone, a roadside barbecue stand with a blue awning and an outhouse in the adjacent field.

There was a truck parked on the other side of the stand, and a long line of soldiers crowding at the barbecue counter. The men were in camouflage. They fanned themselves with their hats and waved when I got out of the car and headed for the phone booth. Some local gypsy kids, handing out pamphlets for a new nightclub in Brac, laughed at me through the glass. Then they ran to the side of the car to bum cigarettes from Zóra.

From the booth, I could see the army truck, with its dusty, folded tarp, and the grill of Boro's Beefs, where a large man, probably Boro himself, was flipping burger patties and veal shoulders and sausages with the flat part of an enormous knife. Behind the stand, a little way across the field, there was a funny-looking brown cow tied to a post in the ground—I suddenly got the feeling that Boro would routinely use that knife for the cow, and the butchering, and the flipping of the burgers, and the cutting of bread, which made me feel a little sorry for the soldier standing by the condiment counter, spooning diced onions all over his sandwich.

I hadn't noticed my headache while I had been driving, but now it hit me when my grandma picked up after the sixth ring, and her voice was followed by the sharp sound of her hearing aid lancing through the phone line and into the base of my skull. There were soft beeps as she turned it down. I could hear my mother's voice in the background, quiet but determined, talking with some other consoler who had come to pay a call.

My grandma was hysterical. 'His things are gone.'

I told her to calm down, asked her to explain.

'His things!' she said. 'Your grandfather's things, they're—your mother went down to the morgue, and they had his suit and coat and shoes, but his *things,* Natalia—they're all gone, they're not there with him.'

'What things?'

'Look, God—'what things'!' I heard her slap her hands together. 'Do you hear me? I'm telling you his things are *gone*—those bastards at the clinic, they stole them, they stole his hat and umbrella, his wallet. Think—can you believe it? To steal things from a dead man.'

I could believe it, having heard things about it at our own hospital. It happened, usually to the unclaimed dead, and often with very little reprimand. But I said, 'Sometimes there's a mix-up. It can't have been a very big clinic, Bako. There might be a delay. Maybe they forgot to send them.'

'His watch, Natalia.'

'Please, Bako.' I thought of his coat pocket, and of *The Jungle Book,* and wanted to ask if it, too, was missing; but as far as I knew, my grandma had not cried yet, and I was terrified of saying something that would make her cry. I must have thought of the deathless man at this moment; but the thought was so far away I wouldn't find it again until later.

'His *watch.*'

'Do you have the number of the clinic?' I said. 'Have you called them?'

18

'I'm calling and calling,' she said. 'There's no answer. Nobody's there. They've taken his things. God, Natalia, his glasses—they're gone.'

His glasses, I thought—the way he would clean them, put almost the whole lens in his mouth to blow on it before wiping it clean with the little silk cloth he kept in his pocket—and a cold stiffness crept into my ribs and stayed there.

'What kind of place is this, where he died?' my grandma was saying. Her voice, hoarse from shouting, was beginning to break.

'I don't know, Bako,' I said. 'I wish I had known he had gone.'

'None of it would be like this—but you have to lie, the pair of you, always whispering about something. He's lying, you're lying.' I heard my mother try to take the phone from her, and my grandma said, 'No.' I was watching Zóra get out of the car. She straightened up slowly and locked the car door, leaving the cooler on the floor of the passenger side. The gypsy kids were leaning against the back bumper, passing a cigarette back and forth. 'You're sure he didn't leave a note?' My grandma asked me what kind of note, and I said, 'Anything. Any kind of message.'

'I'm telling you, I don't know,' she said.

'What did he say when he left?'

'That he was coming to you.'

It was my turn to be suspicious, to calculate who had known what, and how much of it no one had known at all. He had been counting on the pattern into which we had fallen as a family over the years, the tendency to lie about each other's physical condition and whereabouts to spare one another's feelings and fears; like the time my mother had

19

broken her leg falling off the lake-house garage at Verimovo, and we had told my grandparents that we were delaying our trip home because the house had flooded; or the time my grandmother had had open-heart surgery at a clinic in Strekovac while my mother and I, blissfully oblivious, vacationed in Venice, and my grandfather, lying into a telephone line that was too scrambled to be anything but our own, insisted that he had taken my grandma on an impromptu spa trip to Luzern.

'Let me have the phone number of that clinic in Zdrevkov,' I said.

'Why?' my grandma said, still suspicious.

'Just let me have it.' I had a wrinkled receipt in my coat pocket, and I propped it against the glass. The only pencil I had was worn to a stub; my grandfather's influence, the habit of using the same pencil until it couldn't fit between his fingers anymore. I wrote the number down.

Zóra was waving at me and pointing in the direction of Boro and his beefs, and the crowd at the counter, and I shook my head at her and looked on in desperation as she crossed the mud ruts on the shoulder and got in line behind a blue-eyed soldier who couldn't have been more than nineteen. I saw him look her up and down less than discreetly, and then Zóra said something I couldn't hear. The roar of laughter that erupted from the soldiers around the blue-eyed kid was audible even in the phone booth, however, and the kid's ears went red. Zóra gave me a satisfied look, and then continued to stand there with her arms across her chest, eyeing the chalkboard menu above a drawing of a cow wearing a purple hat, which looked a lot like the cow tied up out back.

20

'Where are you girls now?' my grandma said.

'We'll be in Brejevina by nightfall,' I said. 'We'll do the shots and come straight home. I promise I'll try to be home by the day after tomorrow.' She didn't say anything. 'I'll call the clinic in Zdrevkov,' I said, 'and if it's on the way home I'll go by and get his things, Bako.'

'I still don't know,' she finally said, 'how none of us knew.' She was waiting for me to admit that I had known. 'You're lying to me,' she said.

'I don't know anything, Bako.'

She wanted me to say that I had seen the symptoms but ignored them, or that I had spoken to him about it, anything to comfort her in her fear that, despite being with us, he had been totally alone with the knowledge of his own death.

'Then swear to me,' she said. 'Swear to me on my life that you didn't know.'

It was my turn to be silent. She listened for my oath, but when it didn't come, she said: 'It must be hot out there. Are you girls drinking plenty of water?'

'We're fine.'

A pause. 'If you eat meat, make sure it's not pink in the middle.'

I told her I loved her, and she hung up without a word. I held the dead receiver against my head for a few more minutes, and then I called the clinic in Zdrevkov. You could always tell the backwater places because it would take forever to connect, and when it did, the sound was distant and muffled.

I let the line ring to silence twice, and then tried once more before hanging up and getting in line with Zóra, who had already locked horns with

21

Boro trying to order what our city joints called a 'strengthened burger,' with extra onions. Boro told her that this was Brejevina, and that she could have a double burger if she wanted, but he had never heard of a strengthened burger, and what the hell was that? The stand was cluttered with coolers of raw meat and cast-iron soup pots brimming with something brown and oily. Behind the counter, Boro was terse, and he wanted exact change, probably to stick it to us for that strengthened burger. Zóra held her sandwich in one hand and mine in the other while I went through her coat pockets for her wallet.

'You heard of a place called Zdrevkov?' I asked Boro, leaning over the counter with the pink and blue notes in my hand. 'You know where it is?'

He didn't.

At seven-thirty, the sun banking low into a distant cover of blue clouds, we came within sight of Brejevina and turned off the highway to follow the town road to the sea. The town was smaller than I had expected, with a palm-lined boardwalk that ran tight between the shore and the shops and restaurants that spilled out into our path, coffeehouse chairs and postcard stands in the middle of the road, kids on bicycles hitting the back of the car with open hands. It was too early for the tourist season to be in full swing, but, with the windows down, I could hear Polish and Italian as we rolled slowly past the convenience store and the post office, the monastery square where we would be setting up the free clinic for the orphanage.

Fra Antun had told us where to find his parents' house. The place was tucked away in a white oleander grove at the farthest edge of town. It was a modest beachfront house with blue shuttered windows and a roof of faded shingles, sitting on top of a natural escarpment in the slope of the mountain, maybe fifty yards from the sea. There was a big olive tree with what looked like a tire swing out front. There was a henhouse that had apparently collapsed at least once in the last few years, and been haphazardly reassembled and propped up against the low stone wall that ran along the southern edge of the property. A couple of chickens were milling around the door, and a rooster was sitting in one of the downstairs window boxes. The place looked leftover, but not defeated. There was something determined about the way the blue paint clung to the shutters and the door and the broken crate full of lavender that was leaning against the side of the house. Fra Antun's father, Barba Ivan, was a local fisherman. The moment we reached the top of the stairs that led up from the road, he was already hurrying through the garden. He wore brown suspenders and sandals, and a bright red vest that must have cost his wife a fortune at the yarn cart. At his side was a white dog with a square black head—it was a pointer, but its big-eyed, excited expression made it look about as useful as a panda.

Barba Ivan was saying, 'Hey there, doctors! Welcome, welcome!' as he came toward us, and he tried to take all of our belongings at once. After some persuasion, we got him to settle for Zóra's suitcase, which he rolled up the cobbled pathway between the scrub and the roses. Barba Ivan's wife, Nada, was waiting at the door, smoking. She had thin white hair and green-river veins that ran down

23

her neck and bare arms. She kissed our faces matter-of-factly, and then apologized for the state of the garden before putting out her cigarette and herding us inside.

Inside, the house was quiet and warm, bright despite the evening. The corridor where we left our shoes opened out into a small living room with blue-cushioned chairs, and a sofa and armchair that had obviously been upholstered long ago. Someone in the house was a painter: an easel, with an unfinished canvas of what looked like a hound, had been set up by the window, and paint-splattered newspapers were crowded around it on the floor. Framed watercolors were spaced carefully along the walls, and it took me a moment to realize that they were all of the same hound, that beautifully stupid black-headed dog from outside. The windows were all open, and with the outdoor heat came the electric evening song of the cicadas. Still apologizing for the mess, Nada led us through to the kitchen, while Barba Ivan took this opportunity to seize all our luggage—Zóra's suitcase, my duffel, our backpacks—and dart up the stairs at the end of the hall. Nada jostled us into the kitchen and showed us where the plates and glasses were kept, told us where the bread box was, opened the fridge and pointed out the milk and the juice and the pears and the bacon, and told us to have as much of everything as we wanted whenever we wanted, even the cola.

A red and yellow parrot sat in a tin cage between the kitchen window and another lopsided watercolor of the black-headed dog. The parrot had been looking suspiciously at Zóra since we had entered the kitchen, and he took that moment

24

to screech out: 'O! My God! Behold the wonderment!'—an outburst we at first took as a strikingly lecherous reaction to Zóra's bare arms and collarbones. But Nada apologized profusely and dropped a dishrag over the parrot's cage.

'He likes to recite poetry,' Nada said, and then we both realized that the parrot had been trying to begin the prologue of an old epic poem. 'I've tried to get him to say things like "good morning" and "I like bread and butter." '

She showed us upstairs. Zóra and I would be sharing a room with two cots that had been made up with blue paisley quilts. There was a polished wooden dresser with a few broken drawers, and a small bathroom with an old-fashioned tub and a chain-pull toilet we were warned might or might not flush, depending on the time of day. More sketches of the dog under a fig tree, another of him sleeping on the downstairs sofa. Our window looked out over the back of the property, the orange and lemon trees shivering behind it, and, above that, a sloping plain at the foot of the mountain, lined with rows of low, wind-ruffled vines. Men were digging among the vines; we could hear the distant crunch of their shovels, the sound of their voices as they shouted to one another.

'Our vineyard,' Nada said. 'Don't mind them,' she said about the diggers, and closed one of the shutters.

By the time we brought the coolers and the boxes in from the car and stacked them in a corner of our room, dinner was ready. Nada had fried up sardines and two squid, and grilled a few fish that were about the size of a man's hand, and there was nothing to do but accept her hospitality and cluster

25

around the square table in the kitchen while Barba Ivan poured us two mugs of homemade red wine, and the parrot, still under the cover of the dishrag, burbled to himself and occasionally shrieked out 'O! Hear you thunder? Is that the earth a-shaking?' and, every so often, in answer to his own question, 'No! 'Tis not thunder! Nor the earth a-shaking!'

Nada served us black bread, chopped green peppers, boiled potatoes with chard and garlic. She had made a massive effort, arranged everything carefully on blue china that was chipped, but lovingly wiped down after probably spending years in a basement, hidden from looters. The cool evening air came in off the sea from the lower balcony; there were sardines piled high and caked with salt, two charred bass shining with olive oil— 'From our own olives,' Barba Ivan said, tipping the bottle so that I could smell the lip. I could picture him sitting earlier that day in a small dinghy somewhere out in the rolling waters of the bay, the thin net pulling at his hands, the effort it would take for him to pick the fish out of the net with those big-jointed brown hands.

Barba Ivan and Nada did not ask us about our drive, about our work, or about our families. Instead, in order to avoid any potential political or religious tangents, the conversation turned to crops. The spring had been terrible: torrential rains, streams overflowing, floods that had flushed out the soil up and down the coast and destroyed lettuces and onions. Tomatoes had been late coming in, and you couldn't find spinach anywhere—I remembered my grandfather coming back from the market with dandelion leaves that a farmer had passed off as spinach, my grandma buttering the paper-thin dough for *zaljanica* and then pulling the coarse-leafed mass he had brought home out of the grocery bag and shouting, 'What the hell is this?' It was the first time I had thought about my grandfather in several hours, and the suddenness of it pushed me into silence. I sat and listened, half-hearing, as Barba Ivan insisted that the summer, contrary to his expectations, had been incredible: the oranges and lemons plentiful, strawberries everywhere, the figs fat and ripe. Zóra was saying, *for us, too,* even though I'd never seen her eat a fig in her life.

We had scraped most of the flesh off our respective fishes, unwisely downed our mugs of red wine, tried to help the parrot with verses he had apparently committed to memory better than we ever could, when the child appeared. She was so small I suspect that none of us would have noticed her if she hadn't come in coughing—a thick, loud, productive cough that ripped through her on the balcony, and then there she was, tiny and round-bellied, standing in the doorway in mismatched shoes, her head a mass of tight brownish curls.

The child couldn't have been more than five or six, and she held on to the door frame, one hand tucked into the pocket of the yellow summer dress she was wearing. She was a little dusty, her eyes a little tired, and her entrance had caused a lull in the conversation, so that when her second cough came we were all already looking at her. Then she put a finger in her ear.

'Hello,' I said, 'and who are you?'

'God knows,' Nada said, and stood up to clear the plates. 'She's one of *theirs*—those people up in

27

the vineyard.' I hadn't realized, until that moment, that they were staying here, too. To the little girl, Nada said, 'Where's your mother?' leaning forward, speaking very loudly. When the child said nothing, Nada told her, 'Come in for a cookie.'

Barba Ivan leaned back in his chair and reached into the cupboard behind him. He emerged with a tin of pepper cookies, lifted the lid and held it out to the child. She didn't move. Nada returned from the sink and tried to ply her with a glass of lemonade, but the child wouldn't come in: a violet pouch had been tied around her neck with frayed ribbon, and this she was swinging with her free hand from one shoulder to the other, occasionally hitting herself in the chin, and sucking back the green streams of snot that were inching out of her nose. Outside, we could hear people returning from the vineyard, dust-hoarsed voices and the clink of shovels and spades dropping to the ground, feet on the downstairs patio. They were setting up to have their dinner outside, at the table under the big olive tree, and Nada said, 'We'd better finish up here,' and started collecting our utensils. Zóra tried to stand and help, but Nada nudged her back into her seat. The commotion outside had roused the interest of Bis, the dog, who charged out with his ridiculous, ear-swinging lope, nosed the child in the doorway with mild interest, and then got distracted by something in the garden.

Barba Ivan was still holding out the cookie box when a thin young woman swept by the door and swung the child into her arms. Nada went to the door and looked outside. When she turned around, she said, 'They shouldn't be here.'

'Sweets aren't much good for children,' Barba Ivan said to Zóra, confidentially. 'Bad habits before dinner, rots their teeth and such. But what else are we supposed to do? We can't eat all this ourselves.'

'It was ridiculous to let them stay,' Nada said, stacking the dirty plates on the edge of the table.

Barba Ivan was holding the cookie box out to me. 'There was a time when I could eat a whole nut cake, by myself, just sitting around in the afternoon. But my doctor says, *careful*! I'm getting old, he says, I have to be careful.'

'I said this would happen—didn't I?' Nada said, scraping the smeared leftovers of the potatoes and chard onto a plate, and lowering the plate to the floor. 'Two or three days—it's been a week. Wandering in and out all hours of the night, coughing on my sheets.'

'They've got all kinds of rules now,' Barba Ivan was saying. 'Don't eat butter, don't drink beer. This much fruit a day.' He held his hands apart, indicating a small barrel. 'Eat your vegetables.'

'Each one sicker than the next.' This Nada said loudly, leaning toward the door. 'Those children should be in school, or at the hospital, or with people who can afford to put them in school or in the hospital.'

'I tell him, listen. I eat my vegetables. Don't tell me about vegetables: you buy them at the market, I grow them at my house.' Barba Ivan opened his hands and counted off tomatoes, peppers, lettuce, green onions, leeks. 'I'm a man who knows vegetables—but also I've eaten bread every day of my life. My father, too, and he had red wine with every meal. Do you know what my doctor says?' I

29

shook my head, fixing a smile.

Nada said: 'I told you, and I told Antun, I don't want them here—and now the doctors have come, and they're still here, doing God knows what up there, overturning the whole damn vineyard. It's indecent.'

'He says it'll help me live longer. Look, God—why would I want that?'

'Tell me it's not dangerous,' Nada said, touching Zóra's shoulder. 'Tell me, Doctor. Ten of them in two rooms—five to a bed, and all of them sick as dogs, every single one.'

'Why would I want to live longer if I have to eat—rice, and this—what do they call it? Prunes.'

'Not that I am suggesting everyone from up your way sleeps like that. Sleeps five a bed—I'm not saying that at all, Doctor.'

'The hell with your prunes.'

'Have you ever heard of such a thing?' Nada asked us both, wiping her hands on her apron. 'Have you?'

'No,' said Zóra obligingly.

'It's not right,' she said again. 'And with those pouches stinking to high heaven. Whoever heard of such a thing—we Catholics don't have it; the Muslims don't have it.'

'But still, these people have it, and it's not our business,' Barba Ivan said, suddenly serious, turning in his chair to look at her. 'They're staying here—it's not my concern.'

'It's my house,' Nada said. 'My vineyard.'

'The real difficulty is the children,' Barba Ivan said to me, serious now. 'They're very ill. Getting worse.' He closed the cookie tin and put it back on the shelf. 'I'm told they haven't been to a doctor—I don't know, of course.' He made a face, tapped a fist to his neck. 'The bags certainly aren't helping, and they're foul.'

'Foul,' said Nada.

They might have continued like this if one of the diggers, a brown-haired, sunburned boy of about thirteen, hadn't come in to ask for milk. He was shy about asking, and his presence took all the air out of Nada's indignation, so that she didn't go back to it even after he left.

After dinner, Barba Ivan took out his accordion to play us some old census songs he had learned from his grandfather. We cut him off at the pass by asking him when he'd last had a physical and offering to get one started for him, doing his auscultation and taking his temperature and blood pressure before bed.

Later on, upstairs, there were more pressing matters: the toilet didn't flush, and the water in the sink was cold. Their boiler wasn't working. Not one to be disadvantaged out of a shower, Zóra chanced it. Standing at the window, while Zóra yelped under the running water, I could no longer see the vineyard, but I could hear the clink of shovels starting up again, the high sound of voices that sounded like children. The cicadas were trilling from the oleander bush under the window, and swallows were swinging in high arcs just outside the range of the house lights. A speckled gray moth cowered in an outside corner of the mosquito net. Zóra came out of the bathroom and announced, with some triumph, that the purpose of the rusted pliers in the bathtub was to lift up the pin that turned the shower on. She put her wet hair in a ponytail and came to stand by the window.

31

'Are they digging all night?' she said.

I had no idea. 'They must be workers,' I said. 'The Barba must be keeping them here past the season for some kind of charity.'

The state prosecutor had paged her twice while she was in the shower.

'You should call them back,' I said.

She was having an evening smoke, holding an ashtray in her free hand and stirring the ashes with the bright tip of her cigarette. 'As far as I'm concerned, I have nothing to say until I talk to your grandfather,' Zóra said. She smiled at me, carefully blew the smoke out of the window, waved it out of my face with her hand.

She was on the cusp of asking me what was wrong, so I said, 'We'll get them to come down to the clinic tomorrow,' and climbed into bed. Zóra finished her cigarette, but continued to hover, peering out the window. Then she checked the bedroom door.

'Do you suppose they lock up downstairs?'

'Probably not,' I said. 'Doors are probably wide open, and blowing a breeze of paramilitary rapists.'

She turned out the light reluctantly, and for a long time there was silence. She was awake and staring at me, and I was waiting for her to drift off so I wouldn't have to think of something to say.

Downstairs, muffled by the towel covering his cage, the parrot said: 'Wash the bones, bring the body, leave the heart behind.'

2

THE WAR

Gavran Gailé

Everything necessary to understand my grandfather lies between two stories: the story of the tiger's wife, and the story of the deathless man. These stories run like secret rivers through all the other stories of his life—of my grandfather's days in the army; his great love for my grandmother; the years he spent as a surgeon and a tyrant of the University. One, which I learned after his death, is the story of how my grandfather became a man; the other, which he told to me, is of how he became a child again.

*   *   *

The war started quietly, its beginning subdued by the decade we had spent on the precipice, waiting for it to come. Kids at school would say 'any day now' without knowing what they were talking about, repeating what they had been hearing for years at home. First came the election and then the riots, the assassination of a minister, the massacre at the delta, and then came Sarobor—and after Sarobor, it was like something loosening, a release.

Before the war, every week since I was four, my grandfather and I would take that walk to the citadel to see the tigers. It was always just the two of us. We would start at the bottom and come up

33

the back of Strmina Hill, walking the old carriage trail through the shallow valley of the park on the west side of town, crossing the dozens of small clear streams that drizzled through the undergrowth where, as a little girl, I had spent countless hours, stick in hand, dragging the wet leaves of autumn off the mossy rocks in my useless pursuit of tadpoles. My grandfather, his shoulders bent, arms swinging—*rowing,* Grandma would call from the balcony as she watched us leave, *you're rowing again, Doctor*—loped with long strides, the bag with our farm-stand offerings in his hand. He would wear his vest and slacks, his collared shirt with its long white sleeves, his polished hospital shoes, even for summertime uphill treks. Hurrying after him in worn-out sneakers, a foot and a half shorter than he was, my job was only to keep up. After we had crossed the railroad and passed the place where, at age seven, I had taken a dive off my bicycle and bawled through half an hour of treatment via *rakija*-soaked cloth to my ripped-up knees, the trail would begin to slope sharply upward.

When he saw me fall behind, my grandfather would stop, wipe his brow, and say: 'What's this, what's this? I'm just an old man—come on, is your heart a sponge or a fist?'

And then I would speed up and pant all the way up the hill while he complained, with maddening relish, about how hoarse I sounded, about how he wouldn't bring me with him anymore if I insisted on sounding like a weasel in a potato sack, if I was going to ruin his nice time outdoors. From the top of Strmina, the trail descended through a long, flower-speckled meadow across which you could see east over the ruptured Roman wall, stones spilled by long-silent cannon fire, and over the cobbled boulevard of Old Town with its dusty sun-smeared windows, its pale orange roofs, grill smoke drifting through the bright awnings of the coffeehouses and souvenir shops. Pigeons, clustered thick enough to be visible from the hill, shuffled like cowled women up and down the street that curved to the docks where the rivers were smashing into each other all day and all night at the head of the peninsula. And then the view would end as we reached the citadel courtyard and paid at the zoo entrance—always the only people in line on a weekday while the entire City indulged in its afternoon lunch break, always bypassing the green-mouthed camels and the hippo enclosure with its painted egrets, always heading straight for where the tigers were patrolling tirelessly up and down the old grate.

By the time I was thirteen, the ritual of the tigers had become an annoyance. Our way home from the zoo was continually marked by encounters with people I knew: friends, kids my own age, who had long since stopped sharing the company of their elders. I would see them sitting in cafés, smoking on the curb at the Parliament threshold. And they would see me, and remember seeing me, remember enough to laugh mildly about it at school. Their mocking wasn't unkind, just easy; but it reminded me that I was the prisoner of a rite I no longer felt necessary. I didn't know at the time that the rite wasn't solely for my benefit.

Almost immediately after the war began, the Administration closed the zoo. This was ostensibly to prevent anything that might approximate the Zobov incident: a college student in the capital of our soon-to-be southern neighbor had firebombed a zoo concession stand, killing six people. This was part of the Administration's security plan, a preemptive defense of the city and its citizens—a defense that relied heavily on the cultivation of panic and a deliberate overestimation of enemy resources. They closed the zoo, the bus system, the newly named National Library.

Besides interrupting a childhood ritual I was more than ready to put aside, the closing of the zoo was hardly a cause for alarm. Deep down, we all knew, as the Administration did, that the war was being fought almost seven hundred miles away and that a siege of the City was nearly impossible—we had already caught the enemy off guard. We knew that an air strike would never happen because our own paramilitary had taken out the airplane factory and airstrip at Marhan almost six months ago, but the Administration still implemented a curfew and a mandatory lights-out at 10 p.m., just in case. They issued bulletins warning that anyone anywhere could be an informant for the enemy, that it was important to consider the names of your friends and neighbors before you met them at your usual coffeehouse again, and that, in the event of betrayal, you yourself would be held responsible for what you did not report.

On one hand, life went on. Six or seven kids from my class disappeared almost immediately—without warning, without goodbyes, the way refugees tend to do—but I still trudged to school every morning with a packed lunch. While tanks heading for the border drove down the Boulevard, I sat at the window and practiced sums. Because the war was new and distant, because it was about something my family didn't want me to trouble myself with and I didn't particularly care about, there were still art lessons and coffee dates with Zóra, birthday celebrations and shopping trips. My grandfather still taught his seminar and did his hospital rounds and went to the local market every morning, and he still soap-washed apples before peeling them. He also stood in the bread line for six hours at a time, but I wouldn't know this until later. My mother still carried her projector slides to teach art history at the University, my grandma still tuned in to classic movie hour to watch Clark Gable smirk at Vivien Leigh.

The distance of the fighting created the illusion of normalcy, but the new rules resulted in an attitude shift that did not suit the Administration's plans. They were going for structure, control, for panic that produced submission—what they got instead was social looseness and lunacy. To spite the curfew, teenagers parked on the Boulevard, sometimes ten cars deep, and sat drinking on their hoods all night. People would close their shops for lunch and go to the pub and not return until three days later. You'd be on your way to the dentist and see him sitting on someone's stoop in his undershirt, wine bottle in hand, and then you'd either join him or turn around and go home. It was innocent enough at first—before the looting started some years later, before the paramilitary rose to power—the kind of celebration that happens when people, without acknowledging it, stand together on the brink of disaster.

The kids of my generation were still a few years away from facing the inflation that would send us to the bakery with our parents' money piled up in wheelbarrows, or force us to trade shirts in the hallways at school. Those first sixteen months of wartime held almost no reality, and this made them incredible, irresistible, because the fact that something terrible was happening elsewhere, and at the same time to *us,* gave us room to get away with anarchy. Never mind that, three hundred miles away, girls sitting in bomb shelters were getting their periods at the age of seven. In the City, we weren't just affected by the war; we were entitled to our affectation. When your parents said, *get your ass to school,* it was all right to say, *there's a war on,* and go down to the riverbank instead. When they caught you sneaking into the house at three in the morning, your hair reeking of smoke, the fact that there was a war on prevented them from staving your head in. When they heard from neighbors that your friends had been spotted doing a hundred and twenty on the Boulevard with you hanging none too elegantly out the sunroof, they couldn't argue with *there's a war on, we might all die anyway.* They felt responsible, and we took advantage of their guilt because we didn't know any better.

For all its efforts to go on as before, the school system could not prevent the war, however distant, from sliding in: we saw it in the absence of classmates, in the absence of books, in the absence of pig fetuses (which Zóra and I, even then, had eagerly been looking forward to rummaging through). We were supposed to be inducing chemical reactions and doing basic dissection, but

38

we had no chemicals, and our pig fetuses were being held hostage in a lab somewhere across the ever-shifting border. Instead, we made endless circuits with wires and miniature lightbulbs. We left old-money coins out in the rain to rust and then boiled water and salt and baking soda to clean them. We had a few diagrams of dissected frogs, which we were forced to commit to memory. Inexplicably, we also had a cross section of a horse's foot, preserved in formaldehyde in a rectangular vase, which we sketched and re-sketched until it might be assumed that any one of us could perform crude surgery on a horse with hoof problems. Mostly, from eight in the morning until four in the afternoon, we read the textbook aloud.

To make things worse, the conflict had necessitated a rather biased shift of upperclassmen to upper floors; in other words, the older you were, the farther you were from the school basement bomb shelter. So the year we turned fourteen, Zóra and I ended up in a classroom on the concrete roof overlooking the river, a square turret with enormous windows that normally housed the kindergarteners. Everything about that particular rearrangement of space indicated that it had been made quickly: the walls of the classroom were papered with watercolors of princesses, and the windowsill was lined with Styrofoam cups full of earth, from which, we were told, beans would eventually grow. Some even did. There had been family-tree drawings too, but someone had had the presence of mind to take them down, and had left a bare patch of wall under the blackboard. We sat there, drawing that horse's hoof, saying things like, *there's a war on, at least if they bomb us we'll go before the little ones do,* very nonchalant about it. The turret window of that room afforded us a 360-degree view of the City, from the big hill to the north to the citadel across the river, behind which the woods rose and fell in a green line. You could see smokestacks in the distance, belching streams as thick as tar, and the brick outline of the old neighborhoods. You could see the dome of the basilica on University Hill, the square cross bright and enormous on top. You could see the iron bridges—still standing in our city, all but gone up and down the two rivers, rubble in the water. You could see the rafts on the riverbank, abandoned and rusted over, and then, upriver at the confluence, Carton City, where the gypsies lived, with its wet paper walls, the black smoke of its dungfires.

Our teacher that year was a small woman who went by the name M. Dobravka. She had nervous hands, and glasses that slid down so often that she had developed a habit of hitching them up by flexing her nose. We would later learn that M. Dobravka had once been a political artist, and that, after we graduated, she moved somewhere else to avoid persecution. Some years later, she encouraged a group of high school students in the production of an antiadministration poster that landed them in jail and caused her to disappear one night on the walk from her apartment to the newspaper kiosk at the corner of her street. Back then, completely unaware of her determination, unfamiliar with the frustration she felt at not having the tools to teach us her own subject, let alone one with which she was unfamiliar, we

40

thought she was hilarious. Then she brought us a gift.

It was a freak March heat wave, hot as summer, and we had come to school and taken our shoes and socks and sweaters off. The turret was like a greenhouse. We had the door open but we were still moist with perspiration and a tender kind of frenzy that comes from unexpected weather. M. Dobravka came in late and out of breath. She had a large, foil-wrapped parcel under one arm, which she opened to reveal two enormous pairs of lungs, pink, wet, soft as satin. A violation of the meat ration. Contraband. We didn't ask her where she had gotten them.

'Spread some newspapers out on the tables outside,' she said, and her glasses dropped immediately. Ten minutes later, faces dripping with sweat, we hovered over her while she tried to butterfly one pair of lungs with a kitchen knife she had brought along with her. The lung strained against the knife, bulging out on either side of the blade like a rubber ball. The meat was already beginning to smell, and we were swatting the flies away.

'Maybe we should refrigerate them,' somebody said.

But M. Dobravka was a woman possessed. She was determined to make something of the risk she'd taken, to show us how the lungs worked, to open them up like cloth and point out the alveoli, the collapsed air sacs, the thick white cartilage of the bronchial tubes. She sawed away at a corner of the lung, and, as she went on, her range of motion got bigger and bigger, until we all stepped back and watched her tearing into the side of the

41

lung, her glasses going up and down, up and down as she pressed with one arm and pumped away with the other like she was working a cistern.

Then the lung slipped out of her hands and slid across the aluminum foil and over the edge of the table, onto the ground. It lay there, heavy and definite. M. Dobravka looked down at it for a few moments, while the flies immediately found it and began to walk gingerly along the tracheal opening. Then she bent down, picked it up, and dropped it back on the newspaper.

'You,' she said to me, because I happened to be standing next to her. 'Get a straw out of the coffee cabinet and come back here and inflate this lung. Come on, hurry up.'

After that, M. Dobravka was a figure of reverence, particularly for me. Those lungs—the way she'd smuggled them in for us, the way she'd stood over us while we took turns blowing into them, one by one—cemented my interest in becoming a doctor.

M. Dobrovka had also touched upon our relationship to contraband, an obsession that was already beginning to seize the whole City. For her, it was school supplies. For us, it was the same guiding principle, but a different material concern. Suddenly, because we couldn't have them, because they were expensive and difficult to obtain, we wanted things we had never thought of wanting, things that would give us bragging rights: fake designer handbags, Chinese jewelry, American cigarettes, Italian perfume. Zóra started wearing her mother's lipstick, and then began looking for ways to buy some herself. Six months into the war, she developed a taste for French cigarettes, and refused to smoke anything else. All of fifteen, she would sit at the table in our coffeehouse on the Square of the Revolution and raise her eyebrow at boys who had probably gone to considerable lengths to impress her with local varieties. At a party I don't remember attending, she took up with Branko, who was twenty-one and reputed to be a gunrunner. I didn't approve, but there was a war on. Besides, he later turned out to be a punk whose mightiest offense was stealing radios.

Most weekends, Zóra and I would go down to the bottom of Old Town and park at the dock. This was the University hangout, the epicenter of contraband activity, and the boys, gangly and bird-shouldered, sat along the railing with their tables and boxes lined up, videos and sunglasses and T-shirts on display. Zóra, wearing her shortest skirt, pursued by colorful catcalls, would make her way down to where Branko had his stand and sit cross-legged while he played accordion and drank beer and, as the evening deepened, took breaks from peddling his wares to feel her up behind the dumpster. In the meantime, I stayed in the car with the windows rolled down, legs crossed through the passenger window, the bass line of Springsteen's 'I'm on Fire' humming in my lower back.

This was how Ori found me—Ori, who sold fake designer labels he swore he could seamlessly attach to your clothing, luggage, haberdashery. He was seventeen, skinny and shy-grinning, another guy whose wartime reputation made him considerably more appealing than he otherwise might have been, but he had the temerity to stick his head into the car and ask, regarding my music selection, 'You like this stuff? You want more?'

Ori had struck upon my only vice, which I had barely managed to keep in check. The Administration had shut down all but two radio stations, and insisted on repeat airings of folk songs that were outdated even by my grandma's standards. By the second year of war, I was sick of love songs that used trees and barrels as metaphors. Without knowing I was missing them, I wanted Bob Dylan and Paul Simon and Johnny Cash. The first time Ori got me out of the car, he led me across the dock to where his three-legged mutt was guarding an overturned crate, and showed me his stash, alphabetized, the lyrics mistranslated and handwritten on notepaper that had been carefully folded and stuffed into the tape boxes. By some miracle, he had a Walkman, which almost made him worth dating in and of itself, and we sat on the floor behind his table, one earbud each, and he took me through his collection and put his hand on my thigh.

When, after a few weeks of saving up, I tried to buy *Graceland,* he said, 'There's a war on, your money's no good,' and kissed me. I remember being surprised at his mouth, at the difference between the dry outer part of his mouth and the wet inner part, and thinking about this while he was kissing me, and afterward, too.

We went on kissing for three more months, during which my musical holdings must have tripled, and then Ori, like many boys around that age, disappeared. I had borrowed his Walkman and showed up three nights running to our café so I could return it to him—eventually someone told me he was gone, and they didn't know if he had enlisted or fled the draft. I kept the Walkman, slept

44

with it, which must have been some expression of missing him, but the reality of his being gone wouldn't sink in until other things went missing.

*   *   *

The years I spent immersing myself in the mild lawlessness of the war my grandfather spent believing it would end soon, pretending that nothing had changed. I now know that the loss of the tigers was a considerable blow to him, but I wonder whether his optimism didn't have as much to do with my behavior, with his refusal to accept that, for a while at least, he had lost me. We saw very little of each other, and while we did not talk about those years afterward, I know that his other rituals went on uninterrupted, unaltered. Breakfast over a newspaper, followed by Turkish coffee brewed by my grandma; personal correspondence, always in alphabetical order, as dictated by his address book. A walk to the market for fresh fruit—or, as the war went on, whatever he could get, as long as he came back with something. On Mondays and Wednesdays, an afternoon lecture at the University. Lunch, followed by an afternoon nap. Some light exercise; a snack at the kitchen table, almost always sunflower seeds. Then a few hours in the living room with my mother and grandma, sometimes talking, sometimes just sitting together. Dinner, and then an hour of reading. Bed.

We interacted, but always without commiserating, always without acknowledging that things were different. Like the time he forced me to stay home for the family Christmas party, and I drank Cognac

45

all night because I knew he would not reprimand me in front of the guests. Or the time I came home at four—eyeliner smeared and hair a mess following a prolonged encounter with Ori behind a broken vending machine—to find my grandfather on the curb outside our building, on his way back from an emergency house call, politely trying to fend off the advances of a leggy blonde I soon realized was a prostitute.

'You see, there is my granddaughter,' I heard him say as I approached, his voice the voice of a drowning man. Relief tightened the skin around his temples, a reaction I never would have hoped for considering the circumstances of my return. I stepped onto the curb beside him, and he grabbed my arm. 'Here she is,' he said cheerfully. 'You see, here she is.'

'Beat it,' I said to the hooker, acutely aware of the fact that my bra was hanging on for dear life, down to one solitary clasp that might give at any moment and render the whole situation even more uncomfortable.

My grandfather gave the prostitute fifty dinars, and I stood behind him while he unlocked the downstairs door, watching her go down the street on cane-thin legs, one heel slightly shorter than the other.

'What did you give her that money for?' I asked him as we went upstairs.

'You shouldn't be rude like that to anyone,' he said. 'We didn't raise you that way.' Without stopping to look at me when we got to the door: 'For shame.'

This had been the general state of affairs for years. My grandfather and I, without acknowledging it, were at a stalemate. His reductions had dropped my allowance to a new low, and I had taken to locking my door and smoking cigarettes in my room, under the covers.

I was thus occupied one spring afternoon when the doorbell rang. A few moments later, it rang again, and then again. I think I probably shouted for someone to get the door, and when no one did, I put my cigarette out on the outer sill of my bedroom window and did it myself.

I remember the shape of the narrow-brimmed black hat that obscured most of the peephole, and I did not see the man's face, but I was anxious to get back to my room and irritated that no one else in the house had answered.

When I opened the door, the man said that he was there to see the doctor. He had a thin voice, and a doughy face that looked like it had been forcibly stuffed up into his hat, which was probably why he had not removed it in greeting in the first place. I thought I'd seen him before, that he was a hospital official, maybe, and I showed him in and left him in the hall. My mother was on campus, preparing for class; my grandparents sharing a late lunch in the kitchen. My grandfather was eating with one hand, and with the other he held my grandma's wrist across the table. She was smiling about something, and the moment I came in she pointed at the pot of stuffed peppers on the stove.

'Eat something,' she said.

'Later,' I said. 'There's a man at the door for you,' I said to my grandfather.

'Who the hell is it?' my grandfather said.

'I don't know,' I told him.

A few more spoonfuls of stuffed pepper while

my grandfather thought it over. 'Well, what does he think this is? Tell him to wait. I'm eating with my wife.' My grandma handed him the bread.

I showed the hat into the living room, and he sat there for what must have been twenty minutes, looking around. So that no one could accuse me of being inhospitable, I went to get him some water, but when I came back I saw that he had taken a notebook out of his briefcase, and was squinting up at the paintings on our walls, scribbling down some sort of inventory. His eye went over my grandparents' wedding pictures, my grandma's old coffee set, the vintage bottles behind the glass door of the liquor cabinet.

He was writing and writing, and I realized what a serious mistake I had made letting him into the house. I was terrified, and then when he took two gulps of water and peered into the glass to see if it was clean all my fear turned into a wash of rage. I went into my room to put my Paul Simon tape in my Walkman and returned to the living room with my headset on, pretending to dust. I had the Walkman clipped to my pocket so he could see it, the angry wheels of my contraband spinning through the plastic window, and he sat there blinking at me while I ran a moist towel over the television and the coffee table and the pictures from my grandparents' wedding. I thought I was somehow sticking it to him, but he was unfazed by all this, and continued to write in his notebook until my grandfather came out of the kitchen.

'Can I help you?' he said, and the hat got up and shook his hand.

The hat said good afternoon, and that he was there on behalf of the enlistment office. He showed my grandfather his card. I turned down the headset volume and started dusting books one by one.

'Well?' my grandfather said. He did not ask the hat to sit back down.

'I am here to confirm your birth date and your record of service in the army,' the hat said. 'On behalf of the enlistment office.' My grandfather stood across the coffee table with his arms folded, looking the hat up and down. 'This is standard procedure, Doctor.'

'Then proceed.'

The hat put on a pair of glasses and opened the ledger to the page on which he had been scribbling. He ran a large, white finger down the page, and without looking up, he asked my grandfather: 'It is true you were born in 1932?'

My grandfather nodded once.

'Where?'

'In Galina.'

'And where is that?' I didn't know myself.

'Some four hundred miles northwest of here, I suppose.'

'Brothers or sisters?'

'None.'

'You served in the National Army from '47 to '56?'

'That is correct.'

'And why did you leave?'

'To work at the University.'

The hat made a note, and looked up at my grandfather and smiled. My grandfather did not return the expression, and the hat's grin deflated.

'Children?' the hat said.

'One daughter.'

'Where does she live?'

'Here.'

'Grandchildren?'

'One granddaughter.'

'Are there any young men between the ages of eighteen and forty-five living in the house, or who have cited this house as a residence?'

'None,' my grandfather said.

'Where is your son-in-law?'

My grandfather's mouth moved as he ran his tongue over a tooth. 'There are no other men living here.'

'And—I'm sorry, Doctor, standard procedure—your wife?'

'What about her?'

'Was she born in Galina, too?'

'Why, are you hoping to draft her?'

The hat didn't reply. He appeared to be going down the page, counting something.

'Your wife's full name, please, Doctor?'

'Mrs. Doctor,' my grandfather said. He said this in a way that made the hat look up from his notebook.

'Like I said, Doctor, this is standard procedure for the enlistment office.'

'I don't believe you, and I don't like your questions. You're sucking around for something, and you may as well ask me directly so we can get to the point.'

'Where was your wife born?'

'In Sarobor.'

'I see,' the hat said. I had stopped dusting, and was standing there with the moist towel in my hand, looking from my grandfather to the hat. I could imagine my grandma sitting on the other

50

side of the door, in the kitchen, listening to all this. We had heard about this kind of thing happening; I had let it into the house.

'And your wife's family lives—?'

'My wife's family lives in this house.'

'Is your wife in touch with anyone in Sarobor?'

'Of course not,' my grandfather said. Only later would I understand what it meant to him to add: 'Even if she wanted to be, I should think that would be difficult to manage, considering it's been razed to the ground.'

'It is my job to ask,' the hat said with a gracious smile. He was clearly trying to backtrack now, to ingratiate himself, and he waved a hand around the room. 'You are a man of considerable assets, and if your wife has brothers or sisters still in Sarobor—'

'Get out,' my grandfather said. The hat blinked at him stupidly. My neck had stiffened up, and drops of cold water from the towel were running down the outside of my leg.

'Doctor—' the hat began, but my grandfather cut him off.

'Get the hell out.' He had put his hands behind his back and was rocking forward on his heels now. His shoulders had slumped down and forward, his whole face sunk in a grimace. 'Out of my house,' he said. 'Out.'

The hat closed his notebook and put it away. Then he picked up the briefcase and rested it on the edge of the coffee table. 'There's no need for this misunderstanding.'

'Did you hear me?' my grandfather said. Then, without warning, he leaned forward in one motion and grabbed the handle of the briefcase and

51

pulled. The hat did not let go, and he stumbled forward still hanging on, and the coffee table went end over end, the vase and all the old newspapers and magazines on it showering onto the floor, along with the contents of the briefcase, which had flown open. The hat knelt down, red-faced—*God damn it, look at all this, there's no need for this, sir*—trying to put all his papers back in the briefcase, and suddenly my grandfather, like something out of a cartoon, was kicking all those fallen newspapers and letters and magazines and coupons, kicking his feet into the pile and heaving up clouds of paper. He looked ridiculous, long-legged and awkward in his suit, swinging his arms around insanely and saying, without the slightest rise in his voice, 'Get out, get out, get out, get the hell out.' By the time the hat had finished stuffing his belongings back into the briefcase, my grandfather was already holding the door open.

Three months later, the Administration came down especially hard on established doctors. Apparently, my grandfather was not the only one with ties to the old system, to the provinces, to families there. Doctors above the age of fifty, suspected of having loyalist feelings toward the unified state, were suspended from practice, and were informed, in writing, that their University seminars would be closely monitored.

Despite the insistent pull of his instinct to protect us, my grandfather still suffered from that national characteristic of our people that is often mistaken for stupidity but is more like self-righteous indignation. He called a locksmith whom he had once treated for gallstones, and had him install the most complex front-door deadbolt system I had ever seen. It made the inner plane of the door look like something out of a clock, and you needed three separate keys to get in from the outside. The sound of the gears moving would have woken the dead. Although the termination of his practice did not entirely preclude him from teaching at the University, my grandfather tendered his resignation. Then he telephoned the patients he was now forbidden to see—asthma sufferers and victims of rheumatoid arthritis; insomniacs, teachers who had recently given up smoking, construction workers whose backs were on the mend; paraplegics and hypochondriacs; a tubercular horse breeder; a celebrated thespian who was also a recovering alcoholic—and arranged a schedule of house calls that seemed, at least to me, endless.

I sat in the armchair beside his desk while he made the phone calls, rolling my eyes. I couldn't figure out whether his decision was the result of his commitment to his patients, or some remote glimmer of the same adolescent stubbornness I recognized in myself, in Zóra, in the kids on the docks. The possibility that it might be the latter terrified me, but I did not have the courage to challenge him on that front, to ask him if it was possible that he could risk everything on something that in us seemed like towering defiance, but in him amounted to inexcusable stupidity. Instead—in what must have been the most I'd said to him in months—I leveled one disastrous scenario after another at him, all of which left him completely unfazed: What if one of your patients is indiscreet? What if someone follows you on a house call? What if the pharmacy starts asking questions about why you yourself are filling out all these prescriptions for ailments you clearly don't have? What if someone in your care dies, has a stroke, hemorrhages, suffers an aneurysm—what if you're blamed for that death because your patient didn't go to the hospital? What if you end up in prison, charged with murder? What will happen to us?

'Why do I have to be the adult?' I would ask Zóra while we sat at our usual table, waiting for Branko to start baying into the microphone. 'Why do I have to point out when he does something insane?'

'I know,' Zóra would say, smacking her lips in the direction of her compact. 'Really.'

My grandfather must have noticed that he was seeing considerably more of me than he had over the past two years. He must have noticed that I, and not my grandma, was brewing coffee at daybreak; that our breakfast debates over the latest news did not stop with my waving a hand and muttering, *what do you expect, there's a war on,* but spilled down the stairs and onto the street when I went with him to do the marketing; that I protested when my grandma tried to make the beds, or chop too-hard vegetables, or watch television instead of taking a nap. He must have realized that I was doing my homework in the kitchen every evening when he left to make house calls, and that I was up doing the crossword puzzle when he returned. He must have noticed it all, but he never said anything of my new rituals, and he never invited me to share in any of his. This was, perhaps, a kind of punishment, and back then I thought it was for allowing myself to slip, or for

54

letting the hat into our apartment. Now I realize that it was punishment for giving up so easily on the tigers.

In the end, though, I must have earned something back, because he told me about the deathless man.

It was the summer I turned sixteen. Some patient—I didn't know who—had been battling pneumonia, and my grandfather's visits to him had increased from once to three times a week. I had dozed off struggling through a crossword puzzle, fully intending to wait up for him, and I came around some hours later to find my grandfather standing in the doorway, flicking the table lamp on and off. When he saw me sit up, he stopped, and for a few moments I sat in total darkness.

'Natalia,' I heard him say, and I realized he was motioning for me to get off the sofa. I could see him now. He was still wearing his hat and raincoat, and exhaustion turned my relief at seeing him into impatience.

'What?' I said, all hunched and groggy. 'What?'

He motioned toward the door, and then he said, 'Quietly. Come on.' He had my raincoat over his arm, my sneakers in his right hand. Evidently, there was no time to change. 'What's going on?' I said, forcing my foot into an already laced sneaker. 'What's the matter?'

'You'll see,' he said, holding the coat out for me. 'Hurry up, come on.'

I thought: *that's it, it's finally happened—he's killed somebody.*

The elevator would have made too much noise, so we took the stairs. Outside the rain had stopped, but water was still running in the gutters, coming

55

down the street from the market and carrying with it the smell of cabbage and dead flowers. The café across the street had closed early, the patio chained off, wet chairs stacked on the tabletops. An enormous white cat was sitting under the pharmacy awning, blinking at us with distaste as we passed under the lamppost at the end of the block. By this time, I had given up on my coat buttons.

'Where are we going?' I said. 'What's happened?'

But my grandfather didn't answer. He just kept moving down the street, so fast I came after him almost at a run. I thought, *if I start crying, he'll make me go back,* and stayed on his heels. Past the baker, the bank, the out-of-business toy shop where I had bought stickers for my never-completed Ewoks album; past the stand that sold fried dough, the sugared smell of it wedged permanently in the air; past the stationery shop, the newsstand on the next corner. Three blocks down, I realized how quiet it was. We had passed two cafés, both closed, and a late-night grill that was normally packed, but was occupied tonight by only one waiter, who sat spinning coins across an eight-person table.

'What the hell is going on?' I asked my grandfather.

I wondered what my mother would do if she woke up to find us both gone. We were nearing the end of our street where it opened out onto the Boulevard, and I assumed the silence of our walk would be shattered by the bustle along the tramway. But when we got there, nothing, not even a single passing car. All the way from one end of the Boulevard to the other, every window was dark, and a hazy yellow moon was climbing along the curve of the old basilica on the hill. As it rose, it seemed to be gathering the silence up around it like a net. Not a sound: no police sirens, no rats in the dumpsters that lined the street. Not even my grandfather's shoes as he stopped, looked up and down the street, and then turned left to follow the Boulevard east across the Square of the Konjanik.

'It's not far now,' he said, and I caught up with him long enough to see the side of his face. He was smiling.

'Not far to where?' I said, out of breath, angry. 'Where are you taking me?' I drew myself up and stopped. 'I'm not going any further until you tell me what the hell this is.'

He turned to look at me, indignant. 'Lower your voice, you fool, before you set something off,' he hissed. 'Can't you feel it?' Suddenly his arms went over his head in a wide arc. 'Isn't it lovely? No one in the world awake but us.' And off he went again. I stood still for a few moments, watching him go, a tall, thin, noiseless shadow. Then the realization of it rushed over me: he didn't need me with him, he wanted me there. Without realizing it, I had been invited back.

We passed the empty windows of shops that had gone out of business; lightless buildings where roosting pigeons hunched along the fire escapes; a beggar sleeping so soundly that I would have thought him dead if I hadn't realized that the moment had closed around us, stilling everything.

When I finally caught up with my grandfather, I said: 'Look, I don't know what we're doing, but I'd like to be in on it.'

Then suddenly he stopped in the darkness

57

ahead of me and my chin cracked his elbow. The force of the collision knocked me back, but then he reached for me and held my shoulder while I steadied myself. My jaw clicked when I put my hand against it.

My grandfather stood on the curb, pointing into the distance of the empty street. 'There,' he said, 'look.' His hand was shaking with excitement.

'I don't see anything,' I told him.

'Yes you do,' he said. 'You do, Natalia. Look.'

I peered out into the street, where the long blades of the rails lay slick and shining. There was a tree on the other curb, a lamppost with a dying bulb, an eviscerated dumpster lying on its side in the road. I was opening my mouth to say *what*? And then I saw it.

Half a block from where we were standing, an enormous shadow was moving along the street, going very slowly up the Boulevard of the Revolution. At first I thought it was a bus, but its shape was too organic, too lumpy, and it was going far too slowly for that, making almost no noise. It was swaying, too, swaying up the street with an even momentum, a ballasted rolling motion that was drawing it away from us like a tide, and every time it rocked forward something about it made a soft dragging sound on the rails. As we watched, the thing sucked in air and then let out a deep groan.

'God,' I said. 'That's an elephant.'

My grandfather said nothing, but when I looked up at him he was smiling. His glasses had fogged up during the walk, but he wasn't taking them off to wipe them.

'Come on,' he said, and took my hand. We

moved fast along the sidewalk until we drew parallel, and then passed it, stopped a hundred meters down so we could watch it coming toward us.

From there, the elephant—the sound and smell of it; the ears folded back against the domed, bouldered head with big-lidded eyes; the arched roll of the spine, falling away into the hips; dry folds of skin shaking around the shoulders and knees as it shifted its weight—seemed to take up the whole street. It dragged its curled trunk like a fist along the ground. Several feet in front of it, holding a bag of something that must have been enormously tempting, a short young man was walking slowly backward, drawing it forward with whispers.

'I saw them up at the train station as I was coming home,' my grandfather said. 'He must be bringing it to the zoo.'

The young man had seen us, and as he inched back along the tramway he nodded and smiled, pulled down on his cap. Every so often, he would take something out of the bag and hold it out to the elephant, and the elephant would lift its trunk from the ground, grip the offering, and loll it back between the yellow sabers of its tusks.

Later on, we would read about how some soldiers had found him near death at the site of an abandoned circus; about how, despite everything, despite closure and bankruptcy, the zoo director had said bring him in, bring him in and eventually the kids will see him. For months the newspapers would run a picture of him, standing stark-ribbed in his new pen at the zoo, an advert of times to come, a pledge of the zoo's future, the undeniable

59

end of the war.

My grandfather and I stopped at the bus station, and the elephant passed, slow, graceful, enchanted by the food in the young man's hand. The moon threw a tangle of light into the long, soft hairs sticking up out of his trunk and under his chin. The mouth was open, and the tongue lay in it like a wet arm.

'No one will ever believe this,' I said.

My grandfather said: 'What?'

'None of my friends will ever believe it.'

My grandfather looked at me like he'd never seen me before, like he couldn't believe I was his. Even in our estrangement, he had never quite looked at me that way, and afterward he never did again.

'You must be joking,' he said. 'Look around. Think for a moment. It's the middle of the night, not a soul anywhere. In this city, at this time. Not a dog in the gutter. Empty. Except for this elephant—and you're going to tell your idiot friends about it? Why? Do you think they'll understand it? Do you think it will matter to them?'

He left me behind and walked on after the elephant. I stood with my hands in my pockets. I felt my voice had fallen through and through me, and I couldn't summon it back to tell him or myself anything at all. The elephant was moving forward along the Boulevard. I followed it. A block down, my grandfather had stopped beside a broken bench, was waiting for the elephant. I caught up with him first, and the two of us stood side by side, in silence, my face burning, his breath barely audible. The young man did not look at us again.

60

Eventually, my grandfather said: 'You must understand, this is one of those moments.'

'What moments?'

'One of those moments you keep to yourself,' he said.

'What do you mean?' I said. 'Why?'

'We're in a war,' he said. 'The story of this war—dates, names, who started it, why—that belongs to everyone. Not just the people involved in it, but the people who write newspapers, politicians thousands of miles away, people who've never even been here or heard of it before. But something like this—this is yours. It belongs only to you. And me. Only to us.' He put his hands behind his back and ambled along slowly, kicking the polished tips of his shoes up as he walked, exaggerating his movements so they would slow him down. No thought of turning around, of going home. Down the Boulevard for as long as the elephant and his boy would tolerate us. My grandfather said: 'You have to think carefully about where you tell it, and to whom. Who deserves to hear it? Your grandma? Zóra? Certainly not that clown you carry on with at the docks.'

That stung. 'He's gone,' I said quietly.

'I would like to be able to say that I'm sorry,' my grandfather said.

'Well, I am,' I said. 'He was drafted.' This I said to make him feel guilty; I didn't know for certain.

For a while, neither of us said anything. The elephant's breathing fell in around us. It was like being inside an engine room. Every few minutes, it would let out a high, hollow, insistent whistle, the barest threat of impatience, and when it did this the young man held the food out more quickly.

61

Then I asked my grandfather, 'Do you have stories like that?'

'I do now.'

'No, I mean from before,' I said.

I saw him thinking about it. He thought for a long time while we walked with the elephant. Perhaps under slightly different circumstances, he might have told me about the tiger's wife. Instead, he told me about the deathless man.

*   *   *

Hands behind his back, walking in the shadow of our elephant, my grandfather said:

This is late summer, '54. Not '55, because that's the year I met your grandma. I am first triage assistant for the battalion, and my apprentice, God rest him, or intern as you would call it, is Dominic Lazlo, a brilliant little Hungarian fellow who has paid a lot of money to study at our University, and who doesn't speak a word of the language. God knows why he's not in Paris or London, he's that apt with a scalpel. Not apt at much else, though. At any rate: a call comes in from this village, where there is a sickness. Some people have died, and those still living are afraid—there is a terrible cough, and blood on their pillows in the morning. This is about as mysterious to me as an empty milk saucer when there's a big, fat cat in the room, and the cat has a ring of milk on its whiskers and everyone is asking where the milk is.

So. We hitch a wagon ride to this village. The man who greets us is called Marek. He is the son of the big man in town, and has been to

University. He is the man who sent the wire asking us to come. He is short and stocky, and he leads us through the village and into his father's house. Marek's sister is this fat, pleasant-looking woman, very much what you'd expect. She gives us coffee and bread with cheese, a nice change from all the porridge we've been eating back at barracks. Then Marek says, 'Gentlemen, something new is at hand.' I expect he will say: *the epidemic's gotten worse, more death, mass hysteria.* I am partly right, especially about the hysteria.

Apparently, this is how it stands: a man has died, and there has been a funeral. At the funeral, the man, who is called Gavo, sits up in his coffin and asks for water. It is an immense surprise. Three o'clock in the afternoon, the procession is following the casket up the churchyard slope to the plot. First, there's the noise of the body sliding in the coffin, and when the lid slides off there he is, this man Gavo, as pale and blue-faced as the day they found him, floating belly up in a pond some way from the town. Gavo sits up in his pressed suit, hat in hand, folded purple napkin in his pocket. An immense surprise. High up, held aloft in his coffin like a man in a boat, he looks around the procession with red eyes and says: 'Water.' That is all. By the time the pallbearers have realized what's happened, by the time they've dropped the coffin and fled like crazy men into the church, this man Gavo has already fallen back into the casket.

That is what Marek tells us regarding this new development.

From where we are sitting in Marek's house, I can see out the open door and down the road leading across the field and through the churchyard. I have only just noticed that the town is very empty, and that, at the door of the little church, there is a man with a pistol—the undertaker, Marek tells me, Aran Darić, who hasn't slept for six days. I am already thinking it would be far more productive to help this man Aran Darić.

Meanwhile, Marek is still telling the story, and in it the man Gavo does not rise from his coffin again. This is helped by the fact that some unknown member of the funeral procession fires two bullets from an army pistol into the back of Gavo's head while he is sitting up in the coffin right after the pallbearers drop it. Never mind why someone is so very prepared to fire a gun at a funeral. Marek only tells this part of the story after he has had two or three glasses of plum brandy.

I am taking notes this whole time, and wondering about how this Gavo ties into the sickness I am here to treat. When Marek mentions the two bullets, I put my pencil down and say: 'So, the man was not dead?'

'No, no,' Marek says. 'Most assuredly, Gavo was dead.'

'Before the bullets were fired?' I ask him, because it seems to me that this whole business is taking a different route, and now they're just making things up to cover murder.

Marek shrugs and says: 'It is a surprise, I know.'

I continue to write, but what I am writing does not make much sense, and Marek looks with interest across the table and reads what I am writing upside down. Dominic, who I suspect has not understood any of this, is staring intently at me for some sort of explanation.

I say: 'We will have to see the body.'

Marek's hands are on the table, and I can see that he is a man who bites his nails when he is nervous. He has been biting them a lot recently. He says to me: 'Are you sure this is necessary?'

'We will have to see it.'

'I don't know about that, Doctor.'

I have been making a list of all the people I want to speak with—anyone who is sick, all the family members of this revenant fellow, Gavo, and especially the priest and the undertaker, who are most likely to know about how ill this man was before he was shot. I say to Marek: 'Mr. Marek, many people are at risk here. If this man was sick—'

'He was not sick.'

'I'm sorry?'

'He was perfectly healthy.'

Dominic is looking in abject confusion from Marek to myself. He has known me long enough to process that the expression on my face is probably not one of delight, and he is obviously puzzled by what is going on. Marek himself doesn't look too good, either. I say: 'Very well, then, Mr. Marek, I will tell you how I see it. As far as the village goes, including Mr. Gavo himself, I am confident that my findings will probably arrive at a diagnosis of consumption—tuberculosis. It is consistent with the symptoms you've described to me—the bloody cough and so forth. I would like to have all the people who are sick assembled in your town hospital, as quickly as possible, and I would also like to place this town under

65

quarantine until we can assess the extent of the illness.'

And here, he catches me off guard, because he says sharply, 'What do you mean, tuberculosis?' He looks very distraught. And I would expect him to be distraught at tuberculosis, but I would expect a different kind of alarm—the way he looks at me, I feel like my diagnosis doesn't suit him, like it's inadequate, not severe enough for him.

Marek says: 'Couldn't it be something else?'

I tell him no, not with these symptoms, not with people falling dead one by one and leaving bloody pillows behind. I tell him that it will be all right, that I will send out for medicine, for nurses and another city physician to help me.

But he says: 'Yes, but what if that doesn't help?'

'It will.'

'If it's tuberculosis,' he says. 'If you're right.'

'I am not entirely certain where this is going.'

'What if you're wrong—what if it's something else?' Marek says. By this time, he is very agitated, and he says, 'I don't think you understand, sir—I really doubt you understand.'

'Well, tell me about it,' I say.

'Well,' says Marek. 'There is blood on our pillows. And . . . there was blood on the lapels of Gavo's coat.'

'Because you shot him.'

Marek almost falls out of his seat. 'I didn't shoot him, Doctor, he was already dead!'

I am scribbling again, mostly just to look official. Dominic is sweating in frustration. I say: 'I will need to speak with his family.'

'He has no family. He's not from around here.'

'Then why was he buried here?'

'He was some sort of peddler from far away, we didn't know anything about him. We wanted to do right by him.'

To me, this is becoming more and more frustrating—but I think: *maybe that is why they are all suddenly coming down with tuberculosis, maybe he was infected and brought it in, even though he seemed perfectly healthy to them.* But then, he has only been here for a short time, certainly not enough time to get the whole village sick—but obviously long enough for them to shoot him in the back of the head. 'Who will give me permission to dig up the body?'

'You don't need it.' Marek is wringing his hands. 'We nailed the coffin shut, and then we put him in the church. He's still in there.'

I look through the door again, and, sure enough, there is Aran Darić, standing at the church door, pistol in hand. Just in case. 'I see.'

'No,' Marek says. He is almost crying, and he is wringing his hat furiously in his hands. Dominic has all but given up. Marek says: 'No, you don't see. People with blood on their clothes are sitting up in coffins and then there is blood on our pillows in the morning. I don't believe you see at all.'

So there we are, Dominic and I, standing in the little stone church at Bistrina, and the coffin of the man called Gavo is there, lying at an angle from the door, as if it's been shoved in pretty quickly. It's a dusty wooden coffin. The church is stone, and quiet. It smells of sandalwood and wax, and there is an icon of the Virgin above the door. The windows are blue glass. It is a beautiful church, but it is obvious that no one has been in it for a long time—the candles are all out, and this fellow Gavo's coffin is covered with a few spatters of white, which the doves that live in the belfry have been dropping down on him. It is a sad thing to see, because as far as I know, this man Gavo has done nothing to deserve being shot in the back of the head at his own funeral. Twice.

After we come in, Aran Darić closes the door behind us quickly and suddenly, and for a long time everything is quiet in the little church. We've come in with our satchels, and we've also brought a crowbar to open the coffin, and we begin to realize that perhaps we should have brought in more than just the crowbar—a team of oxen, for example, because the coffin has not only been nailed shut, but also crisscrossed with extra boards across the lid, and chained around and around with what looks like a bicycle chain. Someone, probably as an afterthought, has thrown a string of garlic onto the coffin, and the heads are lying there in their paper shells.

Dominic manages to say to me, 'Shame, awful shame.' Then he spits and says, 'Peasants.'

And then we hear something that is altogether incredible, something you cannot even begin to appreciate because, without hearing for yourself the way it sounded in the quiet church, you won't believe it happened. It is the sound of shuffling movement, and then, all of a sudden, a voice from the coffin, a frank, polite, slightly muffled voice that says: 'Water.'

We are, of course, completely paralyzed. Dominic Lazlo stands beside me, gripping the crowbar in a white fist. His breathing is slow and shallow, and his mustache is beginning to sweat, and he is swearing quietly again and again in Hungarian. I am on the verge of saying something when the voice—same tone, very passive, just asking—says: 'Pardon me: water, please.'

And then *quick, quick, he's alive, open the coffin!* Dominic Lazlo is thrusting the edge of the crowbar under the lid, and I am on my knees trying to yank off the bicycle chain. We're hammering away at the coffin like we're trying to pry the whole thing to pieces, and Dominic has his foot against the side and he's heaving down on the length of the crowbar like a madman, and I am not helping by saying, *push push push.* And then the lid, creaking like bone, snaps off and there he is, the man Gavo lying back against the cushions with his folded purple napkin, looking slightly dusty but otherwise unharmed.

We grab him by the arms and pull him into a sitting position, which, in retrospect, isn't something I recommend you ever do with someone who's been shot in the back of the head, because who knows what's kept him alive. But I think, how extraordinary. I have been expecting this man to look older, white hair, maybe a mustache.

But Gavo is young, thirty at most, and he has a fine head of dark hair and a pleased expression on his face. It is hard to believe that a man who has just been pulled out of a coffin where he has spent several days can look anything short of exuberant; but that's the extraordinary thing, he just looks very pleased, sitting there, with his hands in his lap.

'Do you know your name?' I ask him. There is still a lot of urgency for me, and so I widen his eyes with my fingers and peer inside. He looks at me with interest.

'Oh yes,' he says. 'Gavo.' He sits there patiently while I feel his forehead and take his pulse. Then he says: 'I'm sorry, but I would really like some water.'

Half a minute later, Dominic takes off running through the village to the well, and allegedly passes Marek, who shouts, 'I told you, didn't I?' after him. In the meantime, I am opening my medical bag and taking out my things and listening to Gavo's heart, which still beats firmly under the thin rib bones of his chest. He asks me who I am, and I tell him I'm Dr. Leandro from such and such battalion, and not to worry. Dominic comes back with the water, and, as Gavo tips the bucket to drink, I notice the drops of blood on the coffin pillow, and Dominic and I both look around the side of Gavo's head. And sure enough, there they are, two bullets, sitting like metal eyes in the nest of Gavo's hair. Now there is the question of, shall we risk moving him or perform the excision right here—and, should we perform the excision at all, because what if we pull the bullets out and his brains come running after them like undercooked eggs? And then we have a funeral after all, and have to try the whole village for murder, or else we get implicated somehow, and then the whole thing ends in disaster for everybody.

So I ask him: 'How do you feel, Gavo?'

He has finished the bucket and he puts it down on his knees. He looks suddenly refreshed, and he says: 'Much better, thank you.' Then he looks at

Dominic and thanks him in Hungarian and commends him on his masterful handling of the crowbar.

I am careful about what I say next. 'You have been shot in the head twice,' I say. 'I need to take you to the hospital so we can decide how best to treat you.'

But Gavo is cheerful. 'No, thank you,' he says. 'It is very late already, I should be on my way.' And he grips the sides of the coffin and pulls himself out, just like that. A small cloud of dust lifts off him and falls to the ground, and he stands there in the little church, looking up at the stained glass windows and the light drifting in as if it is breaking through water.

I get up and I push him back down, and I say to him: 'Please don't do that again, you are in a serious condition, very serious.'

'It is not so serious,' he says, smiling. He reaches around and fingers the bullets in the back of his head, and the whole time he is smiling at me rather like a cow. I can picture his fingers moving around on the bullets, and the whole time he is touching them I am reaching for his hands to stop him, and I can imagine his eyes moving around, in and out of his head, as the bullets push his brains about. Which, of course, isn't happening. But you can see it all the same. Then he says: 'I know this is probably very frightening for you, Doctor, but this is not the first time this has happened.'

'I'm sorry?' I say.

He tells me: 'I was once shot in the eye at Plovotje, during a battle.'

'Last year?' I say, because there was a political skirmish out at Plovotje, and several people died,

71

and moreover I believe him to be mistaken about the eye, because neither of his eyes is missing.

'No, no, no,' he says. 'In the war.'

This other battle at Plovotje, in the war, was something like fifteen years ago, so this is not impossible. But still, there is the matter of his having both eyes, and I have decided, by now, that there is nothing to do but ignore him, and I tell myself that yes, it is true, the bullets have made mincemeat of his brains. I tell him I know he is in great pain, and that these things are hard to accept. But he is smiling so persistently that I stop and look at him hard. Perhaps it is brain damage, perhaps it is shock, perhaps he has lost too much blood. Suffice it to say that he is looking at us with such profound calm that Dominic whispers a question to him in Hungarian, and even I know he is asking whether this man is a vampire. Gavo merely laughs—pleasant, polite as always—and Dominic looks like he is about to cry.

'You misunderstand,' Gavo says. 'It's not a supernatural matter—I cannot die.'

I am dumbfounded. 'How do you mean?'

'I am not permitted,' he says.

'I'm sorry?'

'I am not permitted,' he says again. Like he is saying, *for my health, I am not permitted to dance the kolo, or to marry a fat woman.*

Something makes me ask: 'Then how were you drowned?'

'I wasn't. As you see.'

'People in this village will swear that you were dead when they pulled you out of the water and put you in that coffin.'

'They are very nice people. Have you met

72

Marek? His sister is a lovely woman.' He makes a pleasant, round gesture with his arms.

'How did twenty people mistake you for dead if, as you say, you were not drowned?'

'I was conversing with a certain gentleman, and he was not too happy about what I had to say, so he held me underwater,' Gavo says. 'I may have passed out. Sometimes, under strain, I tire easily. These things happen.'

'A man held you underwater?' I say, and he nods. 'What man?'

'A villager, no one of particular importance.'

This is becoming more and more complicated, or possibly about to become very simple, so I say: 'Is he the same man who shot you?'

But Gavo says, 'I really don't know—I was shot in the back of the head.' He sees the way I am looking at him, and he says: 'I feel that you and I, Doctor, are not understanding one another as we should. You see, it is not that I won't accept death, or that I pretend it hasn't happened and therefore I am alive. I am simply telling you that, as sure as you are sitting here in this church, in front of God and your Hungarian fellow—who will not let go of his crowbar because he still thinks I am a vampire—that I cannot die.'

'Whyever not?'

'My uncle has forbidden it.'

'Your uncle. Who is your uncle?'

'I am not disposed to say. Especially because I feel you will be laughing at me. Now'—dusting himself off again—'it is getting late, and no doubt some of your villagers will be hovering outside to see what progress you are making. Please let me up, and I will be on my way.'

73

'Do not get up.'

'Please do not pull my coat.'

'I forbid it. Your brains, right now, are plugged up in your head by two bullets, and if one of them dislodges, everything in there is going to come running out like pudding. I would be insane to let you up.'

'I would be insane to stay here,' he says to me in an exasperated voice. 'Any minute now your Hungarian is going to go outside and call in the others, and then there will be business with garlic and stakes and things. And even though I cannot die, I have to tell you that I do not enjoy having a tent peg put in my ribs. I've had it before, and I do not want it again.'

'If I can promise the villagers will not be involved—if I can promise you real doctors, and a clean hospital bed, no stakes, no shouting, will you be still and let me do my work?'

He laughs at me, and I tell him I want to take him to the field hospital, some twelve kilometers away, to make sure he is properly cared for. I tell him I will send Dominic on foot to get some people to come out with the car, and that we will carry Gavo out in the coffin, and make him comfortable on the drive. I even humor him, I tell him that, if he is not going to die, he can at least get out of this church in some acceptable way, some safe way that will ensure he will not be shot at again. I tell him this because I think, on some level, that he is afraid of the man who shot him, and all the while he is looking at me with great sympathy—this great sympathy, as if this is so pleasant for him, he is so moved by my gesture, by the fact that I care so much for his plugged-up brains. He says all right, he will stay until the medics come, and I give Dominic instructions, I tell him to walk back to the field hospital and have them bring the car out with a stretcher and one of the other field surgeons. Dominic is very nervous at the idea of my staying in the church with a vampire, and I can see that he is not at all looking forward to the prospect of walking twelve kilometers in the dark, especially after what he has seen, but he agrees to do it. He will set off immediately and, on his way, he will give the nearest sentry orders to quarantine the nearest bridge so that sick people from the village cannot leave, and no one traveling in this direction can cross to stop at the village. Gavo shakes Dominic's hand, and Dominic gives him a feeble smile, and off he goes.

Now I am alone with Gavo, and I light some of the lamps in the church, and the pigeons in the rafters are cooing and fluttering here and there above us in the darkness. I roll up my coat and I put it down like a pillow in the coffin, and then I take out my bandages and I start to bandage Gavo's head so that the bullets will not fall out. He sits very patiently and gives me that cowlike look, and for the first time, I wonder if somehow he is going to make me feel safe and pleasant enough to fall asleep, and then I will find myself starting awake with him standing over me, growling like an animal, his eyes bulging like a rabid dog's. You know I don't believe in these things, Natalia, but at that moment, I find myself feeling sorry for poor Dominic, who does.

I ask Gavo about his drowning.

'Who is the man who held you underwater?' I

75

say.

'It doesn't matter,' Gavo says. 'It doesn't matter at all.'

'I think it may,' I tell him. 'I think he may have been the man who shot you.'

'Does it matter?' Gavo says. 'He hasn't killed me.'

'Not yet,' I say.

He looks at me patiently. I am passing the bandage over one of his eyes, and now he looks like a mummy, like a mummy from one of those movies. 'Not at all,' he says.

I do not want to go back to this business of deathlessness, so I say to him: 'Why did he try to drown you?'

And like a shot, he answers: 'Because I told him that *he* was going to die.'

Now I am thinking, *my God, I'm bandaging up a murderer, he came here to kill someone and they tried to drown him and they shot him in the head in self-defense, and that is what this whole thing has been about. Dominic has left only a half hour ago, and I have all night to be alone with this man. Who knows what might happen?* I tell myself, *if he starts toward me, I'll hit him in the back of the head and turn over his coffin and I'll run like hell.*

'Did you come to kill him?' I say.

'Of course not,' Gavo says. 'He was dying of tuberculosis—you've heard what they're saying around the village, I'm sure. I only came to tell him, to help him, to be here when it happened. Come now, Doctor—blood on pillows, a terrible cough. What was your diagnosis even before you came here?'

I am very surprised by this. 'Are you a doctor?'

76

'I was once, yes.'

'And now? Are you a priest?'

'Not exactly a priest, no,' he says. 'But I have made it my work to make myself available to the dying and the dead.'

'Your work?'

'For my uncle,' he says. 'In repayment to my uncle.'

'Is your uncle a priest?' I say.

Gavo laughs, and he says: 'No, but he makes much work for priests.' I finish bandaging him up, and he still won't tell me who his uncle is. I am beginning to suspect he may be some political radical, one of those men who have been instigating the skirmishes in the north. If that is true, I would rather not know who his uncle is.

'You may want to identify the man who tried to kill you,' I tell him. 'He could hurt others.'

'I very much doubt that. I doubt anyone else is going to tell him he is about to die.'

'Well, then, I would like to know who he is, so I can give him medicine.'

'He is beyond medicine,' Gavo says. 'It is very understandable that he was angry. I don't blame him for trying to drown me.' He watches me put my things away and close up my medical bag. 'People become very upset,' Gavo tells me, 'when they find out they are going to die. You must know this, Doctor, you must see it all the time.'

'I suppose,' I say.

'They behave very strangely,' he says. 'They are suddenly filled with life. Suddenly they want to fight for things, ask questions. They want to throw hot water in your face, or beat you senseless with an umbrella, or hit you in the head with a rock.

77

Suddenly they remember things they have to do, people they have forgotten. All that refusal, all that resistance. Such a luxury.'

I take his temperature, and it is normal, but he sounds to me like he is getting more agitated.

'Why don't you lie back down?' I tell him.

But he says: 'I'd like some more water, please.' And out of nowhere, probably from inside the coffin, or from inside his coat pocket, he pulls out a little cup, a small white cup with a gold rim, and he holds it out to me.

I tell him I am not going out to the village well and leaving him here by himself, and he points to the vestibule and tells me that holy water will do just fine. You know me, Natalia, you know I don't believe in these things, but you know I cross myself if I go into a church out of respect for people who do. I do not have a problem giving holy water to a man who is dying in a church. So I fill up the cup, and he drinks it, and then I give him another, and I ask him how long he has been without urinating, and he tells me he isn't sure, but that he certainly doesn't feel like it now. I take his blood pressure. I take his pulse. I give him more water, and eventually he agrees to lie back down, and I sit against one of the pews and I untie my shoes and think about poor Dominic. I have no inclination to doze off, but I am deep in thought—I am thinking about these people, and their epidemic, I am thinking about the bridge over the nearby river, the quarantine lanterns lit. I am thinking about why we've quarantined ourselves, who would come this way in the dead of night to this small, faraway village. An hour, maybe an hour and a half, goes by this way, and

78

Gavo is making no noise inside his coffin, so I lean over him to look inside. There is something very unsettling about someone looking up at you from a coffin. He has very large, very round eyes, and they are very open. He smiles at me and he says, 'Don't worry, Doctor, I still can't die.' I go back to sitting against the pews, and from where I am sitting I see his arms come up and he stretches them a little, and then they go back inside the coffin.

'Who is your uncle?' I say.

'I don't think you really want to know,' he says.

'Well, I'm asking.'

'There is no point in telling you,' Gavo says. 'I confided in you as a fellow man of medicine, but I can see you will not believe me, and this conversation cannot go anywhere if some part of it is not taken in good faith.'

I am honest. I say to him: 'I am interested in who your uncle is because you believe it explains your being unable to die.'

'It does.'

'Well?'

'If you do not believe I cannot die—even though a man held me underwater for ten minutes and then shot me in the back of the head twice—I do not see you believing who my uncle is. I do not see it.' I can hear him shuffling around in the coffin, his shoulders moving, his boots on the bottom of the coffin.

'Please hold still,' I say.

'I would like some coffee,' he says.

I laugh in his face, and I tell him is he crazy?—I am not going to give him coffee in his condition.

'If we have coffee, I can prove to you that I

79

cannot die,' he says.

'How?'

'You will see,' he says, 'if you make the coffee.'
I see him sit up, and he leans out of the coffin and
looks inside my traveling bag, and he takes out the
coffee box and the paraffin burner. I tell him to lie
down, for God's sake, but he only says: 'Go on,
make us some coffee, Doctor, and I'll show you.'

I have nothing else to do, so I make coffee. I
make coffee with holy water, the smell of the
paraffin burning inside the church. He watches me
do this while he sits, cross-legged, on the velvet
cushions of his coffin, and I find that I've given up
insisting he lie down. I stir the coffee with a
tongue depressor, and the brown grit spreads
through the water in a thick cloud, and he watches
it, still smiling.

When the coffee is done, he insists we both
drink from the little white cup with the gold rim.
He says this is how he will prove what he means
about being deathless, and by this time I am
intrigued, so I let him reach out of the coffin and
pour me a cup. He tells me to hold it in my hands
and not to blow on it, to sit with it until it becomes
cool enough to drink in one swallow. While I'm
holding the cup, I'm telling myself that I am crazy.
I am sitting, I tell myself, *in a church, drinking
coffee with a man who has two bullets lodged in his
head.*

'Now drink it,' he says, and I do. It is still too
hot, and it burns my tongue, and I cough when
I've finished it. But he's already taking the cup
from my hands and peering inside. He tips it my
way so I can see. The bottom is clotted with grit.
Then I realize what's going on.

80

'You're reading my coffee grit?' I say. I am dumbfounded. This is what gypsies do, or magicians at the circus.

'No, no,' he says. 'Sure enough, grit is involved. In this grit, I can see your death.'

'You must be joking,' I say.

'No, I can see it,' he says. 'It is there. The fact that you have grit, in and of itself, is a certain thing.'

'Of course it's certain,' I say. 'It's coffee. Everybody has grit. Grit is certain.'

'So is death,' he says. Then he holds up his hand, and he pours himself a cup. He holds it in his hands, and I am too angry at myself to speak, too angry that I allowed him to persuade me to make coffee just to be mocked like this. After a few minutes, he drinks his coffee, and a thin little stream of it runs down his neck, and I am thinking about the bullets quivering in his skull and praying they don't dislodge—or, now, maybe I am praying that they do.

Gavo holds out the cup to me, and the cup is empty. I can see the white bottom, and the inside of the cup is as dry as if he had just wiped it with a towel.

'Satisfied?' he says, looking at me like he's just done something wonderful.

'I'm sorry?' I say.

'I have no grit,' he says.

'This is a joke,' I tell him.

'Certainly not,' he says. 'Look.' And he runs his finger across the bottom of the cup.

'That you have no grit in your coffee cup proves to me that you are deathless?'

'It certainly should,' he says. He says it like he

81

has just solved a mathematical equation, like I am being difficult about something that is fact.

'It's a party trick.'

'No. It's not a trick. The cup is special, that is true, but it is not a joke cup—it was given to me by my uncle.'

'To hell with your uncle,' I shout. 'You lie down and shut up until the medics get here.'

'I'm not going to the hospital, Doctor,' he says, flatly. 'My name is Gavran Gailé, and I am a deathless man.'

I shake my head and I turn off the paraffin burner, and put away the coffee box. I want to take his cup away, but I don't want to provoke him. He never stops smiling.

'How can I prove to you that I am telling the truth?' I think I hear resignation in his voice, and I realize he is tired, he has tired of me.

'You can't.'

'What would satisfy you?'

'Your cooperation—please.'

'This is getting ridiculous.' I am so stunned at his audacity in saying this that I have nothing to say to him. He looks like a lamb, sitting there in that coffin with big lamb eyes. 'Let me up, and I promise to prove to you that I cannot die.'

'There is no such thing as a deathless body. This will end in complete disaster. You're going to die, you stubborn bastard, and I am going to go to prison over you.'

'Anything you want,' he says. 'Shoot me, stab me if you like. Set me on fire. I will even put money on it. We can even bet the old-fashioned way—I can name my terms after I win.'

I tell him I will not bet.

'You are not a betting man?' he says.

'On the contrary—I do not waste my time with bets I am sure to win.'

'Now I see that you are angry, Doctor,' he says. 'Wouldn't you like to crack me in the head with one of those planks?'

'Lie down,' I say.

'Too violent,' Gavran Gailé is saying. 'All right, something else.' He is still sitting up in the coffin, looking about the room. 'What about the lake?' he finally says. 'Why not throw me into the lake with weights tied to my feet?'

Now, Natalia, you know I anger easily. You know I've no patience for fools. And I am so angry about the cup and the cheap trick with the coffee—that I allowed myself to be duped into making him coffee, and from my field rations, too—that I do not care, I am ready to let him do whatever he wants, to hang himself. It's dark, it's late, I have been on the road for hours. I am alone with this man who is telling me to hit him with planks, and now he is telling me to throw me into the lake. I have not agreed, but I have not disagreed, and perhaps there's something hallucinatory about it—I don't know. He sees that I am not telling him to lie down. Suddenly, he is getting out of the coffin, and he says to me, 'That is excellent, afterwards you will be glad.' I tell him I have no doubt of this.

There's a lake right beside the church, and we hunt around for something heavy enough. I find two enormous cinder blocks under the altar, and I make him carry them down the stairs. Secretly, I am hoping he will faint, but this does not happen. He rearranges the bandage around his head while

I unwind the bicycle chain from the coffin where the villagers put Gavo. He helps me gather my belongings, smiling, smiling. I go outside first, and find that Aran Darić, probably at Dominic's instructions, is long gone. It is very late, and the village is completely dark. I am certain they are watching us through the windows, but I don't care. I tell him to come out, and then the two of us walk through the mud and the moss, and onto the little jetty that goes out over the pond, where the village children probably fish. Gavo seems very excited by all this. I get him to put his feet in the gaps in the cinder blocks, and then I wrap the chain around his ankles and through the cinder blocks, tight and complicated, until you can't even see that he has feet at the ends of his legs.

I am beginning to feel guilty while this is going on, and afraid. I have not been thinking of myself as a doctor, but as a man of science simply proving that an idiot is an idiot. *Still,* I say to myself, *I do not want this idiot's blood on my hands.*

'There,' I say, when I am done. He lifts his feet, just slightly, first one, then the other, like a child trying out roller skates.

'Well done, Doctor,' he says.

'We must take some precaution,' I say. Gavo looks annoyed. 'It would be irresponsible of me to let you go into that lake without some precaution.' I am looking around for some way to hold him to shore, and there is a length of rope tied up around a post on the jetty, and I take this rope and tie the free end of it around his waist. He watches me do this with great interest.

'I want your word,' I say, 'that you will pull on the rope when you begin to drown.'

84

'I will not be drowning, Doctor,' he says. 'But because you have been so kind to me, I will give you my word. I will pledge something on it.' He takes a few moments to think about this, tugging at the rope around his waist to make sure the knot is tight. Then he says: 'I pledge my coffee cup that I will not die tonight, Doctor.' And he takes it out of his breast pocket and holds it up to me between his fingers, like an egg.

'I don't want your damned cup.'

'Even so. I pledge it. What will you pledge, Doctor?'

'Why should I pledge?' I ask him. 'I am not going into the lake.'

'Just the same, I should like you to pledge something. I would like you to pledge something against my death, so that, when we meet next, we needn't go through this again.'

It is all ridiculous, but I look around for something to pledge. He will be pulling on that rope, I tell myself, and soon. I ask him if I can pledge the paraffin burner, and he laughs at me and says, 'You mock me by pledging that. Come, Doctor. You must pledge something of value to you.'

I take out my old *Jungle Book*—you know, that old one I keep in my pocket—and I show it to him. 'I will pledge this,' I say. He is looking at it with great interest, and then he leans forward with the cinder blocks on his feet and sniffs it.

'I take it this is something you would not want to lose?'

It occurs to me that I had better be clear, as we are both pledging things that mean a great deal to us, so I say: 'I pledge it on the grounds that you

85

will begin to drown.'

'Not that I will die?'

'No, because you have pledged to pull on the rope before that happens,' I tell him. 'This is your chance,' I say, 'to change your mind. The medics are probably already on their way.' This is a lie, Dominic is probably only halfway to the field hospital by now. But I try. Gavran Gailé smiles and smiles.

He holds out his hand, and when I go to shake his, he puts something cold and metallic in my palm. The bullets, I realize. While I've been arranging this trip into the lake, he has taken them out. I am looking down at them, shining with blood, matted with clumps of hair, and suddenly Gavo is stepping back toward the edge of the jetty, and he says to me: 'Well, Doctor, I will be seeing you shortly.' Then he leans over and drops into the lake. I cannot remember the splash at all.

I can hear Dominic's voice saying to me, 'My God, boss. You've send a man with two bullet in his head into lake with stones tied to his feet.' I don't do anything, not while there are bubbles, and also not when there are no bubbles anymore. The rope straightens out a little, but then it is still.

At first, I tell myself that maybe I should have tied Gavo's hands to his ankles—perhaps, with his hands free, he has too much accommodation to untie himself and break off a hollow reed, or push up a lily pad, and conceal a breathing mechanism from me, like something out of a Robin Hood film. Then it occurs to me that I haven't thought this out properly, because, if he dies in that pond, he will not come up easily with those bricks tied to his feet. Then I remember that he was originally buried for having drowned, and I tell myself that this is a man who holds his breath—this is a man who plays jokes on honest people by performing a circus trick so that others will believe themselves guilty of his death, and he can walk away with some sick feeling of triumph, some feeling of having made fools of them.

'I am not going anywhere,' I say to myself, 'until he either comes up or floats up.' I sit down on the bank and I hold on to the rope. I take out my pipe and I start to smoke it. I can picture the villagers sitting at their darkened windows, staring out at me in horror—me, the doctor, who let a miraculous survivor drown. Eventually five minutes pass, and then seven. Ten minutes, twelve. At fifteen I've really got that pipe going, and the rope is as stiff as a board. He's not coming up, and there are no bubbles. I am thinking that I have misjudged the depth of the pond, that the rope has tightened around his waist and broken all his ribs. I am beginning to pull the rope now, but gently, every few minutes, so that, if by some miracle of God he is alive, I do not hurt him, but so that he will be reminded to pull back on it. He does not do this, however, and I am absolutely convinced, at this point, that he is dead, and I've been tricked into a huge mistake. His body is floating limp, I tell myself, like he's been hanged, floating over his own feet like a balloon. *A man is not a porpoise,* is what I am thinking. *A man cannot survive a thing like this. A man does not just slow his heart down because he feels he should.*

After an hour, I have cried a little, mostly for myself, and I am out of tobacco. I have stopped tugging. I can already see my firing squad. Or maybe, I am thinking, a little cave somewhere in Greece. I am thinking about what I could change my name to. The night is going by and by, until, eventually, it is that hour before dawn, when the birds are coming awake.

This is when the most extraordinary thing happens. I hear a sound in the water, and I look up. The rope is moving through the water, rising up, wet. Light is beginning slowly in the east, and I can see the opposite bank of the lake, where the woods come all the way up to the bulrushes. And there he is, Gavran Gailé—the deathless man—climbing slowly and wetly out of the lake on the opposite side, his coat completely drenched, water grasses on his shoulders. He's got the cinder blocks on his feet, and the rope around his waist, and it's been hours. I am on my feet, but I am very quiet. Gavran Gailé's hat is dripping over his ears, and he takes it off and shakes the water out of it. Then he bends down and unwinds the chains from his feet. He does this like he is taking off his shoes, and then he undoes the knot of the rope around his waist and lets it fall back into the water.

He turns around, and it is really him, really his face, as smiling and polite as ever, as he says to me, 'Remember your pledge, Doctor—for next time.' He waves to me, and then he turns around and disappears into the woods.

3

THE DIGGERS

The first night at Barba Ivan and Nada's place, I slept for three hours, and after that my dreams filled up with the music of the cicadas and I woke up stifled by the heat. My bed faced the window that looked out over the vineyards behind the house, and through it I could see an orange half-moon falling down the spine of the hillside. Zóra, facedown and prostrate, had kicked off the covers, legs hanging off the end of the bed; her breath was caught in a tight whistle somewhere between her arms and hair and the pillows. Downstairs, the little girl was coughing again, and her coughs were sticky and unfinished; she was trying to sleep through them. Somewhere among layers of noise was the sea, dragging foam up the beach on the other side of the house.

Months later, long after the forty days were over, when I had already begun to piece things together, I would still go to sleep hoping that he would find his way into my dreams and tell me something important. I was always disappointed, of course, because even when I did dream of him, he would inevitably be sitting in an armchair we didn't own, in a room I didn't recognize, and he would say things like, *Bring me the newspaper, I'm hungry,* and I would know, even in my sleep, that it didn't mean a fucking thing. But that night, I hadn't learned to think of him as dead yet, hadn't processed news that seemed too distant to belong

89

to me, not even when I tried to bring it closer by thinking of his absence from our house.

I thought about our pantry. It was an enormous cupboard built into the kitchen wall opposite the sink, ceiling-to-floor eggshell doors, the plastic bags from Zlatan's bakery swinging from the door handles as you opened it. I could see my grandma's big flour tin, white and blue, with a little cheerful baker in a chef's hat smiling from the front of it. The bottom shelf with its plastic bags and cereals, the salt tin, mixing bowls, the orange and brown coffee bags from the store down the street. And then, higher up on the center shelf, four glass bowls in a neat line across the middle of the cupboard. Almonds, sunflower seeds, walnuts, and cut-up squares of bittersweet baking chocolate. My grandfather's snack regimen, always ready ahead of time. There for thirty-five more days.

The diggers were back in the vineyard again; I couldn't see them in the darkness, but they were there, long shadows moving in the faint beam of a single flashlight that seemed to shift constantly, except for a few minutes here and there when whoever held it put it down to continue digging, and the light shone into the vines until they tightened and drowned it out. Every so often, one of the diggers would cough; and while I was watching the vineyard, the little girl kept coughing, too.

Around four in the morning, I got dressed and went downstairs. Bis was nowhere to be seen, but his likeness, face slightly twisted by an unsteady hand, peered down at me from a sketch above the umbrella pot by the back door. There was an antique telephone on the living room desk, a rotary dial with a heavy brass-and-bone receiver, the numbers in the wheel worn away to nothing. I took the crumpled receipt with the Zdrevkov clinic number out of my pocket and dialed. At first, I got a busy signal, and it raised my hopes; I could picture the night-duty receptionist, blue eye shadow oiling the creases of her eyes, blond hair disheveled, keeping herself awake with a tantalizingly forbidden call to an overseas boyfriend. But when I called again, it rang and rang, this time without even going dead until I replaced the receiver. Afterward, I sat on the couch while gray light crawled into the spaces between the shutters.

When the coughing started again, it sounded wet and close. It occurred to me that the little girl had wandered out of her room, but she wasn't in the kitchen or the laundry, or in any of the other rooms on the main landing, rooms that smelled of fresh paint and were full of shrouded furniture. I held on to the banister so that I wouldn't trip in the dark on the way down, feeling my way along the wall. Downstairs, the air was cool. Two doors in the narrow corridor, both open to rooms that were empty except for beds and a jumble of belongings: piles of blankets on the floor, iron pots stacked in the corner, countless cigarette butts lying in ashtrays. There were bottles by the bed, *rakija* and beer bottles; a few bottles of some herb liquor, long-necked bottles full of clear liquid stuffed with lashed bunches of dead grass. The men were gone, and so were the boys Nada had talked about. But the young woman and the little girl were sitting in an armchair by the window in the second room. The woman was asleep, her head tipped back

91

against the cushion. She had a lavender pouch, too, and held the little girl propped up against her chest, wrapped in a thin sheet that clung like wet paper to the child's shoulders and knees. The child was awake, and staring.

The little girl was looking at me without fear or deference, and I found myself coming into the room, taking a few steps on the balls of my feet. At this distance, I could smell the alcohol, the thin, searing smell of walnut *rakija*. The sheet had been soaked in it; they were trying to bring down her fever, break it by cooling her very quickly. It was a backwater method, a precipitous gamble, and we'd seen it over and over at the urgent care clinic— new mothers who couldn't be steered away from their own mothers' remedies.

I reached over the woman and put the heel of my hand against the little girl's forehead. She was warm, but it was the damp warmth of a fever that had broken. There was no way of telling when and if it would spike again or how high it had been, but the strain in her eyes had unbuckled, and she didn't lift her head from her sleeping mother's neck at all, just looked at me without focus or interest while I backed out of the room.

I waited for the diggers, but an hour went by and they didn't come back. There was no movement, no sign of anyone in the house. The little girl had fallen asleep, and the parrot, who had temporarily climbed down to the cage bottom and clattered around for a while, had gone quiet. In that silence, there was only the incessant ringing of the Zdrevkov clinic line, and then I got fed up, took my white coat off the peg and went out to find the road up to the vineyard.

There was no way to get up the slope behind Barba Ivan and Nada's house, so I walked north toward the main square where the silent spire of the monastery rose out among the roofs. Early morning, and the restaurants and shops were still shuttered, grills cold, leaving room for the heavy smell of the sea. For about a third of a mile, there were only houses: whitewashed stone beach houses with iron railings and open windows, humming neon signs that read *Pension* in three or four languages. I passed the arcade, a firestorm of yellow and red and blue lights under an awning laden with pine needles. The Brejevina camping ground was a moonlit flat of dry grass, fenced off with chicken wire.

A greenish stone canal ran up past the campground, and this was the route I took. Green shutters, flower boxes in the windows, here and there a garage with a tarped car and maybe some chickens huddled on the hood. There were wheelbarrows full of patching bricks or cement or manure; one or two houses had gutting stations for fish set up, and laundry lines hung from house to house, heavy with sheets and headless shirts, pegged rows of socks. A soft-muzzled, black donkey was breathing softly, tied to a tree in someone's front yard.

At the end of the canal, I found the vineyard gate. It was unmarked, rusted over with the salt in the air, and it opened up to a slope of cypresses and limestone ridges. The sun was coming up, whitening the sky above the mountain. I could see the diggers moving around among the vines, men straightening up here and there to stretch and yawn and light cigarettes. There were seven or eight men with shovels scattered across the slope, and they were digging in an irregular pattern, what seemed like complete disarray, under the cypresses and between the rows, as high up as the top of the vineyard where the plot became scrubland, turning over the dew-moistened earth. The clink of their shovels, which had carried all the way down the hill last night, was somehow not so loud here. Up ahead, one of the men was singing.

I was unsteady on the loose dirt of the slope, and there were mounds and shallow holes everywhere. My eyes had adjusted to the half-light, and as I stepped through the rows I came across the nearest man, heavyset and hatted, sitting on the ground a few yards away. He was turned away from me, leaning on his shovel and uncorking what looked like a flask, and I was opening my mouth to greet him when my leg dropped into one of the holes, and I went down.

When he caught sight of me trying to get myself out of the hole, his breath stuck and he staggered back, eyes wild, lips blue, chins shaking. 'Mother of Christ!' he shouted, and I realized he was crossing himself, and for a moment I thought he was going to take a swing at me with his shovel. I had my hands up and was shouting that I was a doctor, I was a doctor, don't.

He took a minute to recover, still breathing heavily. 'Motherfuck you,' he said, still crossing himself. The commotion of our encounter had sent the other men running toward us, and they were emerging now from the vines, heads and shovels, an arm here and there, their faces indistinguishable. Someone stepped forward with the flashlight, and the beam lanced my eyes.

'Do you see her?' my fat victim asked one of the men. 'Duré, you see her?'

He said this to a short man who had materialized out of a corner row down the slope. 'I thought you found something,' the man said. He was switch-thin. His ears were remarkable—sticking away from his face in silhouette like pot handles—and the sweat on his face was breaking through a fine layer of pale dust that had caked solid in the creases around his eyes and mouth.

'But, Duré, do you *see* her?'

'It's all right,' Duré said, clapping the fat man's shoulder. 'It's all right.' And to me, he said, 'What the hell are you doing?' I had no answer. 'Don't you know better than to come creeping up here in the middle of the night? What's the matter with you?'

'I'm a doctor,' I said, feeling stupid.

He squinted at my white coat—splattered now with dust and something I hoped was mud—and then he shook his head. 'Jesus.'

'I'm sorry,' I said to the heavyset man, and he leveled some incomprehensible, regional epithet at me, almost certainly not an acceptance of my apology. Then he picked up his flask and waddled off into the rows, muttering to himself and coughing that same cough I had heard from the house. The men who had been standing around began to disperse, returning to their places among the vines. Duré dusted his hands off on the gray jumpsuit he was wearing, then lit a cigarette. He didn't seem particularly interested in why I was there, or why I wasn't leaving, and eventually he turned around and headed back down the slope. I followed him between the rows until he found his shovel, and stood behind him as he swung it into the hard dirt under the vines.

My hands had broken my fall, and I realized they were scraped up, sticky with blood, dirt pushed in under the skin.

'Got any water?' I said to Duré.

He didn't, but he had *rakija*. He watched me tip a capful of it onto my palms. 'That's homemade,' he told me. It smelled like apricots, and stung.

'I'm a doctor,' I said.

'You keep saying that,' Duré said, taking back his flask. 'I'm a mechanic. Dubi over there is a welder. My uncle shovels shit for a living.' He unscrewed the cap and tilted the flask back.

'I'm staying at Barba Ivan's,' I said. 'I want to talk to you about the little girl.'

'What about her?'

'Is she your daughter?'

'That's what my wife says.' He took a final drag of the cigarette that had been cindering away between his lips, dropped it into the mound of dirt that was slowly piling higher by his sneakers.

'What's her name?'

'What's that got to do with you?' He tucked the *rakija* flask back into the pocket of his gray jumpsuit and swung the shovel off his shoulder and into the ground.

'That little girl is very sick,' I said.

'Really?' said Duré. 'Think it takes you to tell me that—why d'you think I'm out here, for exercise?'

I put my hands in my pockets and watched sunlight sliding up the tips of the hills in the distance. Nada had been right about the other children—two young boys who couldn't have been

96

more than nine, digging with the rest of the men, their faces white, eyelids dark and swollen. They were passing a cigarette between them. I thought to myself, *my grandfather would twist their ears off*—and in that first moment afterward, when I realized that I would not be telling him, I stood there with the dry earth flying and the cicadas scraping their melancholy drone on the cypress slope.

I asked Duré: 'How old are those kids over there?'

'They're my kids,' he said to me, without missing a beat.

'They're smoking,' I said. One of the kids had a long, thick clot of green coming out of one nostril, and as he dug he occasionally licked it away. 'Are they sick, too?' I said.

Duré lanced the shovel, spade down, into the dirt and straightened up to look at me. 'That's not your business,' he said.

'This isn't an ordinary cold. It sounds serious—the little girl could have whooping cough, bronchitis. She could end up with pneumonia.'

'She won't.'

'Has she seen a doctor?'

'She doesn't need one.'

'What about the boys—they don't need one either?'

'They'll be fine,' Duré said.

'I've heard you've got them out here in the afternoons, in the heat. Do you know what that does if someone's got a fever?'

'You've heard, have you?' he said. He was shaking his head, his chuckles weighed down by the way he was leaning forward. 'We do what we have to, Doctor,' he said. 'Don't concern yourself with it.'

'I'm sure you need all the hands you can get for the working season,' I said, trying to sound understanding. 'But you must be able to spare the boys.'

'Work has nothing to do with it,' Duré said.

'Send them down to see us,' I said, pressing on, ignoring him. 'We're from the University—we've got medicines for the new orphanage of Sveti Paškal. There'll be a free clinic.'

'My children aren't orphans.'

'I know,' I said. 'That's all right, it's free medicine.'

'*That's all right,* she says—what's the matter with you?' he said again. 'You think I want my kids around orphans?'

'Well, you'll put them to work when they're sick,' I said loudly. Someone in the vineyard let out a low whistle, and it was followed by an explosion of laughter from the men.

Duré was unfazed. All that time, he hadn't stopped digging for a moment. I could see the gaunt outline of his shoulder blades rising and falling through the gray jumpsuit. By now, this same conversation with my grandfather would probably have come to blows.

'I'll take good care of them,' I said.

'This is family business,' Duré told me. 'They're being cared for.'

I was suddenly incredibly angry. I fought the urge to ask Duré how he would feel about a visit from my friend, the sergeant, back at United Clinics headquarters—how would Duré feel about getting a talking-to from a man who weighed a hundred and fifty kilos and had just spent six weeks supervising the demolition of a third-rate hospital that didn't have running water? But then I felt it might be counterproductive, so I just stood by while Duré lit another cigarette and continued to scrape away. Every so often, he would lean in to examine the dirt carefully, run his fingers through it, and the straightening up—not the cigarette, not the *rakija*—was the effort that forced the wet cough out of him at last.

I said: 'How far do you think you're going to get with that *rakija* wrap, and whatever other insane cures you're trying—smothering them with blankets and putting potato peelings in their socks?' He had stopped listening. 'They need medicine. So does your wife. And I wouldn't be surprised if you did, too.'

There was a shout from the other side of the vineyard. One of the men had found something, and there was a commotion to get to it as quickly as possible. Duré made his way over, probably thinking that leaving me behind would ensure my immediate departure; it didn't. I followed him along the row and then around the corner, to where a slim young man was kneeling over a deep pit in the ground. The men clustered around it. A little way behind them, I stood on tiptoe to see.

Duré leaned down and sifted through the dirt with his free hand. The vineyard had filled with pale light, and the earth was white and moist. He straightened up with something on the palm of his hand—a finger-length shard of something sharp and yellow. Bone, I realized. He turned it over in his fist, looked down into the dirt again.

'What do you say, Doctor?' Duré said, turning around and holding it out to me. I didn't know what he was asking, and I stared stupidly at it.

'Didn't think so,' he said, and dropped it into the dirt. 'Some animal,' he said to the digger who had found it.

One of the boys was standing at my elbow, leaning over the handle of his shovel. He was a scrawny, sandy-haired kid with a wide face, and he was making that wet glazed noise of throat ache between yawns, sucking his tongue back to scrape it along the dry surface of his throat. Just hearing it made my eyes water. When he turned to go, I clapped a hand onto his temples.

'He's got a fever,' I said to Duré, who was heading back down to his little patch at the bottom of the vineyard.

But it was already dawn, and the yellow haze of light had crossed the summit of Mount Brejevina and was coming down the other side toward us, toward the house, our upstairs window behind the oleander bush, and the sea, flat and shining beyond the roof. I felt I'd been awake for days. I couldn't keep up with Duré on the uneven ground, so I was shouting down to him: 'He's sick and underage, you're breaking the law.'

'I'm in my country.'

It was a vehement lie. He had a drawl from just east of the City. 'You're not,' I said.

'Neither are you, Doctor.'

'Still, even out here there are organizations that wouldn't think twice—'

But Duré had heard enough. He came back up toward me so fast we nearly collided, his neck cabled with tendons. I had the higher ground, but he had the shovel, and his eyes were bloodshot. 'You think you're the first coat to tell me something like that?' He was very quiet saying this. I could smell the sting of the apricots on his breath. 'I haven't heard this before, about how you're bringing someone in to interfere, take my kids away? You go ahead, see how long it takes.'

'He's been out here all night—send him home.'

The kid in question had been listening the whole time, standing on the bouldered ground above us, thin shoulders slumped forward. Duré rested the shovel against his thigh and took a pair of work gloves out of his pocket, pulled them over calloused, dark-nailed fingers. 'Marko,' Duré said loudly. 'Doctor advises you to go home.' He did not look at the boy. 'It's up to you.'

The kid hesitated for a moment, looking up and down the vineyard. Then he went back to digging without a word.

Duré watched him with a smile I couldn't categorize. Then he turned to me. 'I've no more time to waste with you. I got a body somewhere under here that needs to come up so my kids can get better.' He turned, dragging the shovel. 'That sound acceptable, Doctor—my kids getting better?'

I watched the thin lines of his hair, slicked back across the bare parts of his head, as he descended, trying to find his footing on the gravel. 'I don't understand,' I said.

'We've got a cousin in this vineyard, Doctor.' He spread his arms and gestured to the vines, from one side of the plot to the other. 'Buried twelve years. During the war.' He was perfectly serious. 'Doesn't like it here, and he's making us sick. When we find him we'll be on our way.'

I was too tired, I thought, and I felt myself

beginning to laugh. He had run out of things to say and had resorted to this to get rid of me. But the digging was shallow, patternless—they hadn't been planting anything, I realized. They hadn't been weeding, either, or smashing the skulls of field mice. I was trying to be funny when I said: 'Have you checked the bridge foundations?'

Duré looked at me for a moment, serious and unblinking. Then he said: 'Sure, it's the first place we looked.'

4

THE TIGER

Having sifted through everything I now know about the tiger's wife, I can tell you that this much is fact: in 1941, in late spring, without declaration or warning, German bombs started falling on the city and did not stop for three days.

The tiger did not know that they were bombs. He did not know anything beyond the hiss and screech of the fighters passing overhead, missiles falling, the sound of bears bellowing in another part of the fortress, the sudden silence of birds. There was smoke and terrible warmth, a gray sun rising and falling in what seemed like a matter of minutes, and the tiger, frenzied, dry-tongued, ran back and forth across the span of the rusted bars, lowing like an ox. He was alone and hungry, and that hunger, coupled with the thunderous noise of bombardment, had burned in him a kind of awareness of his own death, an imminent and

102

innate knowledge he could neither dismiss nor succumb to. He did not know what to do with it. His water had dried up, and he rolled and rolled in the stone bed of his trough, in the uneaten bones lying in a corner of the cage, making that long sad sound that tigers make.

After two days of pacing, his legs gave out, and he was reduced to a contraction of limbs lying in his own waste. He had lost the ability to move, to produce sound, to react in any way. When a stray bomb hit the south wall of the citadel—sending up a choking cloud of smoke and ash and shattering bits of rubble into the skin of his head and flank, bits that would gnaw at his flesh for weeks until he got used to the grainy ache of them when he rolled onto his side or scratched himself against trees— his heart should have stopped. The iridescent air and the feeling of his fur folding back like paper in the heat, and then the long hours during which he crouched at the back of his pen, watching the ruptured flank of the citadel wall. All of these things should have killed him. But something, some flickering of the blood, forced him to his feet and through the gap in the wall. The strength of that drive. (He was not the only one: years later they would write about wolves running down the street, a polar bear standing in the river. They would write about how flights of parrots were seen for weeks above the city, how a prominent engineer and his family lived an entire month off a zebra carcass.)

The tiger's route through the city that night took him north to the waterfront behind the citadel, where the remains of the merchants' port and Jewish quarter spread in flattened piles of brick

103

down the bank and into the waters of the Danube. The river was lit by fires, and those who had gone into it were washing back against the bank where the tiger stood. He considered the possibility of swimming across, and under optimal circumstances he might have attempted it, but the smell rising off the bodies turned the tiger around, sent him back past the citadel hill and into the ruined city.

People must have seen him, but in the wake of bombardment he was anything but a tiger to them: a joke, an insanity, a religious hallucination. He drifted, enormous and silent, down the alleys of Old Town, past the smashed-in doors of coffeehouses and bakeries, past motorcars flung through shopwindows. He went down the tramway, up and over fallen trolleys in his path, beneath lines of electric cable that ran through the city and now hung broken and black as jungle creeper.

By the time he reached Knez Petrova, looters were already swarming the Boulevard. Men were walking by him, past him, alongside him, men with fur coats and bags of flour, with sacks of sugar and ceiling fixtures, with faucets, tables, chair legs, upholstery ripped from the walls of ancient Turkish houses that had fallen in the raid. He ignored them all.

Some hours before sunrise, the tiger found himself in the abandoned market at Kalinia, two blocks up from where my grandfather and my grandma would buy their first apartment fifteen years later. Here, the scent of death that clung to the wind drifting in from the north separated from the pools of rich stench that ran between the cobbles of the market square. He walked with his head down, savoring the spectrum of unrecognizable aromas—splattered tomatoes and spinach that stuck to the grooves in the road, broken eggs, bits of fish, the clotted fat leavings on the sides of the butchers' stands, the thick smell smeared around the cheese counter. His thirst insane, the tiger lapped up pools from the leaky fountain where the flower women filled their buckets, and then put his nose into the face of a sleeping child who had been left, wrapped in blankets, under the pancake stand.

Finally, up through the sleepless neighborhoods of the lower city, with the sound of the second river in his ears, the tiger began to climb the trail into the king's forest. I like to think that he went along our old carriage trail. I like to imagine his big-cat paw prints in the gravel, his exhausted, square-shouldered walk along my childhood paths, years before I was even born—but in reality, the way through the undergrowth was faster, the moss easier on paws he had shredded on city rubble. The cooling feel of the trees bending down to him as he pushed up the hill, until at last he reached the top, the burning city far behind him.

The tiger spent the rest of the night in the graveyard and left the city at dawn. He did not go by unobserved. He was seen first by the grave digger, a man who was almost blind, and who did not trust his eyes to tell him that a tiger, braced on its hind legs, was rummaging through the churchyard garbage heap, mouthing thistles in the early morning sunlight. He was seen next by a small girl, riding in the back of her family's wagon, who noticed him between the trees and thought he was a dream. He was noticed, too, by the city's tank commander, who would go on to shoot himself three days later, and who mentioned the tiger in his last letter to his betrothed—*I have never seen so strange a thing as a tiger in a wheat field,* he wrote, *even though, today, I pulled a woman's black breasts and stomach out of the pond at the Convent of Sveta Maria.* The last person to see the tiger was a farmer on a small plot of land two miles south of the city, who was burying his son in the garden, and who threw rocks when the tiger got too close.

The tiger had no destination, only the constant tug of self-preservation in the pit of his stomach, some vague, inborn sense of what he was looking for, which carried him onward. For days, then weeks, there were long, parched fields and stretches of marshland clogged with the dead. Bodies lay in piles by the roadside and hung like pods, split open and drying, from the branches of trees. The tiger waited below for them to fall, then scavenged them until he got mange, lost two teeth, and moved on. He followed the river upstream, through the flooded bowl of the foothills swollen with April rain, sleeping in empty riverboats while the sun, pale in the blue mist of the river, grew dimmer. He skirted human habitations, small farms where the sound of cattle drew him out of the bracken; but the openness of the sky and the prospect of human noise terrified him, and he did not stay long.

At some bend in the river, he came across an abandoned church, half a bell tower overgrown with ivy, crowded with the hushed shuffling of pigeons. It kept the rain off him for a few weeks, but there was no food for him there, all the corpses in the churchyard having decomposed long ago, nothing for him but the eggs of waterbirds and the occasional beached catfish, and eventually he moved on. By early autumn, he had spent four months in the swamps, gnawing on decaying carcasses that drifted by, snatching frogs and salamanders along the creek bed. He had become a host for leeches, and dozens of them stood like eyes in the fur of his legs and sides.

One morning, in the grip of an early frost, he came across a boar. Brown and bloated, the hog was distracted with acorns, and for the first time in his life, the tiger gave chase. It was loud and poorly calculated. He came on with his head up and his breath blaring like a foghorn, and the hog, without even turning to look at its pursuer, disappeared into the autumn brush.

The tiger did not succeed, but it was something, at least. He had been born in a box of hay in a gypsy circus, and had spent his life feeding on fat white columns of spine in the citadel cage. For the first time, the impulse that made him flex his claws in sleep, the compulsion that led him to drag his meat to the corner of the cage he occupied alone, was articulated into something other than frustration. Necessity drew him slowly out of his domesticated clumsiness. It strengthened and reinforced the building blocks of his nature, honed his languid, feline reflexes; and the long-lost Siberian instinct pulled him north, into the cold.

*   *   *

The village of Galina, where my grandfather grew up, does not appear on a map. My grandfather never took me there, rarely mentioned it, never expressed longing or curiosity, or a desire to return. My mother could tell me nothing about it; my grandma had never been there. When I finally sought it out, after the inoculations at Brejevina, long after my grandfather's burial, I went by myself, without telling anyone where I was going.

To get to Galina, you must leave the City at daybreak, and travel northwest along the highway that cuts through the suburbs where entrepreneurs are building their summer homes—tall, yardless brick houses that will never be finished. Behind their gates, the doors and windows yawn empty, and thin-legged cats stretch out in dirt-piled wheelbarrows. Here and there are signs for a country mending itself: paint store posters, green hardware-stand leaflets pinned to trees, bath-and-tile business placards, banners for carpentry workshops, furniture warehouses, electricians' offices. A quarry, cliff face split open, unmanned yellow bulldozers waiting for the day to begin; an enormous billboard advertising the world's best grill with a picture of a heat-dented lamb turning over a spit.

The way is nothing like the drive Zóra and I made to Brejevina, though here, too, there are vineyards, shining green and yellow toward the east. Old men cross the road in front of you on foot, behind flocks of newly shorn sheep, taking their time, stopping to wave the fat lambs over, or to take off their shoes and look for bits of gravel that have been bothering them for hours. The fact that you are in a hurry is of no particular interest to them; in their opinion, if you are making your journey in a hurry, you are making it poorly.

The highway narrows into a single-lane road and begins to climb—a slight incline at first, forest-rimmed pastures, bright flushes of green that open up suddenly as you come around the curves. Cars heading down the mountain toward you are small, crowded with families, and sliding into your lane. Already your radio is picking up news from across the border, but the signal is faint, and the voices are lost to static for minutes at a time.

You lose sunlight, and suddenly you are driving through a low cloud bank that is unfurling across the road in front of you. It is anchored to the pines and the rocks above you, to the sprawling pastures that open up below, dotted with ramshackle houses, with doorless inns, distant, nameless streams. You realize that you haven't seen a car for miles. You have a map, but it is useless. The church you pass is gray and silent, its parking lot empty. At the gas station, no one can tell you where to go next, and they haven't had a shipment of petrol in weeks.

On that empty stretch of highway, there is a single sign pointing you in the correct direction. It is easy to miss, a wooden board with the words *Sveti Danilo* scrawled in white chalk, and a crooked arrow pointing toward the gravel path that turns down into the valley below. The sign will not tell you that, once you have turned onto the path, you have effectively committed to spending the night; that your car probably will not make it back up in one try; that you will spend eight hours with your knees against your chin, your back against the door, your flashlight pointless and unused in the trunk, because to retrieve it you would have to get out of the car, and that will never happen.

The path cuts steeply down through fenced wheat fields and blackberry patches, pastures

109

where the forest has come back and thrown a spray of white flowers into the grass. Every so often you pass a huge, unattended pig, rooting in the ditch by the path. The pig will look up at you, and it will appear unimpressed.

Twenty minutes in, the road hairpins, and when you take this turn, wait for the blaze that strikes from across the valley, where the pine forest stands dense and silent: that light is the sun glancing off the last surviving window of the monastery of Sveti Danilo, the only sign that it is still there, and is considered a miracle, because you will see it from the same place any time of the day, as long as the sun is up.

Soon afterward, houses will begin to appear: first, a tin-roofed farmhouse whose loft window opens onto the road. No one lives here, and a black vine has grown out into the garden and swallowed up the upper part of the orchard. The next house surprises you as you come around the corner. There will be a white-haired man sitting on the porch, and the moment he sees your car, he will get up and move indoors with surprising speed; know that he has been listening to your tires on the gravel for the last five minutes, and wants you to see him slamming the door. His name is Marko Parović—you'll get to him later.

Pass the chain of small waterfalls, and then you will reach the center of the village, ten or twelve gray and red houses clustered around the bronze, one-armed statue of Sveti Danilo and the village well. Everyone will be at the tavern, sitting on the open benches of the porch; everyone will see you, but no one will look at you.

110

My grandfather grew up in a stone house overgrown with ivy and bright purple flowers. The house no longer exists—for twenty years, it stood empty, and then, brick by brick, the villagers took it apart to mend their stable walls, patch up attic holes, brace their doors.

My grandfather's mother had died in childbirth, and his father died before my grandfather had even formed a memory of him. My grandfather lived, instead, with his own grandmother, the town midwife, a woman who had already raised six children, half of whom were the children of village friends and neighbors. The entire town affectionately called her Mother Vera. There is only one surviving picture of her. In it, Mother Vera is an austere, middle-aged woman standing in front of what appears to be the corner of a stone house, behind which a tree-laden orchard slopes down and away. Her hands, crossed in front of her, are the hands of a laborer; her expression seems to indicate that the photographer owes her money.

In those days, the house had only three rooms. My grandfather slept on a straw mattress in a small wooden cot by the hearth. There was a clean kitchen with tin pots and pans, strings of garlic hanging from the rafters, a neat larder stocked with pickle barrels, jars of *ajvar* and onions and rose-hip jam, bottles of homemade walnut *rakija*. In winter, Mother Vera lit a fire that burned all day and all night without going out, and in summer a pair of white storks nested in the charred stone top of the chimney, clattering their bills for hours at a time. The view from the garden opened out onto

111

the green mountains above town, and the valley through which a bright, broad river still widens and then contracts around a bend with a red-steepled church. A dirt road went by the house, leading from the linden grove to the plum orchard by the water. In the garden, Mother Vera planted potatoes, lettuces, carrots, and a small rosebush which she tended with celebrated care.

They say that, in medieval times, the town sprang up around the monastery of Sveti Danilo. The monastery was the project of an architect whose mapping skills and artful design were undermined by his inability to consider that the seclusion of the monks would be regularly interrupted by the movement of armies over the eastern mountains and into the river valley. The result was the gradual encroachment on the monastery's lands by an ever-growing band of farmers, herders, and mountain people, who, though capable of withstanding long-running battles with bears, snow, dead ancestors, and Baba Roga, came to find that isolation on the eastern slopes was not preferable to the ability to run for the monastery walls at the first sign of a Turkish horde. They eventually devised a small economy of their own, balanced on the varied professions of about twenty resident families, whose lot in life was passed on from generation to generation, and whose solitude, even after the monastery fell in the First World War, was fiercely protected from all outsiders, save the occasional traveling summer market, or a daughter from across the mountain who came into the village as a new bride.

Mother Vera's people had always been shepherds, and, being alone, she had invested so much of her own life in this profession that it seemed the natural path down which to direct my grandfather. So he was brought up with sheep, with their bleating and groaning, their thick smell and runny eyes, their stupefied spring nakedness. He was brought up, too, with their death, the spring slaughter, the way they were butchered and sold. The articulate way Mother Vera handled the knife: straightforward, precise, like everything she did, from her cooking to the way she knitted sweaters for him. The ritual rhythms of this life were built into Mother Vera's nature, an asset she hoped would adhere to my grandfather, too: the logical and straightforward process of moving from season to season, from birth to death, without unnecessary sentiment.

Like all matriarchal disciplinarians, Mother Vera was certain of my grandfather's eventual acceptance of order, and therefore confident in his abilities—overconfident, perhaps, because when he was six, she handed him a small, cut-to-size shepherd's staff and sent him into the fields with a cluster of old sheep, whom she did not expect to give him very much trouble. It was an exercise, and my grandfather was delighted with his newfound responsibility. But he was so young then that later he was only able to remember fragments of what happened next: the lull of the morning fields, the springy cotton flanks of the sheep, the suddenness of the tumble down the deep hole in which he would spend the night, alone, gazing up at the puzzled sheep, and hours later, Mother Vera's thoughtful, dawn-lit face hovering over the mouth of the hole.

This was one of the few stories my grandfather told from his childhood. Another, characteristically, was a medical anecdote. Growing up, he had a friend called Mirica who lived a few houses over, and when they were old enough not to be engaged in the business of pulling each other's hair and calling each other names, they played house, which was the civilized thing to do. One afternoon, my grandfather, playing the part of the woodcutter husband, went down the street, talking to himself and carrying a toy ax in his hand; Mirica, meanwhile, indoctrinated as she was with the principle of what a dutiful wife should be doing, prepared for him a meal of well-water soup in oleander leaves, which she served on the stump of a tree. The problem was not the essence of the game, but the practice: my grandfather dutifully ate the oleander leaf soup and was instantaneously seized with paroxysms of vomiting.

The town apothecary arrived an hour later to induce more vomiting, and to pump my grandfather's stomach, which is a barbaric procedure now and was considerably more barbaric back then. I have heard the apothecary described by others who knew him: enormous hands, great, imposing eyes, and above them the headlamp, and I imagine my grandfather was, from a very early age, lured into a stunned reverence of the medical profession.

Over the years, the apothecary visited more and more often. He was there to administer ipecac and to set broken bones, to pull a shattered molar when my grandfather secretly bought hard candy from a passing gypsy peddler with whom he had been forbidden to interact. When, during

114

an intense game of us-versus-Ottomans, my grandfather shook his makeshift ax a little too enthusiastically and sent the razor-edged tin can tied to the top of it flying into the forehead of a neighborhood boy, the apothecary was there to stitch up the bone-deep cut that ran just under Dušan's hairline. My grandfather, of course, never mentioned the winter of his own great illness, a fever that ripped through the village—despite the apothecary's best efforts, my grandfather was the only child under the age of twelve to survive it, six buried in the snow, his entire generation, even Mirica of the oleander leaves.

I think something in those early childhood memories must have been imperishable. All his life, my grandfather would remember the sensation of standing in the warmth of the apothecary's shop, staring into the cage of the apothecary's great red ibis, quiet and stern. The shop represented a magnificent kind of order, the kind of pleasurable symmetry you just couldn't get from coming home with the right number of sheep. Standing under the counter, one sock lower than the other, my grandfather would look up at the shelves and shelves of jars, the swollen-bottomed bottles of remedies, and revel in their calm, controlled promise of wellness. The little golden scales, the powders, the herbs and spices, the welcoming smell of the apothecary's shop, were all things that signified another plane of reality. And the apothecary—tooth puller, dream interpreter, measurer of medicine, keeper of the magnificent scarlet ibis—was the reliable magician, the only kind of magician my grandfather could ever admire. Which is why, in a way, this story starts and ends with him.

Shepherding, perhaps surprisingly, is conducive to scholastics, and likely advanced my grandfather's studies. He went alone and undisturbed for long periods of time. The fields above Galina are green and quiet, the dwelling place of grasshoppers and butterflies, the pasture of red deer. Sixty sheep to one boy, and all the tree shade he could want. That first summer he spent in the fields, he taught himself to read.

He read the alphabet book, that staple of childhood learning, the first philosophy we are exposed to—the simplicity of language, the articulation of a letter that sounds exactly how it looks. Then he read *The Jungle Book*, a gift from the apothecary himself. For weeks, my grandfather sat in the long-stemmed grass and pored over the brown volume with its soft pages. He read about the panther Bagheera, Baloo the bear, the old wolf Akela. Inside the cover was the picture of a boy, thin and upright, thrusting a stick of flame into the face of an enormous square-headed cat.

*   *   *

I'm told that the tiger was first sighted on the Galina ridge, above town, during a snowstorm at the end of December. Who knows how long he had already been there, hiding in the hollows of fallen trees; but, on that particular day, the herdsman Vladiša lost a calf in the blizzard and went up the mountain to retrieve it. In a thicket of saplings, he came across the tiger, yellow-eyed and bright as a blood moon, with the calf, already dead, hanging in its jaws. A tiger. What did that mean to a man like

Vladiša? I knew *tiger* because my grandfather took me to the citadel every week and pointed to show me, *tiger;* because the labels in the taxidermy museum where we sometimes spent quiet afternoons read *tiger,* because *tiger* crawled, in intricate Chinese patterns, all over the lid of my grandma's knee-balm tin. *Tiger* was India, and lazy yellow afternoons; the sambar, eyes wide, neck broken, twisting in the mangroves while Kipling's jungle creepers bent low to mark the killer's back. But in my grandfather's village, in those days, a tiger—what did that even mean? A bear, a wolf, yes. But tiger? How fear came.

People did not believe poor Vladiša, even when they saw him running down the hill, white as a ghost, arms in the air, no calf. They did not believe him when he collapsed in the village square, breathless with exhaustion and terror, and managed to stutter out that they were done for, that the devil had come to Galina, and call the priest quick. They did not believe him because they didn't know what to believe—what was this orange thing, back and shoulders scorched with fire? They would have been better equipped to react if he had told them he had met Baba Roga, and if, that same instant, her skull-and-bones hut on its one chicken leg had come tearing down the hillside after him.

My grandfather and Mother Vera were among those who were summoned to the square by the sound of Vladiša's shouting. The tiger's wife must have been there, too, but they didn't know it at the time. My grandfather ran out of the house quickly, without his coat on, and Mother Vera came out after him with his coat in her hands and gave him a cuff across the ear as she forced him into the

117

sleeves. Then they stood there, the two of them, while the blacksmith and the fishmonger and the man who sold buttons propped Vladiša up in the snow and gave him water.

Vladiša was saying: 'The devil I tell you! The devil has come for us all!'

To my grandfather, the devil was many things. The devil was Leši, the hobgoblin, whom you met in the pasture, and who asked you for coins—deny him, and he would turn the forest around and upside down and you would be lost forever. The devil was Crnobog, the horned god, who summoned darkness. You were sent to the devil by your elders if you misbehaved; you were allowed to send other people to the devil, but only if you were much, much older. The devil was Night, Baba Roga's second son, who rode a black horse through the woods. Sometimes, the devil was Death, on foot, waiting for you at the crossroads, or behind some door you had been repeatedly warned against opening. But as my grandfather listened to Vladiša, who was sobbing about orange fur and stripes, it became clearer and clearer to him that this particular thing in the woods was not the devil, and not a devil, but perhaps something else, something he maybe knew a little bit about, and his eyes must have lit up when he said: 'But that's Shere Khan.'

My grandfather was a thin child, with blond hair and large eyes—I have seen pictures of him, black-and-white photographs with scalloped edges, in which he looks sternly at the camera with his schoolboy socks pulled all the way up, and his hands in his pockets. It must have been strange, his calmness, his level voice, and the fishmonger and the blacksmith and several other people who had come running from the village all looked at him, puzzled.

The apothecary, however, was there too. 'You may be right,' the apothecary said. 'Where's that book I gave you?' My grandfather ran inside to get it, and as he came back out, he was flipping through the pages frantically so that, by the time he reached the sprawled-out form of Vladiša, he had reached the plate with his favorite picture, the one with Mowgli and Shere Khan. He held it out to the terrified cowherd. Vladiša took one look at it and fainted, and that was how the village found out about the tiger.

*   *   *

If the tiger had been a different sort of tiger, a hunter from the beginning, he probably would have come down to the village sooner. His long journey from the city had brought him as far as the ridge, and even he could not be certain why he had chosen to remain there. I could argue now that the wind and deep snows were no obstacle to him, that he might have pressed on all winter and arrived at some other village, with some other church, maybe some place with some less superstitious people where some matter-of-fact farmer might have shot him and strung him up, as empty as a bag, above the fireplace. But the ridge—with its bowed saplings and deadfall underfoot, the steep flank of the mountain studded with caves, the wild game wide-eyed and reckless with the starvation of winter—trapped him between his new, broadening senses and the vaguely familiar smell of the village

119

below.

All day long, he walked up and down the length of the ridge, letting the smells drift up to him, puzzled by the feeling that they weren't entirely new. He had not forgotten his time at the citadel, but his memory was heavily veiled by his final days there and the days afterward, his arduous trek, burrs and splinters and glass stinging his paws, the dense, watery taste of the bloated dead. By now, he had only an indistinct sense, in another layer of his mind, that, long, long ago, someone had thrown him fresh meat twice a day and sprayed him with water when the heat grew too unbearable. The smells from below meant something related to that, and they made him restless and agitated as he wandered the woods, instinctively sprinting after every rabbit and squirrel he saw. The smells were pleasant and distinct, entirely separate from one another: the thick, woolly smell of sheep and goats; the smell of fire, tar, wax; the interesting reek of the outhouses; paper, iron, the individual smells of people; the savory smells of stew and goulash, the grease of baking pies. The smells also made him more and more aware of his hunger, his lack of success as a hunter, of the length of time since his last meal, the calf that had blundered into him that bitter afternoon when he'd seen the man turn and run. The taste of the calf had been familiar; the shape of the man had been familiar.

That night, he had come halfway down the mountain. Stopped at a precipice where the tree line curved around the bottom of a frozen waterfall, and looked and looked at the burning windows and snow-topped roofs below him in the valley.

And some nights later, there was a new smell. He had sensed it here and there in the past—the momentary aroma of salt and wood smoke, rich with blood. The smell fell into his stomach, made him long for the calf, reduced him to rolling onto his back, head pressed into the snow, and calling for it until the birds shuddered free of their nests. The smell came up to him almost every night, in darkness, and he stood there in the newly fallen snow, with the trees arching in low around him, breathing it in and out. One night, half a mile from his clearing, he watched a lone stag—whose imminent death the tiger had been waiting on, had sensed days before it happened—buckle under the weight of starvation and old age and the bitter cold. The tiger watched him kneel and fold over, watched the stag's one remaining antler snap off. Later, as he ripped the belly open, even the spreading warmth of the stag's entrails couldn't drown out the smell from the village.

One night, he went down to the valley and stood at the pasture fence. Across the field, the silent houses, past the barn and the empty pigpen, past the house with its snow-packed porch, stood the smokehouse. There was the smell, almost close enough. The tiger rubbed his chin up and down the fence posts. He did not return for two days, but when he did he found the meat. Someone had been there in his absence. One of the fence planks had been ripped down, and the meat lay under it, dry and tough, but full of the smell that frenzied him. He dug it up and carried it back to the woods, where he gnawed on it for a long time.

Two nights later, he had to venture closer to find the next piece; it was waiting for him under a

121

broken barrel that had been left out in the field, just yards from the smokehouse door. A cautious return some nights later to the same place, a bigger piece. Then two pieces, then three, and, eventually, a whole shoulder right at the threshold of the smokehouse.

The following night, the tiger came up the smokehouse ramp and put his shoulders in the doorway, which was thrown wide open for the first time. He could hear the sheep bleating in the stable, some distance away, terrified by his presence; the dogs, fenced up, barking furiously. The tiger sniffed the air: there was the smell of the meat, but also the thick, overwhelming smell of the person inside, the person whose scent he had found on and around the meat before, and whom he could see now, sitting in the back of the smokehouse, a piece of meat in her hands.

*   *   *

Galina, meanwhile, had gone nervously about its business. The end of the year was marked with heavy snowstorms, knee-deep drifts that moved like sand in and out of doorways. There was a quiet, clotted feeling in the air, the electricity of fear. Snow had buried the mountain passes, and, with them, any news of the war. Somewhere nearby, high above them in the dense pine forests of Galina ridge, something large and red and unknown was stalking up and down and biding its time. They found evidence of it once—the woodcutter, reluctantly braving the undergrowth at the bottom of the mountain, had come across the head of a stag, fur matted and eyes gone white, the

122

spinal column, like a braid of bone, rolling out gray along the ground—and this, with Vladiša's encounter, sufficiently persuaded them against leaving the village.

It was winter, and their livestock were already slaughtered, or stabled until spring. The season had provided them with an excuse for staying safely indoors, which they already knew how to do, and the tiger, they hoped, would not last the winter. On the other hand, there was the possibility that the tiger—how had it gotten there in the first place, they wondered, if it belonged so far away, in jungles, in fields of elephant grass?—would realize it might not last, and come down into the village to hunt them just the same. So they lit fires in their homes, hoping to discourage it from leaving the ridge. The ground was frozen solid, they had already postponed all funerals until the thaw—only three people died that winter anyway, so they were fortunate, very fortunate—and they packed the undertaker's basement with ice blocks and took the added precaution of stuffing the windows with cloth from the inside, to prevent any smell of the corpses from getting out.

For a while, there was no trace of the tiger. They almost managed to convince themselves that it had all been a joke, that Vladiša had seen a personal ghost of some kind, or perhaps had some kind of seizure up there in the mountains; that the stag had been dispatched by a bear or wolf. But the village dogs—sheepdogs and boarhounds, thick-coated hunting dogs with yellow eyes who belonged to everybody and nobody at once—knew for certain that he was up there, and reminded the village. The dogs could smell him, the big-cat stink of him, and it drove them crazy. They were restless, and bayed at him and pulled at their tethers. They filled the night with a hollow sound, and the villagers, swaddled in their nightshirts and woolen socks, shook in their beds and slept fitfully.

But my grandfather still walked to the village well every morning, and laid out quail traps every night. It was his responsibility to ensure that he and Mother Vera had something to eat—and, besides, he was hoping, all the time hoping, for a glimpse of the tiger. He carried his brown volume with the picture of Shere Khan everywhere he went; and, while he never went far that particular winter, it must have been tangible, the excitement of a nine-year-old boy, because it brought him to the attention of the deaf-mute girl.

She was a girl of about sixteen, who lived on the edge of town in the butcher's house and helped with the shop. My grandfather, probably not the most observant boy, had seen her occasionally, on market days and festival days, but he never noticed her with any particular interest until, that winter, some days before the Christmas celebration in January, she shyly blocked his path as he was heading to the baker's in the early morning and took his book out of the top breast pocket of his coat, where he had kept it since the tiger had come.

My grandfather would remember the girl all his life. He would remember her dark hair and large eyes, interested, expressive eyes, and he would remember the cleft in her chin when she smiled as she opened the book to the dog-eared page with Shere Khan. My grandfather had his gray woolen cap down around his ears, and in the muted hush of his own head, he heard himself say: 'That's what the tiger looks like.' And he pointed to the mountain above the smoking chimneys of the village.

The girl did not say anything, but she studied the picture carefully. She had only one glove, and the cold had turned the fingers of her bare hand an odd shade of purple. Her nose was slightly runny, and this made my grandfather wipe his own nose with the back of his coat sleeve, as discreetly as possible. The girl still hadn't said anything, and it occurred to him that she might be embarrassed because she couldn't read—so he launched into an explanation of Shere Khan, and his complicated relationship with Mowgli, and how my grandfather himself found it strange that in one chapter Mowgli skinned the tiger and draped the tiger-skin over Council Rock, but later on Shere Khan was whole again. He talked very quickly, gulping down pockets of cold air, and the girl, who still didn't say a thing, looked at him patiently and then, after a few minutes, handed the book back to him and went on her way.

In particular, my grandfather remembered his own embarrassment, when, after talking at her about tigers and asking her questions to which she did not reply, he went home confused and asked Mother Vera about her. He remembered how bright his own ears felt when she cuffed him and said: 'Don't bother her, that's Luka's wife. That girl's a deaf-mute, and Mohammedan besides—you stay away from her.'

Luka was the town butcher, who owned the pasture and smokehouse on the edge of town. He was a tall man with curly brown hair and thick, red hands, and he wore an apron that was almost perpetually soaked in blood. Something about that apron made the townspeople uncomfortable. They were, in one capacity or another, all butchers themselves, and they didn't understand why, if he had to make his money cutting up meat and selling it at Gorchevo, he didn't at least change to conduct his business transactions, didn't do his best to smell like something other than the sour insides of cows and sheep. In the nine years of his life at the time, my grandfather had met Luka only once, but the encounter was clear in his memory. Two years before, during a brief but cold winter storm, Mother Vera had sent my grandfather out to the butcher's shop to buy a leg of lamb because the cold had tightened her hands with pain. The front room of the butcher's house was filled with the smell of meat, and my grandfather had stood and looked around at the smoked hams and sausages hanging from the rafters, soup bones and square bacon slabs in the cold vitrine, the skinned red lamb with its sharp little teeth lying on the block while Luka, his glasses hanging around his neck, cleaved the bone of the leg away. My grandfather was leaning in to look at jars full of something brined and white and lumpy behind the counter when the butcher smiled at him and said: 'Pigs' feet. Delicious. They're a lot like children's feet, actually.'

My grandfather couldn't remember whether he had seen the girl when he had gone to the butcher's shop; perhaps she hadn't been married to Luka then. And he would not see her again until the day before Christmas Eve, when the pain in Mother Vera's hands was so agonizing that she groaned in her sleep, and, overwhelmed by his own inability to help her, he went out to bring back water for her bath.

My grandfather wore his wool coat and hat, and carried the empty bucket to the well. Like so much of the village, the well had been erected during Ottoman times. It is still there today, but has been empty for many decades. That night, its pointed roof was dusted with snow, and snow-laden gusts of wind snaked all around it as my grandfather made his way across the village square. He was keenly aware of the moonless cold, the faint fires in the windows he passed, the desolate sound of his own feet shuffling along.

He had just put the bucket down and grabbed the rope when he looked up and saw a thin light at the edge of the pasture. My grandfather stood with the rope frozen in his hands, and tried to see through the darkness. He could see the butcher's house, with the fire dying inside, which meant that Luka was probably fast asleep, but the light was not that; nor was it the barn where the butcher kept his livestock. It was the smokehouse: the door was open, and there was light inside.

My grandfather did not go there looking for trouble; it merely occurred to him that some traveler or gypsy had found shelter for the night and that Luka might be angry, or they might come across the tiger. It was the latter thought that drove him to pick up his bucket and press on to the smokehouse, partly because he wanted to warn the intruder about the tiger, partly because he was filled with a frantic, inexplicable jealousy at the thought of some drifter seeing his tiger first. Carefully, he crossed the empty fold, and picked his way through the pasture.

The chimney was going, and the smell of smoked meat hung in the air. He thought, for a moment, about whether he could get Luka to smoke the Christmas quail he hoped to find in the trap tomorrow. Then he crept up to the ramp, put his hands on it and hoisted himself up. He picked up the bucket. He stood in the doorway and looked in.

There was a lot less light than he had initially supposed. He could hardly see inside, where the hollowed-out hogs and cattle hung in rows, to the little front room in the corner, where the butcher's block stood. The smell was wonderful, and he suddenly felt hungry, but then there was a different smell he hadn't noticed before, a thick, dark musk, and just as he realized this the light went out. In the sudden darkness, he heard a low, heavy sound, like breath all around him, a single deep rumble that strung his veins together and trembled in his lungs. The sound spread around his skull for a moment, making room for itself. Then he dove into the little butchering room and crawled under a tarp in the corner and sat in a shuddering heap with the bucket still in his hands.

It seemed to my grandfather that the sound was still in the air, as sure and constant as his own crazy heartbeat, which could drown out everything except the sound. The smell was there too, everywhere, lingering—the smell of wild things, fox or badger, but bigger, so much more of it, like nothing he could place but something he could identify in so many other things. He thought of the plate in his book, in bed, at home, which seemed infinitely far now, not just twenty seconds of solid

128

running past the houses of people he knew.

Something in the darkness moved, and the butcher's hooks, hanging in rows along the rafters, clinked against one another, and my grandfather knew that it was the tiger. The tiger was walking. He could not make out the individual footfalls, the great velvet paws landing, one in front of the other; just the overall sound of it, a soft, traveling thump. He tried to quiet his own breathing, but found that he couldn't. He was panting under the tarp and the tarp kept drawing in around him, rustling insanely, pointing him out. He could feel the tiger just beside him, through the wooden planks, the big, red heart clenching and unclenching under the ribs, the weight of it groaning through the floor. My grandfather's chest was jolting, and he could already picture the tiger bearing down on him, but he thought of *The Jungle Book*—the way Mowgli had taunted Shere Khan at Council Rock, torch in hand, grabbing the Lame Tiger under the chin to subdue him—and he put his hand out through the tarp and touched the coarse hairs passing by him.

And, just like that, the tiger was gone. My grandfather felt the big, hot, rushing heart brush past and then vanish. He broke out in a sweat, sitting there with the bucket between his knees. He heard the sound of footsteps, and moments later the deaf-mute girl was kneeling at his side in the little room with the butcher's table, digging him out of his tarp, brushing the hair from his forehead with worry in her eyes. Her hands, sweeping over his face, carried the heavy smell of the tiger, of snow and pine trees and blood.

And then, Mother Vera's voice, screaming in the distance: 'My child! The devil has taken my child!'

129

My grandfather eventually learned that Mother Vera, sensing that he had been gone a long time, had stepped out, and from the stairs of their little house, had seen the tiger leave the smokehouse and take off across the field. She was still screaming when the doors of the houses around the square opened, one by one, and the men spilled out into the streets and gave chase to the edge of the pasture. Loud voices, and then light and men filling the doorway, even Luka the butcher, looking furious in his nightshirt and slippers, a cleaver in his hand. The deaf-mute girl helped my grandfather to his feet, and led him to the door. From the smokehouse ramp, he could see the dark, empty field, swimming with shadows: the villagers, the snowdrifts, the fence, but not the tiger. The tiger was already gone.

'He's here, here he is,' my grandfather heard someone say, and suddenly Mother Vera was clutching at him with cold hands, out of breath and stuttering.

Outside, in the snow, were footprints. Big, round, springy footprints, the even, loping prints of a cat. My grandfather watched as the grocer Jovo, who had once killed a badger with his bare hands, knelt down in the snow and pressed his hand into one of them. The tracks were the size of dinner plates, and they ran—matter-of-factly and without pause—down from the woods and across the field, into the smokehouse and back.

'I heard something in the smokehouse,' my grandfather was telling everyone. 'I thought one of the animals had escaped. But it was the tiger.'

Nearby, Luka stood looking out through the smokehouse door, holding on to the arm of the

130

deaf-mute, whose skin had gone white around his grip. She was looking at my grandfather and smiling.

He appealed to the deaf-mute. 'You came out because you heard him, too, didn't you?'

'The bitch is deaf, she didn't hear anything,' Luka told him, before he led her across the field into the house and closed the door.

*   *   *

There was only one gun in the village, and, for many years, it had been kept in the family home of the blacksmith. It was an old Ottoman musket and it had a long, sharp muzzle, like a pike, and a silver-mantled barrel with a miniature Turkish cavalry carved riding forward over the saddle below the sight. A faded, woolly tassel hung from an embroidered cord over the musket butt, which was a deep, oily mahogany, and rough along the side, where the name of the Turk who had first carried it had been thoughtfully scraped off.

The musket had made its way to the village through a series of exchanges that differed almost every time someone told the story, and went back nearly two centuries. It had supposedly first seen battle at Lastica, before disappearing in the mule-pack of a defecting Janissary from the sultan's personal bodyguard, a soldier-turned-peddler who carried it with him for many decades while he roamed the mountains, selling silks and cook pots and exotic oils. The musket was eventually stolen from the Janissary peddler by a Magyar highwayman, and, later still, dragged out from under the Magyar's body by the mounted brigade

131

that shot him down outside the house of his mistress, whose blouse, wet with the highwayman's blood, was still unbuttoned when she begged the brigadiers to leave her the gun as they took her lover's corpse away. The highwayman's mistress mounted the gun above the counter in her tavern. She dressed in mourning, and developed a habit of cleaning the gun as though it were in use. Many years later, an old woman of sixty, she gave it to the boy who carried milk up the stairs for her, so it would protect him when he rode against the bey's citadel in an ill-fated uprising that was swiftly crushed. The boy's head ended up on a pike on the citadel wall, and the gun ended up in the possession of the bey, who hung it in a minor trophy room of his winter palace, between the heads of two leopards with crooked eyes. It stayed there for almost sixty years, through the reigns of three beys, hanging opposite a stuffed lynx—and then, as time passed, a sultan's last battle outfit, the carriage of a Russian queen, a silver tea-set honoring one alliance or another, and eventually a state car belonging to a wealthy Turk who, shortly before his execution, had forfeited all his possessions to the citadel.

When the citadel fell, shortly after the turn of the century, the gun was taken away by a looter from Kovač, who carried it with him while he went from town to town, selling coffee. In the end, switching hands in some skirmish between peasants and Turkish militia, the musket went home with one of the survivors, a youth from the village, the grandfather of the blacksmith. That was 1901. Since then, the gun had hung on the wall above the blacksmith's hearth. It had been fired only once, in the direction of a sheep rapist, and never by the blacksmith himself. Now, my grandfather learned, the old gun would be used to kill the tiger.

The blacksmith was allegedly very brave about the business of the gun, and did not reveal—although perhaps he should have—that he did not know how to use it. He had a vague sense of what he was supposed to do with the powder, the bullets, the greased paper wadding, the ramrod. He felt an obligation to the village, and to the memory of his grandfather, whom he had never known, but who had once shod the sultan's horse. On the eve of the hunt, the blacksmith sat by the fire and watched his wife take the gun down and wipe the barrel in clean, even strokes, slowly and with loving patience. She polished the hood, beat the dust out of the tassel, and then wiped the inside with greased felt.

My grandfather watched them prepare for the hunt the following morning, in the gray hours before dawn. He did not know what to make of his encounter in the smokehouse, but his throat was tight when the blacksmith emerged from his house with the honored gun under his arm. With the blacksmith were two other men: Luka and Jovo. They had dogs with them, too—a short, fat hound with floppy ears, and an old red sheepdog who had lost one eye under a carriage wheel.

It was Christmas Eve, and the entire village had turned out to watch the hunters depart. People stood in a long line by the side of the road, their hands held out to touch the gun for luck as it went by on the blacksmith's arm. My grandfather stood guiltily beside Mother Vera with his sleeves drawn up over his hands, and when his turn came, he touched the barrel with the tip of one sleeve-covered finger, and only for a moment.

That afternoon, as he waited for the hunters to return, my grandfather drew in the hearth dust with that same finger and hated the men on the hill. He hated Luka already, for the pigs' feet and the way he called his wife 'bitch,' but now he hated those other men, and the dogs too, because he believed, fully and wholeheartedly, that the tiger would have spared him even if he had come in just a moment earlier or later, even if he had come in to find the tiger's eyes burning at him from the other side of the barn. He could already see the men coming back, the tiger slung upside down on a pole between them; or else, just the tiger's head, in one of their carry sacks, and he hated them.

He would probably not have hated them if he had known what is easy to guess: that the blacksmith was terrified. Climbing up Galina, knee-deep in snow, the gun, for all its honored past, a deadweight against his ribs, the blacksmith was convinced that this was the end for him. Like everyone in the village, he had faith in the rituals of superstition. He gave money to beggars before traveling, put pennies in the shrines of the Virgin at crossroads, spat on his children when they were born. But, unlike his fellow villagers, he was renowned for having a deficit. He had been born in a lean year, without a ducat under his pillow. To make matters worse, an estranged aunt had once allegedly lifted him from his crib and praised heaven for what a beautiful baby, what a gorgeous, fat, blessed, rosy child he was—forever sealing his destiny to be impoverished, crippled, struck down

134

and taken by the devil at some unexpected time, in some terrifying way.

Of course, it hadn't happened yet. But he could not imagine anything more terrifying than a tiger. And there he was—thirty-nine years old, happily married and with five children—on his way to meet the devil. All his efforts, all his many precautions and prayers, the countless coins he had thrown to gypsies and circus folk and legless soldiers, all the times he had crossed himself while traveling on a lonely road at night, had been counteracted by the simple fact that the gun, like the misfortune, was his birthright, and that, regardless of his qualifications, he was the one intended to carry it against the tiger.

Like his companions, the blacksmith did not know what to expect. He would have been just as surprised to discover that the tiger was a small but cunning cat with very big feet as he would have to find Satan—whether horned and cloven-hoofed or robed in black—riding the tiger around a massive steaming caldera in the forest. He hoped, of course, that they would not meet the tiger at all. He hoped to find himself at home that night, eating goat stew, and preparing to make love to his wife.

The day was intermittently gray and bright. Along the ridges, where the mountains sloped in and out of the pine-filled valleys, they could hear the echoing crack of the red deer stags in rut. A freezing rain had fallen during the night, and the trees, twisting under the weight of their ice-laden branches, had transformed the forest into a snarl of crystal. The dogs plodded along, running to and fro, sniffing at trees and pissing wherever they could, seemingly unaware of their purpose on the trip. Luka was bracing himself up the mountain, using his pitchfork as a staff, and talking, too loudly for the blacksmith's taste, about his plans to raise the price of meat when the Germans came through in the spring. Jovo was eating cheese, throwing slices of it to the dogs, and calling Luka a filthy collaborator.

On the ridge midway up the mountain, the dogs grew excited. They snuffled impatiently through the snow, whimpering. There were yellow patches melted into the snow, an occasional pile of scat here and there, and, most important, a clot of brownish fur clinging to a bramble by the frozen stream. Most assuredly, Jovo told the blacksmith, the tiger had crossed here. They followed. They crossed the sheet of ice and went uphill, following the dense pines through a rocky pass where the sun had melted the snow, and then reaching a small crevasse that they had to help each other across with the dogs, whining, tied to their packs. The blacksmith thought about suggesting they turn back. He couldn't understand Jovo's calmness, or Luka's tight-jawed determination.

It was late afternoon when they came across the tiger in a clearing by a frozen pond, bright and real, carved from sunlight. The dogs saw him first, sensed him, perhaps, because he lay partially obscured in the shadow of a tree, and the blacksmith felt, as he saw him get up to meet the dogs with his ears flat and his teeth bared, that he would have passed the tiger by. He felt his organs clench as the first of the dogs, the bravely stupid, half-blind shepherd, reached the tiger and went end over end when the big cat lashed at him, and

136

then pinned him with all its enormous weight.

Jovo seized the other dog and held it in his arms. From the other side of the pond, they watched the tiger crush the thrashing red dog. There was blood on the snow already, from something the tiger had been eating, something that looked like pork shoulder, something that Luka was observing keenly while his grip on the pitchfork tightened.

Later on, at the village, Luka and Jovo would praise the blacksmith for his strength and resolve. They would talk about how he bravely raised the gun to his shoulder. Over and over again, Luka and Jovo would tell the villagers about how the blacksmith fired, how the bullet struck the tiger between the eyes, sending up a tremendous, rusty spurt. The noise the tiger made: a sound like a tree breaking. The tiger's invincibility: how they watched while it got to its feet and cleared the pond in a single bound and brought the blacksmith down in a cloud of hellish red. A snap like thunder—and then, nothing, just the blacksmith's gun lying in the snow, and the dead dog across the pond.

In reality, at that moment, the blacksmith stood stone-still, staring at the yellow thing in the bracken. The yellow thing stared back with yellow eyes. Seeing it there, crouched at the pond's edge with the body of the red dog under it, the blacksmith suddenly felt that the whole clearing had gone very bright, that brightness was spreading slowly across the pond and toward him. Luka shouted to the blacksmith to hurry up and shoot, idiot, and Jovo, whose mouth had dropped open, had now taken off his hat and resorted to slapping

137

himself in the face with it, while the remaining dog, shivering like bulrush in a high wind, cowered around his legs.

After uttering a little prayer, the blacksmith did actually raise the gun to his shoulder, and did cock it, sight, and pull the trigger, and the gun did go off, with a blast that rocked the clearing and spasmed through the blacksmith's knees. But when the smoke cleared and the noise of it had died down in his ribs, the blacksmith looked up to discover that the tiger was on its feet and moving swiftly to the frozen center of the pond, undeterred by the ice and the men and the sound of the gunshot. Out of the corner of his eye, he saw Luka drop his pitchfork and break for cover. The blacksmith fell to his knees. His hand was rummaging through the clots of yarn and the buttons and crumbs that lined the bottom of his pocket, searching for the encased bullet. When he found it, he stuffed it into the muzzle with shaking hands that seemed to be darting everywhere with the sheer force of terror, and fumbled for the ramrod. The tiger was almost over the pond, bounding on muscles like springs. He heard Jovo muttering, 'Fuck me,' helplessly, and the sound of Jovo's footsteps moving away. The blacksmith had the ramrod out and he was shoving it into the muzzle, pumping and pumping and pumping furiously, his hand already on the trigger, and he was ready to fire, strangely calm with the tiger there, almost on him, its whiskers so close and surprisingly bright and rigid. At last, it was done, and he tossed the ramrod aside and peered into the barrel, just to be sure, and blew his own head off with a thunderclap.

No one would ever guess that the gun had misfired. No one would ever guess that Luka and Jovo, from the branches of the tree they had scrambled up, had watched the tiger reel back in surprise, and look around, puzzled. No one would ever guess, not even after the blacksmith's clothed bones were found in disarray, many years later, that the two of them waited in that tree until the tiger pulled the blacksmith's legs off and dragged them away, waited until nightfall to climb down and retrieve the gun from what was left of the blacksmith. No one would guess that they did not even bury the unlucky blacksmith, whose brain was eventually picked over by crows, and to whose carcass the tiger would return again and again, until he had learned something about the taste of man, about the freshness of human meat, which was different now, in snow, than it had been in the heat of summer.

5

THE ORPHANAGE

Bis was snoring asthmatically on the doorstep of the upper patio, and he started at the sound of my footsteps and bellowed like a moose until I reached him. I pushed past him with my knee, and then he followed me to the upper porch, where I sat at the top of the staircase above the main road. Bis hung around for a moment or two, pushing his wet face into the crook of my arm, sneezing with excitement at the notion of sharing the early morning hours with someone; and then he decided that I was unanimated and useless, and he ran down and over the road and dropped past the palms onto the beach. Moments later, I could hear him splashing around. It wasn't dawn yet, and there was a fine pink sheen to the air, as translucent as a fish. The lights of Zvočana were still bright on the water across the bay.

The shadows were pulling back from the water, gathering at the foot of the road, when Barba Ivan came down the stairs. He came down slowly, putting both feet on each stair. He took one look at me—scuffed-up pant legs and dirt-smeared coat and bloodied palms—and said, 'I see you've been up to the vineyard.'

That I had made this effort on my own seemed to compel him to confide in me. He asked if I wanted to come fishing, and I said no, but I got up and followed him down to his boat anyway. It was a little blue skiff, paint peeling off the sides, green and yellow barnacles clinging to the bottom like something earned. Rubber boots on his feet, two large crates and an empty bucket in his arms, the Barba told me he had some lobster cages near the shore, a small net for dogfish a little farther out, and then the big net, right in the middle of the bay, that Fra Antun helped him with when he wasn't supervising the orphanage. He held his arm out as he explained this to me, cutting the horizon into evenly distanced rectangles with a flat hand.

Then he told me about the diggers. They had shown up on his doorstep last week, two carloads of them, all their pots and pans and, in his words, peddling bric-a-brac, and at first he'd thought they were gypsies. He hadn't known how ill they were then; only Duré had come inside, and he had stood in Barba Ivan's kitchen and told them there was a body in the vineyard, a body Duré had put there, the body of a distant cousin whom he had carried down from the mountains during the war and had to leave behind. The cousin had been stuffed into the ground somewhere up on that plot during the months the house had been abandoned. Now the whole family was sick, and no one had been able to help them until some hag from back in their village told them it was the body making them sick, the body calling out for last rites, a proper resting place. They were going to find him at any cost; earlier this year, they'd lost an aunt to the illness, and they were paying to dig.

'Nada doesn't care for it,' he told me, untying the boat. 'But then, of course, what it comes down to is: they've got children. And do we or do we not want a body in the vineyard?'

He had been watching them for the last week, growing more and more uneasy. 'You've seen the pouches,' he said, pointing to his neck. 'They've got—I don't know—grass and dead things in them to keep away the illness.'

They had brought so many bottles that Barba Ivan suspected they had a trade on the side; rare kinds of *rakija,* perhaps some family concoction. But the young woman had told him about the bottles, full of water from a holy spring—back on Duré's and my side of the border—and herbs and grasses for health.

'But they haven't found him yet?' I said.

'Oh, he's long gone,' Barba Ivan said with a broad smile. 'I keep telling them—long gone. It's hard, shallow earth. He's not where he's supposed to be—floods have flushed him out, dogs have dragged him off. Who knows?'

The Barba put his crates in the boat and I helped him push it out, even though he waved me off. Bis was already in the boat, wagging his tail so hard his hips and whole rear end were swinging manically from left to right. Then Barba Ivan climbed into the boat and, eighty years old if he was a day, rowed himself out to the motorboat he kept moored to the breakwater, switched vessels, lifted Bis out of the skiff and into the motorboat, and then, with the dog standing on the wet prow like a masthead, the two of them set off down the coast, cutting the still morning water. Every hundred yards or so, Bis would launch backward out of the boat, his jowls flapping into an insane grin of canine pleasure, and disappear under the waves; Barba Ivan would kill the motor and drift until the dog caught up, or turn the boat around and go back for him.

*   *   *

Zóra had begun her morning with a call to the prosecutor's assistant, whom she'd succeeded in calling a cow within the first two minutes of conversation. I tried to cheer her up by telling her about the diggers on our way to the monastery, about the illness and the dead cousin, whose bones were perhaps somewhere up in the vineyard, and whom the diggers, as I understood it, would be repotting as soon as he was discovered.

Zóra gave me a look from behind her sunglasses, and said nothing. She was pulling one of two dollies Nada had provided to accommodate

142

us in our effort of delivering the vaccines to the monastery orphanage. We had stood in the doorway of the garden shed while Nada pushed boxes and crates aside to find them—two rusted carts with wheels barely clinging to the axles, leaning against the back wall behind a broken washing machine and some paper-wrapped canvases that we assumed were, undoubtedly, more dog portraits.

Zóra and I walked through town slowly, pulling the dollies behind us, past the little souvenir shops that were just opening up, past a farm stand where a thin, burnt-brown man was spearing handwritten price tags into crates of melons, tomatoes, bright green peppers, and limes. Shirtless men were already tearing down a stone wall at the bottom of an empty, sloping field full of dead yellow grasses and dark scrubs that were growing up here and there, throwing pockets of shade down the hill and onto the road. At the ferry pier, we ran into a small procession of children, presumably from the orphanage, heading our way, clinging to a frayed red rope that was slung between the waists of two supervisors, women who were both talking at the same time, telling the children to stay out of the street and not lick each other.

When we reached the monastery, we forced our crooked-wheeled dollies over the stairs at the gate, through an arbor of vines that clung like spiders to the lattice above. Fra Antun, we were told by the young woman who worked at the tourism counter in the courtyard, was in the garden. We left the dollies with her and went to find him. The garden was through a low stone tunnel, facing the sea, and was surrounded by a wall braced with cypresses

143

and lavender. There was a goldfish pond with yawning papyrus fronds that leaned out over the water, shading a mossy rock that someone had crowned with a grinning turtle ashtray. Evidence of children lay everywhere: abandoned buckets, blue-and-green sand trucks, plastic trains crowding end-to-end in the middle of the path, a headless doll with only one shoe, a butterfly net. At the back of the garden, there was a clear space where herbs and tomato vines and heads of lettuce were growing in tight, sprouting rows, and this was where we found Fra Antun. He was dressed in a cassock, cutting herbs with a pair of scissors, and when he straightened up he had glasses and a ponytail and two overlapping front teeth, and he smiled at us in a comfortable way and asked us if we had met Tamsin, the turtle, yet. He laughed, and we laughed with him. When he bent down to gather up his things, Zóra mouthed a soundless whistle and crossed herself.

He helped us bring the dollies into the inner courtyard of the monastery, past the chapel doors, now closed, and the staircase that led up to the campanile where the big brass bell was swinging hard, sending bursts of sound up the mountain. The children had been set up away from the cloisters, in what Fra Antun called the 'museum.' It was a long, white corridor with a clerestory of little square windows that ran parallel to the inner sanctum of the church. Empty sleeping bags were rolled up neatly along both sides of the hall. Fra Antun explained that, once the new orphanage was built and the children had been moved there, this corridor would house historic displays from the old library and pieces by regional artists.

'Local art,' he said with a proud wink, and showed us a patch of wall where more portraits of Bis were lined up. These drawings were in crayon, and the dog stood, stick-legged, three-eyed, bipedal, toadlike, misshapen in every possible way, on napkins and sheets of newspaper and toilet paper that had been lovingly arranged by someone considerably taller than the artists responsible for the work itself. At the end of the corridor, there was a cannonball wedged into the wall, the plaster and paint spidering around it.

'That is a cannonball,' Zóra said, without feeling.

'Yes,' said Fra Antun. 'From a Venetian ship.' And he pointed out in the direction of the sea.

The children were working in a windowless room that looked like an ancient kitchen. There was an enormous, empty black fireplace, and a spinning wheel in a wooden case in the corner, a shelf with turn-of-the-century irons that looked like instruments with which you could club a person to death. Stone bowls were lined up in small piles along a tiered mantelpiece. The single fold of an old fishing net hung above the door; a scruffy-looking blue plush fish was trapped in it. Fra Antun's kids sat hunched over wooden benches in the middle of the room. There were glasses of pencils and crayons scattered over the tables, and the color rose up in a glaring mess from the pages the kids were writing on, sitting on, sneezing on, folding into paper airplanes or birds. The strange thing about it all was the silence. We stood in the doorway, and we could hear the broad sound of the bell outside in the courtyard, but in the kitchen there was only sniffling and shuffling paper, the occasional rhythm of someone scratching his head. They were white-faced and small, sturdy despite their leanness. They were working with another monk, a man named Fra Parso. He had a beard and a tonsure, and was Italian. He didn't smile at us.

We had intended to save the candy for after the injections, to win the children's cooperation and patience, to comfort the criers and coax the breath holders, revive the fainters and bribe the ones who would go limp and eel out of your grip and onto the floor. But the silence in that room, with the little heads bowed over the flush of paper, did something to Zóra, and she unstrapped the box from the top of the pile and set it down right there and announced: 'We have candy.' And after that, the children were milling around her, still quiet, but milling, looking inside the cooler, walking away with bags of Kiki bonbons, which they probably hadn't seen since the war, and some had probably never seen at all. Zóra sat down on the stairs leading into the room with the tables and held out the candy, and I stood back until an even-eyed little boy with thick brown hair came up and took my hand and led me inside to look at his drawing. He was a little pale, but he looked painstakingly well cared for, and his head, which he put near me when he pointed to his picture, smelled clean. I was not surprised to find that he, too, had drawn Bis; except he had given the dog apple-green udders.

'That's a nice dog,' I told him. From the corner of my eye, I could see Zóra eyeing the leftover candy in the cooler, and then estimating how many kids were walking around with their mouths full or

146

with wrappers in their fists, trying to work out whether she could bring them back for seconds.

'It's Arlo's dog,' the little boy said, without looking at me.

'Who's Arlo?' I said.

The boy shrugged, and then wandered off to look for more candy.

I had been longing for my grandfather all day without letting myself think about it. Sitting in that hot, moist room with the dogs in all shapes and colors spread out in front of me made me remember how, for years during the war, he had collected my old things—dolls, baby clothes, books—to take to the orphanage downtown. He would take the tram there and always walk back, and when he came home I knew not to disturb him. They had lost children themselves, my grandparents: a son and a daughter, both stillborn, within a year of each other. It was another thing they never talked about, a fact I knew somehow without knowing how I'd ever heard about it, something buried so long ago, in such absolute silence, that I could go for years without remembering it. When I did, I was always stunned by the fact that they had survived it, this thing that sat between them, barricaded from everyone else, despite which they had been able to cling together, and raise my mother, and take trips, and laugh, and raise me.

I started setting up, and a little while later, her candy-distributing energy spent, Zóra joined me. With the discipline of the morning lesson shattered, the kids hovered in the doorway and watched us set up in an empty room at the end of the hall. Fra Antun and a few other monks carried

147

plastic tables up from the cellar, and we straightened out the table legs and put down cloth, stacked our boxes of injections and sterile blood vials in the corner that didn't get sun, set the scales, got out towels and tubs and boxes of gel for the lice station, and then Zóra had a fight with Fra Parso about the contraceptives we had brought to hand out to the older girls. When it was all finished, we gave the monks the supplies we had brought just in case, the thermometers and hot water bottles, a box of antibiotics and iodine and throat syrup and aspirin. The children were waiting for more candy, and Zóra was getting more and more agitated by what she was now seeing as our lack of preparation. There were no papers, she had realized—the monks did not have the children's medical histories—so we were going to have to make up the records by hand as we went.

The little boy who had drawn the dog with green udders stood, without a word, on the scale and opened his mouth obediently for the tongue depressor, tilted his head for the ear thermometer, drew deep breaths when we asked him to. He did not want to know how a stethoscope worked. Zóra, always great with children despite her insistence she would never have any herself, failed to impress him with her analogy of lice as warriors, fortified and equipped for siege, while she rifled through his hair with gloved hands, finding nothing. Ivo watched with mild interest as I sawed off an ampoule tip and filled the syringe, swabbed down his arm with alcohol. When I put the needle in, he watched the thin depression on his skin deepen without flinching, and when I did his other arm he didn't look at it at all, just sat in the green plastic

148

chair with his hands on his lap and stared at me. We had special-ordered children's band-aids with pictures of dolphins and a counterfeit Spider-Man in a yellow suit, and when I asked him which one he wanted he shrugged, and I gave him two for each arm, and would have given him more. I had the horrified feeling then that all the kids would be like this, oblivious to pain, unmoved in practice by the things that kids at home reacted against on principle. When the next kid kicked me in the shin, I was relieved.

The wails of children in distress are monstrously contagious: the moment one child strikes up, six more follow it, and the acoustics of the monastery halls amplified this phenomenon so that the whole place was ringing with howls of dread and indignation before we even laid hands on the second child. We had presaged what they were capable of doling out, a life-or-death struggle, an eagerness to bite. The monks, who stood by in terror for the first half hour, eventually came to our aid, pinning down legs and arms, threatening punishment, promising sweets. Beguiled by the prospect of more candy, some of the kids came and went without a fight. But in distributing most of the candy beforehand, we had made a serious tactical mistake: our only leverage in the situation had been that candy, and we watched it disappear, piece by piece, bar by bar, with an upwelling of despair, realizing that any minute now we would be down to just one or two.

At two o'clock, the young woman from the house appeared. I looked up and there she was, hovering in the doorway, and I didn't know how long she had been standing there. She had covered

149

her shoulders and head with a shawl to come into church, and the little girl was braced against her hip, asleep on her shoulder. When I motioned for her to enter she turned around and went back into the courtyard. By the time I got the next kid squared away and went to follow her, Fra Antun had cut her off at the door. I couldn't see her face, but I could hear what she was saying. They had found the body.

She was holding a yellowed envelope out to Fra Antun, tilting it toward him, and he had his hands up, refusing to touch it. 'Afterwards,' he was saying. 'Afterwards.' I waited for him to notice me in the doorway, and then I pointed to the child in the young woman's arms. He smiled and turned the young woman to face me, took her elbow, gestured for her to follow me indoors. But she was shaking her head, backing away from him to leave, and the two of us stood and watched her go, her shoulders striped with shadows from the vine awning that led out to the street.

Zóra appeared at my elbow with an empty box. 'We can't go on,' she said, holding it out to me, 'without candy.'

It was lunchtime, so we seized the opportunity to regroup, devise a new strategy for maintaining order. Zóra had turned her pager off, but the prosecutor had called her six times since that morning, so she went to the monastery office to return the calls while I stayed behind to sort out the paperwork. Sleepy, band-aided stragglers were milling around the courtyard in the dense heat of the afternoon; I tried to herd them out of the sun, and by the time I got back to the examining room, Fra Antun was already there, sorting the children's papers in alphabetical order.

He was eyeing my blood pressure pump, and I laughed and told him his was sure to be high, considering he was working with sixty children. He rolled up the sleeve of his cassock and patted the inside of his arm, and I shrugged and pointed to the chair. He sat down, and I pushed the cuff over his fist. He had a thin, young-looking face. Later on, I would find out from Nada that he had been the kind of boy who caught bumblebees in jars and then harnessed them carefully with film from cassette tapes, so that it was not uncommon to see him walking down the main road with dozens of them rising around him like tiny, insane balloons while the film flashed wildly in the sun.

'I hear you caused a stir up in the vineyard this morning,' he said.

I was about to admit to being too confrontational in my conversation with Duré—in my defense, I had listened to the little girl cough all night. But Fra Antun was talking, instead, about the entrance I had made. 'You scared the hell out of them,' he said. I was tightening the cuff over his forearm, and I didn't know what to make of his saying *hell.* He was smiling. 'Imagine: you're digging for a body. You've been digging all day and all night. In the hours before dawn, on the verge of finding what you've been looking for, you are surprised by the sudden appearance of a woman wearing what looks like a white shroud.'

'I fell into a hole,' I said, putting my eartips in and sliding the chestpiece onto his skin.

'That's how it's being told around town,' he said. 'What would you think, in their place?'

'I'd think: *why am I making my children dig for a*

body I put here myself?'

He looked at me like he couldn't decide whether or not to trust me with what he had to say. I was standing over him, inflating the cuff, and he was sitting with his cassock folded down between his knees. I released the air valve and watched the dial and listened to the whumping sound of his blood.

'We have one here, you know.'

I didn't know.

'A haunt,' he said. 'They call it a *mora*. A spirit.'

'We'll have to do this again,' I said, and started over.

'Everyone's shocked about this business with the body, but they forget we've had the *mora* a hundred years. We put coins and presents on the graves of our dead because the *mora* takes them. Word around town is that your diggers' crone knows about our *mora,* and that's why she's having them sanctify the body here.'

'How would she know?'

'That's just what they're saying,' Fra Antun said. 'I don't pretend it makes any sense to me.'

It made no sense to me, either; Duré and his family were from near the City, and we had no shortage of our own *mora*s and spirits, rarely glimpsed beings that willowed about, demanding graveside offerings that inevitably ended up in the hands of churchyard caretakers or passing gypsies.

'So what happens tonight?'

'I'm not sure,' he said. 'Duré says the village woman told him to "wash the bones, bring the body, leave the heart behind."' This charge, which Duré had repeated in confidence to Barba Ivan, had nevertheless spread through town, so that only a week later, it had become a sinister chant

152

regurgitated by the boys who hung out at the arcade, whispered by women at the grocery store, invoked by drunkards who passed the vineyard on their way home.

'Even your parrot knows it,' I said. 'You realize, of course, that no body buried twelve years out here is actually going to have a heart in it.'

'That's none of my business,' Fra Antun said with a defeated smile. 'They've asked me to supervise, and so I will, but unless the devil himself jumps out of the vineyard tonight, what happens to the body is no concern of mine.'

'I'm surprised you condone it,' I said. 'It doesn't sound like a Catholic process.'

'It isn't—it's not really an Orthodox one, either, but I'm sure you know that.' He was smiling. 'They have to settle for me in case something goes wrong,' he said. 'The other monks wouldn't even consider it.'

'And your mother—does she know you'll be officiating?'

'She knows.' His grin was laced with guilt. 'One of the advantages of being a monk is not having to get permission from your mother to carry out holy work.'

'I hear she's not happy about the vineyard.'

'No, it's difficult for her. First there's a body in the vineyard and now people from your side— excuse me, Doctor, but they *are* from your side— digging the whole place up.' He pushed his glasses up his nose and looked at me. 'She'd rather not have me near the vineyard when they're digging. It's not just about the body, or the vines being disturbed—all kinds of accidents happen in the field here.' I gave up on the blood pressure cuff

153

and listened to him. 'Mines,' he said, 'there are still land mines, even around here, up the mountain where the old village used to be. Most of them have been cleared, but the ones that haven't get found when somebody steps on them. A shepherd or farmer, or somebody's child, cuts through an unpaved area. Then there's a rush to keep it quiet.' He watched me roll up the cuff and cord. 'Even just last week, those boys in Zdrevkov.'

I misheard him at first, or the name didn't register because he was pronouncing it differently than my grandma did. Perhaps I didn't make the connection because it was the last thing I expected him to say, the last place I expected him to name, and the collision of my grandfather's death and Fra Antun sitting in that little room with the sun glaring in past the orange tree outside was sudden and senseless until I sorted it out.

Fra Antun had already moved on, talking about the mines above the old village, about an undetonated land mine in the neighbor's plot, by the time I said: 'Where?'

'Next door,' he said, pointing through the window.

'No—the place,' I said. 'You said something about boys there?'

'Zdrevkov,' he said. He took off his glasses and wiped them on the front of his cassock. 'It's even more backwater than this, but there's a clinic there,' he told me, blinking up, eyes unfocused. 'They've been keeping this kind of thing quiet for years. This happened last week. Two teenagers coming home late from town at Rajkovac. Mine got them coming through their own lettuce patch.' He thought my silence was surprise, or fear, or

154

hesitation to ask about the boys' well-being. 'Twelve years since the war, it was in their family's lettuces the whole time.' He got up and dusted off his cassock. 'That's why the digging's bad news.'

'How close is it?' I said.

'Zdrevkov? It's on the peninsula,' he said. 'Maybe an hour's drive.'

*   *   *

I said I was getting more candy, and Zóra believed me, believed me, too, when I said I would be back in an hour or less. She had wanted to come along, but I convinced her we'd look unreliable if we both left, insisted on going alone, insisted it would be faster this way, ignored her when she asked me why I needed the car, why I didn't just walk to the convenience store in town.

North of Brejevina, the road was well paved, stark and new because the scrubland had not grown back up to it, the cliffs rising white and pocked with thorn trees. A wind-flattened thunderhead stood clear of the sea, its gray insides stretching out under the shining anvil. Past the villages of Kolac and Glog, where the seaward slope was topped with new hotels, pink and columned, windows flung wide and the laundry hanging still on the balcony lines. Then came the signs for the peninsula turnoff, twelve kilometers, then seven, and then the peninsula itself, cutting the bay like a ship's prow between the shore and outer islands, wave-lashed cliffs and pineland. Fra Antun had predicted it wouldn't take more than an hour to reach the village, but the closeness of the peninsula stunned me.

My grandfather, it seemed, had been coming to see me after all; but while Zóra and I had gone the long way, sidetracked by having to check into the United Clinics headquarters before crossing the border, he had come straight down by bus, and somewhere around Zdrevkov he had been unable to come farther. Or he had heard, somehow, about the two boys, and stopped to help.

All this time I had been disconnected from the reality of his death by distance, by my inability to understand it—I hadn't allowed myself to picture the clinic where he had died, or the living person who would have his belongings, but that was all drawing in around me now.

The final six kilometers to Zdrevkov were unmarked, a dirt trail that wound left through a scattering of carob trees and climbed into the cypresses, which fell away suddenly in places where the slopes dropped away to the water. In the lagoon where the peninsula met the land, the sun had blanched the water bottle-green. The air-conditioning was giving out, and the steady striping of the light between the trees was making me dizzy. The crest of the next hill brought me out of the forest and into a downward-sloping stretch of road, where the abandoned almond orchards were overgrown with lantana bushes. I could see the light-furrowed afternoon swells in the distance, and, straight ahead, the flat roofs of the village.

Even at this distance, I could see why Zdrevkov was so obscure: it was a shantytown, a cluster of plywood-and-metal shacks that had sprung up around a single street. Some of the shacks were windowless, or propped up with makeshift brick ovens. Household junk spilled out of the doorways

156

and into the yellowed grass: iron cots, stained mattresses, a rusted tub, a vending machine lying on its side. There was an unattended fruit stand with a pyramid of melons, and, a few doors later, a middle-aged man sleeping in a rolling chair outside his tin-roofed house. He had his legs up on a stack of bricks, and as I drove past I realized his right leg was missing, a glaring purple stump just below the knee.

The clinic was a gray, two-story house that stood on the edge of town, easy to find because it was the only brick building in sight. Years ago, it had probably been a serious structure with clean walls, a paved courtyard lined with enormous flower urns that were now empty. Since then, the rain gutters had stained red-brown rivers into the walls.

The lot was empty, the clinic curtains drawn. I got out of the car. The stone stairway was littered with leaves and cigarette butts, and it led to a second-story door on which a square green cross had been painted above a plaque that read VETERANS' CENTER. I knocked with my knuckles, and then with my fist. Nobody answered, and, even with my ear against the door, I heard nothing inside. I tried the handle, but it wouldn't budge, and then I went out along the catwalk and peered around the corner of the clinic. The window facing the valley was shuttered.

The street below dead-ended in a flattened patch of pale grass, bordered on either side by netless goal frames. A slide and some tire swings had been set up on the lip of a wheat field that caught the afternoon light and held it in a shivering glare. Beyond that lay the graveyard, white crosses turned out toward the sea. The wind had subsided,

157

and the road was deserted except for a single mottled goat, tethered to the fence post of what looked like an enormous metal box opposite the clinic. If the BEER sign braced against an oil drum under the awning was to be believed, this was the bar.

I crossed the street and looked inside. The ceiling was very low, the place lit only by the open door and an enormous jukebox, whose sound was drowned out by the humming of a yellow refrigerator that looked like it had been salvaged from a radioactive dump. Four men were on high stools around a single barrel in the corner, drinking beer. It was just the four of them, but they made the room look crowded. One of them straightened up when I came in, a tall man with an ashen, leathery face and thinning gray hair. He didn't ask if he could help me, or invite me to seat myself, but I didn't go away, so he didn't sit back down.

I finally said: 'Is the clinic closed?' This forced him to come around the barrel and toward me. A prosthetic arm dangled weightlessly from his elbow on metal joints.

'You a reporter?' he said.

'A doctor,' I said.

'If you're here about those kids, they're dead.'

'I'm sorry,' I said.

The barman looked at the others in surprise. 'Makes no difference to me, they always die when they get hoisted around here.'

'I'm not interested in that.' I waited for some further acknowledgment, but when none came, I said: 'Is anyone on duty?'

I'd said enough for him to realize that I wasn't

from around there, which he confirmed now with a glance to the others. One of them, a huge, salt-and-pepper man, had an eye patch and a burn-stippled face; the other two seemed whole, but the blond man had an eye that looked away. The way they were staring at me made me wonder how fast I could get to the car and how much power I could get out of the engine if someone here really decided that I wasn't leaving.

'No one's been by in two days,' the barman said, putting his good hand in his pocket.

'Could somebody let me in?'

He picked up his beer bottle and downed what was left, put it back on the barrel top. 'What do you need?'

'Someone from the clinic.' The jukebox had gone quiet, shifting tracks, and the refrigerator kept pitching in with a fierce hum. 'I drove all the way from Brejevina,' I told him. And then, to present myself in the best possible light, I said: 'From the orphanage.'

The barman took a phone out of his pocket and dialed. He had a cell phone, all the way out here. I didn't; I had a pager and maybe two or three bills of the right currency. I stood by and listened while he left a message saying only, 'We got someone out here for you,' and then hung up. 'They'll call us back,' he said to me. 'Have a seat.'

I climbed onto a stool behind a two-top on the opposite end of the bar, and ordered a cola, which overwhelmed the room with a hiss when the barman opened it. I paid. He got four more beers and returned to the barrel where the others were waiting. I drank my cola, buttoned up in my white coat, trying to hide my reluctance to put my mouth

159

to the lip of the bottle, trying not to think about the phone call, which could have been to a nurse, but could also have been to anybody, or to no one at all. *We got someone out here for you*—one way or another, he'd called reinforcements. Nobody knew where I was; Fra Antun had pointed the place out on the map, but I hadn't told him I was coming, especially not like this, in the middle of the day when I was supposed to be inoculating his kids.

'You from the other side?' the eye patch said to me.

'I'm just a doctor,' I said, too quickly, putting my hands on my knees.

'I didn't say you weren't, did I? What else are you supposed to be?'

'Shut up,' the barman said.

'I didn't say she wasn't,' the eye patch said. He pushed his stool away and got up, pulling his shirt down with one hand. He made his way over to the jukebox, the sound of his shoes on the floor filling up the air. As he pushed buttons along the console, the albums flipped with a crunching sound that seemed to indicate something in the machine was broken.

'You like Extra Veka?' he said to me. 'You heard of her?'

Common sense said *say nothing,* but I couldn't pretend he wasn't there, not with the three of them sitting at the barrel. 'I haven't,' I said.

He shifted from one foot to the other, cleared his throat. 'You like Bob Dylan?'

'I like Springsteen better,' I said, and marveled at my own idiocy.

He pushed more buttons. 'Don't have him,' he said.

160

The jukebox whirred to life, an up-tempo Dylan song I didn't recognize. The eye patch moved away from the jukebox slowly, toward the middle of the bar, bobbing a little from side to side in time to the music. As he shifted around on the balls of his feet I saw that the burn scars wrapped around his scalp, leaving a bare, glazed scallop of flesh behind his right ear. The others were watching him. The barman was half-seated behind the bar, one leg propped on the rung of his stool and the other on the floor. The blond guy was smiling.

The eye patch turned slowly, all the way around, chugging one foot and one arm. Then he stopped and held out his hands to me.

'No, thanks,' I said with a smile, shaking my head, pointing to my cola.

'Come on, Doctor,' he said. I took another drink of my cola, shook my head again. 'Come on, come on,' he said, smiling, gesturing for me to get up, fanning himself with his hands. 'Don't make me dance alone,' he said. He clapped his hands and then held them back out. I didn't move. 'It's real, you know,' he said of the eye patch. 'It's not just for show.' He took one corner and flipped it up, the flesh underneath moist with the heat, puckered and white-red where it had been stitched shut.

'Sit down, you idiot,' the barman said.

'I was just showing her.'

'Sit down,' he said again, and stood to take the eye patch's elbow and lead him away from me.

'I've only got one.'

'I'm sure she's seen worse,' the barman said, and pushed him back into his chair at the barrel. Then he got me another cola.

I had no pager service, and Zóra had probably

161

started calling by now, wondering, doubtless, where the fuck I'd gotten to, why I wasn't back yet. I could picture the monastery hallway, the kids already reassembling, soup-stained shirts and sleepy, after-lunch eyes. Zóra, livid, making a mental list of things she would say to me in private, choice expletives. There had been traffic, I would say. An accident on the road. I had gotten lost. The store had been closed, and I had to wait for them to come back for the afternoon shift.

The barman's phone rang. He lifted it to his ear and called the person on the other end 'angel.' Then he waved me over and handed it to me.

'Doctor doesn't come in until next week,' the young woman on the line said right away. 'This an emergency?'

'I don't need the doctor,' I said. I told her I was interested in the discharge records for her patient who had died a few days ago, the one whose body had been returned to the City. The four men at the barrel were silent.

'Oh yes,' she said flatly, and she didn't say what I thought she might—nothing about my grandfather being a nice man, nothing about how it was a shame that he had died.

'I'm here for his clothes and personal belongings.'

'Those are usually sent back with the body,' she said, without interest.

'They didn't arrive,' I said. There was a hum of distant noise behind the nurse, music playing, blips from a pinball machine. She sounded like she had a cold, and every few seconds she would sniffle thinly into the receiver. The way she did this made me think that she was the kind of girl who might be

162

very much at home sitting in a bar not unlike this one.

'I really don't know anything about it,' she said. 'I wasn't on duty back then. You'll want to talk to Dejana.' I heard her light a cigarette and take a drag. Her mouth sounded dry. 'But Dejana's in Turkey now.'

'Turkey.'

'On holiday.'

Then I lied: 'The family needs his things for burial.'

'I don't come out there until Sunday.'

'The funeral is Saturday. I drove here from the City.'

She sounded unimpressed. 'I got no one to drive me out until Sunday. And I can't give you the coroner's notes without the doctor.'

I told her I didn't need the notes, I knew what they'd say. I needed his watch and his wedding band, the glasses he'd worn all my life. The four men around the barrel top were looking at me, but I didn't mind now. 'I don't know if you're familiar with the situation, but this man was dying for a long time, and then he left his family to do it away from home. They're devastated. They want his things back.'

'Dying makes people do strange things—I'm sure you told the family about that. You know how they sometimes go off, like animals do when they're going to die.'

'I need his things,' I said.

She was drinking something; I heard the ice in her glass clink against her teeth. She said: 'Give me Bojan.' The barman called her 'angel' again. She was still talking when he went to the refrigerator, opened it and rummaged around, still talking when he went outside. I hung back in the doorway and watched him cross the street and climb the clinic stairs.

'Well?' he said to me from the top of the stairs, the phone still against his ear. By the time I crossed the street, the door had been propped open, the lights still off. Inside, the air was stale and close, the floor sheeted with pale dust that had settled on the waiting room chairs and the top of the reception counter. There were trails in the dust where people had passed by, and they disappeared under a green curtain that had been drawn across the room.

'In here,' the barman said. He drew the curtain aside, walking slowly from one end of the room to the other, pulling it behind him as he went. The curtain opened out to a whitewashed infirmary, paint-chipped iron cots lined up against the walls, sheets empty and smooth, drawn tight under the mattresses. The room was unfinished, the rear wall missing, and in its place, from ceiling to floor, an enormous, opaque tarp that the afternoon light pasted with a dull yellow sheen. Outside, the wind picked up and the hem of the tarp lifted, crackling.

'Wait here,' the barman said. He unlocked a second door at the other end of the room, and I listened to him going down the stairs until I couldn't hear him anymore.

The fan above me wasn't working, and a dead fly was suspended on the lip of one of the blades. I crossed the room to lift the tarp, my shoes ringing on the tile even when I tried to preserve the silence by dragging my feet. Already, it seemed like the barman had been gone a long time, and I was

164

trying to remember what I had been doing the day he died, and how I'd ended up here, in the room where my grandfather had died, which looked nothing like how I'd pictured it, nothing like the yellowed rooms in the oncology ward back home, trying to remember how he'd sounded when I spoke to him last, his hands holding my suitcase out to me, a memory which was probably not our last goodbye, but some other goodbye before it, something my brain substituted for the real thing.

There was something familiar about the room and the village, a crowded feeling of sadness that crawled into my gut, but not for the first time, like a note of music I could recognize but not name. I don't know how long I stood there before I thought of the deathless man. When I did, I knew immediately that it was the deathless man, and not me, my grandfather had come looking for. And I wondered how much of our hiding his illness had been intended to afford my grandfather the secrecy he would need to go looking for him. The heat overwhelmed me, and I sat down on the end of one of the cots.

The barman reappeared with a pale blue plastic bag under his right arm. I watched him lock the stairwell door and come over to me. Goose bumps paled the flesh of his arm.

'This it?' he asked me. The bag was folded, stapled closed.

'I don't know.' I stood up.

He turned the bag over and looked at the label. 'Stefanović?'

I reached for the bag, but it was so cold it fell out of my hands. Bad arm dangling, the barman stooped to pick it up, and when he held it out to

165

me, I opened my backpack for him and he folded it inside.

He watched me zip up the backpack. 'All I know is, he collapsed,' the barman finally said.

'Where?'

'Outside the bar. A couple of nights after they brought those kids in. Before they died.'

'Were the nurses here? Did they take long to help him?'

The barman shook his head. 'Not long,' he said. 'Not long. They thought maybe he was drunk, at first. But I told them no. I told them he only ordered water.'

'Water? Was he alone?'

The barman wiped the sweat that had congealed on his temples in a grainy film. 'I couldn't say. Think so.'

'A tall man,' I said. 'With glasses, and a hat and coat. You don't remember him sitting with anyone at all?'

'No.'

'With a young man, maybe?'

He shook his head.

'They would have been arguing,' I said.

'This is a veterans' slum, what do you think people do all day?'

In the freezer below us, something shifted with a hollow clang.

'Look,' said the barman. 'Place was crawling with people I didn't know—nurses, assistants, two doctors, people who brought those kids in from the fields. I haven't seen it so full since the war ended. Had the whole village in the bar that afternoon. I only know the old man collapsed. I barely remember him, let alone who he was with.' He

166

went on, 'And I wouldn't go door-to-door round here, Doctor. On the chance that someone might have seen him. Not with that accent.'

I lifted my backpack onto my shoulder. 'You better sign for this,' he added, looking around for a piece of paper. There were no forms, so he turned over a receipt for saline solution and handed me a pen, watched me sign, *Natalia Stefanović,* which I did slowly, hoping he would make the connection. But his eyes told me he had already done this on his own.

6

THE FIRE

Gavran Gailé

Every Sunday afternoon, even when the war was at its worst, the City's greatest doctors would convene on the patio of Banević's restaurant in Old Town to smoke and drink and reminisce, to trade stories of astonishing patients and impossible cases, to praise one another's diagnoses and resourcefulness over a three-o'clock lunch reservation that had stood firm for almost sixty years.

The doctors were professors and nephrologists, cardiologists and University chairs, oncologists and orthopedic surgeons, a rotating parade of retirees whose accomplishments, though sometimes several decades old, still carried considerable weight in the medical community. They knew each other's stories by heart, but over walnut *rakija* and warm bread, red peppers with garlic and platefuls of grilled meat, they reminded each other of difficult times, pleasurable to revisit now that their legacy was secure in a timeline that by the grace of the spoken word only grew more and more incredible.

My grandfather was always among them. They were men alongside whom he had struggled up the tortuous rungs of the School of Medicine in his youth; and, though he was always humble about his work, I guess he, too, needed to remind himself of who he was and had once been. He had not founded a cancer clinic or won a national research prize; but, a great doctor in his own right, he was known for turning out flawless diagnosticians and surgeons during his time at the University, for advocating the medical rights of poverty-stricken villagers, and above all, for the privilege of having saved the Marshall's life—which, for better or worse, was an honor he shared only with certain surgeons in Zurich.

Because my grandfather was far more comfortable with extolling my accomplishments than his own, my knowledge of the incident was vague until I got to medical school. I knew about the Marshall's handwritten letter of thanks, sitting in the top drawer of my grandfather's desk; I knew, also, about the bottle of the Marshall's finest quince *rakija,* made from fruit harvested in the Marshall's own orchards, sitting unopened in the back of my grandfather's liquor cabinet for as long as I could remember.

The person who finally filled me in on the details was a starstruck assistant in first-semester pathology, who related it all sixth- or seventh- or eighth-hand. Apparently, one summer more than

168

thirty years ago, my grandparents were hosting a wedding party for the head of the oncology department of the Military Academy of Medicine at our family lake house in Borovo.

'Verimovo,' I corrected him.

'Right,' the assistant said.

Still, there was a wedding. It was evening, the party in full swing, when an innkeeper from the nearby village came running down the drive in desperation. It's a strange scene to picture: doctors and their wives dancing to the alcohol-impaired efforts of the village trumpet players; interns and laboratory assistants drunkenly lip-locked in the woods behind the house; inebriated dermatologists hanging over the porch rails; the University's entire medical department swarming our old lake house and garden; and my grandfather, a frowning and irritated sentry, extracting the chief of rheumatology from where he had fallen into the rosebushes. The innkeeper coming up the road, waving his arms, saying, *we need the doctor, where is the doctor?—in God's name, give us the doctor, the man is dying!* My grandfather, miraculously the only sober doctor on hand, shrugging into his coat and heading into the village to veto the stupefied local herbalist, who, as the only qualified person in town, had misdiagnosed the condition as food poisoning, and administered raw mint as a remedy.

The patient, of course, was the Marshall himself. He had been taken ill en route to a conference in Vrgovac after overindulging in date shells and garlic broth. Caught without his personal physician, he had been rushed to the nearest medical facility—a two-room shack—with an entourage of thirty men, all armed to the teeth.

169

The innkeeper was terrified: the date shells had been prepared at his establishment. By the time my grandfather reached the clinic, the patient was halfway to looking like a corpse already, and my grandfather knew instinctively that neither food poisoning, nor any of its cognates, was the issue.

My grandfather took one look at the patient—whose green face was ostensibly unrecognizable. 'You stupid son of a bitch,' he said to no one in particular (though everyone present was said to have immediately wet his pants). 'Why didn't you just shoot him in the head, you would have freed up the bed faster.' Fifteen minutes later, the patient was lying half-conscious on an operating table, his midsection unzipped, while my grandfather pulled feet and feet of infected intestine out of the Marshall's body in great red loops over his shoulder, and several bystanders— the innkeeper, assorted security personnel, probably a nurse or two, all terrified into competency by my grandfather's rage—stood in an assembly line of blood-spattered coats and goggles, patting away at the man's entrails, trying to clean off the appendix pus.

I remember the assistant looking at me expectantly when he finished the story, waiting for me to return the favor, to tell him something about my grandfather that could surpass what he had just told me.

*　　　*　　　*

After the University's admission lists were posted, and Zóra and I had confirmed, several times over, that we had both made the stipended top 500

170

cutoff, my grandfather asked me why I had decided to become a doctor. He had already bragged about it at the doctors' luncheon, told a number of his patients about it, and I didn't know what he wanted me to say, so I said, 'Because it's the right thing to do.'

This was true—I had been inspired largely by guilt that was manifesting itself among members of my generation as a desire to help the people we kept hearing about on the news, people whose suffering we had used to explain our struggles, frame our debates, and justify our small rebellions.

For years, we had fought to show nonchalance in the face of war, and now that it was suddenly over, over without having touched us in the City, indignation was surfacing. Everything was a cause, a dignified labor. We fought through biology and organic chemistry and clinical pathology; fought to adopt the University's rituals, from the pre-exam binges to the gypsy woman who took advantage of superstitious exam-takers in the courtyard, threatening them with bad luck if they didn't give her money. We fought, above all, to show that we deserved to be there, to defeat emerging newspaper projections that declared the City's postwar generation destined for failure. We were seventeen, furious at everything because we didn't know what else to do with the fact that the war was over. Years of fighting, and, before that, a lifetime on the cusp of it. Conflict we didn't necessarily understand—conflict we had raged over, regurgitated opinions on, seized as the reason for why we couldn't go anywhere, do anything, be anyone—had been at the center of everything. It had forced us to make choices based on circumstances that were now no longer a part of our daily lives, and we kept it close, a heavy birthright for which we were only too eager to pay.

For a while, I thought I wanted to help women—rape victims, women who were giving birth in basements while their husbands were walking through minefields, women who had been beaten, disfigured, maimed in the war, usually by men from their own side. It was impossible to accept, however, that those particular women would no longer need my help by the time I was qualified to give it. At seventeen, things like that make you self-righteous. You don't know anything about the aftershocks of war. Slightly younger, we had been unable to ration our enthusiasm for living under the yoke of war; now, we couldn't regulate our inability to part with it. Major decisions trended toward the assumption that the war and its immediate effects would always be around. Aspiring to orthopedic surgery was considered underachieving—you wanted, instead, to be an orthopedic surgeon specializing in amputation recovery. Plastic surgery was unthinkable—unless you wanted to deal with facial reconstruction.

One late afternoon, a week before midsemester exams, my grandfather asked me if I had given any thought to my own specialization, as if it were just around the corner. I had an answer for him: 'Pediatric surgery.'

I was sitting cross-legged at the dining room table, my secondhand cellular biology textbook lying on a kitchen towel to spare our white lace tablecloth. My grandfather was eating sunflower seeds directly from the small tin tray he usually toasted them on. Like all of his rituals, this was a process. He would remove the tray from the toaster oven and set it down on two cork coasters, and lay out a napkin for the disposal of shells. He would sift through the seeds before he started eating them; no one, not even my grandma, knew why he did this, what he was looking for. While he was sifting, he would wrinkle his nose to raise his glasses, which were enormous and square, to a position through which he could comfortably focus. It gave him the appearance of a diamond expert, and also made him look slightly suspicious.

'You'll be leaving God out of it, then,' he said.

'What does that mean?' I said. I couldn't remember when he had last mentioned God.

But he was back to the business of sifting through the seeds. Every so often, he would pick one out and chew on it, mostly with his front teeth; he would invariably end up eating them all, rendering the sifting exercise pointless. It took him a long time to ask, 'Been around children much?'

He wasn't looking at me, so he didn't see me shrug. After a while, I shrugged again, tapped my book with a pencil. Eventually, I asked: 'Why?'

He sat up, pushed his chair away from the table and rubbed his knees. 'When men die, they die in fear,' he said. 'They take everything they need from you, and as a doctor it is your job to give it, to comfort them, to hold their hand. But children die how they have been living—in hope. They don't know what's happening, so they expect nothing, they don't ask you to hold their hand—but you end up needing them to hold yours. With children, you're on your own. Do you understand?'

*   *   *

Of everything we fought for that year, we fought hardest for notoriety, for the specific word-of-mouth reputation needed to earn respect, recognition, and above all the favor of an obese technical assistant named Mića the Cleaver, the man who prepared cadavers, and who, like an unmet husband or your passport representative at City Hall, was a figure we were expected to factor into our plans long before we ever actually laid eyes on him.

It was a daunting but critical endeavor. Mića's attention had to be attracted well in advance. His gruff admiration was the prize for having attached some impressive anecdote, some reputable deed, to your name. Earning this attention before second-year anatomy was crucial. The point was to elicit some spark of awareness in his tar-clotted voice during the first roll call in the laboratory basement, so that when he read your name, he would raise an eyebrow at you and say, *Bogdanovic—aren't you the one who smoked pot in your room during the Kobilac retreat, and then put a towel on your head when the firemen came, and tried to say the vapor from your shower had set off the alarm?* You would nod, and, by the grace of God, Mića the Cleaver would smile, and then you were ensured a corpse every week, even in weeks of shortage, which were coming now that the war was over.

Without a weekly cadaver, a corpse to practice on, you were predictably fucked for the remainder of your career in medical school. It was a special privilege to be in those well-scrubbed rooms with

174

the prepared cadavers that looked like damp schnitzel. You wanted to get a head start on your colleagues by entering that mental space where you were used to a dead body, where you could look at a corpse without cringing or throwing up or collapsing. In order to succeed, you needed to move beyond the notion of respect for an autopsy victim, to resist the urge to pass out if the assistant referred to the corpse by its living name. You had to be the kind of person who could rise above the coping mechanism of painting the corpse's eyelashes with green mascara. For this, you needed a weekly corpse. You needed Mića the Cleaver's acknowledgment. You needed it so you could take that first step toward nonchalance in the face of death.

'What the hell do you have to be worried about?' Zóra said to me when some older male colleagues, in an effort to ingratiate themselves to us, revealed that we would be dedicating our first year to this effort. 'Haven't you inherited that anecdote about the Marshall's guts?'

We learned very quickly that nepotism was one of the many ways you did not want to be known to Mića the Cleaver. You did not want to be the perpetrator of some medical disaster, some self-defeating spectacle or slip of the tongue that made you look like an idiot rather than a respectable person for whom a steady influx of cadavers would pave a path to miracles. You did not want to be known for the kind of insolence to your predecessors that Zóra carried around our first semester. In a cavalier bid to secure future connections, Zóra had beaten eight hundred applicants to win a much-lauded internship with the Department of Genetics. To say that the position was lowly would be an understatement; her duties included mopping the floors. Her fifth morning on the job, carrying a box of files from the storage room, she ran into a rickety old man who was shuffling down the hall toward her, and who stopped her to suggest that she should put her excellent hips in a skirt, because pants indicated that she was too forward. Zóra, towering over the old man with a file box she probably considered dropping on his head, responded with: 'Don't be so fucking provincial.' Of course, the old man was the Chair of Genetics, and she spent the rest of the semester filing paperwork in the basement while the pandemic news of her insolence spread throughout the University, abetted by a fifth-year assistant who began producing don't be so fucking provincial T-shirts, which made a killing at the October fund-raiser.

My own notoriety was equally unsatisfying as far as Mića the Cleaver was concerned. I was making a little money helping out twice a week in the biology lab. Three weeks in, I was asked to help a laboratory assistant prepare brain samples for a study. Unfortunately, the brains belonged to a bagful of baby mice. Convincing myself that my sympathy for animals did not extend to small mammals, and taking into consideration the striking eyes of the laboratory assistant, I asked him how we would dispose of the mice. The assistant then explained there were two ways to go about it: seal them up in a box and wait for them to suffocate, or lop off their heads with nail clippers. The latter method he demonstrated rather than described. Zóra didn't witness the incident herself, but she had already heard several colorful renditions of it two days later, with which she was able to regale me while we sat at the orthodonist's office, waiting for them to cap the tooth I'd broken biting the floor.

We ended the term in December, ashamed of our respective debacles and fully expecting them to influence our inevitable encounter with Mića in the fall. But then came preparations for spring anatomy, and the long-awaited search for skull replicas. You'd think that, after the war, they would have had enough real skulls to go around; but they were bullet-riddled skulls, or skulls that needed to be buried so they could wait underground to be dug up, washed, buried again by their loved ones.

Skulls were nearly impossible to come by. The trade embargoes hadn't lifted, and the channels through which the University had acquired medical supplies—questionable to begin with—were considerably more difficult to access now. People from previous years were selling ridiculously overpriced fourth- or fifth-hand skulls, advertising their availability by word of mouth. We were desperate. In the end, a friend of a friend told us about a man called Avgustin, who specialized in producing plastic replicas of human parts, which he sold to dentists, orthopedists, and cosmetic surgeons—on the black market, of course.

We lied to our parents, drove four hours down a snow-packed highway, past army trucks that were inching, bumper to bumper, in the opposite lane; we smiled through two customs lines, at six reluctant officials, so we could meet Avgustin at his office in a Romanian border town, which had windows overlooking the docks and the ice-banked waters of the Grava River. He was a short man with a bald head and square cheeks, and he offered us lunch, which we refused. We stood close together while he told us about the skulls he had for us. They were apparently both replicas of the head of some magician from the 1940s, a man called the Magnificent Fedrizzi. It was a specimen, he said, he had acquired with great difficulty. That was probably a version of the truth, although he didn't mention the part about the obligatory haggling with the gravekeeper, whom he had probably bribed to dig up the Magnificent Fedrizzi after enough time had elapsed for there to be nothing left but bones. In life, this Magnificent Fedrizzi had apparently performed dazzling feats of magic on a Venetian stage—until 1942, when a German audience member, whose woman the Magnificent Fedrizzi had evidently been sharing for some time, put an end to them rather abruptly.

'The skull of Don Juan,' Avgustin said, winking at Zóra. We didn't know why he was telling us this until he finally brought out the replicas, swathed in bubble wrap. The skulls looked like cousins at best, and it immediately became apparent that the German who killed the Magnificent Fedrizzi liked to settle his fights the old-fashioned way—with a wine bottle or nightstick, or perhaps a lamp or rifle butt.

'Couldn't you have at least plastered over the fractures?' Zóra said, pointing to the slightly dented left side of the cranium, the burst of grooves in the plastic.

Apart from the fractures, the skulls were white and matter-of-fact and clinical, and the jaw opened

178

and closed without squeaking, which was, ultimately, all we were looking for. We managed to get Avgustin to knock the price down by 10 percent, and, as we left, he warned us repeatedly against taking the skulls out of their boxes and packaging—labeled SHOES. But in the inbound customs line later on we thought better of this; they were searching people's trunks, and we had two suspicious-looking boxes with black market goods in ours. I put my Magnificent Fedrizzi in my backpack, and Zóra hid hers in the First Aid compartment under the back seat. It didn't end well, but least it ended at our customs booth, and not the Romanian one—the officials searched the car, and then proceeded to hold us up at gunpoint, confiscate my backpack, and take the Magnificent Fedrizzi away.

We would joke, later on, about how he was probably much happier there, in the Grava River Valley, working with the customs officials. But calling home from the customs station, dreading what I would say to my grandfather—whom I hoped to convince to get on the train and rescue us—it was not funny at all.

'Bako,' I said, when my grandma picked up. 'Put Grandpa on.'

'What's the matter?' she said sharply.

'Nothing, just put him on.'

'He's not here. What's happened to you?'

'When is he coming home?'

'I don't know,' she said. 'He's at the zoo.'

Zóra and I sat in the interrogation room at the customs station for six hours until he came to sort out our mess, and that entire time, for some reason, I couldn't work the image of my

179

grandfather sitting at the zoo by himself out of my head. I could see him, a bald man with enormous glasses, sitting on the green bench in front of the tiger pit with *The Jungle Book* closed on one knee. Leaning forward a little in his coat, both feet on the pavement, hands clasped. Smiling at the parents of children going by. In his pocket, the empty, balled-up plastic bag from which he had fed the pony and the hippopotamus. I felt ashamed for thinking of him. It hadn't occurred to me that the zoo would have reopened, or that my grandfather might have resumed going despite my no longer having the time to keep him company. I told myself to ask him about it, but in the end I never found the right moment. Or I was too embarrassed to do anything that might be perceived as questioning the ritual comforts of an old man.

My grandfather cut a different figure, of course, when he stormed into the customs station with his emeritus badge from the University hanging around his neck, white coat on, hat in hand, and demanded the return of his granddaughter and her friend—'the one who smokes.'

'That skull was a medical necessity,' my grandfather said to the customs official holding us prisoner. 'But this will never happen again.'

'The import restrictions are on the other side of the border, Doctor, I couldn't give a shit if they were bringing in six dead bodies and a liquor cabinet,' the customs official said. 'But my son does have a birthday coming up.'

My grandfather paid him off, advised him to invest the money toward his son's moral upbringing, and then motioned us to the back seat of Zóra's car and drove us home in silence. That silence, which was the only thing worse than his rage, his disappointment, his worry, was intended to give me ample time to brace myself for what he would have to say to me when we got home. I was too old for punishment. What I had coming was a carefully versed speech intended to make you feel as ashamed as possible of your own incompetence, stupidity, and lack of respect for things that were above you. But I couldn't get beyond the zoo—he had been at the zoo, all alone, and something about that devastated me.

An hour into the drive, Zóra leaned forward and took our remaining, hidden skull out of the First Aid compartment and put it on the seat between us with a smile that was intended to comfort me. My grandfather was looking in the rearview mirror.

'Who the hell is that?' he said.

'The Magnificent Fedrizzi,' Zóra said flatly, and afterward we shared the skull and the story and, eventually, the smile from Mića.

*   *   *

The war had altered everything. Once separate, the pieces that made up our old country no longer carried the same characteristics that had formerly represented their respective parts of the whole. Previously shared things—landmarks, writers, scientists, histories—had to be doled out according to their new owners. That Nobel Prize-winner was no longer ours, but theirs; we named our airport after our crazy inventor, who was no longer a communal figure. And all the while we told ourselves that everything would eventually return to normal.

181

In my grandfather's life, the rituals that followed the war were rituals of renegotiation. All his life, he had been part of the whole—not just part of it, but made up of it. He had been born here, educated there. His name spoke of one place, his accent of another. None of this had mattered before the war; but as time went on, and the Military Academy did not officially invite him back to practice medicine, it became clear that a return to professional normalcy would not be possible, and he would be tending to his under-the-table patients until the day he chose to retire. With this knowledge came an overwhelming desire to revisit lost places, to reestablish unmaintained rituals. The zoo was one of these.

Another was the lake house at Verimovo, across the border now, where we had spent every summer until I turned eleven. It was a beautiful old stone house at the edge of one of the big valley lakes, just off the main highway that connected Sarobor and Kormilo. A few steps down the cobbled path and you would be in the water, the clear, blue-green waters of Lake Verimovo, fed by the Amovarka. None of us had been to the house in almost seven years, and there was silent acknowledgment in the family that the house was probably no longer standing, or that it had been looted, or that the second you came through the door you would be hoisted by a mine that some careless soldier, probably from your own side, had left behind. There was also acknowledgment, however, that the house had to be seen, the damage assessed, a decision made. My mother and grandma wanted to see if our neighbor Slavko had turned on us, if he'd given up on the house, reneged on his promise to keep it safe until after the war. For my grandfather, however, the urgency sprang from a need to resurrect a past pleasure into the sphere of the everyday, as if nothing had happened.

'Wouldn't it be something if the vine was still up on the garage balcony?' he said in the fourteenth month of the cease-fire, three days after the grand reopening of the southbound railroad. He was packing for the train ride to Verimovo: his small blue suitcase with the built-in combination lock was open on the bed, and he was folding several pairs of gray cotton shorts and white undershirts into it. I was sitting at the foot of the bed, and had come in to tell him not to be ridiculous, to just sell the house. But he was smiling the way he smiled when we used to go to see the tigers, and I suddenly felt overwhelmed by my own lack of optimism—who was I to tell him what was appropriate and inappropriate? Who was I to hold him back when he wanted so much for things to go his way? So instead, I offered to go with him. To my surprise, he accepted. When I think about it now, I realize how willful he was, as though, by bringing me along, he was ensuring it was safe enough to bring me along.

As with everything we did together, there was a plan. We were going to evaluate the damage. Assuming it was still standing, we were going to open up the house, air out the rooms, see what furniture had been stolen or broken, restock the pantry. We were going to bring down summers and summers of swallows' nests that had caked up the balcony walls, trim the bright green vines that slithered along the awning above the garage, pick

183

whatever figs and oranges were ripe, all in preparation for my grandma, who had agreed to join us the following week. Depending on what we found, we were also going to get the new dog accustomed to lakeside life.

He was a very small, but very fat, white dog my grandma had been tricked into buying at the Sunday market in the City. She had fallen victim to circumstance because he had been the last one left in the puppy box, and the farmer, squatting in the summer heat since dawn with a box of wormy, smelly farm puppies, all throwing up and peeing on one another, had finally held the dog up in desperation and said, 'I expect I am going to have to eat you,' just as my grandmother walked by. My grandma paid the man far too much money and came home with the dog cupped in her hat, and the farmer presumably went to buy some crispy pig and never thought about it again.

The dog went unnamed for a long time. He liked to be held, and he sat on my knees wrapped in a pink towel while our train sped through the parched mid-country, following the river past wheat fields and clapboard towns perched at the water's edge, and then, as we got closer to the lakes, through soaring blue mountains tangled with scrubs and sprouting clumps of lavender. We had the compartment, meant for six, all to ourselves, because my grandfather wanted to avoid any other passengers catching sight of our passports at border control. The windows were down, and the smell of that pine scrubland came in sharp and strong.

My grandfather sat beside me, drifting in and out of consciousness. Every so often, he would

184

wake up with a start, and then take his right hand off his belly and pet the dog, who couldn't sleep, and was peering anxiously through the window. My grandfather would pet the dog, and, in a voice that made him sound like some kind of children's program puppet, he would say: 'You're a dog! You're a dog! Where are you? You're a dog!' and the dog's tongue would drop out of its mouth and it would start keening.

After a few hours of this, I said, 'Jesus, Grandpa, I get it, he's a dog,' not knowing that, just a few years later, I would be reminding every dog I met on the street that it was a dog, and asking it where it was.

The house was a five-minute walk from the train station, and we took this walk slowly, both of us stiff-limbed and silent. The afternoon was dry, and my shirt was sinking into my skin before we even reached the drive. And then it was there—the drive, the house, the garage drowning in vines. There was rust on the fence, and I suddenly remembered how easily things rusted at the lake house, and how, long ago, my grandfather would repaint the fence every year, patient, meticulous, standing with a sort of pleasurable grace in his clogs, with his socks on, his bony knees very white with sun protection.

Our neighbor Slavko was standing on the porch, and when he saw us he stood up and began rubbing his hands on his pants. I couldn't really remember him from my childhood at the lake, but my mother had often talked about him: they had grown up more or less together. Somewhere along the line, my mother had started wearing jeans and listening to Johnny Cash; this, according to Slavko and

185

some of the other local boys, distinguished her as part of the 'wild crowd,' and made her a target of prepubescent window peering. I could see that boy in the guilty look he was giving us now. His face was clean-shaven, scrubbed raw, and he had a mop of gray curls that lay flat against his forehead. This, combined with big feet and shoulders that dropped suddenly into a concave chest and potbelly, made him look unnervingly like an oversized penguin.

Slavko had brought us a few pies for dinner, and was rubbing his hands on his pants nervously, nonstop. I thought for a minute that my grandfather would overdo it and embrace him, but they shook hands, and then Slavko called me 'Little Nadia' and rubbed my shoulder cautiously and I shot him a dry smile. He showed us the house. Soldiers had come through almost immediately when the war began, and taken some valuables: my great-grandmother's china, a portrait of a distant aunt, some brass Turkish coffee cups and pots, the washing machine. For the most part, there had been no upkeep. Some of the doors had been taken down, and the countertops were covered with dust and plaster that had fallen from the ceiling, and yellow stuffing was coming out of my grandma's living room set, which, we would soon discover, was also the nesting site of some very uncooperative moths. In the bathroom, the toilet was gone, and the little blue tiles that made up the floor had been reduced to a shattered mosaic.

'Goats,' Slavko said.

'I don't understand,' said my grandfather.

'They needed to smash it up,' said Slavko, 'so their goats wouldn't slip on the tiles.'

As we followed Slavko through the house, I held on to the dog, and kept searching my grandfather's face for signs of disappointment, discouragement, the slightest hint of giving up. But he was smiling, smiling on, and through my own frustration I started to feel that nagging sense of shame again, an acute awareness of my own inability to share in his optimism. My grandfather told Slavko that he hoped it hadn't been a terrible inconvenience for him, keeping the house safe for us, and Slavko laughed nervously, and said, no, no of course it hadn't, not for my grandfather, not for a great doctor like him, everyone in town remembered him.

When Slavko left, my grandfather turned to me and said: 'It's so much better than I expected.' We unpacked, and took a walk through the orchard. My grandma's rose garden was dead, but oranges and figs sat fat in the trees, and my grandfather went along, kicking the soil here and there, sifting for something. Every so often, he came across an artifact that didn't belong in the dirt: bolts, bullets, broken pieces of metal that could have been crowbars or frames. In the back of the property, we found our toilet, which someone had abandoned there, unable to reconcile carrying it up the steeper slope, and also the bones of a dead animal. They were small bones, broken, sharp as glass, and my grandfather picked up the skull and looked at it. It had horns—probably a goat—but my grandfather only turned it toward me very slowly, and said: 'Not the Magnificent Fedrizzi.'

While my grandfather carried the toilet indoors, I climbed the stairs to the garage with a broom under my arm, and I swept dead vine leaves off the

187

cracked stone. There were beer bottles and cigarette butts, probably a lot more recent than the war, and I found a few used condoms, which I forked with the end of my broom and heaved furtively over the wall into the neighbor's yard. In the late afternoon, my grandfather and I ate our dinner on boxes on the garage balcony, cold pie greasing our hands. The lake was still and yellow, dotted with seagulls that had flown in from the coast. Every few minutes, we heard a speedboat, and, eventually, a couple on a pedal-boat went slowly by.

We were sitting like this—my grandfather telling me about repairs that had to be done, things that had to be bought in town, like an air conditioner for Grandma, and a small television, new blinds, of course, and maybe even new windows altogether, a more secure door, some tick medicine for the dog, seeds for reviving the rose garden—when the fire started on the hill. It was not Verimovo's first fire by any means, and, we would later learn, it started like all the others: with a drunkard and a cigarette. We could see black smoke lifting in waves above the summit where the old mines stood, and then, an hour or so later, a bright snake of flame coming down the hill, throwing itself down and down on a path of dry grass and pinecones, following the wind along the mountain. Slavko came to watch it from the garage with us.

'If it blows east, we're going to be picking china out of the ashes of our houses tomorrow morning,' he warned us. 'You better keep an eye on it.'

For a while, my grandfather was certain that the wind off the lake would keep the fire contained on the upper slope, above the dangerous scrubland that would catch like a Christmas tree. He was so adamant in his belief—in what I, at the time, was convinced was his naïveté—that he sent me to bed, and stayed up by himself, sweeping the stairs and poking around the pantry, all the time going outside to look.

Around midnight, when it came as far as the ridge below the tree line, my grandfather got me out of bed—where the dog and I had been wrestling for space, following the fire's progress through the window—and I stood in the hall, watching my grandfather put on his shoes. He told me to get our passports and get out of the house. He was going to help the men from town with the fire. This entailed walking through the fields where the fire had come down from the trees, beating the low flames with coats and shovels so the blaze couldn't start on the gardens and the lawns and the rows of plum and lemon that people were growing for market—but I remember that, even though he knew he was going to spend the night in dirt and ash, he shined his shoes. I remember his hands, and the way they held the shining rag, the way he skimmed it back and forth over the toes of his shoes like he was playing a violin. The dog shuffled around, and my grandfather touched its nose with the shoe rag. Then he took me outside, to the back of the house, where the rear wall of the balcony met the slope of the orchard in the dead rose garden and the orange and fig trees, already reddening with the light from the hill.

'Take this,' he said, putting the garden hose in my hand and turning the faucet on. 'And start watering. Keep the water on the house. Keep the walls and the windows wet, and whatever you do,

189

don't leave the door open. If it gets bad—Natalia—if it jumps the wall and starts on the house, you run for the lake.' Then he clapped my grandma's long-lost saucepan—the old apple-red one from Italy, which had resurfaced that evening for the first time in ten years during his inspection of the pantry, and which he must have felt would afford me some kind of special protection—onto my head, and left. I remember the sound of his shoes on the gravel, the sound of the gate opening, the fact that it was the only time he left the gate open.

My mother always says that fear and pain are immediate, and that, when they're gone, we're left with the concept, but not the true memory—why else, she reasons, would anyone give birth more than once? I think I understand what she means when I look back on the night of the fire. Part of me knows that there was tremendous pain, that the heat of the blaze as it came down through the old village on the hill and Slavko's farmland and our orange grove and ripped through the fig and almond trees, the pinecones sizzling like embers for what seemed like forever before they exploded, was unbearable; that to say that it was difficult to breathe is an impossible understatement; that the hair on my bare arms was already singed when the fire dropped down through the pines and rushed the brick wall. I know that I stood there with one side to the fire and the water trained on the walls and the doors and the shuttered windows, amazed at how quickly the stream of water evaporated, how it sometimes didn't even touch the house. But what I really remember is a sort of projected image of myself, looking ridiculous, there in my red flip-

190

flops and my bootleg BORN TO RUN tube top with the frayed hem, Grandma's best saucepan on my head, handle akimbo, and that hysterical fat white dog under my arm, his heart hammering like a cricket against my wrist, and the stream of water from the hose hissing against the back of the house to keep the fire out.

I do, however, remember the woman from next door with complete clarity. At a certain moment in the night, I turned to find her watching me water the fire from the doorway of her house. I remember she was wearing a buttoned housedress with flowers on it, and her white hair had come out of her updo and was hanging limp with sweat around her face in the firelight. I had no idea how long she had been standing there, but I thought that maybe I recognized her, felt sure she was going to offer me help, and I must have smiled at her, because suddenly she said: 'What are you smiling at, you sow?'

I went back to my watering.

Eventually, as they always do, people would find a way to extract humor even from that evening. They would laugh openly about it, make jokes about the barbecue up at Slavko's place—the pigs and the chickens and the goats cindering down in their pens as the night wore on—and nobody would ever mention that they had five or six hours as the fire wound closer to get the animals out, to stop the screaming that would eventually rise over the deafening noise of the fire. Nobody ever mentions that, at the time, they were so absolutely certain of more war that it was easier for them to let the livestock burn where they stood than to save them, only to have our soldiers return and take it all from them again.

By morning, the fire had died, or spread elsewhere, but with the sun rising there was nowhere to get away from the heat. Indoors, the furniture was white with ash, and I turned on the fans and closed the shutters against the morning stillness that lay on the black slope above the house.

My grandfather got back a little after dawn, wheezing. He came in through the gate, closed it behind him and stepped inside. He didn't embrace me, just put his hand on the top of my head and held it there for a long time. Ash had slid into the lines of his face, the crow's-feet around his eyes, the contours of his mouth. He washed up and then sat at the small table in the kitchen, digging the soot out from under his fingernails, bouncing the dog on his knee, with *The Jungle Book* open on a handkerchief in front of him while I made eggs and toast and cut up slices of watermelon for breakfast.

Then he told me about the deathless man again.

*   *   *

Dabbing the gray corners of The Jungle Book *with his handkerchief, my grandfather said:*
In '71, there's this miracle in a village a little way from here, on the sea. Some kids are playing near a waterfall, this small white waterfall that feeds a deep hole at the bottom of some cliffs, and one day, while they're playing like that, they see the Virgin in the water. The Virgin's just standing there, her arms outspread, and the children run home and tell their parents, and suddenly they are calling the water miraculous. The children are

192

coming to the waterfall every day to see the
Virgin, and suddenly they're renaming the local
church—the Church of the Virgin of the Waters—
and people are coming in from all over. They're
coming in from Spain and Italy and from Austria
to see this little watering hole and sit in the church
and look at the children who are sitting all day,
staring into the water, and saying, 'Yes, we see
her—she is still there.' Pretty soon some cardinal's
coming out to bless it, and suddenly you've got
buses coming out of nowhere, trips from hospitals
and sanitariums so people can come and look at
the waterfall and swim in the water and be healed.
I'm talking about really sick people—I'm talking
about people with cerebral palsy and faulty hearts,
people with cancer. A lot of them are coming in
from tuberculosis clinics. And then there's the
people who can't even walk, people on their last
breath being carried in on stretchers. There's
people who've been sick for years, and no one can
say what's wrong with them. And that Church of
the Waters is handing out blankets, and they're all
sitting out there, the sick people, in the gardens
and in the courtyard, all the way out to the
sidewalk, just waiting. The sick people, in that
heat with the flies around them, with their feet in
the water, their faces in the water, bottling it up to
take home with them. You know me, Natalia—
nothing, for me, has quite the effect of a man with
no legs dragging himself down a rocky slope for
penance so he can sit in a swimming hole and tell
himself he is getting better.

So the University asks me to get a small team
together and get down there right away. There's
risk, they're thinking—all these people, already

dying, are under constant strain. They want me to set up a care center, maybe offer some free medicine. I go out there with about twelve nurses and right away we come to understand that these Waters are a thousand miles from anywhere, and the only building on that side of the mountain is the church, and everything that happens here is happening in or around the church. There's no hospital around, no hotels—not like there will be in twenty years. The miracle is too recent, no one has had the time to profit from it. The church provides shelter for the dying, but the only place they have to put them is the crypt. There's this door under the altar, and you go down down down the stairs into the stone cellar of the crypt, where the dead are laid like bricks into the walls, and there you see the dying on the floor, wrapped in blankets, and the stink is enough to make you want to kill yourself, because, besides the diseases, these dying are eating what the church provides for them: they are eating apples and olives the local farmers bring from the other side of the island, and they are eating bread, and the whole place has this sour, sour smell that goes into your clothes and your hair and there is no place to get away from it.

To make matters worse, in addition to the dying who are there to pray, people are taking the ferry in from the mainland to rejoice, to feast and drink in honor of the Virgin. At night, the priests are always finding six or seven drunks on the church grounds, and they are putting these drunks in a little annex in the crypt so they can sober up overnight. They have no other place to put the drunks—they lock them in so they do not go wandering, but you can imagine what happens when these drunks wake up in the dead of night to find themselves in a lightless stone room. All the time, the drunks are making noise. All night long, you can hear them hooting and sobbing in there, and the dying, who are crowded around the columns and sleeping in the baptismal font, can hear them through the crypt walls, and to them it must sound like the dead are calling them home.

You are going to see what it is like, someday soon, being in a room full of the dying. They're always waiting, and in their sleep they are waiting most of all. When you're around them, you're waiting too, measuring all the time their breaths, their sighs.

On the night I'm telling you about, it is more quiet than usual in the little drunk cell next door. I have given the nurses a night off to have a weekend dinner on the mainland by themselves, and I am not expecting them until morning. It is impossible to sleep, but it is not so bad, being by myself like that. No one is on watch with me, reminding me about the dying. I've got a small lamp, and every so often I go walking up and down the rows of sleepers, leaning over them, looking into their faces. Sometimes, a person runs a fever or begins to vomit, and I give them medicine and stand by them with the light. The light they find more comforting than the medicine. There is a man there who is coughing a great deal, and I am not optimistic about him, or about how much help I will be when the time comes, but whenever the light is near him, he coughs a little less.

I am walking like this, back and forth, when I

hear someone say: 'Water.'

It's very dark, and I can't tell where the voice is coming from, so I say, quietly, 'Who's speaking? Who wants water?'

For a long time there is no reply, and then I hear it again, someone very quietly saying: 'Water, please.'

I lift up my lamp, and all I see around me are the backs and faces of blanket-covered sleepers. No one is lifting a hand to call to me, there are no open eyes looking at me, asking for water.

'Hello?' I say.

'Yes—here,' says the voice. 'I beg your pardon, but—water.'

The voice is very faint, and it's almost as though it is being held up very high in the air, above my head, so that no one else can hear it. I am raising my lamp and turning around and around, looking for the owner of the voice, and then the voice, with so much patience, says to me: 'Doctor, over here. Water, please.' And then I understand that the voice is coming from the little cell where the drunks are kept. I think at first, *some boozer has woken up and gotten out somehow, and now he is going to make trouble for me.* But then the door is shut tight, and I pull on it and it doesn't open, and the voice says, 'Here I am—Doctor, down here' and I search the wall with my hand and I find a space between the stones near the floor, a place where the stones have been taken out or chipped away, a very small opening, and I hold up my light but on the other side I see only darkness. I put my face near the hole, and I say: 'Are you there?'

The voice says: 'Yes, Doctor.' The owner of the voice is sitting by the hole and talking out at me, asking for water. I don't know how I am going to give him the water through the small opening, but I intend to try. Before I can tell him this, however, the voice says: 'This is a wonderful surprise, Doctor.'

'I'm sorry?' I say.

'How nice it is to see you again,' the voice says agreeably, and waits. I am seriously confounded, and I try to put a face to this voice. I say to myself: *who do I know back home who would make a pilgrimage to this island in the middle of nowhere just to end up in the drunk tank?* I think maybe it is some idiot boyfriend of your mother's, in which case I am going to leave him there without any water, but there is something about this business of asking for the water, the way he is asking for the water, that makes me think the voice belongs to someone from long ago. The voice is patient with my silence for a while, and then it says: 'You must remember me.' But still I don't. 'It's been fifteen years, Doctor, but you must remember the coffee grounds. The ankle weights and the lake?' And then I realize it is him—it is the deathless man—and my silence continues because I do not know what to say. He must think I am not saying anything because I do not remember, so he keeps reminding me: 'You must remember me, Doctor—from inside the coffin.'

'Of course,' I say, because I am astounded enough already, and I do not want him to say anything more about the weights and the lake. It is a despicable dream to me, an unthinkable risk some other doctor, some young fool, took long ago, and I cannot put my mind to it just like that. 'It is Gavran Gailé.'

'Oh, I'm so glad,' he says. 'So very glad you remember me, Doctor.'

'Well,' I say. 'This is remarkable.' It is the strangest thing, coming face-to-face with this man, Gavran Gailé, in the dark, without being able to see if he is real. You must realize—to know that a man has not died after going into a lake for most of the night is one thing. You do not explain it to yourself because you know you will never come across this kind of thing again, you will never meet another man who also doubles as a lungfish. You do not explain it to yourself, and, as I have said before, you certainly do not explain it to other people, and then it becomes the sort of thing that slips away from your own grasp of the truth, until you have very nearly forgotten about it.

So the deathless man wants water, but none of my bottles or ladles will fit through the hole, and we sit there, the deathless man and I, in silence, and he is very thirsty, you understand, but never irritable. He does not complain. He asks me what I am doing here, and I tell him I am here for the dying, and he says, what a coincidence, he is too.

And I am thinking to let this go, to not address it at all, when he says: 'Is he dead yet?'

'Who?' I say.

'The man with the cough, the one who is going to die.'

'No one has died tonight, thank you, and I'm confident no one will.'

'You are mistaken, Doctor,' he says with enthusiasm. 'Three will go tonight. The man with the cough, the man with the cancer of the liver, and the man who appears to have indigestion.'

'Don't be ridiculous,' I say, but something

198

about all of this makes me weary, so I get up and walk around anyway, with my lamp up, looking at the sleepers, and among them I do not see anything strange. I come back and I say to the deathless man: 'That's enough. I've nothing to say to you tonight. I have no interest in taking medical cues from a drunk man.'

'Oh, no, Doctor,' he says, and he sounds deeply apologetic. 'I am not drunk. I haven't been drunk in forty years. They put me in here because I was unruly this morning, and wouldn't leave.' I do not ask him what he was doing to be unruly, but I am hovering, and I do not go, so he tells me: 'I have been selling coffee, you see, and today I told that man with the cough that he was going to die.'

Suddenly, I realize I've seen him—I've been seeing him without knowing it, because for the last three or four days there has been a coffee seller at the Waters dressed in the traditional Turkish style, selling coffee to the masses by the waterfalls. I have never looked at him closely, and now it seems to me that, yes, perhaps it is possible that he had the face of the deathless man, but then that face must have changed over the years, and so I do not know. *I cannot believe it,* I say to myself, *I cannot believe that anyone would disguise himself as a coffee seller to play a terrible practical joke.*

'You mustn't do that,' I say to him. 'The people who come here are very sick. You mustn't frighten them like that, they are here to pray.'

'And yet, you are here, so you must not believe entirely in the fact that they will get what they are praying for.'

'But I still let them pray.' I am very angry. 'You must not do this again. They are very sick, they need peace.'

'But that is what I do,' the deathless man says. 'That is my work: to give peace.'

'Who are you, really?' I say. 'What are you doing here?'

'I am here for my penance.'

'You're here for the Virgin?'

'No, on behalf of my uncle.'

'Your uncle. Always there is something with your uncle. Haven't you paid enough penance to your damned uncle?'

'I have been in his debt almost forty years.'

This again, I think. And to him I say: 'It must be incredible, this debt you're paying.'

The deathless man gets very quiet, and after a few moments, he says: 'That reminds me, Doctor. You've a debt of your own.'

The way he says this, the whole room lies still. I have led him straight to the memory of our wager on the bridge so many years ago, but I also feel that he has tricked me, that perhaps he is the one who has been leading *me* to it. I am certain he knows I have not forgotten. Just in case I have, he is helpful, and reminds me: 'The book, Doctor. You pledged the book.'

'I know what I pledged,' I say.

'Of course,' he says, and I can hear he has not doubted me.

'But I do not concede that you won the bet,' I say, angry at his entitlement, angry at myself. I open my coat and feel for the book, which I find is still there.

'I did win it, Doctor.'

'The bet was for proof, Gavran, and you proved nothing,' I say. 'Everything you did could have

200

been a trick.'

'You know that's not true, Doctor,' he says. 'You said you were a betting man. The terms were fair.'

'It was a late night,' I say, 'and I hardly remember it. There could have been a thousand ways for you to stay underwater for so long.'

'Now that's not true either,' he says, sounding, for the first time, disconcerted. 'You are welcome to shoot me,' he says. 'But I am walled up.'

And you'll damn well stay that way, you lunatic. I am thinking we must have someone from the asylum on standby before we let him out of the drunk tank in the morning. We must have someone here to help him, so that he does not go wandering like this, scaring people to death. They will end up calling him a devil—they will say the devil has come to the Waters—and there will be a panic. I find myself wanting to shame him, to ask him to put the back of his head against the wall so I can feel for bullet holes from the last time we met—but I do not do this. Some part of me feels shame, too, for I have not forgotten the bet, and the confidence with which he is offering to let me shoot him—and not for the first time—makes me doubt myself. Besides, it is late, and there is nothing to do but talk to him.

'All right,' I say.

'All right what?' the deathless man says.

'Let's say you're telling the truth.'

'Really, let's.'

'Explain to me how it's possible. You cannot prove it, so at least explain. Let's say—you are deathless. How does that kind of thing come to happen? Are you born with it? You're born and

201

your priest says—*well, here is a deathless man.*
How does it happen?'

'It's not some gift, that I should be born with it.
It's punishment.'

'I doubt most people would say that.'

'You'd be surprised,' he says.

'None of the people in this room would say it.'

'They would in the condition they are in.
Deathless does not mean un-ailing.'

'So—how does it happen?'

'Well,' he says slowly. 'Let's begin with my
uncle.'

'Praise God—the uncle. Tell me about your
uncle.'

'Let's suppose my uncle is Death.' He says this
like he is saying *my uncle is Zeljko, my uncle is
Vladimir.* He lets it hang between us for a while,
and then, when he doesn't hear me say anything,
he says: 'Are we supposing?'

'All right,' I say eventually. 'All right. Let's
suppose your uncle is Death. How is this
possible?'

'He is the brother of my father.' He says this
naturally. *Cain is the brother of Abel; Romulus is
the brother of Remus; Sleep is the brother of Death;
Death is the brother of my father.*

'But how?'

'That's not important,' the deathless man says.
'The important thing is that we are supposing.'

'We are, so we'll keep supposing. Being the
nephew of Death, I assume you are then born
deathless?'

'Not at all.'

'It does not make much sense to me.'

'Even so, that's how it is. I am hardly the first

202

nephew of Death, and those before me have not been deathless.'

'All right.'

'Now. Let's suppose my having this uncle entitles me to certain rights. Let's say that when I turn sixteen, my uncle says to me, "Now you are a man, and I will give you a great gift." '

'I understood it was a punishment.'

'It is. The gift he is talking about is not deathlessness. That comes later. He says to me, "Anything you want." And I think very hard. I think for three days and three nights, and then I go to my uncle and I say: "I should like to be a great physician." '

This doesn't seem very plausible to me, asking Death to make you a doctor. I tell him so. 'Your business would be putting him out of his,' I say.

'That does not matter to my uncle,' the deathless man says. 'Because in the end, even if I heal every man who comes my way, the last word in all the world falls to him. He says to me, "Very well. I will give you this gift—you will be a great physician, and this you will do by being able to tell immediately whether or not a man is going to die."'

'That would make you the first,' I say. 'Physician, I mean, who can reasonably predict whether or not he is going to lose a patient. Truly, after you, there have been no others.' I am smug about saying this.

'We'll not get anywhere with you interrupting to make smart remarks,' the deathless man says. 'You've asked me to tell you about myself, and now you are laughing at me.'

'I'm sorry,' I say, because it is rare to hear him

203

so impatient. 'Please, continue.'

I hear shuffling, and he is doubtless getting into a more comfortable position for his story. 'Now, my uncle gives me a cup. And he says: "In this cup, the lives of men come and go. Give a man coffee from this cup, and once he has had it, you will see the journeys of his life, and whether he is coming or going. If he is sick, but not dying, the paths in the coffee will be still, and constant. Then you must make him break the cup, and you must send the drinker on his way. But if he is coming to me, the paths will point away from the drinker, and then the cup must remain unbroken until he crosses my path." '

'But we are all dying,' I say. 'All the time.'

'I'm not,' he laughs. 'But then, I am the only one for whom the cup shows nothing at all.'

'But really—don't the paths toward your uncle Death appear in the coffee cup of every living man? Isn't every living man a dying man as well?'

'You are determined to make me look useless, Doctor,' he says. 'The paths appear in the cups of men for whom Death is fast approaching. It is as if, having stepped into a room, a man can no longer see the door through which he has come, and so cannot leave. His illness is absolute; his path, fixed.'

'But how is it that you still have the cup?' I say. 'If you were meant to break it when the patient was well?'

'Ah,' he says. 'I am glad you asked. Whenever a patient breaks a cup, a new one takes its place in my coat pocket.'

'Convenient,' I say, with some bile, 'that you are telling me this from behind a wall, and cannot

204

demonstrate your endless, regenerating cups.'

'A demonstration wouldn't prove a thing to you, Doctor,' he says. 'You would only say that I am a magician, another trickster. I can see us now: you, flinging cups to the floor; I, handing you new ones from my coat pocket until you can no longer think of a name bad enough to call me. Smashed crockery everywhere. Besides'—Gavran Gailé says this last part good-naturedly—'what makes you so sure you'd be lucky enough to be breaking your cup tonight?'

And though I do not believe him, Natalia, I feel cold all over. Then there is silence, and after a while he says: 'By God, I should really like some water.' I tell him there is nothing I can do about that, and he says, 'Never mind, never mind. So, off I go with my cup, a great physician now, able to tell a dying man from a living one, which, I can tell you, was a feat back then. First, the people who come to me are villagers, people with small ailments and terrible fears, because everything they do not understand frightens them. And some die, and some live; but what surprises them is that, sometimes when other physicians tell them they are certain to die, I tell them, against all the odds, that they will live. And they fuss and fear, they tell me, *how can I live when I feel as terrible as ever?* But eventually they get well, and then they thank me. And I am never wrong, of course, about this kind of thing, and pretty soon the ones who will get well do not doubt at all, and this, in and of itself, is a kind of medicine for them.'

'Certainty,' I say.

'Yes, certainty,' Gavran Gailé says. 'And then, as time goes by, even the ones whose fates are sealed are calling me a miracle worker, saying, *you saved my sister, you saved my father, if you cannot help me then I know I am meant to go.* And, even though I am a very young man, I am well known, and suddenly craftsmen are coming to me, then artists—painters and writers and players of music—and then merchants, and after them, town magistrates and consuls, until I am seeing lords and dukes, and, once, the king himself. 'If you cannot help me,' he says, 'then I know I am meant to go,' and they bury him six days later, and he goes to his grave smiling. And I realize, even though I have not known it, that when it comes to my uncle, all their fears are the same, and all their fears are terrible.'

One of the sleepers begins to cough, and then he is silent again, breathing slowly through his mouth.

'But the greatest fear is that of uncertainty,' Gavran Gailé is saying. 'They are uncertain about meeting my uncle, of course. But they are uncertain, above all, of their own inaction: have they done enough, discovered their illness soon enough, consulted the worthiest physicians, consumed the best medicines, uttered the correct prayers?'

I say, 'That is why they come to this place.'

But the deathless man is not paying attention: 'And all the while, out of their fear, I am becoming a great and respected man, known the whole kingdom over as a healer, and an honest physician who will not take money if the situation cannot be helped.'

'I have never heard of you,' I say.

'This was many, many years ago,' he says,

206

undeterred. It is incredible.

'And how does this perfect profession go wrong?'

'I make a mistake, of course.'

'It wouldn't happen to involve a woman?'

'It would—how did you guess?'

'I think I've heard this kind of story before.'

'Not like this, you haven't,' he says to me cheerfully. 'This time it's true. This time, I am telling it. Yes, it is a young woman: the daughter of a wealthy silk merchant has fallen ill and the physicians are saying she is as good as dead. She has fallen ill quite suddenly, they are saying, and there is no hope. A terrible fever, a terrible ache in the neck and the back of the head.'

'What was the matter with her?' I say.

'Back then, there were fewer names for illness,' Gavran Gailé says. 'Sometimes, when there was no name, you simply died of Death. She is well liked, this young woman, and about to be married. Her father, I see, has brought me there so he may resign himself, tell himself he has done all he could. The young woman, she is very ill and very frightened. But she has not given up. Though all those around her want me to tell them it is all right, it is all right they have given up, she has not, and she wants nothing from me but to understand that she is not ready to go.'

I do not say anything.

The deathless man continues: 'I give her the coffee, I look inside the cup. And there it is: a journey beginning. All the dregs point to it, they make a little path away from her, and she is very sick, very weak. But still she does not give up, even when I tell her the news, when I tell her I am

207

never wrong. She does not strike me or tell me to get out; instead, for three nights she clings like this to her refusal while I do what I can to make her comfortable.' He is quiet for a while, and then he says, 'It does not take me three whole days to fall in love with her. Only one. But on the third day I am still there while her anger keeps her alive, and fills me more and more with despair and with love. She is so weak that when I tell her to break the cup, I have to hold her wrist while she does it, and she has to hit the cup three times on the side of her bed before it breaks, and even then it is a clumsy break.'

For a little while, he doesn't say anything, he just sits there behind the wall, shuffling quietly. I say: 'Your uncle, I suppose, is furious after that.'

'Furious, yes,' the deathless man says. 'But not as furious as he is going to be later on. He warns me, you see. He says, "What you have done is despicable, and you have betrayed me. But as you are a young man, and very much in love, I will turn my head just this once." '

'That seems generous.'

'It is more than generous. But of course, as it turns out, my love did not just fall ill. She *was* ill. And after we have fled together, after we have begun to build a life, it happens again, the same way over. She is in bed. I give her the coffee. I see what is there, and it is written as plain as a ticket or an agreement at a bank. But still I help her break the cup. What is there for me without her? Then my uncle comes. And he says: "You are a fool, and not my brother's child. I indulged you once, but I'll not do it again. From this day on, I've no need of you, and no want. Your time will

208

never come, and you shall seek all the days of your life and never find it." ' Here, the deathless man laughs, and my head is filled with a dreadful kind of silence. 'You see, Doctor,' he says. 'At that moment, my uncle takes my woman anyway, and so for years I go about my life believing that this is what he is talking about, that I will never find her again, or someone like her again. But it is only when six or seven years have passed that I notice my face, my hands, my hair have not changed. And then, I begin to suspect what has happened. Then I confirm it.'

'How?' I say, slowly. 'How do you confirm it?'

'I throw myself from a cliff in Naples,' he says, quite flatly. 'At the bottom, there is no Death.'

'How high is the cliff?' I say, but he does not answer this.

'I still have the cup, though, and I go about my business, convinced that my uncle will forgive me in time. Years and years go by, and I find, suddenly, that I am no longer giving my cup to those I hope will live, but instead to those I think are certain to die.'

'Why is that?' I say.

'I find myself,' he says, 'seeking the company of the dying, because, among them, I feel I will find my uncle. Except he never lets me see him. The newly dead, however, I see for days. It takes me a long time to realize what they are, for, of course, as a physician I could not see them, I could not see the dead. But my uncle, I think, does this on purpose, and I begin to see them standing alone in fields, near cemeteries and crossroads, waiting for their forty days to pass.'

'Why crossroads?' I say.

209

He sounds a little surprised at my ignorance. 'Crossroads are where the paths of life meet, where life changes. In their case, it changes to death. That is where my uncle meets them once the forty days have passed.'

'And cemeteries?'

'Sometimes they are confused, unsure of where they are going. They drift naturally toward their own bodies. And when they drift this way, I begin to gather them.'

'Gather them how?' I say.

'A few at a time,' he says to me. 'A few at a time, in places where many of them come together. Hospitals. Churches. Mines, when they collapse. I gather them and keep them with me for the forty days, and then I take them to a crossroads, and leave them for my uncle.'

'Got any with you right now?' I say.

'Really, Doctor.' He sounds disappointed.

I feel a little ashamed of making light of the dead. I say: 'Why do you gather them if they are going to him anyway?'

'Because for him it makes things easier,' the deathless man says, 'knowing that they are safe. Knowing that they are coming. Sometimes, when they wander, they do not find their way home again, and become lost after the forty days have passed. Then it is difficult to find them, and they begin to fill up with malice and fear, and this malice extends to the living, to their loved ones.' He sounds sad saying this, like he is talking about lost children. 'Then the living take matters into their own hands. They dig up the bodies to bless them; they bury the dead man's belongings. Money for the dead man. This is sometimes helpful. Sometimes, it brings the spirit back, and then it will come with me to the crossroads even if it has been years and years since its death.' Then he says: 'I confess, too, that I am hoping, all this time, that my uncle will forgive me.'

I am thinking here that, if this is true—which it is not—he has come up with a good way to tell the story so that he seems generous in it, and helpful, too, when in fact his help is ultimately intended for himself. I do not say this, of course.

Instead, I say: 'Why do you tell them that they are going to die?'

'So they can prepare,' he says right away. 'That, too, is supposed to make it easier. You see, there is always a struggle. But if they know—if they have thought about it—sometimes the struggle is less and less.'

'Still,' I say, 'it does not seem fair to frighten the dying, to single them out for punishment.'

'But dying is not punishment,' he says.

'Only to you,' I say, and suddenly I am angry. 'Only because you've been denied it.'

'You and I are not understanding one another,' he says. He has said this to me before, and he is always so patient when he says it. 'The dead are celebrated. The dead are loved. They give something to the living. Once you put something into the ground, Doctor, you always know where to find it.'

I want to say to him, *the living are celebrated too, and loved.* But this has gone on long enough, and he seems to think so, too.

'Now, Doctor,' says the deathless man, with the voice of someone who is getting up from a meal. 'I must ask you to let me out.'

211

'I can't,' I say.

'You must. I need water.'

'It's impossible,' I say. 'If I had the keys to let you out, don't you think I would have given you water by now?' But I am wondering it a little myself, wondering whether or not I would let him out if I had the keys. I'm not saying what I really think, which is that I am glad he cannot come out, glad he can't take the book from me, even though I still do not believe that I lost my bet. Even though I believe he would take it unfairly if he took it now. Then I say, 'I wonder, assuming I believe you—which I don't—how could I be responsible for letting out the man who is here to gather my patients for the grave?'

The deathless man laughs at this. 'Whether I am in here or out there, they are going to die,' he says. 'I do not direct the passage—I just make it easier. Remember, Doctor: the man with the cough, the man with liver cancer, and the man who appears to have indigestion.'

It is like we are playing Battleship with the dying. I tell him this, hoping that he will laugh a little, but all he says to me is, 'Remember for next time, Doctor, that you still owe me a pledge.'

I sit for a long time by that door, and then I am convinced he has fallen asleep. I get up and I continue my walking, but Natalia—I am telling you this honestly—that night they go, one by one: the man with the cough, the man with the liver cancer, and the man who appears to have indigestion. They go in that order too, but by the time we have lost the last one, the monks have returned and are helping me, performing the rites, closing the eyes and crossing the arms, and the dying all around are in distress, in fear, feeling themselves all over and asking me, *it's not me yet, is it, Doctor?*

By the time I go back to see the deathless man, the monks have already opened the cell and let the drunks out to the morning, and he is long gone.

7

THE BUTCHER

When Luka and Jovo returned from the mountain, carrying with them the gun of the fallen blacksmith—about whose fate they lied through their teeth, and whose final moments they played up to such an extent that stories of the blacksmith's skill and fortitude were being told in surrounding towns long after the war had ended—my grandfather was relieved to discover that the hunt had not been successful. In the long afternoon and night while the hunters were away, he had contemplated his encounter with the tiger in the smokehouse. Why had the girl been there? Had she been there the whole time? What had she been doing?

He knew for certain that her purpose had not been to harm the tiger, that she had smiled knowingly at him when it became obvious that the tiger had escaped. My grandfather considered what he would say to the girl when he saw her next, how he could ask her, knowing she could not reply, about what she had seen, what the tiger was like.

213

They were sharing the tiger now.

My grandfather felt certain that he would see her at the service to honor the blacksmith. Sunday afternoon, and he stood in the stifled back of the church, with its hanging white tapestries, and scanned the frost-reddened faces of the congregation, but he did not see her. He did not see her outside afterward, either, or later that week at the Wednesday market.

What my grandfather didn't know was that, in addition to the gun, Luka had brought something else back from the mountain: the pork shoulder the tiger had been eating when the hunters had come upon him in the glade. My grandfather did not know that, after Luka had entered his quiet house at the edge of the pasture on the afternoon of his return, and slowly placed the blacksmith's gun by the door, he had swung that pork shoulder into the face of the deaf-mute girl, who was already kneeling in the corner with her arms across her belly. My grandfather didn't know that Luka, after he had dislocated the deaf-mute's shoulder, had dragged her into the kitchen by her hair, and pressed her hands into the stove.

My grandfather did not know any of these things, but the other villagers knew, without having to talk about it, that Luka was a batterer. People had noticed well enough when she went missing for days, when new rungs appeared in her nose, when that unmoving blood-spot welled in her eye and did not dissipate, to guess what was happening in Luka's house.

It would be easy for me to simplify the situation. It might even be justifiable to say, 'Luka was a batterer, and so he deserved what was coming to

214

him'—but because I am trying to understand now what my grandfather did not know then, it's a lot more important to be able to say, 'Luka was a batterer, and here is why.'

*   *   *

Luka, like almost everyone in the village, had been born in Galina, in the family house he would occupy until his death. From the start to the end of his days, he knew the ax, the butcher's block, the wet smell of autumnal slaughter. Even during the hopeful decade he spent away from home, the sound of a sheep's bell in the market square produced in him a paralyzing rush too complicated to be mere nostalgia.

Luka was the sixth son of a seventh son, born just shy of being blessed, and this almost-luck sat at his shoulders all his life. His father, Korčul, was an enormous, bearded man with big teeth, the only person in the house, it seemed, who ever laughed, and never at the right thing. In his youth, Korčul had spent some fifteen years in 'the Army'—when asked about it, he always said 'the Army,' because he did not care to advertise that he had, in fact, volunteered with several, and had not been particularly selective regarding the alliance or aim of the side on which he was fighting, as long as he could see Turkish pennants flying above the distant, advancing line. Over the years, he had amassed an impressive collection of Ottoman war artifacts, and Sunday mornings found him at the tavern on the upper slopes of the village, coffee in one hand, *rakija* in the other, trading stories with other veterans, always eager to exhibit some bullet or spearhead or dagger fragment and tell the story of how he had earned it in battle. Long before Luka was born, word had spread that Korčul's trove included items far older than anyone could remember—helmets, arrowheads, links of chain mail—and that the butcher spent his spare time expanding his collection by robbing graves, digging in old battlegrounds for the clothes and weapons of men centuries dead. This, by all standards, was unforgivable, a curse-inviting sin. This was why, they would later say, none of Korčul's children survived to have children of their own.

It was also why the villagers—assessing the goings-on of the butcher's household from a distance—could not reconcile the pairing of Korčul and Luka's mother, Lidia. She was a round woman with patient eyes and a quiet manner, a polite and evenhanded daughter of Sarobor, a merchant's child, reduced from the nomadic luxuries of her youth by the failure of her father's business. Her love for children was boundless, but always greatest for her youngest child—a position Luka occupied for only three years, and from which he was demoted following the birth of the family's first and only daughter. There were five boys before him, the oldest ten years his senior, and while he watched them file, one by one, into the rituals of manhood prescribed by Korčul's own upbringing, Luka found himself clinging to the foundations of his mother's life, the stories of her girlhood travels, her insistence on education, on the importance of history, the sanctity of the written word.

So Luka grew up with the feeling of a world that was larger than the one he knew. As he became

216

more and more aware of himself, it began to occur to him that his father—that feared, well-respected, but illiterate man—knew nothing of that greater world, and had done nothing to arrange for the futures of his children in the context of it. During the time he spent with his father, learning, with his brothers, the life of a butcher, he understood that his father's knowledge extended to cuts of meat and types of blades, the warning signs that an animal was ill, the smell of meat gone bad, the right technique for skinning. For all his prosperity, Luka found Korčul's ignorance ugly, his disinterest in a larger life, apart from battle trophies, profane, and came to abhor Korčul's tendency to overlook cleaning his apron, or to eat bread with blood-rusted nail beds. While his brothers were pretending to bash one another over the head with makeshift cudgels, Luka busied himself reading history and literature.

For all his resistance, however, Luka could not avoid the rites that came with family. By the age of ten, he was butchering sheep, and when he turned fourteen, his father, following a tradition of many generations, gave him a knife for cutting bread and locked him into the barn with a young bull whose nose had been filled with pepper. Like his brothers before him, Luka was expected to subdue the bull and kill it with a single knife-thrust to the skull. Luka had spent most of his life dreading this ritual—the violence, the pointlessness of it—but he found himself hoping that, despite his unfortunately wiry frame and thin hands, he might have some unexpected success, some miraculous burst of strength that would enable him to just get it over with. But the bull came tearing out of the

217

back of the stable and smeared Luka across the dirt in front of the butcher and his five other sons, and twenty or thirty villagers who had come to watch the show. Someone who witnessed the event told me that it was like watching a tank crumple a lamppost. (I have since surmised that this rich analogy could not have come about until at least a decade after the actual event, when the witness would have had occasion to see his first tank.) Luka had the bull by the top of the skull, his armpits braced against the boss of the horns. The bull—sensing, perhaps, that victory was imminent—dropped to its knees on top of Luka's torso, pressed the boy into the ground and plowed the dirt with him, crashing into crates and troughs and hay bales until a physician who had come all the way from Gorchevo climbed into the barn and lodged an ax in the dome of the bull's back. Luka had a concussion and three broken ribs. A few days later, his father also broke Luka's left arm in a fit of rage.

After that, Luka bought an old gusla off a gypsy peddler, and went into the fields to shepherd for a few of the local families who needed hired hands. A lot of this is probably tainted by hindsight, but people say that he was too easy in his manner. His voice was too soft, his mind too eased by quiet evenings playing his new gusla. He was too eager to strip naked and bathe with other young men in the mountain lake above the pasture—although no one will ever accuse the other young men of his generation of being too eager to bathe with him. This may be because the young men of Luka's generation are the fathers of the men telling these stories.

218

All this aside, Luka became renowned for sitting under the summer trees and composing love songs. I have heard, from more than one source, that Luka was unnaturally good at this, even though he never seemed to be in love himself, and even though his musical talent never quite caught up to his prowess as a lyricist. Though there are those who say that any man who heard Luka play the gusla, even in wordless melody, was immediately moved to tears. One spring—and this, like so much of what is said about someone in admiration, is probably a lie—a wolf came to hunt in the pasture, and Luka, instead of throwing rocks or calling for his father's dog, subdued it with music.

When I think of Luka in his youth, I sometimes picture a thin, pale boy with large eyes and lips, the kind of boy you might see sitting with his feet bare and his arms around a lamb in a pastoral painting. It is easy to see him this way when you hear the villagers talk about his songs, about the gravity and maturity of his music. In this early image, he is a beloved son of Galina. Maybe it is easier for them to remember him as this mild boy instead of the enraged youth he must have been, the adolescent consumed with the smallness of his life, and then, later on, the man in the red apron who beat a deaf-mute bride.

This much is certain: Luka was angry enough, determined enough, good enough to leave Galina at sixteen and make his way to the river port of Sarobor in the hope of becoming a guslar.

At that time, the Sarobor guslars were a group of young men from all over the neighboring provinces, who had found one another through some small miracle, and who would converge nightly on the banks of the Grava to sing folk songs. Luka had first heard about them from his mother, who had described them as artists, philosophers, lovers of music, and for years Luka had been convincing himself to join them. Without a word of objection from his father—who had hardly uttered a word of any sort to him since the incident with the bull—Luka crossed three hundred miles on foot to reach them. He had a vision of men with serious faces sitting around a pier with their feet in the bright water below, singing about love and famine and the long, sad passage of their fathers' fathers, who knew a lot, but not enough to cheat Death, that black-hearted villain who treats all men equally. It was, Luka believed, the only kind of life for him, the life that would certainly lead him farther, perhaps even to the City itself.

In his first week in Sarobor, while renting a thin-ceilinged room above a whorehouse on the eastern side of town, Luka learned that there was a strictly observed hierarchy to all musical proceedings on the river. The musicians did not assemble, as he had supposed, in a convivial atmosphere to share and trade songs; nor were they proper guslars. Instead of solitary men playing the one-stringed fiddle he had come to know and love, he found two considerably sized warring factions—one that favored the brass sound that had come out of the West, and one that retained the frantic string arrangements that harkened back to Ottoman times. Each group, often twenty strong, would assemble nightly on opposite sides of the river and begin to play; then, as the evening progressed, and revelers, drunk with perfume and the moist heat of

220

the river, began to fill the street, each band would take a little bit of the bridge. Slowly, song by song, dance by dance, the musicians would advance along the wide cobbled arch, each band's progress depending solely upon the size of its audience, the grace of those who had been moved to dance, the enthusiasm of the passersby who stopped to join in the chorus. The songs were not, as Luka had hoped, serious meditations on the fickle nature of love and the difficulties of life under the sultan; instead, they were drinking songs, songs of indulgent levity; songs like 'There Goes Our Last Child,' and 'Now That the Storm Has Passed (Should We Rebuild the Village?).'

As to the musicians themselves, they were more complicated than Luka had originally expected, a little more ragtag, disorganized, a little more disheveled and drunk than he had imagined. They were wanderers, mostly, and had a fast turnover rate because every six months or so someone would fall in love and get married, one would die of syphilis or tuberculosis, and at least one would be arrested for some minor offense and hanged in the town square as an example to the others.

As Luka became better acquainted with them—crowding in with the string section, night after night, his gusla silent in his hands except for the two or three times he picked up a few bars of some song—he came to know the regulars, the men who had lingered on the bridge for years. There was a fellow who played the goblet drum, a Turk with pomade-glossed hair who was known for being a sensation among rich young ladies. There was also a straw-haired kid whose name no one could ever get right, and whose tongue had been cut out as a result of some mysterious transgression, but who kept good time with a tambourine. On accordion: Grickalica Brkić, whose teeth, whenever a buxom woman stopped to hear his playing, would begin to chatter uncontrollably, and thus made for interesting accompaniment. The fiddler was a man known only as 'the Monk.' Some say this was because he had left the Benedictine order because God's calling for him was in music, not in silence. In reality, however, this nickname was derived from the Monk's highly unusual haircut: the man was thirty, but bald from forehead to ears, eyebrows included, the result of a disastrous drunken night when he had suggested that, because the fire would not hold in the hearth, someone go up and pour oil down the chimney while he himself lit the wood below.

None of them knew much about history or art. None of them had much ambition for moving on to better things. None of them cared much for the traditional gusla, or its use in epic poetry; but they thought it added an interesting sound to their amateur-crowded group. Luka played on with them for months, at the Monk's elbow, until they came to understand that he wasn't going anywhere; until he was a welcome and unequivocal constant among those core players; a drinking companion, a confidant, a recognized wordsmith. People would go on to recite his songs in their homes, hum them in the marketplace, and throw coins into his hat so they could hear them again.

And all the while, carrying on like this, Luka did not give up his devotion to the gusla, or his desire to move on to a position that would afford him more distinguished notoriety. After a certain point, he was forced to admit to himself that the people of Sarobor were beginning to tire of the sad songs that were his passion, but he did not abandon the belief that demand for those songs would exist elsewhere. Lazy afternoons, when the other musicians slept in tavern basements, in the shade of porch screens or in the pale arms of women whose names they did not know, Luka made a project of seeking out real guslars. They were thin-boned old men who had long since stopped playing, and who sent him away from their doors again and again. But he kept coming back, and eventually they relented. After a few glasses of *rakija,* pulled back to some earlier time by the sound of the river and the sight of the merchants' ships arriving along the green curve of the bank, the old men would reach for Luka's gusla and begin to play.

He immersed himself in the movement of their hands, the soft thump of their feet, the throbbing wail of their voices winding through tales remembered or invented. The more time he spent in their company, the more certain he was that this was how he wanted to live and die; the more they praised his growing skill, the more he was able to stand himself, tolerate what he saw as the wretchedness of his roots, accept the disparity between the love he voiced in his songs and the lack of desire he felt for women, from the veiled girls who smiled at him on the bridge to the whores who tried to push themselves over his knees while he sat at the tavern in the company of the other musicians.

There was never enough money to move on, so he stayed in Sarobor; first for one year, then two, then three, playing at weddings, composing serenades, fighting for room on the bridge.

About ten years into his life as a guslar, he met the woman who would destroy his life. She was the daughter of the prosperous Turkish silk merchant, Hassan Effendi, a boisterous, clever, and charming girl named Amana, who was already somewhat of a legend in the town, having vowed, at the age of ten, to remain a virgin forever, and to spend her life studying music and poetry, and painting canvases (which supposedly weren't particularly good, but were nevertheless valued on principle). A great deal was known about her life, mostly because Hassan Effendi was a notorious bellyacher, and on his daily visit to the teahouse would divulge—and probably embellish—the details of whatever new obstinacy Amana had adopted. As a result, she was often the subject of broader market gossip, renowned for her arrogance, wit, and charm; for the many delicacies to which she was prone; for the determination and inventiveness with which she threatened suicide every other week, whenever her father suggested a new suitor; for sneaking, unveiled, out of her father's house to join in the revelries on the bridge in a practiced routine obvious to everyone but Hassan Effendi.

Luka had seen her here and there, from a distance—recognized her as the bright-eyed girl with the braid and the disarming smile—but he would never have exchanged words with her if she had not grown curious about his instrument. One evening, after the band had rounded out a lively rendition of 'Is That Your Blood?' Luka looked up from his gusla to see her standing over him, one hand on her hip, the other holding a gold coin over

224

the old hat at his feet.

'What do they call that, boy?' she said loudly, though she already knew, and touched the bottom of his fiddle with a sandaled foot.

'This is a gusla,' he said, and found himself grinning.

'Poor little fiddle,' said Amana, in a voice that made the people who had gotten up to give him money stop and hover behind her. 'It has only one string.'

Luka said: 'They might offer me a bigger fiddle tomorrow, but still I would not give up my one string.'

'Why? What can it do?'

For a moment, Luka felt his face burn. Then he said: 'Fifty strings sing one song, but this single string knows a thousand stories.'

Then Amana dropped the coin into his hat, and without moving from his side she said: 'Well, play me one, guslar.'

Luka took up his bow and obliged, and for the ten minutes he played alone, silence fell over the bridge. I'm told he played 'The Hangman's Daughter,' but Luka himself could never remember what he played; for years afterward, he would recall only the way the string sent a grating pulse through his chest, the strange sound of his own voice, the outline of Amana's unmoving hand on her hip.

People began to talk: Luka and Amana sitting on the bridge together at daybreak, Luka and Amana at the tavern with their heads bent close over a piece of paper.

That they loved each other was certain. The nature of that love, however, was not as simple as people supposed. Luka had found someone who admired his music, and wanted to hear every song he could play; someone who knew about poetry and the art of conversation, about finer things he had long since given up on trying to address with the other musicians. Amana found the intellectual weight behind Luka's aspirations attractive, the idea of the journey he had already made—and the journey he hoped to make still—incredible. The problem was, however, that she had long since decided she wanted nothing to do with men; and he did not make the effort to convince her otherwise, because he had long since realized he wanted nothing to do with women. Amana was determined to die a virgin; Luka had come to terms, by then, with what it meant to find himself aroused by the sight of the town youths diving into the river on summer days. Taking the final step would mean summoning failure to himself in a world that had already thrown too much against him; one hopes, however, that despite what would happen later with the tiger's wife, that Luka did find some happiness during the days and nights of which he never spoke.

For a year, his friendship with Amana grew on song and philosophical debate, on stories and pointless arguments about poetry and history. Balmy evenings found them on the bridge together, standing apart from the old bands: Luka singing with the fiddle against his belly, and, sitting behind him on a broken-backed chair, Amana with her chin on his shoulder, lending her voice to his songs, deepening them. On their own, neither was a spectacular singer; but together their voices blended into a low and surprising sadness, a twang that pulled even the most optimistic crowds away from the foot-stomping revelry of the traditional bridge bands.

Luka, with Amana's help, was well on his way to the life he had designed for himself so many years ago. He had begun to make up his own songs—sometimes even spontaneously, right there on the bridge—and he had begun to form a following among the younger guslars. He still lacked the means, however, to move to the City; and, even if he had been better funded, he was reluctant to leave Amana behind, and he could not ask for her hand without having something to offer in return. Around this time, there appeared in Sarobor a soft-spoken, bearded scholar named Vuk, who, according to the town gossips, had been traveling from town to town for almost ten years, listening to songs and stories and writing them down.

'He is a thief of music,' said those on the bridge who refused to speak to him. 'If he comes to you, you send him to hell.'

The scholar cornered Luka in the tavern one night and explained to him about the School of Music that had recently been founded in the City. In an effort to gain more popularity and support, the School had begun a collaborative program with the government: any traditional musician from a municipality outside the City would be awarded a small fee for any song he consented to submit for a recording. Luka, the scholar informed him, was the man he wanted to sing for Sarobor; Luka and that charming young lady of his, even though it was not traditional for women to participate in gusla playing.

Luka had seen his first radio earlier that spring;

this, combined with his encounter in the tavern, was enough to make him dream. He couldn't see how he would get them there, himself and Amana—how a journey like that could be justified at all. The solution came one week later, in the form of a letter from Luka's younger sister. She was writing on the pretense of informing him of her recent marriage to a man whose father owned a car factory in Berlin. Her actual goal, however, was to break the news of their mother's death to him gently, and to negotiate his conditional return to Galina at the behest of his father, who had found himself alone and helpless. She wrote to him with news of his only remaining brother, the firstborn: he had died of pneumonia the previous winter. Two of the four who had gone into the army had died long ago, in the service of the kaiser; the second-youngest had just been killed in a fight over a woman outside a tavern two towns over. No one knew the whereabouts of the fifth brother, but some people said that he had fallen in love with a gypsy, and had gone to France with her many years ago. His father, she said, was on the brink of death. And now, despite the unfortunate incident with the bull, despite what may or may not have been said about Luka over the years, it was up to him to carry on the family name and business. *With a woman,* his sister made sure to write, *of fine character, who will bear you many children.*

Luka, who had for so long resisted his past, suddenly found himself contemplating a strategic return to Galina. His father was old, grief-stricken. He knew that there would be no love between them upon his return; but he also knew that his father could not live long, and after that, the inheritance that would have otherwise been split between six brothers would fall to Luka alone. If he sacrificed two years now—spent them perfecting his songs in Galina while he waited for the old man to die—he could make his future with the earnings of the man who had made him wretched, use Korčul's own fortune. The closeness of that possibility, the reality of it, made it fragile.

For a few days, he hardly spoke to anyone. Then, just after nightfall, he climbed the lattice up to Amana's room and asked for her hand.

'Well, I knew you were mad,' she said, sitting up in bed. 'But I didn't realize you were a fool.'

Then he explained it all to her, explained about his father and his fortune, and about the radio in the City, waiting for their songs—songs they would sing together, because he could not see himself pursuing this without her. And when he was finished, he said: 'Amana, we've been good friends all these years.' He had been kneeling by her bed. He pushed himself up and sat down on the covers beside her. 'Your father will charge you, one way or another, to marry somebody someday—wouldn't you rather it be me than some stranger who will force himself on you? I promise not to touch you, and to love you as I love you now until the day I die. No other man who comes into this room asking for you will ever make that promise knowing with certainty that it will be kept.'

It was the first time he had voiced anything close to a confession of himself, and even though she had known for a long time, Amana put a hand out and touched his face.

They began to plan their marriage. Amana

agreed to confine herself to the house and avoid jeopardizing their situation; and for two months Luka made himself presentable every night and appeared at her house and ate and drank with Hassan Effendi, and the two of them smoked *narghile* and played music until the sun came up. Hassan Effendi, who deduced rather quickly that an offer of marriage would soon be at hand, resigned himself to the idea of having an enterprising butcher for a son-in-law rather than an obstinate virgin for a daughter, and with patience let Luka woo him for as long as necessary to secure a socially appropriate proposal.

If Luka had been a slightly better judge of character—if he had realized that Hassan Effendi was sold at a month and a half, and asked for Amana's hand almost immediately—this story might have turned out quite differently. Instead, while the two of them were playing at social graces, strumming away on Hassan Effendi's balcony and listening to each other's opinions, they left Amana entirely out of the proceedings, left her to her own devices, left her to wait. And while she was waiting, contemplating her future as Luka's wife, anticipating their eventual move to the City, it began to occur to her that the life of virginal solitude she had so publicly laid claim to on so many occasions had been secured. It was done. She no longer had to fear, as she had feared all her days, the presence of a domineering, oafish husband, the ordeal of the wedding night, the drudgery of marriage, the gruesome prospect of childbirth. A single decision, and those possibilities had vanished. Her life lay before her without them, and at first she was glad. But then she began to

230

think about what a long life it was, and how the way she pictured herself lay in the presence of those fears, in the conflict they provided; it occurred to her that the struggle had not been nearly as great as the struggle for which she had steeled herself, and that, above all, with it had gone that other possibility, the unnamed one: the possibility of changing her mind. It suddenly seemed to her that her whole life had come and gone.

Two weeks before the wedding, Amana fell into bed with a fever. News concerning the severity of her illness spread around town. People said that her curtains could not be opened, that she clutched at her bedclothes, sweating and raving, that the mere act of nodding her head caused her excruciating pain.

Luka was not a friend, not a family member, not yet even an official fiancé. He listened for news of her welfare in the market and on the bridge, and this was how he found out that physician after physician came and went from Hassan Effendi's house, and that his girl was still no better. From Hassan Effendi, he was able to extract only hopeful news—*she's very well, it is a minor autumnal cough, she will get better soon enough*—but on street corners he heard that the situation had become desperate, and that Khasim Aga, the herbalist, had written to a physician who lived across the kingdom, and who was known as something of a miracle worker.

No one in town saw the miracle worker arrive; no one would have been able to recognize him in the street. It was well known that for three days and three nights, the miracle worker stood over

Amana's bed, holding her wrist, wiping her brow. It was also soon evident that this miracle worker, with one or two earnest glances, and hands that unsteadily ran the cold sponge down her neck, obliterated all of Amana's notions of virginity and scholastic isolation, all her lifelong plans, her devotion to music and to Luka. As soon as she had begun to recover, she was sneaking out of her bedroom to meet with the physician who had saved her, just as she had snuck out to play with the guslars—except now, she was sneaking around abandoned mills and barn lofts with dots of perfume on her wrists and navel.

Relieved at the news that she had recovered, still not permitted to visit her sickbed, Luka did not suspect a thing. He did not know that when Hassan Effendi told Amana he had consented for her to be wed to Luka, she kissed her father's hands and then went up to her bedroom to hang herself with the curtains. Luka did not know that the story might have ended there had the tiger's wife not come in at the right moment, and found her sister sprawled out on the bed, weeping with frustration at not being able to get the curtain thin enough to wrap around her neck for the jump. He would never know that it was the tiger's wife who held Amana's head on her knees until she came up with a better plan; that the tiger's wife carried Amana's letter of desperation to the physician the following morning. The tiger's wife was the lookout when Amana climbed down the lattice the following night; she was there, in Amana's bedroom, to give their mother Amana's letter of farewell the morning of the wedding.

Hassan Effendi, standing over the two

remaining women in his life, found himself saying words he never would have imagined Amana putting him in a position to say: 'God damn her, the whore has disgraced me.' And right then and there, with his wife weeping profusely over his decision, he took the opportunity to rid himself of the child he thought he would be saddled with forever by dressing the deaf-mute girl in her sister's wedding clothes and putting her in Amana's place.

And so Luka, who spent the wedding in a contemplative daze, imagining his future with Amana in the City, did not know that all his plans for his father's fortune, all the songs he was hoping to sing, all the many freedoms he saw opening up before him, were being dashed to hell even as he was taking his vows.

He did not realize Hassan Effendi's deceit until he lifted the veil in the ceremonial gesture of seeing his wife for the first time and found himself looking, with almost profane stupidity, into the face of a stranger. Afterward, while the men were toasting the bridegroom, all Hassan Effendi had to say was, 'Even so, she's yours, as prescribed by custom. She is the sister of your betrothed, and I've the right to demand that you take her. You will disgrace yourself to refuse her now.' And so Luka found himself married to a deaf-mute child of thirteen, who looked at him with big, fearful eyes, and smiled absently every so often in his direction at the feast while her mother was crying and kissing her forehead.

That night, he looked at her in her terrified nakedness, and made her face away from him while he took off his clothes, expectation hanging

233

between them. The following day, he took her back to Galina in the wagon, a child bride for the butcher's son. No laughter, no friendship, no hope for the future. The ride lasted five days, and on the second day he realized that, though he had probably heard it at one time or another, he had forgotten her name.

'What do they call you?' he said to her. When she did not respond, he took her hand and shook it a little. 'Your name—what is your name?' But she only smiled.

To make matters worse, the house—which Luka remembered as a place teeming with loud bodies, running feet, crying children, two frying pans on the stove at all times—was silent. Luka's father, worn by old age into a crooked-backed cripple, sat alone by a low fire. Without greeting, he looked at the new bride as she stepped over the threshold and said to his only remaining son, 'Couldn't you do any better than some bitch of Mohammed?' Luka did not have the strength to tell his father, with relish, that he had meant better, that somehow he would remedy everything once Korčul was gone.

With this distant hope growing in him again, Luka resigned himself to his temporary life. Even without Amana, he would find a plan for the gusla, for his songs, for the School of Music. In the meantime, he had only the deaf-mute girl, an old incontinent man, the ceaseless death screams of the sheep in the smokehouse, and his own rage at the unfairness of it all.

What surprised him most was how quickly he came to tolerate his wife. She had big eyes and a quiet gait, and sometimes when he looked at her he saw Amana, even called her Amana once or twice. She needed some guidance—he had to show her how to warm the stove, where the cistern was, had to take her into the village several times to show her how to do the marketing—but he realized that once she knew how something was done, she took it over herself completely, developed her own routine for doing it. She was everywhere: helping in the smokehouse, washing his clothes, changing his father's soiled trousers. Without complaining, without uttering a syllable, she carried water from the well and walked the old man down the porch stairs every day for a breath of fresh air. Sometimes it was even pleasant to come home in the evenings, and have someone to smile at him.

Could Luka have left her there, in Galina, with the old man, once he had recovered from the initial shock of what had happened to him? Could he have taken some of his father's money from the coffer hidden under the baseboards of the house, left for the City on his own, found someone to take Amana's place? Almost certainly. After the first few times he followed the deaf-mute girl into town to disperse the children who would assemble behind her to make faces and shout the obscenities they had picked up from their parents at her retreating back, he realized that he had worsened matters by bringing her here, that people were beginning to talk. *Look at that girl,* people were saying, *look at the deaf-mute he's brought home— where did he get her? What is he trying to hide?* Their attention drove him to panic, made him more determined to flee than ever; but, in doing so, it also deepened his predicament, pointed out to him the many ways he would have to uncouple his life in order to abandon it again.

Then there was the afternoon he came home to find her with Korčul in the attic: his father, in a gesture masquerading as affection, had brought out his box of war relics, and Luka came upstairs to find the deaf-mute girl sitting cross-legged with the box across her knees while the old man knelt behind her, one hand already on her breast.

'She's a child!' Luka kept screaming after he had thrown Korčul against the wall. 'She's a child, she's a child!'

'She's a child!' Korčul screamed back, grinning wildly. Then he said: 'If you don't start producing sons, I will.'

He could not leave her there, he realized, because, Mohammedan or not, child bride or not, Korčul was going to rape her, if he hadn't already—force her down while Luka was out of the house—and she would be powerless to stop him.

And so Luka stayed, and the longer he stayed the farther that burning dream seemed; the more insults Korčul flung at him, the more questions people entering the butcher's shop asked him about his wife, the more he came to see her as the reason he was still there. In those moments, his wife's silence terrified him. It terrified him because he knew, and knew absolutely, that she could see every thought that passed through his head. She was like an animal, he thought, as silent and begrudging as an owl. And what made it considerably worse was that, despite his belief that it was his right to think whatever he wanted—he had, after all, been cheated, and what did she want from him, this girl, when he had been unfairly

236

crippled by fate?—he found himself wanting to explain it to her, wanting to tell her that none of it was her fault, not the silence, not the marriage, not Korčul's advances. He wanted to explain, too, that none of it was his fault, either, but he was having a difficult enough time convincing himself.

The day things finally broke, it was high summer, incredibly hot, and Luka hadn't been able to get away from the heat. She was scrubbing the laundry in a corner of the kitchen, and his father was snoring wetly in one of the many empty bedrooms. Luka had come in to rest for the afternoon, to wait out the worst of the day before heading back to the shop. Plums had ripened in the orchard, and he had brought three inside, was slicing them on the empty table when he turned the radio on; and then, just like that, he recognized the Monk's nasal twang, an octave higher than it should have been, cutting through the melody of one of Luka's own songs like some kind of terrible joke. His body seemed to fall away from him.

It was 'The Enchantress,' a song he had written with and about Amana, reduced from its slow tempo, intended for the gusla, to a frenzied ode about debauchery. He half expected to wake up moments later and find that he had passed out drunk the night before—but he didn't, he just sat and sat there on the kitchen chair while the song moved through the verses, and then it was over, and the radio had moved on to something else. His songs had moved on without him, too, moved on to the School of Music.

He looked up to see the girl standing over him, his wet shirt slung across her shoulder like skin.

'Listen,' he said to her, and touched his ear and

then the radio. He ran his fingers over the top of the mahogany box. She stood there, smiling at him. In that moment, he was still himself. Then she made a gesture, something like a half shrug, and she leaned forward, took one of the plum slices from under his knife, put it under her tongue, and turned away to go outside. He was up before he knew what he was doing, pushing the table onto her, pinning her facedown under the full weight of it. The sound her body made when she struck the floor stayed in him, and he stood over her and kicked her ribs and head until blood came out of her ears.

Everything about that first time surprised him. His own inexplicable rage, the dull thud of his boot against her body, her soundless, gaping mouth and closed eyes. He realized that he had gone on hitting her far longer than he had intended, because he had been expecting her to cry out in fear or pain. He realized afterward, while he was helping her up, that his curiosity about whether she could even produce sound had just been fulfilled, and, now that it had, there was even more rage than ever: rage at himself, rage at her for looking so surprised and forlorn and subdued when he brought the water in to wash the blood off her face.

He told himself that it would never happen again. But, of course, it did. Something had opened in him, and he could not close it again. It happened the night of his father's funeral, when it was just Luka and the girl and the house, silence everywhere. He thought, *after me, there will be no children, no one left,* and rolled on top of her. He would try, he told himself, to fuck her—he would

238

try. But it had been months since he had managed it, and, feeling her under him, small and tense, as still as death, he couldn't. He couldn't even hurt her that way. Hitting her didn't help, either—but it made him feel like he was doing something, interrupting her judgment at the very least. The injustice of it, that judgment he knew was there but couldn't force out. He couldn't force her to voice it, and he couldn't force her to put it away.

Eventually, it was just the fear in her eyes when he walked in, just the way her shoulders shrank back when she was scrubbing the floor and felt his footsteps through the floorboards. The fact that she could see him that way, a side of himself that surprised him. Sometimes he would throw things at her: fruit, plates, a pot of boiling water that hit her at the waist and soaked through her clothes while she panted and her eyes rolled in terror. Once he held her against the wall with his body and slammed his forehead into her face until her blood seeped into his eyes.

*   *   *

People in Galina now, they give a thousand explanations for Luka's marriage to the tiger's wife. She was the bastard child of a notorious gambler, some say, who was forced on Luka as payment for a tremendous debt, a shameful secret that followed him back from those years he spent in Turkey. According to others, he purchased her from a thief in Istanbul, a man who sold girls at the souk, where she had stood quietly among the spice sacks and pyramids of fruit until Luka found her.

Whatever Luka's reason, there is general

239

agreement that the girl's presence in his life was intended to hide something, because a deaf-mute could not reveal the truth about the assorted vices he was presumed to have during his ten-year absence: his gambling, his whoring, his predilection for men. And perhaps, in some part, that is true; perhaps he had allowed himself to think he had found someone to put between himself and the village, someone whose appearance, if not her disability, would discourage people from making contact while he secluded himself and planned a return to his dream that would never be fulfilled—she would remind them too much of the last war, their fathers' fears, stories they'd heard of sons lost to the sultan. Never mind, the villagers thought, that he had found a wife who could never demand anything of him, never reproach him for being drunk, never beg for money.

But, in keeping her, Luka had also stumbled into an unwelcome complication. He had underestimated the power of her strangeness, the village's potential for a fascination with her, and now people were talking more than ever. The secrecy she had been intended to afford him had turned his life into a public spectacle. He could hear them chattering now, gossiping, speculating and flat-out lying about where she'd come from and how he had found her, asking each other about the bruises on her arms, about why Luka and his wife were rarely seen in public together, why she'd yet to bear him a child—every possible answer leading only to further questions, further humiliations. It was worse than the first winter of their marriage, when he had brought her with

240

him to church on Christmas, and the entire congregation had whispered afterward, *What does he mean by bringing her here?* Worse even than the following Christmas, when he had not, and they said, *What does he mean by leaving her at home?*

And now they were talking about the smokehouse. In the two days since the tiger was spotted in the village, there were whispers everywhere. *What had she been doing,* they were asking in doorways, *in the smokehouse with that tiger? And what did it mean,* they wanted to know, *that Luka couldn't keep her in his bed?*

For weeks, he had suspected that the smokehouse was missing meat, but he had second-guessed his own judgment, refusing to believe that she had the audacity to steal from him. And then he had seen the tiger, and the sight of that pork in the big cat's jaws had stunned him—that little gypsy, he had thought, that Mohammedan bitch, sneaking out and giving his meat to the devil. She was making him look like an idiot.

The night he returned from the hunt, he took her outside and tied her up in the smokehouse. He told himself that he wanted only to punish her, but, while he was eating his supper and getting ready for bed, he understood that some part of him was hoping that the tiger would come for her, that it would come in the night and rip her apart, and in the morning Luka would awake to find nothing.

*   *   *

If you go to Galina now, people will tell you different things about Luka's disappearance. In one version of the story, the village woodcutter,

241

waking from a dream in which his wife has forgotten to put the pie in the oven and served it to him raw, looks through the window and sees Luka wandering down the road in his nightgown, a white scarf tying his chin to the rest of his head so that the mouth will not fall open in death, his red butcher's apron slung over one shoulder. In that version, Luka's face is as loose as a puppet's, and there is a bright light in his eyes, the light of a journey beginning. The woodcutter stands with the window curtains flung open, his legs stiff with fear and lack of sleep, and he watches the butcher's slow advance through the snowdrifts that are running across the dead man's bare feet.

Others will tell you about the baker's eldest daughter, who, getting up early to warm the ovens, opens the window to let the winter air in to cool her and sees a grounded hawk sitting like something ancient on the fallen snow of her garden. The hawk's shoulders are dark with blood, and when it hears her open the window it turns and looks at her with yellow eyes. She asks the hawk, 'Is all well with you, brother—or not?' and the hawk replies, 'Not,' and vanishes.

Whatever the details, the consensus is that there was an immediate awareness of Luka's death, and an immediate acknowledgment that the tiger's wife was responsible—but many of the people telling you the story couldn't have been alive when it happened, and then it becomes clear that they have all been telling each other different stories, too.

No one will ever tell you that four or five days went by before anyone began to suspect a thing. People didn't like Luka—they didn't visit his house, and his docility while he stood there, his glasses around his neck in the yawning white space of the butcher's shop with his hands on the meat, made them universally uncomfortable. The truth is that, even after the baker's daughter went to buy meat and found the shutters of the butcher's shop closed and the lights out, it took several days before anyone else tried again, before they began to realize that this winter they would have to do without.

There is the very real possibility that people assumed Luka had gone away—that he was out trapping rabbits for the midwinter feasts, or that he had given up on the village and decided to brave the snowed-in pass and make for the City while the German occupation there was still new. The truth is, the whole situation did not strike anyone as particularly unusual until the deaf-mute girl appeared in town, perhaps two weeks later, with a fresh, bright face, and a smile that suggested something new about her.

My grandfather had spent the morning carrying firewood from the timber pile, and was pounding the snow from the bottoms of his shoes on the doorstep when he saw her coming down the road, wrapped in Luka's fur coat. It was a cloudless winter afternoon, and villagers were leaning against their doorways. At first, only a few of them saw her, but by the time she reached the square the whole village was peering through doors and windows, watching her as she made her way into the fabric shop. They could see her through the window, hovering there indulgently, pointing to the Turkish silks that hung from the walls and running her hands over them lovingly when the

243

shopkeeper spread them out on the counter for her. A few minutes later, my grandfather saw her cross the square with a parcel of silks under her arm, followed by a small procession of village women, who, while keeping their distance, were still too intrigued to maintain the illusion of nonchalance.

Who came up with that name for her? I can't say—I have never been able to find out. Until the moment of Luka's disappearance, she was known as 'the deaf-mute girl,' or 'the Mohammedan.' Then suddenly, for reasons uncertain to the villagers, Luka was no longer a factor in how they perceived the girl. And even after that first time, even after she wrapped her head in Turkish silk and admired herself in front of the mirror in the fabric shop, when it was clearer than ever that Luka was not coming back, that she had no more fear of him, she still did not become 'Luka's widow.' They called her 'the tiger's wife'—and the name stuck. Her presence in town, smiling, bruiseless, suddenly suggested an exciting and irrevocable possibility for what had happened to Luka, a possibility the people of Galina would cling to even seventy years later.

*   *   *

If things had turned out differently, if that winter's disasters had fallen in some alternate order—if the baker had not sat up in bed some night and seen, or thought he had seen, the ghost of his mother-in-law standing in the doorway, and buckled under the weight of his own superstitions; if the pies of the cobbler's aunt had risen properly, putting her in a good mood—the rumors that spread about the tiger's wife might have been different. Conversation might have been more practical, more generous, and the tiger's wife might have immediately been regarded as a *vila,* as something sacred to the entire village. Even without their admission, she was already a protective entity, sanctified by her position between them and the red devil on the hill. But because that winter was the longest anyone could remember, and filled with a thousand small discomforts, a thousand senseless quarrels, a thousand personal shames, the tiger's wife shouldered the blame for the villagers' misfortunes.

So their talk about her was constant, careless, and unburdening, and my grandfather, with *The Jungle Book* in his pocket, listened. They were talking about her in every village corner, on every village doorstep, and he could hear them as he came and went from Mother Vera's house. Truths, half-truths, utter delusions drifted like shadows into conversations he was not intended to overhear.

'I seen her today,' the Brketič widow would say, chins shaking, slung like thin necklaces, while my grandfather stood at the counter of the greengrocer's, waiting for pickling salts.

'The tiger's wife?'

'I seen her coming down from that house again, alone as you please.'

'She's driven him away, hasn't she? Luka's never coming back.'

'Driven him away! Imagine that. A man like Luka being driven away by a deaf-mute child. Our Luka? I seen Luka eat a ram's head raw.'

245

'What then?'

'Well, that's plain, isn't it? That tiger's got him. That tiger's got him, and now she's all alone, nobody bothering her, no one but the tiger.'

'I can't say I'm all that sorry. Not all that sorry, not for Luka.'

'Well, I am. Don't anyone deserve to be done that way.'

'What way?'

'Well, isn't it obvious? Isn't it plain? She's made a pact with that tiger, hasn't she? She probably done Luka herself, probably cut off his head in the night, left the body out for the tiger to eat.'

'That little thing? She's barely bigger than a child.'

'I'm telling you, that's what happened. That devil give her the strength to do it, and now she's his wife.'

My grandfather listened without believing everything—with caution, with guarded curiosity, with a premonition that something inferior was going on in those conversations, something that did not include the horizon of his own imagination. He understood that some part of the tiger was, of course, Shere Khan. He understood that, if Shere Khan was a butcher, this tiger had some butcher in him, too. But he had always felt some compassion for Shere Khan to begin with, and this tiger— neither lame nor vengeful—did not come into the village to kill men or cattle. The thing he had met in the smokehouse was massive, slow, hot-breathing—but, to him, it had been a merciful thing, and what had passed between my grandfather and the tiger's wife had been a shared understanding of something the villagers did not

246

seem to feel. So because they did not know, as he knew, that the tiger was concrete, lonely, different, he did not trust what they said about the tiger's wife. He did not trust them when they whispered that she had been responsible for Luka's death, or when they called the tiger *devil*. And he did not trust them when, a few weeks after her appearance in the fabric shop, they began to talk about how she was changing. Her body, they said, was changing. She was growing bigger, the tiger's wife, and more frightening, and my grandfather listened in the shops and in the square when they said it was because she was swelling with strength, or anger, and when they decided, that no, it wasn't her spirit, just her belly, her belly was growing, and they all knew what that meant.

'You don't think it was an accident do you?' the beautiful Svetlana would say to her friends at the village well. 'She saw, that girl, what was coming. And Luka, he never was too clever. Still, that's what comes to you when you marry one of them Mohammedans from God knows where. Like a gypsy, that girl. Probably strung him up with his own meat hooks, left him there for the tiger.'

'That can't be true.'

'Well, you believe it or don't. But I'm telling you, whatever happened to that Luka was no accident. And that baby—that's no accident, neither.'

'That's no baby. She's eating—Luka's been starving her for years, and now she's free to eat.'

'Haven't you seen her? Haven't you seen her coming into town, so slow, those robes of hers coming up bigger and bigger in the front? That girl's got a belly out to here, are you blind?'

'There's no belly.'

'Oh, there's a belly—and I'll tell you something else. That belly ain't Luka's.'

*　　　*　　　*

It never occurred to my grandfather to accept what the others were thinking—that the baby belonged to the tiger. To my grandfather, the baby was incidental. He had no need to guess, as I have guessed, that it was a result of some drunken stupor of Luka's, or rape by some unnamed villager, and that the baby had been there before the tiger had come to Galina.

However, there was no way to deny that the tiger's wife was changing. And whatever the source of that transformation, whatever was said about it, my grandfather realized that the only true witness to it was the tiger. The tiger saw the girl as she had seen him: without judgment, fear, foolishness, and somehow the two of them understood each other without exchanging a single sound. My grandfather had inadvertently stumbled onto that understanding that night at the smokehouse, and now he wanted so much to be a part of it. On the simplest possible level, his longing was just about the tiger. He was a boy from a small village in the grip of a terrible winter, and he wanted, wanted, wanted to see the tiger. But there was more to it than that. Sitting at the hearth in Mother Vera's house, my grandfather drew the shape of the tiger in the ashes, and thought about seeing and knowing—about how everyone knew, without having seen, that Luka was dead, and that the tiger was a devil, and that the girl was carrying the tiger's baby. He wondered why it didn't occur to

248

anyone to know other things—to know, as he knew, that the tiger meant them no harm, and that what went on in that house had nothing to do with Luka, or the village, or the baby: nightfall, hours of silence, and then, quiet as a river, the tiger coming down from the hills, dragging with him that sour, heavy smell, snow dewing on his ears and back. And then, for hours by the fireside, comfort and warmth—the girl leaning against his side and combing the burs and tree sap out of the tiger's fur while the big cat lay, broad-backed and rumbling, red tongue peeling the cold out of his paws.

My grandfather knew this, but he wanted to see it for himself. Now that Luka was gone, there was no reason for him to stay away. So when he saw the tiger's wife one day as she was walking home from the grocer's, her arms heavy with tins of jam and dried fruit, he found himself brave enough to grin up at her and pat his own stomach in a pleased and understanding kind of way. He wasn't sure if he did this in approval of her choice of jams, or because he wanted to let her know he didn't care about the baby. She had been smiling from the moment she spotted him across the square, and when he stopped to acknowledge her—the first person to do so for what must have been weeks—she piled four of her jam tins into the crook of his arm, and the two of them walked slowly together down the road and through the pasture, past the empty smokehouse and the gate, which was breaking in the winter cold.

*   *   *

At church, the women who made the candles were

249

gossiping together: 'She'll have a time with that baby and only a tiger for a husband. I tell you, it makes my skin crawl. They ought to run her out. She'll be feeding our children to the tiger next.'

'She's harmless.'

'Harmless! You ask poor Luka if she's harmless. He'd tell you how harmless she is—if he could.'

'Well, I'm sure she'd have a thing or two to say about Luka, if *she* could. Mother of God, I'm glad she's killed him, if that's what she's done. The broken bones he laid on that girl. I hope she fed him to that tiger, nice and slow. Feet first.'

'That's what I heard. I heard she carved him up, right in his own smokehouse, and then in comes the tiger for dinner, and she feeds him strips of her dead husband like it's feast day.'

'Good.'

'Well, can't you see why she did it? She didn't do it for herself. She did it to protect that baby, didn't she?'

'What do you mean?'

'That's the tiger's baby growing in her. Imagine what would have happened when it came out—that Luka, being the way he is, seeing the tiger's baby come out of his wife. He'd just kill her, wouldn't he? Or worse.'

'What do you mean, worse?'

'Well, he'd do like a wolf.'

'Like a wolf how?'

'Don't you know? A wolf'll kill another wolf's pups when he comes up in a pack. Sometimes he'll even kill the bitch what carries them. Don't you know anything?'

'I didn't know that.'

'Well, that's why she killed him, isn't it? So he

wouldn't go mad like a wolf and kill her devil-baby when it come out.'

'That makes a lot of sense to me. Her killing him to make room for the tiger. Even so, that Luka was a bastard ten times over. What do you think that baby will look like?'

'I don't know, I'm sure, and I don't want to know. I hope they run her out. All my life, I've never laid eyes on a devil—fifty years, and I never seen one. I don't intend to start now. I hope she knows well enough to keep that child in the house, and not bring it out here for my children to look at.'

'I'll say one thing. I'll say this: I'm not Vera. I'll not have my children running around with the devil's brood.'

Mother Vera had already caught him coming back from the butcher's house: she had been standing on the porch steps when he came back in the twilight that first time, waiting for him, and as he stole back across the field he saw her and hung his head, expecting a reproach. To his surprise, she did nothing, only looked him over and pulled him into the house. After she got wind of what they were saying about her, she herself packed up a basket of food, pies and jams and pickles, a few cloths and a sprig of rosemary, and she sent my grandfather to take it to the tiger's wife that same afternoon, in full view of the entire village, while she stood in the doorway and shouted for him to hurry up. My grandfather grinned obligingly at passersby as he braced the basket against his hip, pushing his feet through the snow. Halfway across the field, he heard Mother Vera's voice behind him say: 'What are you looking at, you fools?'

                    *   *   *

All month, my grandfather carried food and
blankets to the tiger's wife. The winter sat, still and
insensate, on the ridges of Galina, and while it
clung like this to the world, my grandfather
brought her water and firewood, measured the
girl's forehead for a new bonnet Mother Vera was
knitting, a task the old woman was performing
publicly, defiantly, on the porch so the village
could see her, wrapped in six or seven blankets, her
hands blue with cold. She would never cross the
pasture to greet the tiger's wife; but every so often,
she would give the half-finished bonnet, a snarl of
yellow and black yarn, to my grandfather, and he
would carry it as gently as you would carry a bird's
nest, cross the road with it and climb the porch
stairs and, holding the needles aside, tuck the
shining hair of the tiger's wife under it, and look
across to his own house for Mother Vera's motion
of approval.

Because my grandfather was not permitted to
linger at the girl's house after dark, there was still
no sign of the tiger. But he hadn't given up hope.
Most afternoons, he would put blankets on the
floor by the hearth in the girl's house, and help her
sit down, and then he would take out *The Jungle
Book*. It had taken him a few days to determine
that she did not know how to read; at first, he had
sat beside her with the book open on his knees,
believing that the two of them were reading
together in silence. But then he noticed that she
would flip impatiently through to the pictures, and
he understood. So he began to draw the story of

252

Mowgli and Shere Khan for her instead, mangled, disproportionate figures in the hearth ashes: tiger, panther, bear. He drew Mother Wolf, the suckling cubs, and then the jackal Tabaqui—or, at least, how he envisioned Tabaqui, because Kipling had not drawn him at all, and my grandfather drew something that looked like a squirrel, a strange, big-eared squirrel that hovered watchfully around the den and prey of Shere Khan. He drew the wolf pack and Council Rock, showed her in layers of ash how Baloo taught the man-cub the Law of the Jungle. He drew a frog to explain what Mowgli's name meant, and the frog he drew looked stupid, but obliging.

He always began and ended with a drawing of Shere Khan, because even his feeble, flat-nosed cat with the stripes that looked like scars made her smile, and every so often the tiger's wife would reach out and fix his drawing, and my grandfather felt that he was getting closer.

*   *   *

My grandfather sat on a bench by the door of the apothecary's shop, waiting for Mother Vera's hand ointment. Two women, the wives of men he didn't know, stood at the counter, watching the apothecary prepare herbs, and saying: 'The priest says if the devil-child come into this town, we're all done for.'

'Don't make much difference, having a devil-child, if the devil's already here.'

'What do you mean?'

'That tiger. I seen him crossing the pasture by moonlight, big as a horse. Wild eyes in that tiger's

253

head, I'm telling you. Human eyes. Froze me right down to my feet.'

'What were you doing out so late?'

'That doesn't matter. Point is, that tiger come all the way up to the door of Luka's house, and then he get up and take off his skin. Leaves it out on the step and goes in to see his pregnant wife.'

'Imagine that.'

'Don't have to, I seen it.'

'Sure you did. Me, I keep wondering about that baby.'

Then my grandfather said: 'I think she's lovely.'

The women turned to look at him. They had cold-reddened faces and chapped lips, and my grandfather shuffled where he sat on the bench, and said, 'The girl. I think she's lovely.'

Without raising his eyes from his mortar and pestle, the apothecary said: 'Nothing is as lovely as a woman with child.'

The two women stood in silence after that, their backs turned toward my grandfather, whose ears were burning. They paid for their herbs in silence, took their time putting on their gloves, and when they were gone, the apothecary's shop was filled with an unwelcome emptiness that my grandfather had not expected. The ibis in the cage by the counter stood with one leg tucked under the blood-washed skirt of its feathers.

The apothecary was taking balms down from the shelves that lined the back of the shop, unscrewing the lids of tins and jars, mixing white cream in a bowl. Quietly, he said: 'Everyone is afraid of Shere Khan.'

'But I haven't seen Shere Khan in the village— have you?' my grandfather said. The apothecary looked my grandfather over, and then went back to mixing the white cream with a twisted wooden spoon. Then my grandfather said: 'Are you afraid?'

'Not of Shere Khan,' said the apothecary.

*   *   *

Crossing the square one morning with a basket of bread for the tiger's wife, my grandfather heard: 'There he goes again.'

'Who?'

'That little boy—Vera's grandson. There he goes again with a basket for that wretched girl. Look how cowed he looks—he's shaking in his boots. It's wrong to send a child into the house of the devil.'

'What I don't understand is—how can our apothecary just sit by and watch that child go back and forth and back and forth and never say a word? Never say, *look you, old woman, keep your child from the devil's door.*'

'That man doesn't know, that apothecary. He's not from around here. He doesn't know to say.'

'It's his place, though. It's his place to say. If he doesn't, who will?'

'I tell you, I'll have a thing or two to say about what's what when that child gets eaten.'

'I think you're wrong about that. That girl wouldn't harm him.'

'Probably not the way Vera's carrying on. Do you know this is the third basket she's sent over this week? What's she sending?'

'By the grace of God, holy water.'

'Why's she sending baskets?'

'Maybe she's feeling sorry.'

'What for? Who feels sorry for a girl carrying

255

the devil's child?'

'I don't know. That Vera used to be a midwife. I suppose she feels like she has to help, like that girl shouldn't carry alone. She's sending food. I seen the boy packing up that basket when he's dropped it once or twice, and always there's bread inside, and soup, too.'

'Imagine that, feeding that girl, when the rest of us have no meat. Feeding the tiger's wife when there's been no meat. When that girl's been saving it all for the tiger.'

*   *   *

My grandfather told the tiger's wife about the Bandar-log and about Kotick, the white seal—but whenever he reached the end of Shere Khan's story, he could not bring himself to tell her its real conclusion. He found himself often in the gully of the ravine, with Rama and the water buffaloes stampeding at Mowgli's command, smudged shadows in the ash, but somehow he could never reveal the way the man-cub claimed the tiger's life. He could not make himself draw Shere Khan lying in the dust, or Shere Khan's skin on Council Rock, clewed up, as dead as a sail. Instead, every day it was something different. Sometimes Rama stumbled and gave up, or there was a fight between Shere Khan and the buffaloes, for which he would draw his finger through the ashen figures, sending up powdery clouds, chaos, until he found some way to bring Shere Khan out of the fray alive. Sometimes it never even came to Rama— sometimes Mowgli frightened the lame tiger off with fire, or the wolf pack ambushed and drove him away. Every so often, their fights ended in a stalemate, and they came down to the Water Truce together and Bagheera grew jealous at this false, tentative peace.

Who knows if the tiger's wife understood my grandfather's story, or why he was doing her this courtesy. It is easy enough to guess that, after the first few times he changed the story, she realized that he was hiding some deeper tragedy from her. Perhaps her gratitude for the tiger was matched by this new gratitude, the gratitude for help and human companionship, for this persistent and animated man-cub who drew stories in the hearth. Whatever the reason, a few days before the arrival of Dariša the Bear, my grandfather earned from her a little paper bag tied with string, hardly big enough to be a button bag. When he opened it in the darkness of his own house later that night, his fingers felt emptiness, emptiness, and then short, coarse, rusty hairs that scraped that distant, living smell of the smokehouse into his fingers.

8

THE HEART

On the way back from Zdrevkov, I stopped at Kolac for the children's candy, intercepted the cashier of the gas station convenience store just as she was closing up for the evening. I had no bills left, and I grappled with her for twenty minutes, finally persuading her by paying double the amount in our currency to cover the cost of her

257

having to go to the money exchange in the morning. She helped me load two boxes of local chocolate into the car and then drove away in a little run-down hatchback that roared out a line of smoke as she pulled onto the road.

There was a pay phone by the deserted gas pump, and I used my last four coins to call my grandma. The blue bag was in my backpack, folded in half. The mortuary cold of it had stunned me, and I hadn't touched it since Zdrevkov.

My grandma had been making funeral arrangements all day, and when she asked me if I was ready to come home, I told her about Zdrevkov, about going to the veterans' clinic, about how hospitable and consoling they had been. She listened to me in silence, and I realized the news of this journey was as incomprehensible for her as the idea of my grandfather's death had been to me, all of it just words on a bad line. The fact that Zdrevkov had been within driving distance seemed to comfort her, reaffirm in some way that he had been coming to see me after all. She could forgive a misunderstanding, but not an outright lie. Driving off the peninsula, I had been thinking about the deathless man, how my grandfather could have heard about the boys who had stepped on the land mine. The veterans' village, stragglers clinging to life after the dead had gone away. I didn't mention any of this to her.

'Were they disappointed?' she said. 'Were they hoping no one would come by to collect his things?' She had been envisioning a despicable scenario in which I walked into the hospital to find my grandfather's belongings had been distributed among the staff, his hat on the head of an assistant janitor, his watch on the receptionist's wrist.

'They're very busy there,' I said. 'They apologized for the mix-up.' I didn't have the heart to tell her what kind of place it was, that we had been lucky to have them find us at all, lucky he hadn't ended up on that sea-facing slope behind the clinic. 'Would you like me to tell you what's in the bag?'

There was a long silence. The phone clicked. My grandma finally said, 'You opened it?'

'Not yet.'

'And don't,' she told me. 'Don't you dare. How can you even think it?' She started in about the forty days again, about unwittingly interrupting the progress of the soul. How the bag was a blessing, an untouched blessing, and what the hell was I thinking? She was shouting by the time she said: 'What else do I have left to pay my respects with, Natalia? When I didn't know he was sick? And you didn't say anything when you knew?'

The phone beeped twice, and then the line went dead. My pager rang almost immediately, and it continued to ring while I drove back to Brejevina, but I had no money left, and the afternoon was fading into evening. She gave up eventually, my grandma, and I drove with all four windows down, the draft keeping me awake.

By the time I got back to the monastery, the gate was closed. I could see the low sun mirrored in the clerestory windows from the road, but the garden was empty. All along the boardwalk, the shops were dark and shuttered, the postcard stands and trays of snorkeling gear crammed behind iron screens. Some hundred yards later, I came to the corner canal, and here Brejevina's townspeople and tourists were standing in animated, sunburned throngs, smoking, leaning against cars, making their way slowly between the eucalyptus trees to the vineyard fence. I rolled the car into the ditch and left it there, went up the slope with my backpack in my arms, the bag still inside. There was a hot stillness over the sea, and it had crawled onto the land and stilled everything, even the vineyard. From the gate, I could see the diggers, deeper among the vines than they had been that morning. Duré was there with his pot-handle ears, standing like a scarecrow, back bent, hips thrown out. The heavyset man from that morning was there, too, drinking a can of cola, his neck reddened by the sun. The boys from that morning were sitting against a dirt-filled wheelbarrow among the vines; there was no sign of the young woman, or the little girl.

Fra Antun saw me from the vineyard gate, opened it without a word. I apologized, told him about the traffic and the candy, but I'm sure he could tell I was lying. He was sweating under his cassock, his glasses fogged up and his hair curling in thin wisps away from his neck.

From the hill, I could see the sun cutting an unhurried line through the water, the ferry returning from the islands, and the shaded back of Barba Ivan's place. People were ranged along the vineyard fence all the way down into the overgrowth behind the house. Nada stood on the downstairs balcony, smoking with about six or seven other women, widows hunched like birds in their black dresses and a few middle-aged housewives in fish-splashed towels who had just come up from the beach. Nada had set food out on

260

a long rectangular table under the olive tree, and every few minutes she would lower a tray down to the people crowding the fence.

Zóra stood by an oil-drum fire behind the diggers, frowning at something on the bottom of her shoe. When she straightened up and saw me, she gave me a look formerly reserved for Ironglove and the records administrator who worked at the University registrar's office. Armed with disinfectants, several liters of water, and some knowledge of what was to come, she was there to salvage the community's faith in us by forestalling a medical disaster. She did not want my help.

Out among the vines, Duré was bending over something with a damp cloth, wiping it down slowly from end to end, making a visible effort not to move it around too much. It was a suitcase of some kind, an old-fashioned valise, patent leather cracked, handles frayed gray. This, I realized, was why Duré had been confident that the body would eventually make an appearance, why he had been willing to overlook the reality of dogs and floods: he had safeguarded the cousin—whom I had previously imagined to be the occupant of a shallow grave—by stuffing him into a suitcase. Duré was wiping the sides down slowly, with great care, enormous relief at having recovered the case evident in his face. Twelve years of accounting for his inability to return the body, his negligence in leaving a family member behind, loyalty suspect, always defending himself from the conclusions they must have been drawing when he explained himself—had he abandoned a dying man? Killed him and disposed of the body? And the illness itself, how his thoughts must have turned straight

261

to the body when his wife and children began falling ill, one by one; how he must have circled around his own guilt, hinted at it while he searched for cures from the village crone, until the old woman finally caught on and told him what he wanted to hear, pointed to his recklessness and irresponsibility with the body, absolved him by confirming that the burden was his.

The evening began with a blessing. This had been scrawled on a piece of neon-green paper in handwriting that was presumably illegible; Duré read it aloud, slowly, stumbling over the words, over the name of the Father and of the Son, and over some invocation that mystified him so thoroughly he was forced to summon help from some of the other diggers. While they tried in vain to decipher their guidelines, I imagined the old woman who had sent them here, alone in a small, cold house high above Duré's village, as milky-eyed and supple-limbed as a toad, devoting every ounce of strength to composing this blessing she knew by heart, but had never written down. Her notes urged the diggers to wail, but their hesitation made their efforts seem halfhearted. Shawled and bent, the old woman would have given the process dignity, produced a sound long and hollow and endless, a sound that would have dispersed the audience along the vineyard fence. Instead, the discordant howl of the diggers roused the onlookers into a steady chorus of 'wash the bones, bring the body, leave the heart behind' that started first among the most inebriated of the men, but pretty soon spread up and down the line.

Undaunted, the heavyset man turned away from the fire and shouted 'Motherfuck you!' to everyone.

'Stop fucking around,' Duré said to him, and lost his place on the page. 'That's not part of this,' he said, turning to Fra Antun, 'should I start over?'

'I really don't know,' the monk said.

Fra Antun had incense, and he was swinging it back and forth helplessly over the valise while Duré read on, and the diggers coughed and crossed themselves. There was still no sign of the little girl.

The heat of the day, compounded by my early morning in the vineyard, had caught up to me. I felt I'd waited years for the body to be found, though I'd only heard about it that morning—somehow being in Zdrevkov had changed everything, and I didn't know what I was waiting for anymore. My backpack was on my knees, my grandfather's belongings folded up inside. I wondered what they would look like without him: his watch, his wallet, his hat reduced by his absence to objects you could find at a flea market, in somebody's attic.

The opening of the valise was preceded by a baptism with holy water from one of the diggers' herbed bottles. Fra Antun sprinkled it himself, and then Duré tried the zipper—not surprisingly, after more than a decade underground, the zipper did not budge. In the end, they agreed to cut the suitcase open, and someone ran for a kitchen knife from the house, which Nada handed over from the balcony. The diggers were deliberating over where to make the incision. Total silence from the spectators for Duré's backswing and then the knife went in. A strained creak, followed almost immediately by the stench of decay. The body

263

groaned. The sound, straining like a violin, stretched between the fire and the fence. Someone behind me called for God. Arms swung into action; up and down the fence, people were crossing themselves.

Zóra, meanwhile, had been standing by all this time, watching the proceedings, her whole body tensed up like piano wire. I would later find out that, before things got under way, she had asked Duré if he really expected to find a heart in the valise, and he'd said: 'What do you think I am, some sort of idiot?' to which Zóra—by no small miracle—did not reply. But now that groans from the valise had shaken the entire town into paroxysmal supplication, she couldn't restrain herself any longer. 'That's just the gases depressurizing,' she said, loudly and to no one in particular.

But the diggers were undeterred. More chanting and wailing, Fra Antun refusing to touch the herbed bottle, renouncing their holy water but still swinging that incense patiently over the suitcase, the pot catching the light of the falling sun. Zóra waited for another opportunity to offer her opinion, but minutes went by and none came. She drew back to my side of the vineyard, came up the slope dusting her hands against her coat, and stood over me. I pushed myself across the rock ledge to make room for her.

'I have a message for you,' she said. She handed me her coat, and then took off her sweater. She laid the sweater out on the ground beside me and sat down on it, took her coat back across her knees. 'Your grandma says: you open the bag, you'd better not bother coming home.' Zóra said

264

this without looking at me. Her throat was beaded with sweat from standing too close to the fire. 'She was emphatic on that point.'

Zóra had begun wearing a new perfume two months ago, and I hadn't been able to get used to the smell of it yet—but, sitting there with the smoke in her hair and the day coming out of her skin, the smell of alcohol and soap and cigarettes, her mother's detergent in the starchy smell of her coat, the iron in her earrings tinged by sweat, she came back to me completely. Everything I had expected her to say she let fall between us, and I couldn't remember the answers I had been preparing.

Duré had moistened a clean rag with water from the herbed bottle and was taking the cousin out of the suitcase, bone by bone, rubbing the long yellowed blades of the legs gently with the cloth, laying them down on a clean sheet on the ground. The other diggers hovered over him, smoking, their backs to the fence. They had closed off the ritual, speaking quietly, with smaller gestures, either following the directions of their village crone or owing to the animated reaction of the onlookers—who, having guessed that the liveliest portion of the proceedings had come and gone, were beginning to lose interest anyway.

'What would you do?' I said.

'That depends,' said Zóra. 'What would your grandfather say?'

'He'd tell me to humor my grandma, not to open the bag.' After a while, I said: 'And he'd tell you to testify.'

'We'll never get back by Saturday,' Zóra told me. 'But you know that.' She took my hand and held it on her knee, and didn't say anything.

The wet rag was passing from hand to hand, and they were squeezing the water out of it onto the bones, the cracked dome of the skull, wiping down the empty sockets and the crooked lines between the teeth. The spinal column was materializing on the sheet, the vertebral discs like toys. So many hands in the suitcase it was hard to tell who was removing what, but someone was meticulous and organized, sorting the pieces out on the sheet, joints here, fingers there, even though the whole thing would be folded up into itself later. Then they were breaking the thighbones, sawing through them with a cleaver so that the body could not walk in death to bring sickness to the living, and Duré was rolling up the rag, winding it tight over his fist and calling it the heart—and I felt stupid for not considering this possibility, the metaphorical heart, and for doubting the old crone, wherever she was.

Silence while Duré moistened the rag again, three splashes of water for the newly baptized heart, the clenched wad of it tight and heavy in his fist. The heavyset man brought out a small brass pot, and Duré lowered the rag into it carefully, poured oil on it and set it on fire, and for a long time the little brass pot stood on the ground with the family leaning forward to look at it, and all I could think about while we were waiting for it to end was the deathless man and his coffee cup.

They were adding water to the brass pot, which was smoking now, putting it over the oil-drum coals, and Duré baptized the fire and the bones with what was left of the water and then tossed the bottle aside. All along the fence, the onlookers were beginning to dissipate, buckling under the

266

weight of their expectations. A couple of boys were kicking a soccer ball along the vineyard fence.

Then the water was boiling, and Duré took the pot off the fire, and the men began passing it around quietly, without emotion, steadfast drinkers all, trying not to spill the ash-water. Some of the men removed their hats as they did this; some didn't bother to put out their cigarettes. Fra Antun carried his incense over to us and stood there, watching the slow progression of the brass pot, and the faces of the men who had already had their share of the heart.

'Where's the little girl?' I asked him.

'Inside,' said Fra Antun, 'sleeping. They had her out here with a fever this afternoon, my mother threatened to call the police if they tried to bring her back out again.'

It was getting dark now. The sun had dipped below the side of the peninsula, and the sky in the west was draining quickly into the water. While we watched, one of the boys from the burial party put on his hat and went by us quickly. Zóra was already holding out an offering of water and disinfectant, but he pushed past her and went through the gate at the end of the vineyard. And with him, it was over, the tight secrecy of the circle around the valise had unraveled. One of the men wiped his mouth and laughed about something.

'What now?' Zóra said.

'Now comes the vigil,' Fra Antun told her.

'Where's that kid going?' she said.

'To get someone from outside the family to bury the ashes on the hill.'

'Why doesn't he do it himself?'

'Family member,' Fra Antun said. 'He can't.'

267

'What about you?'

'Well, I won't.' Peering down at us from the underside of his glasses, he looked like an enormous dragonfly. 'He'll have a hard time getting anyone to go up to the crossroads after a body's come up.'

'The crossroads?'

'For our *mora,*' said Fra Antun with a smile. 'The spirit who comes to gather the dead.'

I was saying, 'I'll do it,' before my mind had fully come around what he might mean.

'Don't be stupid,' Zóra said, looking at me. Fra Antun was biting his nails, letting the two of us sort it out ourselves.

I said: 'Tell Duré and the family I'll go to the crossroads on their behalf if they send the mother and the kids down to the clinic in the morning.'

9

THE BEAR

While the villagers of Galina are reluctant to talk about the tiger and his wife, they will never hesitate to tell you stories of one of the lateral participants in their story.

Ask someone from Galina about Dariša the Bear, and the conversation will begin with a story that isn't true: Dariša was raised by bears—or, he ate only bears. In some versions, he had spent twenty years hunting a great black bruin that had eluded other hunters from time out of mind, even Vuk Sivić, who had killed the fabled wolf of

Kolovac. In the end, the advocates of that narrative say, the bear grew so weary of Dariša's pursuit that it came to his camp in the night and lay down to die, and Dariša talked to it while it was dying like this in the snow, until its spirit passed into him at first light. My personal favorite, however, was the story that Dariša's tremendous success as a hunter was derived from his ability to actually turn into a bear—that he did not kill, as men killed, with gun or poison or knife, but with tooth and claw, with the savage tearing of flesh, great ursine teeth locked into the throat of his opponent, making a sound as loud as the breaking of a mountain.

All these variations come down to one truth, however: Dariša was the greatest bear hunter in the old kingdom. That, at least, is fact. There is evidence of it. There are pictures of Dariša before the incident with the tiger's wife—pictures in which Dariša, light-eyed and stone-faced, stands over the piled hides of bears, almost invariably in the company of some spindly-legged member of the aristocracy whose cheerful grin is intended to conceal knees still shaking from the hunt. In these pictures, Dariša is guileless and unsmiling, as charismatic as a lump of coal, and it's hard to understand how he managed to generate such a loyal following among the villagers of Galina. The bears in these pictures tell a different story, too, one of death in excess—but then, no one ever looks to them for answers.

Dariša came to Galina once a year, right after the Christmas feasts, to indulge in village hospitality and to sell furs in anticipation of the hardening winter. His entrance was expected but sudden: people never saw him arrive, only awoke to the pleasant realization that he was already there, his horse tethered, oxen unhitched from their cart, fare spread out on a faded blue carpet. Dariša was short and bearded, and, in passing, might have been taken for a beggar; but, like his quiet manner and his tendency to indulge the morbid curiosity of children, he seemed to bring with him a wilder, more admirable world. He brought news and warmth, too, and occasionally stories of the wilderness and the animals that peopled it, and the villagers of Galina associated his arrival with good luck and seasonal stability.

Until that particular winter, my grandfather had looked forward to the yearly visit of Dariša the Bear with as much enthusiasm as anyone else in the village; but, distracted by the tiger and his wife, my grandfather had forgotten all about him. The other villagers, however, had not; instead, the inevitability of his appearance had loomed on and on in their collective consciousness, something that they avoided mentioning, lest their reliance on its surety prevent his arrival. So, when they emerged from their houses one late January morning and saw him there, brown and dirty and as welcome as a promise, their hearts rose.

My grandfather, who would otherwise have been first in line to walk up and down the faded blue carpet and stare at the open-jawed heads of bears, eyes glass, or stone, or altogether missing, looked through the window and realized, with dread, what was going to happen. Across the square, the tiger's wife was probably looking out at Dariša, too, but she did not know the gravity of the commotion that was animating the village. She did not guess, as my

270

grandfather must have guessed, that the priest rushing toward Dariša with open arms was not just saying hello, but also: 'Praise God you've come safely through—you must rid us of this devil in his fiery pajamas.'

All along, my grandfather had hoped for a miracle, but expected disaster. He was nine, but he had known, since the encounter in the smokehouse, that he and the tiger and the tiger's wife were caught on one side of a failing fight. He did not understand the opponents; he did not want to. Mother Vera's unexpected assistance had been a sign of hope, but he didn't know what the hope was toward. And with the hunter's coming, my grandfather realized immediately that the odds were now heavily weighted against the tiger. Dariša the Bear, who, for so long, had represented something admirable and untouchable, became a betrayer, a murderer, a killer of tigers, a knife-wielding, snare-setting instrument of death that would be directed at something sacred, and my grandfather had no doubt that, given enough time, Dariša would succeed.

*　　　*　　　*

Unlike most hunters, Dariša the Bear did not live for the moment of death, but for what came afterward. He indulged the occupation he was known for so that he could earn the occupation that gave him pleasure: the preparation of the pelts. For Dariša, it was the skinning, the scraping, the smell of the curing oils, the ability to frame the memory of the hunt by re-creating wilderness in his own house. That is the truth about Dariša: the

271

man was a taxidermist at heart.

To understand this, you have to go back to his childhood, to things no one in the village had heard about, to a prominent neighborhood of the City, a redbrick house on a lamp-lit thoroughfare overlooking the king's manicured parks; to Dariša's father, who was a renowned Austrian engineer, twice widowed, and who spent the better part of his life abroad; to Dariša's sister, Magdalena, whose lifelong illness prevented them from following their father when he left, for years at a time, to oversee the construction of museums and palaces in Egypt, and kept them confined to each other's company, and to the landscape of their father's letters.

Magdalena was epileptic, and therefore restricted to small distances and small pleasures. Unable to attend school, she made as much progress as she could with a tutor, and taught herself painting. Dariša, seven years her junior, doted on her, adored everything she adored, and had grown up with the notion that her welfare was his obligation, his responsibility. Standing in the hallway of their house, watching the footman carry his father's valises out to the waiting carriage, Dariša would cling to the lapels of the engineer's coat, and his father would say: 'You're a very small boy, but I am going to make you a gentleman. Do you know how a small boy becomes a gentleman?'

'How?' Dariša would say, even though he already knew the answer.

'With a task,' his father said. 'With taking responsibility for others. Shall I give you a task?'

'Yes, sir.'

'Help me think of one. What do you think most

272

needs doing while I am away? While you are the only gentleman in the house?'

'Magdalena needs to be looked after.'

'And will you look after her for me?'

During the months that followed he busied himself with doing what he could for her, establishing order on a miniature but ferocious level. They had a housekeeper who prepared the meals and cleaned the house—but it was Dariša who carried the breakfast tray up to his sister's room, Dariša who helped her pick the ribbons out for her hair, Dariša who fetched her frocks and stockings and then stood guard outside her door while she got dressed, so he could be there to hear her if she felt dizzy and called for him. Dariša laced her shoes, posted her letters, carried her things, held her hand when they took walks in the park; he sat in on her piano lessons, scowling like a fish, interfering if the teacher grew too stern; he arranged baskets of fruit and glasses of wine and wedges of cheese for her so she could paint still lifes; he kept an endless circulation of books and travel journals on her nightstand so they could read together at bedtime. For her part, Magdalena indulged him. He was a great help to her, and she realized very quickly that by looking after her he was learning to look after himself. His efforts invariably earned him the first line in Magdalena's letters: *Dearest papa, you should see how our Dariša takes care of me.*

He was eight years old when he first witnessed one of her attacks. He had crept into her room to tell her about a bad dream. He found her twisted up in the covers, her body taut with spasms, her neck and shoulders drenched with sweat and something white and sticky. Looking at her, he suddenly felt ambushed, stifled by the soundless arrival of something else that had eased into the room with him when he opened the door. He left her there. Without putting on his coat, without putting on his shoes, he left the house and ran down the street in his nightshirt, his bare feet slapping on the wet pavement, all the way to the doctor's house halfway across town. All around him, he felt only absence, as wide and heavy as a ship. The absence of people on the street, the absence of his father, the absence of certainty that Magdalena would be alive when he got home. He cried only a little, and afterward, in the doctor's carriage, he didn't cry at all.

'Let's not tell Papa about any of this, all right?' Magdalena said two days later, when he was still refusing to leave her bedside. 'You were such a brave little man, my brave, brave little gentleman—but let's not tell him, let's not make him worry.'

After that, Dariša learned to fear the night—not because he found the darkness itself terrifying, or because he was afraid of being carried off by something supernatural and ugly, but because he realized suddenly the extent of his own helplessness. Death, winged and quiet, was already in the house with him. It hovered in the spaces between people and things, between his bed and the lamp, between his room and Magdalena's— always there, drifting between rooms, especially when his mind was temporarily elsewhere, especially when he was asleep. He decided that his dealings with Death had to be preemptive. He developed a habit of sleeping for two hours, while

274

it was still light out, and then waking to wander the house, to creep into Magdalena's room, his breath withering in front of him, and to stand with his hand on her stomach, as if she were a baby, waiting for the movement of her ribs. Sometimes he would sit in the room with her all night, but most often he would leave her door open and go through the rest of the house, room by room, looking for Death, trying to flush him from his hiding places. He looked in the hall cupboards and the china cabinets, the armoires where boxes of old newspapers and diagrams were kept. He looked in his father's room, always empty, in the wardrobe where his father kept his old military uniform, under the beds, behind bathroom doors. Back and forth he went through the house, latching and unlatching windows with useless determination, expecting, at any moment, to look inside the oven and find Death squatting in it—a man, just a man, a patient-looking winged man with the unmoving eyes of a thief.

Dariša planned to say: 'I've found you, now get out.' He had planned no course of action in the event of Death's refusal.

Dariša had been doing this for several months when the Winter Palace of Emin Pasha opened its doors. For years, the fate of the pasha's winter residence had been a subject of some debate among the City's officials. As a relic of the City's Ottoman history, it had been unused for years. Unable to use it for himself, unwilling to rid the City of it entirely, the magistrate from Vienna called it a museum, and turned it over that year to the enjoyment of royal subjects who were already patrons of the arts, people who were regulars at places like the National Opera, the Royal Library, the King's Gardens.

WONDER AND MAJESTY, said a red-and-gold placard on every lamppost in Dariša's neighborhood. A DAZZLING LOOK INTO THE HEATHEN WORLD.

The upper floor of the palace was a cigar club for gentlemen, with a card room and bar and library, and an equestrian museum with mounted horses from the pasha's cavalry, chargers with gilded bridles and the jangling processional saddles of the empire, creaking carriages with polished wheels, rows and rows of pennants bearing the empire's crescent and star. Downstairs, there was a courtyard garden with arbors of jasmine and palm, a cushioned arcade for outdoor reading, and a pond where a rare white frog was said to live in a skull that had been wedged under the lily pads by some assassin seeking to conceal the identity of his now-headless victim. There were portraiture halls with ornate hangings and brass lamps, court tapestries depicting feasts and battles, a small library annex where the young ladies could read, and a tearoom where the pasha's china and cookbooks and coffee cups were on display.

Magdalena seized the opportunity to take her little brother there right away. She was sixteen, aware of the full extent of her illness, and increasingly tortured by the fact that she had never been anywhere, and that she was to blame for Dariša's isolation (about which he did not complain) and Dariša's endless nighttime patrolling (which he would not give up). She had read in the newspaper that the palace contained something called the Pasha's Hall of Mirrors, and

276

she took him there because she wanted Dariša to know something of the world outside their thoroughfare and their park and the four walls of their house.

To enter the Pasha's Hall of Mirrors, you had to cross the garden and go down a small staircase to a landing that looked like the threshold of a tomb. A rearing dragon was carved on the tympanum, and a gypsy with a lion cub sat on a small box and threatened to curse your way if you did not pay for guidance. This was mostly for the benefit of children, because both the gypsy and the lion cub were on the payroll of the museum. You would put a grosh in the gypsy's hat, and she would say 'Beware of yourself' and then shove you inside and slam the door. Wary of Magdalena's condition, the family's doctor had advised her against going inside, so Dariša went alone.

The first part of the labyrinth was innocent enough, a row of joke mirrors that blew you up and cut you in half and made your head look like a zeppelin, but past that you would suddenly have the notion of standing upside down and back to front. The ceiling and floor were done in gold tile and carved palm crowns, and the mirrors stood so that every step you took was into an alcove with nine, ten, twenty thousand of yourself. You would inch along slowly, the tiles on the floor shifting and changing shape, the angles of the mirrors slanting in and out of reality while your hands touched glass, and glass, and more glass, and then, finally, open space where you least expected it. Coming around invisible corners, you would occasionally encounter a painted oasis, or a mounted peacock in what appeared to be the distance, but was, in reality, somewhere behind you. Then the marionette of an Indian snake charmer, with a wooden cobra rearing out of a basket. Making his way through the labyrinth, Dariša felt that his heart might stop at any moment, felt that, even though he was seeing himself everywhere as he advanced, he did not know which one of him was real, and his movement was crippled by indecision and fear of becoming lost, of never finding his way out of the fog, and despite Magdalena's best intentions, he began to feel the same emptiness that found him in the darkness of his room at home. Every few feet, his face would hit the mirror and leave a chalky stain on the glass. He was crying by the time he reached the pasha's oasis, a curtained atrium with six or seven live peacocks milling around a green fountain, and beyond it, the door to the trophy room.

The trophy room was a long, narrow corridor with blue wallpaper. A tasseled Turkish carpet unrolled down the length of the hall, and the south wall was studded with the shining mounted skulls of antelope and wild sheep, the broad horns of buffalo and moose; picture-boxes of pinned beetles and butterflies; carved perches from which the wide dead eyes of hawks and owls stared down; the tusks of an elephant, crossed like sabers next to a case containing the spiraled single horn of a narwhal; a large swan, spread-winged and silent, kiting on string; and, at the end of the hall, the mounted body of a hermaphroditic goat, with several photographs of the living animal preserving moments of its life in the pasha's menagerie to prove that its existence had been real, and not fabricated after death.

278

The opposite wall was illuminated with lamps that tilted upward from the floor into enormous glass cases where the wild things of the world were posed in agitated silence. One case for every corner of the earth, every place the pasha or his sons had hunted. Yellow grass and the staircase crowns of flat-topped trees painted in the background of a case that held a lion and his cub, an ostrich, a purple warthog, and a small gazelle cowering in a flush of thorns. Dark woods with canvas waterfalls, the mouth of a cave, and a bear standing rigid, paws folded, eyes up, ears forward; behind the bear, a white hare with red eyes and a pheasant in flight pinned to the wall. A pastel river, thick with the foreheads of drinking zebra, kudu, oryx, horns slanting up, ears turned here and there to catch the silence. An evening tableau: bent bamboo forest, green as summer, and a tiger, washed with fire, standing in the thicket with its face pulled up in a snarl, eyes fixed forward through the glass.

Young boys are fascinated with animals, but for Dariša the hysterical dream of the golden labyrinth, coupled with the silent sanctuary of the trophy room, amounted to a much simpler notion: absence, solitude, and then, at the end of it all, Death in thousands of forms, standing in that hall with frankness and clarity—Death had size and color and shape, texture and grace. There was something concrete to it. In that room, Death had come and gone, swept by, and left behind a mirage of life—it was possible, he realized, to find life in Death.

Dariša did not necessarily understand the feeling that came over him. He knew only that for a long time he had feared absence, and now here was presence. But he realized that it had something to do with preservation of spirit, with the maintenance of an image you most loved or feared or respected, and afterward he came to the Hall of Mirrors often, by himself, and walked up and down the trophy room, admiring the wax nostrils and fixed postures, the roll of the tendons and muscles, and the veins in the faces of stags and rams.

Dariša began his apprenticeship with Mr. Bogdan Dankov of Dankov and Slokić long before Magdalena died. He began it because of a chance encounter with Mr. Bogdan at the palace when the old master had come to repair a mounted fox that needed re-bristling. Mr. Bogdan mounted the most respectable heads in town and, in Dariša's twelve-year-old eyes, was an artist of the highest caliber. His clients were dukes and generals, people who lived and hunted in the kinds of places Dariša's father wrote about in his letters, and, more and more often, Dariša found himself at the Bogdan workshop on the south side of town, waiting for the morning deliveries, waiting for the servants of great men to bring in the skins and the skulls, the horns and the heads. Of course, it wasn't all pleasant—the capes arriving, smelling of something faint and funny, the way the dead skins lay there in a matted heap. But the preparation was worth the reward of watching Mr. Bogdan draw up the sketches for the mannequin, and then, as weeks went by, raise the wooden frame, sculpt the plaster and the wax, carve out the muscles and the lines where the tissues held together under the skin, select the eyes, stretch the skin over and sew it up around the body until it stood, full again, knees and ears and tail and all. Then came the painting of the rough spots, the glazing of the nose, the smoothing of the antlers.

To practice, Dariša set up a small workshop of his own in his father's cellar. It was a permanent and unassailable solution to the problem of his inability to sleep, which had never gone away. Still the gendarme of the house, he would read until Magdalena and the housekeeper were asleep, and then go down to his workshop, take the skins out of the icebox, and begin the process of restoring the dead. He must have reasoned, in some way, that if Death were already in the house, it would be attracted to his activity, interested in the magic of reversal, puzzled, perhaps, by how the unformed skin was made to rise over new shoulders, new flanks, new neck. If he kept Death there, kept it riveted and preoccupied, thought about it while it shared the cellar with him, it would not wander the house. He practiced first on vermin he picked out of the trash, cats that had met their ends under carriage wheels, and then on squirrels he trapped with a clumsy box-and-bait apparatus he set up in the back garden. After Magdalena's kingfisher died, he showed the mounted bird to Mr. Bogdan and won the right to take small commissions home with him: fox, badger, pine marten. Whatever satisfaction he gained from the finished product, he did not admit, either to himself or to the quiet, empty room.

He continued this way for years, even after the attack that killed Magdalena, which, predictably, happened one sunny afternoon in March at the park, when he let go of her hand to lace up his

281

shoes, and she seized and fell and hit her head, and after a long time in the hospital, slipped away without waking up or ever saying a word to him again. Afterward, other things collapsed in small piles around him—the kingdom went first, and the wars that united it into a new one bankrupted his father, who hanged himself from one of the many bridges that spanned the Nile, far away, in Egypt. Alone, penniless, without task, Dariša moved into Mr. Bogdan's basement and continued his apprenticeship in the business of death. *At least,* he told himself, *this is something I know how to do,* and he went to the Hall of Mirrors more and more often to perfect the technique of his craft, until at last he was permitted to touch up one of the pasha's great boars, which was much later mounted in the office of the Marshall, although Dariša would never know about it. He had plans, then, to open up a business of his own, or to take over from Mr. Bogdan when the old master retired. But then came the Great War, and years of poverty, and any business he might have made of it dried up in the coffers and pockets of the rich who fled or died or went broke, assumed other identities, adopted other kingdoms.

At twenty, having buried Mr. Bogdan and faithfully distributed almost all the old man's money among his many legitimate and illegitimate children so that he could keep the basement for himself, Dariša was scrounging for work. He found himself running errands for a tavern owner he detested, a sallow-faced, tubercular old gypsy whose name was Karan, and who insisted on paying him in old currency. The tavern was a one-room shack, so there was never enough sitting

282

room inside, and the patrons would instead spill out into the square, where Karan had steadily been carving out space with boxes and moving crates, overturned butter churns and broken pickling barrels, anything found or unused that might serve as a tabletop.

Contributing to the tavern's popularity—particularly in the eyes of children—was Lola, Karan's dancing bear and the love of his life. She was an old, soft-muzzled, doe-eyed thing who had spent countless years traveling the world with her master, performing on street corners and in circuses, in theatrical productions and palace galas, and once—as evidenced by Karan's only framed photograph, proudly on display above the spit—for the late archduke himself. She was so old she no longer needed a tether, and was content to spend her waning years in the shade of the oak outside the tavern, letting the neighborhood children clamber all over her and peer inside her nostrils. On the rare occasion she did get up to dance, she lumbered through it with unforced grace that still showed some traces of her former glory.

Dariša had never seen a living bear before, and when he wasn't scrubbing dishes or butchering the morning's shipment of meat, he was outside with Lola. Old age had worn away her sight and sense of smell, and it was often all she could do to raise herself to her feet and move from one shaded area to another; but her range of expressions still betrayed the wild animal in her. There was, of course, the almost canine sideways tilt of the eyes when she wanted something she was not supposed to have (a prime cut of meat, for example, or a drink of *rakija,* in which she was occasionally

283

permitted to indulge), or the way her muzzle melted into contentment at the sound of Karan's voice; but there was also the sudden upward pull of the facial muscles when she managed to hear a dog in the distance, and the darkened, drawn, focused look that came over her at feeding time.

When Lola finally died that winter, Karan was beside himself with grief. He closed the tavern down, and kept her wrapped in an enormous blanket in the dining room for four days before he finally let Dariša take her away. In Mr. Bogdan's basement, Dariša worked slowly, a little each day, his hands trying to remember the movement of the knife and the needle as smoothly as possible while his mind stayed fixed on Lola in the golden labyrinth. When he brought her back to Karan, almost a month later, the gypsy was speechless. Dariša had positioned her standing, her body half-turned and her ears alert, somewhere between dancing and rearing for a better look at her prey; her paws were outspread, her fur combed and clean, her eyes wide and fixed on something in the distance. Dariša had found the ground between her docile nature and her long-lost, feral dignity; Karan immediately gave him a raise, and put Lola on the slope beneath her tree and laid her silver-tasseled dancing muzzle under one enormous hind paw.

Lola stood outside the tavern this way for months, and when the spring brought trappers back from the mountains after the season's hunt, they marveled at her authenticity, and demanded to meet the man who had done her such remarkable justice. The trappers were hard-faced, ugly men, ugly in every way, but they got less ugly

284

the more they drank, and they drank a lot that night, buying round after round for Dariša. There was no more money to be made in taxidermy in the City, they told him; but there were forests the whole world over, forests belonging to kings and counts, even forests belonging to no one, and these forests were stocked with bear and wolf and lynx, whose hides were now worth a great deal to City men trying to distinguish themselves in social circles to which they had no birthright. In this world, the trappers told Dariša, the aristocracy had fallen from their frivolous pursuits, and a man could no longer rely on them to bring him work. Instead, he must go out and find the beasts himself, hunt them on his own time and with his own skill. If a rich idiot should happen to tag along, he was an added blessing; but rich idiots were harder and harder to come by, unreliable even when they expressed interest, and a man could not spend a lifetime waiting for them.

Dariša mopped floors for the rest of the spring and summer, but when autumn came he followed the trappers into the mountains. The hunt, he had convinced himself, was just a new avenue of the death business, and one way or another it would accommodate a return to independence and to the work he loved. He himself would bring home the hides that would revive Mr. Bogdan's workshop; he would kill the bears whose pelts doctors and politicians would buy on market stands, the bears whose unseen deaths retired generals would embellish in fireside stories.

That first year, following one trapper and then another, Dariša became a hunter. They say he fell to hunting as if he had been born for it; but perhaps it was the possibility of having a purpose again that fueled him to adopt his new life with such ferocious energy and dedication. He learned to set up camp and mend weapons; to build a blind and sit motionless in it for hours; to read his quarry's track in the dark and in the rain. He learned, by heart, the movement of deer herds across the mountains so that he could anticipate the bears who came to pick off the stragglers. He learned to hunt in late autumn, when the bears, slow-gaited and fattened, were fiercest in their last months of foraging before winter sleep. What the other trappers could teach him, he absorbed voraciously; what they could not, he figured out for himself. He hunted with traps and guns, with snares and poisoned meat, grew accustomed to the loud and stinking way bears died, and the way their skin came away from the body if you cut it right, heavy, blood-filled, but as accommodating as a dress pattern. He learned to love solitude, unbroken except for an occasional encounter with other trappers, or the unexpected hospitality of some godforsaken farm where the men always seemed to be gone, and the women always happy to see him. He learned that seven months of hunting could earn him the pleasure of three months of work in Mr. Bogdan's basement, shut away from the world, rebuilding the skins he had brought with him.

He learned, also, to tolerate and understand the necessity of taking on rich idiots—a trickle of young men trying to cling to the noble birthrights of their fathers and grandfathers. By his third year of hunting, these youths would follow him through the brush, as sure-footed as fawns, their alarm wild

286

and loud and completely unpredictable. They were the kind of men who came oversupplied and underprepared, whose teeth would chatter and arms go dead at the crucial moment. Every so often, one of them would inexplicably rise to the occasion and deliver the thunderclap blow at the correct moment and precise angle; these rare boys, few and far between, could never recover completely from the shock of their first kill, and their faces, in hunting photographs and for weeks afterward, would register smiles of stupefaction and little else.

But more and more, as times grew harder, Dariša found himself hunting specific bears, problem bears. Stories of his prowess had spread, and messengers would scour the woods to find him: a black bruin had made off with somebody's child in Zlatica; an unseen devil-bear was coming down to a farm in Drveno, slaughtering horses in the field. A red sow the size of a house had lost her cubs to a male bear in Jesenica, and was jealously guarding the cornfield in which they had died, attacking the farmers during harvest; an old gray boar had made a lair for himself in a barn in Preliv, and was hibernating in there.

One by one, he found them all; and when the killing was done, he took their hides with him to the next village. The villagers would welcome him and take him in, feed and clothe him, buy the pelts he did not keep for himself; and then, when the time came for him to help them, too, they would line up in awe along the village streets and watch him leave the village for the forest beyond. Whether or not Dariša took the precaution of burying his weapons somewhere in the forest is irrelevant. Suffice it to say that he made an impressive sight, all five foot seven of him, disappearing into the forest unarmed, with the great bear pelt rolling over his shoulders.

Dariša the Bear. Behind him, knowledge of the golden labyrinth, and somewhere ahead of him, advancement toward it. And in the meantime, nothing but bears.

*   *   *

And now, a tiger. It is said, of course, that Dariša interfered on Galina's behalf as soon as he heard of the villagers' misfortune; the truth, however, is that Dariša had little interest in hunting a tiger in the bitter winter. He was already in his late forties by then, reluctant to tangle with the unfamiliar; and, besides, he knew the war was coming closer, sensed it in the stories he had heard along the road. He was not compelled to stay in this part of the mountains with the troops moving quickly through the foothills, ready to come up at the first hint of spring. And though his refusal to the priest was firm, it was the apothecary who finally convinced him to stay, the apothecary who appealed to Dariša's sense of compassion—not through righteousness or desperation or even the novelty of the quarry.

It was well known that Dariša, during his stays in the village, was content to sit in the square, sharpening his knives and eavesdropping on the breathless, well-side conversations of women; or to tease them in the marketplace, where they stood cross-armed behind their stands, eyes alert and unwavering. Dariša's affection for women

288

extended to an intolerance of the things that harmed or humiliated them: loud men, loutish behavior, unwanted advances. Whether or not this stemmed from his days of responsibility toward Magdalena, I also cannot say; but he was notorious wherever he traveled for dislocating the shoulders of aggressive drunks, or pulling the ears of neighborhood boys who stood about whistling at young women coming back from pasture.

So at daybreak, the apothecary took him to the edge of the forest on the pretense of showing him the tiger's tracks.

'At least come see what we've got on our hands,' he said, 'and tell me what you think of it.'

The two of them knelt over the previous night's paw prints, and Dariša marveled at the size of them, the strong and unhesitating track that wound up the mountain and into the trees. Dariša climbed into the bracken to look for urine, and traces of the tiger's fur snagged on the low-hanging thickets, and when he came back, they followed the tiger's trail back to the village, to the pasture and over the fence. It led them, of course, to the butcher's house, and the tiger's wife came to the doorway and watched them pass by. She was already obviously pregnant, but something—perhaps the pregnancy itself, or Luka's absence, or something else entirely—had made her come into grace.

Dariša took off his hat when he saw her, and kept it folded in his hands while the tiger's wife studied him with flat eyes. The apothecary took Dariša's arm. 'That tiger seems to have taken a liking to her,' he said, 'which worries me. She lives alone.' He did not call her 'the tiger's wife,' and he did not mention the liking she herself had seemed to have taken to the tiger.

'Isn't that the butcher's wife?' Dariša asked.

'His widow,' the apothecary told him. 'Recently widowed.'

Nothing about the story indicates that Dariša had any other reaction to the girl; but because he agreed, later that afternoon, to stay awhile and see what could be done about the tiger, people say he was a little in love with her. He was a little in love with her while he walked the woods at the bottom of the mountain, reading signs of the tiger in the snow, and a little in love with her as he opened the jaws of bear traps along the fence where the tiger would come through. He was a little in love with her that second morning, when he went out to check the traps and found them closed empty, shut over nothing, slammed down over dead air; a little in love with her when he made an announcement to the whole village that he could work only with everyone's co-operation, and that none of the children must go near the traps again, because this time they might not be so lucky, might lose an arm or leg to the iron jaws. With gossip blazing through the village—what was this new sorcery? how could the traps have closed on their own with nothing to set them off?—no one dared tell Dariša what they really thought: *she* had done it herself, the tiger's wife. Their fears, to them, seemed smaller with Dariša there, shameful to bring up to him, so the girl's magic was allowed to lie over the pasture, the village, probably the entire mountain; nothing could undo it.

Later that afternoon, Mother Vera pulled my grandfather's ear and demanded: 'Did you do it, boy? Did you go to the traps last night?'

290

'I did not,' he said sharply.

And he hadn't. He had, however, explained Dariša's efforts to the tiger's wife in the ash of the hearth, and spent a sleepless night, praying that the tiger would not blunder into the traps, going to the window to look out over the empty streets in the moonlight. Mother Vera's insistence that he stay out of it did not prevent him from taking advantage of Dariša's tolerance of children, tailing the Bear as he went about his work; it did not prevent my grandfather from sitting innocently on a nearby tree stump while Dariša prepared bait carcasses, asking a thousand questions about the hunt; it did not prevent him from following Dariša out to the pasture—and then, as the days went on, to the edge of the woods, to the lowest bank of the forest—and puzzling over the sight of the empty traps.

When the tracks disappeared from the pasture altogether, the apothecary knew that the tiger's wife was responsible in some capacity for Dariša's lack of success. With this in mind, he did his best to steer the Bear away from revealing too many of his plans to my grandfather.

'Of course, he doesn't want you to kill it,' he said to the Bear one evening.

'I'll let him keep one of the teeth when it is done,' Dariša said, smiling. 'That always helps.'

The tiger, it seemed, had disappeared from the village. This forced Dariša to hunt deeper in the woods; and after that came things that are difficult to explain. His snares, they say, were always full of crows—crows already dead, their wings stiff against their sides, and the bait untouched. Dariša's traps were spread out and well hidden, and she found them all, found them night after night, filling them with dead birds. How could she—small as she was, carrying the added weight of her belly—make that nightly journey, covering her own tracks, covering the tiger's? How could she bury each poisoned carcass Dariša left out—not rabbits or squirrels, but deer, sheep, boar—so that no trace of it could be found in the morning? When Dariša, growing frustrated, set a pit-trap over a frozen streambed, how could she break the trap herself and leave, in place of the twigs and ropes, a worn blanket thrust down over the tip of the spear? How could she do all this and come back to the village unbruised, unharmed, her eyes full of innocence, and watch the villagers pretend not to know it was her?

I cannot explain any of it—but the baker's daughter thought she could. Unable to restrain herself, she stopped Dariša one evening in the street, and held on to his arms as she told him all about the blacksmith, about Luka and the baby.

'People have seen it,' she said, her eyes full of tears. 'The tiger is her husband. He comes into her house each night and takes off his skin. That apothecary—he knows, but he will not tell you this. He's not from here.'

I cannot say whether or not Dariša believed this; but he was a practical man, and he was aware of his own tendency to prey, through his reputation, on the superstitions of the people of Galina. It did not surprise him to learn that the villagers had hatched a theory of their own. But he realized, then, that the apothecary had taken advantage of him; that he had led Dariša to protect the girl above all the others without presenting the possibility that she did not want this protection. He had been suspicious of deliberate sabotage for some time, and he was a fool for ignoring the signs. That night, Dariša flew into a rage. 'You've lied to me,' he shouted. 'There's far more to this than you led me to believe.'

'Why would I tell you village stories?' the apothecary demanded, holding his ground between Dariša and the ibis in the cage. 'What are they besides superstitions? How could listening to this nonsense have helped you?' Nevertheless, that night Dariša sat at the window of the shop, and the apothecary, for better or for worse, was forced to keep him company. They sat in silence for hours, watching the village street and the distant square of light in the window of the butcher's house. But for all his years as a hunter, the countless vigils he had learned to endure, Dariša found himself falling into dreams that made no sense to him— dreams in which he stood in front of the house of the tiger's wife and watched the return of her husband. He would see the tiger, broad-shouldered, red skin glinting in the moonlight, cross the square and come down the road, the night behind him drawing in like the hem of a dress. The door of the butcher's house would open, and then, through the window, Dariša could see the tiger rise upright and embrace the girl, and the two of them would sit down at the table together to eat—and always they were eating heads, the heads of cattle and sheep and deer, and then they ate the head of the hermaphroditic goat from the pasha's trophy room.

The villagers were not surprised to find Dariša preparing to leave the following morning, and they stood out in the snow, silent and pale while he rolled up his carpet and piled the remaining pelts onto his cart without looking at any of them. They were not surprised, but they were angry; he had been their surest line of defense, the last reliable weapon they'd been able to offer up against the tiger, and the girl's magic had proved too powerful even for him. They were alone now, with the tiger and his wife, alone again for good.

*   *   *

The tiger had been in the thickets above the ruined monastery for days, his ears straining for the faint sound of the hunter setting traps along the bottom of the hill, obvious to him now that he recognized the sound and smell of them. He had not come close enough to determine what they did. She had brought him here, walked with him patiently with her hand on the ridge between his shoulders, the meat she'd brought him hidden somewhere inside her coat. He had gone a week without the warmth of the village and the smokehouse smell of her hair, though he had found faint traces of her in the air now and then, almost always at night. Once or twice he had gone to her, had tracked her down in the blackness of the trees, but she had always led him back. And so he had lain there among the ruins of Sveti Danilo while the snow fell through the caved-in roof above the altar, and watched the birds huddled along the golden arch of the altarpiece.

He did not fear the hunter because he did not know how or why he should. He knew only that the smell that clung to this man was different—a

294

cluttered smell, the smell of earth and heavy rot, of possessions over which death had been repeatedly smeared—and he found that it did not invite him. It did not invite him when he watched the man from his clearing from the ridge, or when he found it around his old hiding places, along paths he had walked the day before. It was not the hunter's smell, but the scent of a badger, unsteady and warm with winter sleep, that he followed down from Sveti Danilo the day he came across the ox cart, hidden in a pine grove.

The tiger had come up from behind, upwind of the cart, and the surprising shape, the sheer size, of the cart had pulled him down onto his belly. Crouching behind it, he could see beyond the bracken to where the wheels had sunk into the snow, and to where the oxen stood, half-blind with hair, flank to flank for warmth, their breath curling out. The smell of the hunter was everywhere.

The tiger lay in the black thicket behind the wagon for a long time, waiting for something, something just out of reach of his understanding of the situation. Then the wind turned, and the oxen got his scent and they began to shift nervously, their harnesses clanking, the chains that yoked them to the wagon shuddering with silver sound. This pulled him forward a little, only a little, out of the bracken, and their side-slit eyes caught sight of him, and the wagon rumbled forward as they bolted. The tiger, finding his instincts slammed open, was up and running, a full rush of blood already in his chest as he cleared the wagon and sprang for the hindquarters of the ox on the right. He had him, for a moment—claws ripping into the hips and his teeth on the thick base of the tail—but then there was the harness and the cart and the other ox, and somewhere in the confusion something struck him in the ribs and he let go and dropped away, and was left behind, watching the cart's wavering path until it came to rest beyond the clearing.

The hunter was nowhere in sight.

*   *   *

My grandfather should have been comforted by Dariša's departure. But he awoke that night, after hours of half-dreams, with hysteria raging through his bloodstream in the dark. Sitting up in bed, he could not rid himself of the feeling that something had shifted, crawled between himself and the tiger and the tiger's wife until the distances between them, which he had slowly and carefully been closing, had gone back to something insurmountable. The idea of the walk to her house alone exhausted him.

The sky was cloudless, and the moon made shadows on the floor by his bed. The fire was already dead, embers breathing on the hearth. He got up and slipped into his boots and his coat, and, like that, in his nightshirt, his head bare, he went outside and ran through town, the wind biting his face and fingers.

There was no light in the village. All around him, the pasture was shining with new snow. Somewhere behind, a dog was barking, and another dog took up the call, and their voices rang to each other in the dark. The weight of the afternoon's snowfall had freed the slanted shoulders of her roof, piled the hedges thick and uneven, and my grandfather stood at the bottom of the porch steps and stared up at the black attic turret and the black windows. The house seemed strange to him, unfamiliar, and he could not summon a memory of being indoors with the tiger's wife. He could see that something had crossed the stairs and the porch, leaving white furrows behind. He tried to tell himself that perhaps the tiger had done this coming home; but the footprints were small, the trails short and two-footed, and they led away from the door. He thought about going up, letting himself in, waiting for her by the hearth. But the house was empty, and he would be alone.

My grandfather ran down to the end of the pasture and under the fence, following the trail, which was becoming deeper as the snow thickened out in the field. All winter, he had not come this far, and now, with the snow groaning under his boots, he ran blindly forward, his breath beating wide clouds that fanned out around him. His eyes were watering with the cold. At the edge of the field, the ground dipped down into a streambed, where he got stuck, briefly, among the icy rocks, and then began to slope upward sharply through the thickets at the lip of the forest.

The tracks were heavy with hesitation here, and they made twisted, uneven holes in the places where her coat and hair had snagged, forcing her to swivel to free herself, or where the trees had come up quickly and into her eyes. My grandfather kept his head low and reached for the boughs of saplings, pulling himself up, exhausted already, but urging himself on and on. Snow, piled thick in the high silence of the pines, slapped down on him as

297

he went. His hands were raw, and he was choking on his own fear, on his inability to move faster, on the urgency of his own disbelief. Perhaps the house would stay dark forever. Perhaps she had gone away for good. He fell, once, twice, and each time he went down into the snow, suddenly much deeper than it seemed, and when he came up, his nostrils were full, and he had to wipe the sting out of his eyes.

He did not know how much farther he had to go. Perhaps the tiger's wife had left hours before. Perhaps she had already met the tiger, somewhere far ahead in the woods, and the two of them had gone ahead, into the winter, leaving him behind. And what if the stories were not as false and ridiculous as he had previously thought—what if, by the same magic that made him a man, the tiger had changed the girl into a tiger as well? What if my grandfather stumbled onto the two of them, and she did not remember him? As my grandfather went, arm over arm, his heart making sour little shudders against his ribs, he kept listening for a sound, the sound of the tiger, the sound of anything but his own feet and lungs. He was pulling himself up, up, up where the roots of the trees made a curve over what looked like the lip of a hill. Then he was standing in a clearing, and he saw them.

There, where the trees sloped briefly down onto a cradle in the side of the mountain, the tiger's wife, still herself, still human, shoulders draped with hair, was kneeling with an armful of meat. The tiger was nowhere in sight, but there was someone else in the clearing, fifteen or twenty feet behind her, and my grandfather's relief at finding

298

the girl was overwhelmed now by the realization that this unexpected figure—changing before his eyes from man to shadow and back again—was Dariša the Bear, enormous and upright, advancing through the snow with a gun on his arm.

My grandfather wanted to shout a warning, but he stumbled forward instead, breathless, his arms high to pull himself out of the snow. The tiger's wife heard nothing. She was kneeling quietly in the glade, digging. And then Dariša the Bear was on her. My grandfather saw him grab the tiger's wife and pull her to her feet, and already she was thrashing like an animal in a head-snare; Dariša had her by the shoulder, and her body was arching forward, away from him, her free arm jerking over her head to claw at his face and his hair, and all the while she was making a hoarse, rasping sound, like a cough, and my grandfather could hear her teeth clacking together, hard.

She was enormous and clumsy, and then Dariša stumbled forward and pushed her into the snow, and she fell and disappeared, and my grandfather couldn't see her in the darkness, but he was still running. Then Dariša was getting to his knees, and my grandfather put his hands out and shouted— one long, endless howl of fear and hatred and despair—and launched himself onto Dariša's shoulders, and bit his ear.

Dariša did not react as quickly as you might expect, probably because, for a moment, he may have thought the tiger was on him. Then he must have realized that something small and human was gnawing on his ear, and he reached around, and my grandfather hung on and on, until Dariša finally caught hold of my grandfather's coat and peeled him off with one arm, off and onto the ground. My grandfather lay stunned. Above him, the trees were steep and sharp and lost in the darkness, and the sounds around his head vanished in the snow. Then the furious face of Dariša the Bear, neck dark with blood, and weight coming down on my grandfather's chest—Dariša's knee or elbow—and then, before he even knew it was happening, my grandfather's hand was closing on something cold and hard it contacted in the snow and raising it straight up against Dariša's nose. There was a crack, and a sudden burst of blood, and then Dariša fell forward over my grandfather and lay still.

My grandfather did not get up. He lay there, the coarse hairs of Dariša's coat in his mouth, and he listened to the dull thud of a heartbeat, unsure whether it was his own or Dariša's. And then the blood-brown, sticky hands of the tiger's wife rolled the man over, and pulled my grandfather to his feet. She was ashen, the skin beneath her eyes tight and gray with fear, and she was turning his face this way and that, uselessly bundling him deeper into his coat.

And then my grandfather was running again. The tiger's wife was running beside him, gripping his hand like she might fall. She was breathing hard and fast, small sounds that lodged in her throat. My grandfather hoped she might call to the tiger somehow, but he didn't know how, and he didn't know whether he was supposed to be holding her hand or the other way around. He knew, with certainty, that he could run faster, but the tiger's wife had her other arm across her belly, so he kept pace with her, her bundled-up body and her bare feet, and he held her fingers tight.

10

THE CROSSROADS

'No,' Duré said to Fra Antun, 'No, I don't want her, get me somebody else.'

But the crowd along the fence had thinned out, the campground lighting up, restaurants along the boardwalk reopening, and the kid who had gone looking for a volunteer had not come back. Duré tried to wait him out, but night was falling, and after a few minutes without better prospects he was forced to consult his green paper for any rules that might explicitly prohibit me from taking the rag heart up to the crossroads.

'For God's sake,' he said at last, his face falling. 'Have you at least got a patron saint in your family?'

'Where's that written?' I said, trying to get a look at the paper.

'Doesn't matter,' said Duré. 'Who's your patron saint?'

'Lazarus,' I said, uncertain, trying to picture the icon hanging from the handle of my grandma's sewing drawer. This seemed sufficient for Duré, and he gave in.

'Tomorrow,' he said. 'I'll send the boys around tomorrow.'

'Send them all tonight,' Zóra said. 'And the little girl.'

Even before he handed me the jar I had

admitted to myself that my desire to bury the heart on behalf of his family had nothing to do with good faith, or good medicine, or any kind of spiritual generosity. It had to do with the *mora,* that man who came out of the darkness to dig up jars, and who was probably just someone from the village playing a practical joke—but who was, nevertheless, gathering souls at a crossroads sixty kilometers from where my grandfather had died, a ferry ride from the island of the Virgin of the Waters, three hours from Sarobor, and there was no way around these things, not after I had been thinking about them all afternoon, not with my grandfather's belongings in my backpack. I was prepared, of course, for a prankster. I was prepared for an awkward exchange, an encounter in which I caught three teenagers digging up the jar to steal coins from the hole, putting their cigarettes out in the well-loved ashes of the heart. It was also possible—more than possible, in fact, probable, really, the likeliest of all possibilities— that no one would appear, and that I would wait at the crossroads all night, watching the wind come through the slanted green plot of the neighboring vineyard. Or that, in my exhaustion, I would fall asleep or begin to hallucinate. Or it would be the deathless man, tall and wearing his coat, coming down through the fields of long grass above the town—smiling, always smiling—and then I would sit, without breathing, in some bush or under some tree while he dug up the jar, probably whistling to himself, and when he had it in his hand, I would come out and ask him about my grandfather.

The sun had set, bringing the sky low and spreading thin clouds into corners of the horizon where the light was still standing. The tide had risen suddenly, gray and heavy and massive on the shore below. Fra Antun volunteered to show me the way to the crossroads, and we took a road up from the vineyard into the open space between the town and the mountain, and were walking south along the ridge, through a field of bristles and purple and red flowers scattered in tight clusters, out of which grasshoppers, black and singing, fell like arrows as we passed. Fra Antun was walking a few steps ahead, in silence, probably considering how he would broach the subject of my disappearance earlier that afternoon. I followed with a garden spade in my pocket and the little clay jar in my hands, terrified that I was going to drop it, or that it was going to tilt and spill ash-water over me. I had the backpack thrown over one shoulder, and as it swung back and forth, I could hear the muted crackle of the blue bag from Zdrevkov. We passed a young boy bringing six gray-faced sheep down from the mountain—we heard them before we saw them, and long after they had gone, we could hear the steady clang of the ram's bell.

'It's very kind of you to do this,' Fra Antun said suddenly, looking back at me, and I shook my head.

'At least they'll come for medicine now,' I said, and I thought of Zóra down in the graveyard, waiting patiently to start wiping people's mouths and handing out water.

'I'm sure your time could be better spent,' he said, and for a moment I thought he was reproaching me, but then he turned and smiled back at me, and I smiled back and kept walking.

'You're looking after sixty children, Father,' I said eventually. 'I'm just burying a jar.' Fra Antun was holding up the hem of his cassock, and I could see sandals and frayed jeans underneath. 'There are a lot of paintings of your dog in town,' I said. 'At the monastery, at your mother's house.'

'Bis isn't mine,' he said, 'Bis is Arlo's dog—my brother, Arlo.'

'Did your brother do the paintings at Nada's house?'

'Some of them,' he said. 'But then a lot of people took to it after the war.'

'The children seem really attached to him,' I said, and it all seemed to make sense to me. 'Does Arlo bring the dog around for them to play with?'

'My brother is dead,' he said shortly. We had come up to a slight rise in the road, and here the path through the grass veered off and up the hill, but Fra Antun pressed on into the field, where the sticky, switch-thin blades were sawing against each other. I was still going after him, and trying to think of something to say to that, something besides *I'm sorry,* when he stopped abruptly and turned. 'For my mother, it's been very hard.' I nodded, and Fra Antun scratched the back of his neck with his hand. 'Arlo was fifteen the year before the war started, and he made friends with some boys who were staying with us on vacation. One day they all went camping up at Bogomoljka, just five or six kids, for a night or two. A few nights went by—he was fifteen you know, we thought maybe he was acting up, acting out. This was a few months before the war. We didn't look for him. He'd been gone a week. My father went down to throw the trash out in the dumpster in our drive,

304

and there he was.'

I said: 'I'm sorry,' and regretted it immediately, because it just fell out of my mouth and continued to fall, and did nothing.

'Anyway,' he said, without hearing me, 'that whole week he was gone, Bis sat next to the dumpster and didn't move, and we all thought he was waiting by the road for Arlo to come back. Except we had it wrong—he was waiting for us to find Arlo.' Fra Antun took off his glasses and wiped them on his cassock. 'So—we found out a few years later that those kids he had gone camping with were serving with the paramilitary on the border. And now, people paint Bis.'

He had his hands inside the sleeves of his cassock, and then he said again that it had been very hard for his mother, and I wanted to say I knew, but I didn't know. He could have said *your paramilitary,* but he didn't. I kept waiting for him to say it, but he didn't, and then I let him not say anything, and I didn't say anything, either, and then he told me, 'It's not much further now.' We kept walking, side by side, over the rise and then down a slight dip in the field, where a low evening fog was pinning itself to the side of the mountain. Below us, at the bottom of the incline, lay a dirt track that led straight up and onto the steepest part of the slope, where the scrub grew close and dark, and, going across it, another track that led out of the field and into the spider-leafed plot of the vineyard.

When we got to the crossroads, Fra Antun showed me the shrine of the Virgin. It was on a shelf that had been carved into the seaward side of a boulder that stood in the grass where the two roads met. The Virgin, a wooden icon with dark edges where water had damaged the wood, stood propped up on the stone shelf, and flowers, dry as paper, lay piled in neat, dark bunches around the base of the stone. Several feet away, the grass was bright with beer cans and cigarette butts, which Fra Antun began picking up with his hands while I knelt down and got out my spade and thrust the point of it into the dirt. The ground was hard, packed tight, and eventually I settled on scraping it away instead of trying to spoon it out. Every so often, I looked over my shoulder at Fra Antun, who was piling the cans and bottles and leftover wrappers into the apron he had made out of the front of his cassock. When he was done, he lit the candle on the shrine, and I put the jar into the hole I had made, and then dropped three coins in with it. I mounded the earth, like he told me to, packed it tight over the top of the jar, and then straightened up, dusted off my hands. I asked him if it would be difficult to get back to town in the dark, in case I had to before morning.

He looked at me with surprise. 'You're not thinking of staying?'

'I said I would.'

'No one ever stays,' said Fra Antun, and he sounded serious. 'There are foxes out here, Doctor, that carry rabies—and obviously people who come to drink. I can't let you stay.'

'I'll be all right,' I said.

Fra Antun tried again. 'Men, Doctor, who get drunk around here.' He looked like he was contemplating how he was going to force me to come with him. 'I absolutely insist,' he said.

'I was in Zdrevkov earlier today,' I said. It was

306

supposed to make him feel better about my decision to stay, but he took off his glasses and touched his wrist to each eye, very slowly.

'Doctor,' he said again.

'I'll stay here,' I said. And then I said: 'Part of the goodwill service.' It wasn't entirely a lie, and he couldn't argue with it. And I couldn't tell him the truth.

He looked around, and then he said: 'I must ask you to stand in the vineyard, then, and you must promise not to leave it till morning.'

'Why?'

'They say the vines are holy,' he said. 'The blood of Christ.' He pushed his glasses up nervously, and then he took my arm, and we walked twenty feet off the road and into the first rows of the vineyard. He was tucking me in, I realized, tucking me as far back into the vines as possible. He held my hand, and he kept looking up the mountain and then down toward the water, picking his way between the vines, pulling me behind him. 'It doesn't matter, of course,' he said, once he'd picked a spot. 'No one is actually going to come, Doctor. You know that, you must know that.' I nodded hard. 'But it will give me peace of mind to know you're off the road,' he said, smiling. 'We're all entitled to our superstitions.'

I watched him as he walked out between the vines. He waved to me once he got out, and I could barely see him, but I waved back, and then I stayed where I was and watched him as he went through the field slowly, without looking over his shoulder, and his failure to do this worried me now that I was alone. The cans in his cassock were rattling, and I could hear them after he had disappeared over the

307

rise and down the road that led to the graveyard below.

It was very late, but the remaining light of the day was still falling on the sea, settling in cones behind the peaks of the offshore islands. At eleven it was late evening, a cloudless night, and the moon was surfacing above the summit of Mount Brejevina, casting before it a net of brightness that crept up and up and made new shadows on the ground. There was nowhere to sit, so I stood with the vines shuddering around me until I got tired, and then I crouched down in the dirt and watched the flickering light of the Virgin's candle through the wooden legs of the vineyard. I put the backpack down in front of me and opened the flap so I could see the blue bag, but with the fading of the light it had gone gray like everything else.

For the first two hours, I had no visitors, and it's possible that I fell asleep, because I don't remember how that time passed. Then, I expect, it got late enough for the movement of nocturnal things, and an owl fared in from somewhere behind me and landed in the field, the white ruff of its feathers rearing up around the swiveling head while it listened for something I couldn't hear. It sat with me for a long time, wide-eyed and silent, shifting from side to side, and then, when I got up to stretch my legs, it was gone. Mice were in the vineyard, the quick movement of their feet. The cicadas sang in waves, in lulls and roars of sound that drifted in from the field. Around two-thirty, I heard what I thought were footsteps, and I stood up and tried to get a look at the shrine, but it was only a donkey coming down from the mountain, brown, big-headed, disinterested. It had shy eyes,

308

and it entered the vineyard a little way down from me, and I could hear it moving off through the leaves, making a dry snorting sound as it went. It left a warm, sweet smell behind it.

My grandfather, I realized, would have called me a lot of things for staying there. It hadn't occurred to me that, if anyone came, they might come through the vineyard, too, and we might surprise each other, in which case I could get shot, or stabbed, or worse.

At three-fifteen, a fox ran by out of nowhere. I had confined myself to my square of vineyard, and hadn't moved at all, and it came in with a shriek that rose up through me from the ground and rattled me completely. It sounded like a child, and I was looking around for it before I was even on my feet, but then I saw the fox, or, at least, the rings that were the fox's eyes, and then the silver flash of the tail receding into darkness, and then I thought, *the hell with this.*

My feet were asleep. I waited out the pins and needles and made my way to the edge of the vineyard, and then I saw that somehow the candle on the shrine had gone out.

Someone was already there.

From where I was standing I could see the curved back of a figure hunched over the ground by the boulder. When I saw it, I backed quickly into the vineyard and continued to stare between the leaves. I didn't know where the man had come from, I couldn't understand how I hadn't heard his approach.

He was digging: slowly, methodically, with both hands, throwing up small black showers of dirt, its shadow spread out like a wing across the white boulder. Then he found the jar, and I heard the sound of his hand on the coins—one, two, three. All that certainty I had felt that nothing would come, and now this. And I found myself barely able to stand, let alone come out and say, *Are you the deathless man? Are you?* in a voice convincing enough to deserve an answer.

He had the jar, and he turned away from the shrine. He did not start down the road to Brejevina then, but instead began a slow ascent up the mountain. I waited until I could see the outline of him on the first roll below the tree line, and then I followed.

11

THE BOMBING

Gavran Gailé

A few years before my grandfather died, bombs were falling on the City. It was the final collapse, years after it had first begun, and it had finally reached us. Bombs were falling, and they were falling on government buildings and banks, on the houses of war criminals—but also on libraries, on buses, on bridges that spanned the two rivers. It came as a surprise, the bombing, especially because the way it started was so mundane. There was an announcement, and then, an hour later, the scream of the air raid siren. All of it was going on outside, somehow, even when the sound of the bombs hitting started coming in through the open

310

windows, and even when you went outside, you could tell yourself it was some kind of crazy construction accident, that the car, flung seventy-five feet into the façade of a brick building, was just some kind of terrible joke.

Bombs were falling, and the entire City shut down. For the first three days, people did not know how to react—there was hysteria, mostly, and people evacuated or tried to evacuate, but bombs were falling up and down the two rivers, and there was nowhere to go to avoid them. Those who stayed in the City were convinced that it wouldn't last more than a week, that it was ineffective and expensive, and that they would just give up and go away, and there was nothing to do but stick it out. On the fourth day of the bombing, compelled by the irresistible need for certain kinds of freedoms despite the circumstances—or, perhaps, because of them—people started going to coffeehouses again, sitting on the porches, often staying out to drink and smoke even after the sirens sounded. There was an attitude of outdoor safety—if you were outside, people reasoned, you were a much smaller, moving target, while if you sat in your building, you were just waiting for them to miss what they were actually aiming for and hit you instead. The coffeehouses stayed open all night, their lights darkened, the television hissing in a back room, people sitting quietly with their beers and iced teas, watching the useless red waterfalls of light from the antiaircraft guns on the hill.

While it was happening, my grandfather didn't read about it, and didn't talk about it, not even to my mother who, for the first three days of bombing, became the kind of person who yelled at the television and didn't turn the set off even when she went to bed—as if keeping it on would somehow isolate her from the thunder outside, as if our city's presence on the screen could somehow contain what was happening, make it reasonable and distant and insignificant.

I was twenty-two, interning at the Military Academy of Medicine. To me, the persistence of my grandfather's rituals meant that he was unchanged, running on discipline and continuance and stoicism. I didn't notice, and didn't realize, that the rituals themselves were changing, that there was a difference between the rituals of comfort and the preventive rituals that come at the end of life. He still went out as though he had a full roster of house calls to make, but his lifelong patients were beginning to die, to fold slowly to the maladies of old age, even with him there. His daily exercises continued, but they were the perfunctory exercises of an old man: facing the living room window in the pale morning light, his sweatpants loose and hitched up above his socks, his hands clasped behind his back in a matter-of-fact way while he rose to the balls of his feet and fell back onto his heels, rhythmically, with a thump that reverberated through the whole apartment. He did this daily, and without deviation, even with the sirens grinding a howl on the next block.

For twenty years, we had watched the four-o'clock showing of *'Allo 'Allo!* together. Now, there were afternoon naps. He slept sitting up, with his head bent. His feet stuck straight out in front of him, and his body was propped up entirely on the heels of his clogs. His hands were folded across his stomach, which was usually growling, because in

312

addition to everything else, he was now frowning, without precedent, over the things my grandma cooked for us, over *burek* and *paprikash* and stuffed peppers, things I remembered him eating with relish in the past, meals he would sigh delightedly over during otherwise silent dinners. It happened while I wasn't looking, but Grandma was preparing separate meals for him now, because she couldn't bear to subject the rest of us to the punishment of eating boiled greens twice a day and poached meat for dinner, which was all he ate, strictly and uncomplaining.

His trips to the zoo had become a thing of the past long before the bombing forced the City to close its gates. There was a lot of speculation about this closure—people, not just my grandfather, were furious, felt it was a sign of giving up, accused the City of using the bombing as an excuse to slaughter the animals to save on resources. Indignant, the authorities set up a weekly newspaper column that ran current pictures of the animals and reported on their well-being, on the birth of their cubs, on plans for zoo renovation when the raids were over.

My grandfather began to cut out newspaper clippings about the zoo. I would come home in the early mornings, after my shift at the hospital, to find him taking breakfast by himself, removing the back section of the newspaper and looking through it angrily. There was disaster, he would tell me, at the zoo.

'This business is very bad for us,' he said, tilting his head up to look through his bifocals, his tray of seeds and nuts half-finished, his water glass tinted with the orange of fiber supplements.

The story in the newspaper focused on the tiger,

and only on the tiger, because, despite everything, there was still some hope for him. It said nothing about how the lioness aborted and the wolves turned and ate their cubs, one by one, while the cubs howled in agony and tried to run. It said nothing about the owls, splitting open their unhatched eggs and pulling the runny red yolk, bird-formed and nearly ready, out of the center; or about the prized Arctic fox, who disemboweled his mate and rolled around in her remains until his heart stopped under the lancing lights of the evening raids.

Instead, they said that the tiger had begun to eat his own legs, first one and then the other, systematically, flesh to bone. They had a picture of the tiger, Zbogom—the aging son of one of my childhood tigers—sprawled out on the stone floor of his cage, his legs, stiff as boards, tied up behind him like hams. You could see the thick black marks where the flesh of his ankles had been soaked in iodine, and the newspaper said that nothing could abate that particular compulsion—they had tried tranquilizers, chains, bandages dipped in quinine. They had modified a dog funnel and taped it to his neck, but he had eaten the funnel during one of the night raids, and afterward he had eaten two of his own toes.

Two days after the tiger article ran, bombers hit the bridge over the South River and, within two hours of its collapse, they hit the abandoned car factory beside the zoo and Sonja, our adopted African elephant—beloved zoo mascot, small-eyed matriarch of the citadel herd, lover of peanuts and of small children—fell dead on the spot.

For weeks, the City had been trying to process

the suddenness of the war, the actuality of its arrival, and we had treated it as something unusual and temporary; but, after that particular raid, something changed, and all the indignation and self-righteousness that had seeped over from the end of the last war was now put to good use. Every night afterward, people marched for miles to stand shoulder to shoulder at the citadel gate. Others, meanwhile, stood packed in inebriated rows on the stone arches of our remaining bridges. You had to be drunk for the bridge guard, because the chances you would be hit were higher, and after that the chances got higher still that you would die, because standing on either end would not spare you from a fall into the water if the middle was hit.

Zóra, braver than anyone I knew, spread out her defensive agenda—she spent her nights with thousands of people by the stone knees of the dead Marshall's horse on the east bank of Korčuna, wearing a toucan hat in solidarity with the people guarding the zoo. She can tell stories about the bombing of the First National bank, how she watched a missile hit the old brick building across the river, the vacuum of sound as the blue light went down, straight down, through the top of the building and then blasted out the windows and the doors and the wooden shutters, the bronze name on the building, the plaques commemorating the dead—all of this followed by the realization, once the smoke cleared, that despite everything, the building didn't fall, but stood there, like a jawless skull, while people cheered and kissed and, as the newspapers would later point out, started a baby boom.

During the war, I had begged my grandfather to

315

give up on his nightly house calls, on the rituals that made him feel productive; now, against his wishes—which he expressed with a more colorful vocabulary than even I had allowed myself at fourteen—I was holding vigil at the zoo on my nights off. The crowd there was different, older. People would begin to arrive around seven o'clock, in time for the last round of the popcorn cart, and then we would stand in small groups on the sidewalk that ran around the citadel wall, wearing the regalia of our beast of choice. The lion-woman was there, wearing a yellow mop as a wig. One man had tied wire hangers around his head and put white socks on them as ears and come to stand for Nikodemus, our giant Welsh rabbit. A few people came as the wolf pack, wearing toilet rolls as snouts, and there was a woman who had been to the zoo only once, as a child, and had come dressed the way she remembered her first and only giraffe: yellow and with stumpy horns. I didn't have the heart to tell her she'd forgotten the blotches. I came for the tiger, of course, but the best I could do was paint a Davy Crockett-style cap from my old dress-up box in the basement with orange and black stripes, and stand there with the monstrous fake raccoon tail hanging over my back. The fox was a man dressed in a red suit, bow tie, and glasses. The zoo had never had a panda, but we had six or seven pandas guarding the citadel gate, loofah tails sticking out of their pants. The hippo wore a purple sweater, with a pillow tucked underneath.

People were also writing on the zoo wall with chalk and spray paint, and, a few weeks in, they began arriving with placards that favored an attitude of friendly reportage over the standard FUCK YOUS that were being held aloft up and down the bridges. A gray-clad man with a pink towel over his head appeared one evening at the zoo gates holding up a sign that said: AIM HERE, I AM AN ELEPHANT. There was also a famous guy from lower Dranje, where the water tower had been hit, who originally posed as a duck, but then showed up on the sidewalk the day after the cotton factory bombing with the announcement: I NOW HAVE NO CLEAN UNDERWEAR. After that, the newspapers were flooded with overhead shots of his poster, the red lettering, his frayed gray gloves clutching the cardboard. He appeared again, in a week or two, bearing the message: NO UNDERWEAR AT ALL. Someone else held up a sign that read: ME NEITHER.

Zóra and I swapped stories over our shifts at the clinic, where we bandaged heads and arms and legs, helped make room for the wounded, assisted in the maternity ward, supervised the distribution of sedatives. From the office window on the third floor of Sveti Jarmo hospital, you could see the trucks coming in from the bomb sites, the tarps laid out on the stone courtyard, laden with parts of the dead. They were not like the parts we saw in anatomy, fresh, connected to their related tissues, or to the function that gave them meaning. Instead, they made no sense, lying there red and clotted, charred at the sides, in piles to which you could only guess they belonged—legs, arms, heads. They had been picked out of ditches, trees, the rubble of buildings where they had been blown by the force of the bombs, with the purpose of identifying the dead, but you could barely

317

distinguish what they were, much less try to assign them to the bodies, faces, persons of loved ones.

*   *   *

I came home one day to find my grandfather standing in the hallway in his big-buttoned coat, wearing his hat. I came in while he was tying his sash carefully, tucking *The Jungle Book* back into the coat's inside pocket. The dog was sitting on the footstool by the door, and he was talking to the dog in that voice, and the dog was already leashed, waiting.

I kissed him, and I said: 'Where are you going?'

'We've been waiting,' he said, of the dog and himself. 'We're coming with you tonight.'

It was the last time we went to the citadel together, and we walked the whole way. It was a bright, clear autumn evening, and we went down our street until we reached the Boulevard of the Revolution and then turned uptown along the cobbled road that ran beside the tramway. Trams went by, quiet and old, as empty as the street, the tracks slick with the afternoon's rain. There was a soft, cold wind blowing up the Boulevard toward us, raising leaves and newspapers against our legs, and against the face of the dog, who was running openmouthed, in short, fat-legged strides, between us. I had put an orange bow on the dog, to honor the tiger, and I had offered my raccoon hat to my grandfather, and he had looked at me and said, 'Please. Leave me some dignity.'

It had been predicted that there would be no air raid that night, so the sidewalk at the zoo was practically empty. The lion-woman was there, leaning against a lamppost, and we exchanged hellos and then she went back to her newspaper. A guy I'd seen only once or twice was sitting on the zoo wall, turning the dials of a handheld radio. We sat down on the bus-stop bench and my grandfather put the dog, with its fat muddy feet, on his knees, and for about twenty minutes we watched the general confusion of the intersection with the broken traffic light that no one had fixed in almost a month. Then the siren across town went off, followed by another, closer siren, and two minutes later we saw the first blast to the southwest, across the river, where they were starting on the old compound of the Treasury. I remember being surprised that the dog just sat there, looking noncommittal, while the ambulance vans from Sveti Pavlo lit up and streamed out of the garage down the street. I was comforting my grandfather about the tiger, telling him about how they dealt with crippled cats and dogs in America, how sometimes they made little wheelchairs they'd harness onto the animal's side, and then the cat or dog could live a perfectly normal life, with its haunches in a little pet wheelchair, wheeling itself around and around the house.

'They're self-righting,' I said.

For a long time, my grandfather said nothing. He was taking treats out of his pocket and giving them to the dog, and the dog was scarfing them down noisily and sniffing my grandfather's hands for more.

All through the war, my grandfather had been living in hope. The year before the bombing, Zóra had managed to threaten and plead him into addressing the National Council of Doctors about recasting past relationships, resuming hospital collaboration across the new borders. But now, in the country's last hour, it was clear to him, as it was to me, that the cease-fire had provided the delusion of normalcy, but never peace. When your fight has purpose—to free you from something, to interfere on the behalf of an innocent—it has a hope of finality. When the fight is about unraveling—when it is about your name, the places to which your blood is anchored, the attachment of your name to some landmark or event—there is nothing but hate, and the long, slow progression of people who feed on it and are fed it, meticulously, by the ones who come before them. Then the fight is endless, and comes in waves and waves, but always retains its capacity to surprise those who hope against it.

Our vigil at the zoo came more than a year before we found out he was ill, before the secret visits to the oncologist, our final alliance. But the body knows itself, and part of him must have already been aware of what was starting when he turned to me, and told me for the last time about the deathless man.

*   *   *

My grandfather rubbed his knees and said:
The siege of Sarobor. We've never talked about it. Things were bad then, but there was a chance that they would improve. There was a chance they wouldn't go all to hell immediately. I was at a conference on the sea, and I was about to drive home when I got a call about some wounded men at Marhan.

I get to Marhan and it's this mass of tents and men, and some people have been shot in a skirmish a few miles up the road, and they tell me while I'm bandaging them up, while I'm waiting for the medical relief, that they're there to take out the airplane factory in the Marhan Valley, first with heavy artillery and then with men. After that, they say, they're going into Sarobor. Sarobor—can you imagine? Sarobor, where your grandma was born. So, I find the general and I ask him, *what the hell is this?* Do you know what he says to me?

He says: 'The Muslims want access to the sea, so we'll send them to it, downriver, one by one.'

What can I tell you about that? What is there to say? I married your grandmother in a church, but I would still have married her if her family had asked me to be married by a *hodza*. What does it hurt me to say happy Eid to her, once a year—when she is perfectly happy to light a candle for my dead in the church? I was raised Orthodox; on principle, I would have had your mother christened Catholic to spare her a full dunking in that filthy water they keep in the baptismal tureens. In practice, I didn't have her christened at all. My name, your name, her name. In the end, all you want is someone to long for you when it comes time to put you in the ground.

I leave Marhan. But I don't go home. You're at home, and your mother, and your grandma, but that's not where I go. My relief comes, and it's this young doctor. I can't remember his face. He comes, and I say my goodbyes and I leave, and then I go out onto the road and I walk all afternoon until I get to Sarobor. It's fifty centigrade going into the Amovarka Valley,

321

everything is dry and pale green and very quiet, except for the shelling, which is starting now in Marhan. This is thirteen years ago, you understand, and the war is hardly even a war yet. This was when they had the big olive grove on the hills above the town. You probably can't remember what that town was like before they started on it, before they shelled the Muslim neighborhoods and dropped that old bridge into the river like a tree, like nothing.

I go down into Sarobor, and it's deserted. Night is falling. Up and down the Turkish quarter, you can hear our men shelling the factory out in the Marhan valley, and you can see the lights over the hill. You can tell what's coming next, you know what's coming. Everyone knows, so no one is outside, and there are no lights in the windows. There's a smell of cooking—people are sitting down to dinner in the dark. There's a rich dinner smell that makes me think of that irrational desire that comes over you when it is almost the end— instead of saving for a siege they're feasting in the houses along the river, they've got lamb and potatoes and yogurt on their tables. I can smell the mint and the olives, and sometimes when I pass the windows I can hear frying. It makes me think of the way your grandma used to cook while we lived in Sarobor, standing by the window with the big willow tree outside.

The Turkish quarter has that narrow street that runs along the river on the Muslim side of town, with the closed-up Turkish coffeehouses and the restaurants where you buy the best *burek* in the world, the places that sell hookah pipes, glassmakers' workshops, and then the flower gardens that are all dug up now for the new graveyards. All along the street, as you follow it down to the riverbank, you can look up to see the Old Bridge in the distance, with those gleaming, round guard-towers. And every few feet, you pass Turkish fountains. Those fountains—that is the sound of Sarobor, Sarobor always sounds like running water, like good clean water, from the river to the cisterns. Then there's the old mosque, with that lonely minaret lit up like a shell.

I cross the Old Bridge, and I go down to the Hotel Amovarka, where your grandma and I spent our honeymoon before we found an apartment to live in. It's where foreign dignitaries and ambassadors stay when they come to Sarobor. The director of the airplane factory in Marhan—the one we're bombing—sometimes stays there for months on end. The hotel stands on this stone shelf at the river's edge, banked by olive trees and palms, overlooking the water at the top of the cataract. It has these white-curtained windows and a balcony that looks like a woman's skirt, all these round stone folds that come out over the water. There's brass Turkish lanterns on the balcony. You can see the balcony from the Old Bridge, and if you take an evening walk from the hotel you can stand on the bridge and look down over the cataract and the balcony restaurant, where they have a four-man orchestra that goes from table to table, playing love songs.

Inside, the hotel has those wooden screens and red-and-white painted arches. It's got the pasha's tapestries hung up on every wall, and old wingback chairs and a fire in the lobby. I come in, and the place is empty, completely empty. I cross through without seeing anybody, not a soul, not even at the counter. I go down a long hallway, and then I find myself in the front room of the balcony restaurant.

There's a waiter there, just one waiter. He's got very little hair, and it's all white and combed forward over his head, and he's got a big black bruise on his forehead, clear as day, that devout Muslim bruise you can always recognize. He's strapped into his suit, and he's got his tie on and his napkin over his arm. He sees me come in and he lights up. Like he's thrilled to see me, like it's the best news of his day that I am there. He asks me if I want dinner, and he says it in a way that is intended to encourage me to stay even though no one else is having dinner, and I say yes, I want dinner, I want dinner, of course. I am thinking of my honeymoon, and I am thinking they have lobster there, all kinds of fish they bring up on riverboats from the sea.

'Where would sir like to sit?' he says to me, and he gestures around the room. The restaurant has a high, yellow ceiling with a battle painted on it, and these brass lanterns and red curtains hanging from the ceiling, and the whole room, like the rest of the hotel, is completely empty.

'On the balcony, please,' I say. He leads me out to the balcony and seats me at the best table in the house, which is made up for two, and he takes away the other fork and knife and napkin and plate.

'With apologies, sir,' he says to me. He has this hoarse, rasping voice, even though I can tell from his hands and his teeth he's never smoked a day in his life. 'We have only the house wine tonight.'

324

'That will do just fine,' I say.

'And we have it only by the bottle, sir,' he says. I tell him to bring me the bottle, and also that I will be staying the night, if he would be so good as to find someone at the front desk who can help me. I know you're thinking this is not a good idea. I know you're thinking, those men shelling over the hill are getting ready to come down on Sarobor in the morning. But staying is my plan at the time, and so I say that to him, maybe also to be kind. He is a very old man. And you don't know what our waiters used to be. How they were trained for the old restaurants. They would go to a school, the finest table-service school, right here in the City. They learn their craft, they learn their manner. They're practically chefs. They can recognize a wine with their eyes closed and carve up the carcass themselves, they can tell you what fish swims where and what it eats, they dabble for years in herb gardens before they're permitted to serve. This is the kind of waiter he is, and a Muslim besides, and the whole thing makes me think of your grandma, and I feel ill, suddenly, watching him leave to get my wine.

I sit back and I listen to them down in Marhan. Every few minutes this blue blast lights up the hilltops at the crown of the valley, and a few seconds later comes the cracking sound of the artillery. There's a southerly breeze blowing down to me through the valley, and it brings in the singed smell of gun-powder. I can see the outline of the Old Bridge on the bank above the hotel, and a man is walking up it from the tower on the other side, lighting the lampposts the old-fashioned way, the way it's been done since my

325

time. The river is making a song against the bank under the hotel ledge. I am leaning forward a little to look through the florets in the balcony railing down to where the water is dark against the white rocks of the riverbed. When I lean back, I notice the smell of cigarette smoke nearby, and I look around, and—to my surprise—there is another guest sitting at a table in the opposite corner, with his elbow up on the stone balcony rail. He is wearing a suit and tie, and he is reading, holding the book up so I cannot see his face. The table in front of him is empty, except for a coffee cup, which makes me think he has finished his dinner, and I feel glad he will be leaving soon, he will be finishing his coffee and leaving. He seems completely unaware of the way the bombing is lighting up the sky—like it's a celebration, like fireworks are happening over the hill and the celebration is coming closer. Then I find myself thinking—*maybe it* is *a celebration for him, maybe he has crossed the river tonight to gloat in the old Muslim palace. Maybe, for him, this is something funny, a night he will talk about years from now to his friends when they ask him about sending the Muslims downriver.*

At this moment, the old waiter comes back, bringing with him my bottle. I can remember it now. It's an '88 *Šalimač*, from a famous vineyard that will soon be on our side of the border. He serves it to me like that means nothing to him—and I get the sense that he is bent on showing the great strength of character it takes for him to serve me this wine like it doesn't make the slightest bit of difference to him whether or not the owner of the vineyard is bayoneting his son in the airplane factory right now. He peels the foil off the top of the bottle, and then he uncorks the wine in front of me. He flips my glass and pours me a little, and he blinks at me while I taste it. Then he pours me the whole glass and leaves the bottle on the table. He disappears for a moment, and then he comes back, wheeling in front of him a cart that's covered in big lettuce leaves and bunches of grapes, slices of lemon, all of which are crowded around a centerpiece of fish. The fish are clear-eyed and firm, but they look like something out of a circus.

The waiter says to me: 'Well, sir. Tonight we have the sole, the eel, the cuttlefish, and the John Dory. May I recommend the John Dory? It was freshly caught this morning.'

There are not very many of them, not very many fish—perhaps five or six, but they are neatly arranged, with the two eels curled around the edges of the display. The John Dory is lying on its side like a spiked flat of paper, the spot on its tail staring up like an eye. Of all the fish on the cart, it is the only one that actually looks like a fish, and also the only one not giving off a vaguely dead smell. Now, I love John Dory, but tonight I find myself wanting lobster, and I ask about it, about the lobster. The old waiter bows to me, and apologizes, says that they have just run out.

I tell him I will need a moment to think, and he leaves me with the menu and disappears. I am pretty disappointed about that lobster, I can tell you, as I sit there looking at the dishes they have to go with the fish. They have, of course, what you would expect: they have potatoes several ways, salad with garlic, four or five different sauces to go with the fish, but all the time I am thinking about the lobster, about how they have just run out. And then I think: *my God, it would be awful if this man, this gloating man who is here reading a book, has just had the last lobster, the lobster that should have come to me when I am not here to gloat.*

And just at that moment, as I am thinking this, the old waiter reappears and bows over the man's table.

'And now, sir,' I hear the waiter say to the man. 'Have you had a chance to consider? Is there anything I can offer you to drink?'

'Yes, please,' says the man. 'Water.'

I put my menu down and I look at him. He has lowered the book so that he can speak to the waiter, and I recognize him immediately. The waiter goes to get him the water, and Gavran Gailé does not raise his book back up; instead, he looks out over the river, and then around the balcony, and finally his gaze settles on me, and it is the same gaze of the man from inside the coffin—the same eyes, the same face, unchanged and whole, as it must have been in the drunk tank that night at the Church of the Virgin of the Waters, when I did not have the opportunity to see it.

The deathless man is smiling at me, and I say to him: 'It's you.'

He calls me doctor, and then he gets up and dusts off his coat and comes over to shake my hand. I stand up and hold my napkin, and while we are shaking hands in silence like this, it comes to me why he is here, but I cannot tell myself that I am surprised to see him. No, I realize, I am not surprised at all. His being here can mean only one

328

thing, and, like the rest of us, he knows what is going to happen. He has come to collect, the deathless man.

'What a wonder,' he is saying to me. 'What a remarkable, remarkable wonder.'

'How long have you been in town?' I say.

'Several days now,' he tells me.

I am tired, and all business, and I tell him: 'Without doubt, you have been buying people a great deal of coffee.'

He does not smile at this, but he does not reproach me either. He does not confirm, he does not deny. He is just there. It occurs to me that he never looks tired, he never looks worn. I tell him I insist he join me for dinner, and he does, gladly. He goes to get his book and his cup, and the waiter brings us another place setting for him.

'Do you gentlemen know what you would like?' the waiter asks.

'Not yet,' my friend says to him. 'But we will take *narghile*.'

I wait until the old man has left to get us the pipes, and then I say: 'The best meal of my life, I ate here.' The deathless man nods at me in appreciation. 'During my honeymoon,' I say. 'You have never met my wife. We stayed here for our honeymoon, my wife and I, and we had lobster. Two years after the first time you and I met in that little village—do you remember it?'

'I remember,' he says.

'I was very young,' I say. 'It was a beautiful honeymoon. For a week, I ate nothing but lobster. I could eat it still.'

'Then you should.'

'They haven't any tonight.'

329

'That's a shame.'

'You did not happen to get the last one?' I say.

'As you see,' he tells me, 'I have not eaten.'

We sit in silence for a while, and he does not ask me what I am doing here. This is when it occurs to me that perhaps he knows something I don't—that perhaps it is not someone else he is here to see, but, instead, that he has come to see me, that he is here for me in particular, and that thought fills me up. And I tell you, it is one thing not to believe, but quite another to entertain a possibility, and I don't know if it's the shelling or the evening or the Old Bridge on the water, but that is what I am doing as I sit there, hanging on to that napkin on my knees—I am entertaining the possibility.

'And have you been very busy?' I ask him.

'Not particularly,' he says to me, and he wants to say more, but at this moment the old waiter comes shuffling back with the *narghile,* which he sets up for us, cleaning the pipe lips, setting up the tobacco and *tumbak* in the bowl. When he finishes, there is a sweet roasting smell coming from the pipe, honey-and-rose smell, and he is taking out a pencil and piece of paper to write down our order.

'What do you say to the perch?' the deathless man asks me.

'I am a great lover of John Dory,' I say. 'In the absence of lobster.'

'Shall we have the John Dory?'

'Let's have the John Dory.'

'We'll have the John Dory,' the deathless man says to the old waiter, looking up at him and smiling. The waiter bows from the waist, like we've made a very good choice. Which we have, we've really made a very good choice. It is probably the last John Dory the hotel will ever sell.

'Can I entice the sirs with some *mezze*?' the old waiter says. 'We have an excellent *ajvar* with garlic, and also an octopus salad. We have wonderful *sarma,* and cheese with olives.'

'I feel some indulgence is needed,' the deathless man says. 'Some indulgence is needed tonight. We'll have it all. And, to go with the fish, the boiled potatoes with chard.'

'Very good, sir,' the waiter says while he is writing it all down with a stubby pencil.

'And, naturally, the parsley sauce.'

'Naturally, sir,' says the waiter.

He refills our wine glasses and leaves, and I am sitting there looking at the calm, smiling face of the deathless man, and asking myself why, in particular, indulgence is needed tonight. The deathless man takes the pipe of the *narghile* and begins to puff on it slowly, and big thick clouds of smoke are rising out of his nostrils and mouth and he looks very content, sitting there, with the blasts rocking the valley at Marhan.

I must be looking pretty stupefied at all this, because he asks me: 'Is something wrong?' I shake my head, and he smiles. 'Do not worry about the price, Doctor. This is my treat. It is important—so important—to indulge in these pleasurable things.'

My God, I say to myself, *and now it has come to this. My last meal, and with a deathless man, at that.*

'My best meal,' he says out of nowhere, as if we are still on that subject, 'was at the Big Boar,

331

about sixty years ago.' I do not know why this happens now, but I do not find myself saying, *how? How could you have had a meal like this, when your face says you are thirty, and even that is generous.* He says: 'The Big Boar was a wonderful tavern in the king's hunting park, and you would shoot the game yourself and then the chef would prepare it in his special way. The woman I told you about—the woman who died—she and I went there when we first fled. When we fled from here.'

'I didn't realize she was from Sarobor,' I say.

'Everybody's from somewhere, Doctor. She used to play the gusla there—' he says, pointing down to the Old Bridge, 'just over there.'

The pepper and the octopus salad and the *sarma* arrive, and the waiter arranges the plates, and the deathless man digs right in. It all smells so wonderful, and he is spooning those cabbage leaves and that red pepper onto his plate, and all those oils are running into each other, and the pink-purple octopus tentacles are shining with oil, and I put some on my plate and I eat, too, but I eat slowly, because who knows, maybe it's poisoned, maybe the old waiter is working with a vengeance, maybe that is why the deathless man is here. But it is too difficult not to eat with the lights going off in Marhan, and now Gavran Gailé will not stop talking about the meal we are eating. Every time the waiter comes close, Gavo is talking loudly about how wonderful the flavors are, how fresh the oil—and it is true, the food is wonderful, but I am feeling that he is rubbing it in, this business of it being my last meal, and I am thinking, *My God, what I have done, coming here?*

The waiter brings the John Dory and it is

glorious. The fish is dark and crisp on the outside, and it has been grilled whole. He cuts it up slowly with the fish knife, and the flesh goes soft and feathery under the knife, and he serves it to us on our plates and then ladles out the potatoes with the chard. The potatoes are bright yellow and steaming, and the chard is thick and green and clinging to the potatoes, and the deathless man is eating and eating and talking about how glorious the meal is—which is true, really, it is a glorious meal, and even though you can hear the shelling in Marhan, it is all right with the meal on the balcony and the river and the Old Bridge.

Because I have to know, at a certain point I say: 'Are you here to tell me that I am going to die?'

He looks up at me with surprise. 'I beg your pardon?' he says.

'This meal,' I say. 'Indulgence. If you are here to let me indulge in my last meal, I would like to know this. I would like to call my wife, my daughter, my grandchild.'

'I take it, since you ask that question without provocation, that you have accepted what I am— does that mean you are ready to pay your debt to me, Doctor?'

'Certainly not,' I say.

'Still more proof?'

'We've not even had coffee yet.'

Gavran Gailé picks up a corner of his napkin and he dabs his mouth with it.

'May I see it?'

'What?'

'Your pledge, Doctor. The book. Let me see it.'

'No,' I say, and I am worried.

'Come now, Doctor. I am only asking to see it.'

'I do not ask to see your cup,' I say. But he is not giving up, not taking up his fork and knife, just sitting there. And after a while, I take out my *Jungle Book* and I hold it out to him. He wipes the tips of his fingers before he takes it from me, and then he runs his hand over the cover.

'Oh yes,' he says, as if he remembers it well, remembers the story. He opens it and flips through the pictures and the poems. I am afraid he is going to take it, but I am also afraid that it will upset him to know I don't trust him.

'Rikki Tikki Tavi,' he says to me, handing the book back across the table. 'I remember him. I liked him best.'

'How surprising,' I say, 'that you should like the weasel.' He does not reproach me for saying this, even though we know I am both rude and incorrect: Rikki Tikki is, of course, a mongoose.

Gavran Gailé watches me put the book back in my pocket. He is smiling at me, and he leans forward across the table and quietly says, 'I am here for him,' and he nods at the waiter. He does not say he is not here for me, and I am weary, but suddenly I feel awful for the little old waiter.

'Does he know?'

'How would he know?'

'In the past, you've told them.'

'Yes, and I've learned a thing or two, haven't I? You've been there, Doctor, while I've been learning. If I tell him, he is going to spear me with a kebab stick and I am going to have a difficult recovery, which mustn't happen because—as you say—I am due to be very busy.' He sits back and wipes his mouth with a napkin. 'Besides, what good would it do him to know? He is happy, he is serving an enormous meal to two pleasant people on the eve of war. Let him be happy.'

'Happy?' I am dumbfounded. 'He could be home—he could be with his family.'

'We are indulging ourselves, and so indulging him,' the deathless man says. 'This fellow takes great pride in what he does—and he is serving a glorious and wonderful meal, a memorable one. Tonight, he will go home to his family and talk about serving the last meal of the Hotel Amovarka, and tomorrow when he is gone, those still alive will have this to talk about. They will be talking about it after the war has ended. Do you see?'

The waiter comes and clears away our plates, the big plate with the John Dory on it, the little glass bones all picked clean. He balances the plates on one arm, and still the white napkin is folded over his free arm, and I am filled up with the idea of this memorable meal, which I have not been enjoying for fear.

'May I tempt the sirs with a dessert drink?' the old waiter says. 'Or dessert?'

'All of it,' I am suddenly saying. I am saying: 'We will have the *tulumbe* and the baklava and *tufahije,* and also the *kadaif,* please.'

'With quince *rakija,*' the deathless man says, and when the old waiter leaves, he tells me he is glad that I am getting into the spirit of things.

We do not talk, because I am thinking of how to convince the deathless man to tell the waiter, or perhaps how to tell him myself without the deathless man noticing, and the waiter brings the dessert on an enormous silver tray and sets it down. The *tulumbe* are there, golden and soft and dripping, and the baklava sticks to my mouth, and the roasted apple with the walnuts is lovely and it melts under the fork and all these things come with the quince brandy that burns your throat between bites, and I am a little drunk, now, and watching the fire in the sky over Marhan, I am missing your grandmother's cooking, because her pastries are better than this.

When we are finished, Gavran Gailé pushes his chair back and says: 'Truly.' And he folds his hands over his belly and there is something about him that makes me sad, too.

'Are you going to die tomorrow, too?' I say. 'Is that why you're here?' It is a foolish question, and I realize this as soon as I have asked it.

'Of course not,' he tells me. His fingers are drumming on his belly like a little boy's fingers. 'Are you?' he says.

I do not laugh, even though I think he is joking. 'Even after all this—after this city is razed to the ground, which is what is going to happen tomorrow, without question—you don't believe he will give you permission to die?' I say.

'Of course he won't.' Gavo wipes his mouth with his napkin, and raises his hand for the waiter. The waiter comes and gathers the plates, and before he even asks, the deathless man is saying: 'And now we'll have some coffee.'

And now I am thinking, this is serious. He takes up the *narghile* pipe again and begins to smoke it, and every few puffs he offers me a try, and I refuse. His tobacco smells like wood and bitter roses. The smoke unfurls and goes into the fog that is hanging low, smearing the lights above the bridge. The waiter comes back with our coffee. He

336

begins to set the table, to put down the coffee cups, but the deathless man says, 'No, we will share from this one,' and he pulls out his little white cup with the gold trim.

I make one last attempt, and, while the waiter is in earshot, I say: 'I suppose, now, that you will be asking the gentleman to share our coffee?' I say this rudely, so the waiter will leave and not drink from the cup.

But the deathless man says, 'No, no, the two of us, we had coffee this afternoon—didn't we?' And the old waiter smiles and bows his bald head and I am very sad, suddenly, I am stricken with sadness for the old man. 'No, my friend, this coffee is for you and me,' says the deathless man. When the waiter leaves, Gavo pours the hot coffee into the cup, and hands it to me, and sits back and waits for it to be cold enough. This takes a long time, but eventually I drink down my cup, and my friend is smiling at me.

'Well now,' he says, and takes it from me. It is dark on the balcony, and he is peering inside the cup, and I am leaning forward, and his face is like stone.

'Look here,' he says suddenly. 'Why did you come into Sarobor? You are with the other side.'

'I beg you not to say that,' I tell him. 'I am begging you not to say that aloud again. Do you want that old man to hear?' Gavo is still holding my cup in his hand, and I say: 'I am not with the other side. I have no side. I am all sides.'

'Not by name,' he says.

'My wife was born here,' I tell him, and I am tapping the table with my finger. 'My daughter, too. We lived here until my daughter was six.'

337

'But you seem to know what is going to happen tomorrow. I ask, why did you come? You were not summoned. You did not come here to retrieve anything of value. You came to have dinner—why?'

'That *is* of value to me,' I say. 'And apparently to that poor old man, whom you will not even give a chance to be with his family.'

'He will be with his family tonight, Doctor, when he goes home,' the deathless man says, and he is still patient. I cannot believe how patient he is. 'Why should I tell him that tomorrow he is going to die? So that, on his last night with his family, he will mourn himself?'

'Why did you bother warning the others, then?'

'What others?'

'The others—the man who drowned you, and the man with the cough at the Virgin of the Waters. Why do you not warn him? Those other men were dying, really dying. This man could save himself, he could leave.'

'So could you,' he says.

'I am going to.'

'Are you?' he says.

'I am,' I say. 'Give me that cup, you smiling bastard—there is nothing in it for me.'

But he will not give me the cup, and he says to me: 'You did not answer, Doctor, when I asked you why you had come to Sarobor.'

I drink a lot of wine very quickly, and then I say: 'Because I have loved it all my life. My finest memories are here—my wife, my child. This, all this, is going to hell tomorrow.'

'By coming here, you realize you risk going with it. They could fire off a missile right now and hit

338

this building.'

'Is that going to happen?' I say. I am too angry now to be concerned.

'It may and it may not,' he says.

'So you are not warning me either?'

'No, Doctor—I am talking about something,' he says patiently. 'I am not talking about illness, about a long slow descent into something. I am talking about suddenness. I am trying to explain. I am not warning that man because his life will end in suddenness. He does not need to know this, because it is through the not-knowing that he will not suffer.'

'Suddenness?' I say.

'Suddenness,' he says to me. 'His life, as he is living it—well, and with love, with friends—and then suddenness. Believe me, Doctor, if your life ends in suddenness you will be glad it did, and if it does not you will wish it had. You will want suddenness, Doctor.'

'Not me,' I say. 'I do not do things, as you say, suddenly. I prepare, I think, I explain.'

'Yes,' he says. 'And those things you can do reasonably well for everything—but not this.' And he is pointing into the cup, and I think, *yes, he is here for me, too*. 'Suddenness,' he says. 'You do not prepare, you do not explain, you do not apologize. Suddenly, you go. And with you, you take all contemplation, all consideration of your own departure. All the suffering that would have come from knowing comes after you are gone, and you are not a part of it.' He is looking at me, and I am looking at him, and the waiter comes with the check. The waiter must think something very terrible and private is going on, because he leaves

339

very quickly.

'Why are you crying, Doctor?' the deathless man says.

I wipe my eyes and tell him I hadn't realized I was.

'There is going to be a lot of suddenness, Doctor, over the next few years,' says Gavran Gailé. 'They are going to be long, long years—you can have no doubt about that. But those years will pass, eventually they will end. So you must tell me why you came to Sarobor, Doctor, where you take a risk every minute you sit here, even though you know that one day this war will end?'

'This war never ends,' I say. 'It was there when I was a child and it will be here for my children's children. I came to Sarobor because I want to see it again before it dies, because I do not want it to go from me, like you say, in suddenness.' I have been bunching up the tablecloth and I smooth it out. The deathless man puts crisp, clean bills that will be worth nothing in the morning onto the plate with the check. Then I say: 'Tell me, Gavran Gailé—does the cup say that I will be joining you, tonight, in suddenness?'

He shrugs, and he is smiling at me. There is nothing angry, nothing mean in his smile. There never is. 'What would you like me to say, Doctor?'

'No.'

'Then break your cup,' he says to me, 'and go.'

*   *   *

Months later, for weeks and weeks after the bombing ended, Zbogom the tiger continued to eat his own legs. He was docile, tame, to the keepers,

340

but savage on himself, and they would sit in the cage with him, stroking the big square block of his head while he gnawed on the stumps of his legs. The wounds were infected, swollen, and black.

In the end, without announcing it in the newspaper, they shot that legless tiger there, on the stone slab of his cage. The man who raised him—the man who nursed him, weighed him, gave him baths, the man who carried him around the zoo in a knapsack, the man whose hands appeared in every picture ever taken of the tiger as a cub— pulled the trigger. They say the tiger's mate killed and ate one of her cubs the following spring. To the tigress, the season meant red light and heat, a sound that rises and falls like a scream; so the keepers took the remaining cubs away from her, raised them in their own houses, with their own pets and children. Houses without electricity, with no running water for weeks on end. Houses with tigers.

12

THE APOTHECARY

The man who discovered the death of Dariša the Bear is still living in Galina today. His name is Marko Parović, and he is seventy-seven years old, a great-grandfather. His grandchildren have recently purchased a new lawn mower for him, and he operates this monstrosity by himself, a tiny, hatted, brown-armed man who still somehow manages to aim the orange machine in a straight line across his

341

lawn. He does not talk about Dariša the Bear at night, and he will not talk about him at all without enlisting encouragement from several glasses of rakija.

When he does talk, this is the story he tells:

An hour before first light, Dariša the Bear awoke from his interrupted journey in the bloodied snow. When he sat up and looked about himself, he saw the tiger was eating his heart. There among the black trees of Galina, the yellow-eyed devil sat with his teeth deep in the wet wedge of Dariša's heart. Terrified at first, Dariša felt his ribs and found them empty, and he drew on his only remaining strength, the strength of bears whose hearts he had stilled over the years. His human heart gone, Dariša fell to all fours, and his back rose like a mountain, his eyes full of darkness. His teeth fell like glass from his jaws and in their place grew the yellow tusks of the bear. He reared high over the tiger, black-backed in the moonlight, and the whole forest shook with his roar.

To this day, on such and such a night, you can still hear the ringing of their battle when the wind blows east through the treetops of Galina. Dariša the Bear threw his great, ursine weight into the tiger's side, and the yellow-eyed devil sank his claws into Dariša's shoulders, and the two of them rolled through the snow, jaws locked, leveling trees and laying bare the rocks of the ground.

In the morning, nothing of the terrible battle remained but the empty skin of Dariša the Bear, and a blood-smeared field that will not flower to this day.

*　　　*　　　*

Some hours after daybreak—he had felt certain he would not be able to sleep at all, but somehow, at first light, he had found himself submitting to his own exhaustion, to the terrible cold, to the relief of having brought the tiger's wife safely home—my grandfather awoke to a world that already knew Dariša the Bear was dead. Marko Parović, checking his quail traps at the foot of the mountain, had stumbled upon the red-clotted skin, and he had come running into the village, dragging it behind him, calling for God.

By the time my grandfather climbed out of bed and went to the doorway, a great crowd was already assembling in the square, and the women, their heads wrapped in flower-stippled handkerchiefs, were already shrieking it out:

'Dariša is dead. God has abandoned us.'

My grandfather stood at Mother Vera's side, watching the crowd grow bigger and bigger at the bottom of the stairs. He could see Jovo, the greengrocer, and Mr. Neven, who repaired plows; he could see the priest in his stained black cassock, and the spinster sisters from two doors down, who had come out with their slippers on. Half a dozen other people with their backs turned to him. The first wave of panic at Marko Parović's news had hit, and now my grandfather watched the disbelieving faces of the men and women he had known all his life: the baker, rigid and red-faced with his dough-numbed fingers; the shaking shoulders of the baker's daughter, who was gasping and twisting her hair in her fists like a mourner at a burial. Standing slightly apart was the apothecary, quiet with his coat thrown over his shoulders, looking down at the formless, blood-soaked pelt, all that was left of Dariša the Bear, which lay at their feet as if Dariša had never been alive at all.

The apothecary stooped down and picked up one end of the pelt. Half-lifted, it looked like a wet, hairy wing.

'Poor man,' my grandfather heard a woman say. 'It is too much.'

'We must honor him. We must have a funeral.'

'Look, God—what shall we bury?'

'Here,' my grandfather heard the apothecary say, 'here, are you quite sure there was no trace of him?'

'Sir,' Marko Parović said, spreading his hands. 'Only the trails in the snow where the battle was fought.'

A mutter of horror and admiration passed through the crowd, and people began crossing themselves. The villagers' collective disappointment in Dariša, their rage at his abandonment, the fact that they had been denigrating his name and what he stood for little more than two hours ago—all of this had fallen by the wayside with the news of his death.

One of the village hounds chose that moment to investigate the outspread pelt and raise a leg against it; there was a cry of outrage as six or seven hands reached for the pelt and somebody's boot kicked the dog out of the way, and Vladiša, whose nerves had never recovered from his encounter with the tiger, went down in a dead faint.

'By God, let us take it into church,' the priest said. And while a handful of aghast villagers carried the pelt off in the direction of the church, the apothecary propped Vladiša against the porch steps, and for the first time looked at my grandfather in the doorway.

'Get water,' the apothecary said, and my grandfather ran to the kitchen basin and obliged. He was aware, when he came back, of being carefully studied, of the eyes of the village women on him like shadows. But my grandfather looked only at the apothecary, who smelled of soap and warmth, and who smiled at him as he handed down the water basin.

And then there was a flurry of female voices.

'So, it's you, is it?' the baker's daughter shouted at him, embattled. My grandfather backed up the porch steps and stared down at her. 'Don't you go back in, you just stay out here and show your face. Just look. Look at what's happened.' Mother Vera came out to stand behind my grandfather, and the baker's daughter said, 'Aren't you ashamed? At what cost have you befriended the devil's bitch, made her welcome here? Aren't you ashamed?'

'You mind your own business,' Mother Vera said.

The baker's daughter said: 'It's everybody's business now.'

My grandfather said nothing. With daylight and a few hours' sleep separating him from it, the journey of last night seemed a thousand years ago. His mind could not frame it properly. He suspected—even as the baker's daughter was blaming him for his involvement—that no one actually knew its true level. But there was still a chance that someone would come forward and say they had seen him sneak out of the village the previous night; or, worse still, that they had witnessed his return with the girl, seen him sinking into the snow under the weight of her exertions; or that they had found his tracks before the midnight snowfall had covered them up.

Lying on his cot, his feet cold and his legs twitching, trying to still the nervous jerking of his limbs, certain that the force with which his heart was shuddering through his hair and skin must be audible to Mother Vera, my grandfather had allowed himself to believe that they had gotten away with something. But now, it was impossible not to think of Dariša—and even though my grandfather was too young to completely understand what had happened to the Bear, some feeling of responsibility must have clung to him all his life. As it was, nine years old and terrified, all he could do was stand in the doorway and watch the panic that was shaking the village loose of any sense it had left.

'It has gone too far,' the woodcutter said. 'She'll dispatch us one by one.'

'We must leave, all of us.'

'We must drive the bitch out,' Jovo said, 'and stay.'

In the movements of the men my grandfather saw a new sense of purpose. They had not coordinated themselves yet, but they were on the verge of some decision, and my grandfather felt the inevitability of disaster run by him like a river against whose current he was completely helpless.

He was certain of only one thing: she needed him now more than ever. He had realized it last night, when they stopped in a glade a little way down the mountain, and he had stood over the tiger's wife while she knelt in the snow, watching the breath smoke out of her mouth in long, thin trails, and he had been unable to let go of her hand. He had the sense that whatever made her a grown-up, kept her calm and unafraid, kept her belly as round as the moon, had given way to the terrors of night, and had left her alone, and left him alone with her. It was as if they had lost the tiger, as if the tiger had abandoned them, and it was just the two of them, my grandfather and the tiger's wife.

He had helped her up the stairs of her house last night and he had told her, even though she couldn't hear him, that he would come back in the morning. He would come back with warm tea and water, with porridge for her breakfast, and he would keep her company. Would take care of her. But now, he realized, this was impossible. To leave his house and walk through the square with all of them watching him, to cross the pasture and go into her house, would set something off, a decline without end. He could not do it; he had no authority, no way to brace himself against the shock outside, against the anger of the grown-ups, who were, after all, grown-ups. And she, the tiger's wife, was entirely alone. This thought, above all others, strangled him.

He wanted to explain it to Mother Vera as she forced him back into the house. He wanted to tell her about the previous night, how cold and terrified the girl had been. But he couldn't find a way to explain himself. It occurred to him, then, that she had allowed him to sleep in: she had neglected to wake him at dawn for his chores, or at eight for his breakfast; she had neglected to wake him when Marko Parović had stumbled out of the pasture and past the butcher's house with the

347

bloodied hide in his hands and struck up a cry. She had let him sleep because she had sensed that he needed it. There was nothing more he could tell her. She already knew. And, for whatever reason, she had cut herself away from it, and her eyes told him that, as far as she was concerned, she no longer had a place in the battle.

Hopeless, my grandfather stood at the window and looked on. There was a thin, mud-tinged ring of slush where last night's snow pile was beginning to melt; the village dogs, dirty and matted, were milling around; the fence posts and wide-flung doors of the village houses stood wet and cold, and beyond them the little butcher's house on the edge of the pasture, with its smoking chimney, which seemed impossibly far now. When the apothecary helped Vladiša to his feet and set off for his shop, my grandfather ran outside and went after him.

*   *   *

When people talk about the apothecary of Galina, they rarely mention his appearance. As I find out from Marko Parović, there is a reason for this. 'Dignified,' he says of the apothecary, drawing his hand across his face, 'but very ugly.'

The implication is that, despite whatever unfortunate configuration of his features—or, perhaps, because of it—the apothecary looked trustworthy, at ease with himself, someone to whom people would turn for counsel.

It is less easy to imagine him in one of his many lives before Galina, as a ten-year-old boy, the first time he appears in the stories of other people, when he was found wandering the charred ruins of the monastery of Sveti Petar by a hajduk band, twelve men mounted on scruffy nags who had arrived too late to interrupt a raid by an Ottoman battalion. The monks of Sveti Petar had been accused of hiding a rebel who had killed the nephew of the captain of the battalion in a tavern brawl several weeks earlier—and the captain had personally undertaken the task of avenging both his nephew's death and the more important, slanderous casting of the young man as a drunk. Four days of siege, and then indiscriminate slaughter; for the hajduks, who had spent the morning extracting the dead from the fragile cinders of the chapel, the sight of the apothecary crawling out from under an overturned wagon by the south wall was redemption from God's own hand. Here was a child that had been spared for them; they did not know who he was, could not guess he had been an orphan at the monastery, would never know about his fear, his hatred, his blind recklessness when he had lost patience praying and charged out to face the Turkish cavalry alone. A saber had promptly caught him in the ribs, and he lay there, gasping for air in the smoke-stained dawn while the captain, Mehmet Aga, bent over him and demanded his name, so that he would know who he was about to impale on the stake. He did not tell the hajduks—and no one in Galina would ever find out—that it was not the Aga's admiration for the boy's courage that won him his life, but that name: 'Kasim,' the apothecary said, using, for the last time, the name under which he had been abandoned at the monastery door, 'Kasim Suleimanović,' and the Aga, turned to improbable mercy by the hand of his own God, left him there to seep out into the ashen earth. Saved by his name once, the boy did not expect it to save him again. When the hajduks asked him for it while they bandaged him, he said he couldn't remember.

Then the hajduks gave him a new name—Nenad, the unhoped-for one—but to the apothecary, the new name meant nothing: changed once, he would change it again and again. Yet his old name, and what it had meant, would follow him, unshed, for the rest of his life.

Kasim Suleimanović would follow him during his years with the hajduks, with whom he lived and pillaged with considerable reluctance until he turned eighteen. The name brought uncertainty, the awareness of a certain kind of betrayal whose consequences he would always anticipate. Like a vulture, the name sat at his shoulders, keeping him apart so that he was able to see the flaws that made the hajduks ridiculous: they were determined to give back to the poor, but in their unbridled generosity failed to keep any funds for themselves, which often left them scraping for resources and severely undermined their valiant marauding; they craved victory, but defeat was more honorable, more character-forming, more pleasant to reflect on; their pursuits demanded discretion, but they would break into songs that lauded their own exploits at the first hint of tavern adoration. The apothecary, while he was among them—while he prepared their meals and sharpened their swords, cared for their wounded—did not voice his reservations, could not confess that he thought their endeavors celebrated their own certainty to fail, and were therefore senseless and stupid and unsafe. In every collective tendency of the hajduks, he recognized a willful attempt to forestall security.

The name followed him, too, when the hajduk camp fell to a band of Magyar bounty hunters. It was with him when he dragged his only surviving compatriot, Blind Orlo, out of the debris of their camp and into the woods; it was with him while he tended to Orlo, bound his fractured skull, set the bullet-grazed fibula until an infection swelled Orlo's right leg to twice its size, thundered through his bloodstream for weeks. It was a bitter winter, and the apothecary kept the old man outdoors as much as he dared, applying salves, keeping the leg cold, terrified he would wake up one morning to find that it had gone black during the night.

Following Blind Orlo's recovery, the apothecary could have broken away, found some other life. But he was duty-bound to his blind companion, and so he stayed; and this, perhaps, was only an excuse for his fear of a world in which his standing was uncertain. Protected, for the first half of his life, by monks, and guarded by hajduks these past ten years, he did not know how to give up the certainty of unquestioning brotherhood. Without it, he would be powerless.

At Blind Orlo's side, the apothecary acquired the foundations of deceit he would come to abhor. For years, he followed Blind Orlo from village to village, preying on the superstitions of the simple and easily led. They played the same trick in each town: the blind soothsayer and his companion with the unfortunate face. Officially, Blind Orlo read tea leaves, bones, dice, innards, the movement of swallows, and his condition lent credibility to his claims. But all the intuition his lies required was relayed to him in unspoken signals by the apothecary, who learned to read the desires and fears of his followers in the lines of their mouths and eyes, foreheads, the minute movements of their hands, vocal inconsistencies, gestures of which they themselves were unaware. Then Blind Orlo told them what they wanted to hear.

'Your crop will prosper,' he would say to the farmer with callused palms.

'A handsome boy from the next village is in your thoughts,' he would say to the virgin who stared at him across the pink entrails of the dove she had brought. 'Do not worry, you are also in his.'

Serving as Blind Orlo's eyes, the apothecary learned to read white lies, to distinguish furtive glances between secret lovers that would precipitate future weddings, to harness old family hatreds dredged up in fireside conversations that allowed him to foresee conflicts, fights, sometimes even murders. He learned, too, that when confounded by the extremes of life—whether good or bad—people would turn first to superstition to find meaning, to stitch together unconnected events in order to understand what was happening. He learned that, no matter how grave the secret, how imperative absolute silence, someone would always feel the urge to confess, and an unleashed secret was a terrible force.

While the apothecary was learning this way about deceit, he stumbled, quite accidentally, onto his own medical prowess. It started slowly at first, with services that supplemented the soothsaying profession: herbs for migraines, fertility incantations, brews for impotence. But pretty soon

352

he was splinting bones and feeling spleens, putting his fingers against the swollen lymph nodes of influenza sufferers. Once, without prior training, he excised a deeply embedded bullet from the shoulder of a town constable. It was a gift, they said wherever he went; they had never seen such a calm, authoritative, compassionate young man. It was a gift to them all, but it was a gift to the apothecary as well: as healer he was the giver of answers, the vanquisher of fear, the restorer of order and stability. Blind Orlo, with his lies and manipulations, had power, yes; but real power, he came to understand, lay in the definite and the concrete, in predictions backed by evidence, in the continued life of a man you claimed you could save, and the death of a man you pronounced was certain to die.

Of course, neither the apothecary nor Blind Orlo could account for the unpredictability of their ventures, the unreliability of people, omitted details that made an enormous difference in situations that were impossible to read. It was probably not their first grave mistake; but it was the only one for which they were still around, and they paid dearly. In the town of Spašen, they counseled a well-to-do merchant, who was considering expanding his business, to take on an ambitious young protégé about whom the merchant had entertained serious doubts.

'Give the boy a position,' Blind Orlo had said. 'Youth reinvigorates the soul.'

Of course, neither he nor the apothecary could have guessed that the soul the young man was reinvigorating belonged, in fact, to the merchant's wife; or that the merchant would return home one night to find that the lady of the house had absconded with both the youthful protégé and the jar of money the merchant had kept hidden in the baptismal font of his family chapel. The merchant then drank for three days and three nights, on tab, without stopping, and, thus lubricated, shot Blind Orlo one evening as he and the apothecary were returning from supper at the miller's house.

The apothecary, who barely escaped with his life, would learn several weeks later that the jilted husband was a man of considerable determination: he had placed a modest but compelling bounty, and a charge of fraudulence, on the apothecary's head, making it necessary for him to move on. The apothecary mourned for his fallen compatriot, the last link to his first life; but by that time, the apothecary was certain of what he wanted, what he longed for: stability, lawfulness, belonging. And he found them, some years later, in a remote corner of the Northern Mountains, in a tiny village through which he had been passing when a mother of four had fallen ill, and he had stopped to care for her, and never left.

Marko Parović was not yet born when the apothecary began, slowly but surely, to set up shop in Galina—but he tells the story of the apothecary's arrival as though he himself witnessed it: the wagon with its unnamed trinkets, the dozens and dozens of crated jars slowly carried in through the door of the abandoned cobbler's shop, the counter built with the help of young men from the village, the gasp that went up at the arrival of the caged ibis. How, for years, the children of the village reveled in attempting to teach the ibis to talk; and how the apothecary, out of sheer delight, never attempted to correct them. How his only fee, for many years, was a log for his fire; how a single log from your stockpile earned you the privilege of sitting in one of his varnished wooden chairs, of revealing to him the secrets of what ailed you, your headaches and nightmares, the discomforts of certain foods and the difficulties of lovemaking, and how the apothecary, as if he had all the time in the world, would listen and nod and take notes, open your mouth and peer into your eyes, feel the bones of your spine, recommend this dried grass and that.

Unaware as he is of the apothecary's past, Marko Parović can tell me nothing of what the apothecary must have felt during those blissful years, when he finally earned the trust of the village, the security of their faith, the power that came from enchanting them with his ability to mend their small pains and arrest the advance of death. How it must have relieved him, after a lifetime of violence, to find himself being asked to preside over trivial land disputes and trade squabbles in a village with only one gun. And of course Marko Parović can tell me nothing of how the apothecary must have felt at the first appearance of Luka's deaf-mute bride, a Mohammedan like him, or how the villagers' treatment of her must have reinforced his need to keep himself a secret, to keep them mesmerized and unsuspecting, however ashamed he must have been for neglecting to intervene on her behalf.

He barely remembered Luka as a child, but he was wary of the butcher's son as soon as he'd returned: Luka, who'd seen the world; Luka, who was a brute without being a fool, an inexcusable

355

combination; Luka, who had, despite the distrust between them, appeared ashen-faced at the shop door late one night two autumns ago, eyes bloodshot, voice cracking. 'You'd better come—I think she's dead.'

There in Luka's house he had at last seen proof of what he had suspected for months: the girl was in the corner, twisted up under a broken table that had been driven against the wall. He couldn't imagine how the table had ended up there, how she had fallen under it. He couldn't bring himself to drag her out. Her neck looked loose, broken, and if she was still alive he could kill her by moving her. So he dragged the table across the room while Luka sat on the kitchen floor, sobbing into his fists. The girl's face was unrecognizable, gelled with blood, her hair matted down and the scalp bleeding into the floor. Her nose was broken—he was certain of that without touching her. He put his hands on the floor, brought his face close, knelt like this for a long time before he finally found her breath, caught in a thick, blood-clotted bubble of spit that stretched out between her lips.

He assessed the damage: kneecap shattered; the scalp studded with shards of some kind of crockery; left hand mangled, twisted back toward the arm, a spear of bone stretching the skin just above her wrist. At first, he thought three of her front teeth were gone—but then he put his fingers in her mouth and found them, slammed back into the ridges of her palate. He used a spoon to brace them, brought them forward again with a wet crack that he would feel in the tips of his fingers. They would never set properly, but at least she wouldn't lose them. He sponged the blood from her face,

356

bandaged her head, splinted up what he could and immobilized the rest, tied the jaw shut with dressings, chinned her up like a corpse, and that was how she looked, lying on a cot in the front room, four days going by before she opened her good eye. The apothecary had been going to Luka's house twice daily to ice her face and ribs and smooth balm into the cuts on her head, all the while convinced that she would slip away between visits, and he was stunned when she looked at him.

The last time he stopped by to look in on her, the apothecary said to Luka: 'If this happens again, I will run you out.'

He had meant it, too; and, back then, he'd had enough heft in the village to manage it. But then came the epidemic that claimed the children of the village—Mirica of the oleander leaves, my grandfather's friend Dušan—and the long, terrifying fight in which he had seen them slip out of his grasp one by one. After that, the line at his door had dwindled; patients came around twice, three times, to make sure they were on the path to recovery, to question the herbs he had prescribed to them. His power—which had, until that moment, elevated him even above the priest, that last-resort mediator for the next world—was suddenly poised on the edge of a knife. He was, and always had been, an outsider, and when his dependability failed, he had felt his hold on the village slipping. He had resolved that he would defend the girl; but, on the heels of his defeat, that promise, made largely to himself, had fallen behind his efforts to regain the villagers' trust, reestablish their faith in and submission to him. It was becoming apparent to him that these efforts, too, had failed.

*   *   *

The men of the village had started a small bonfire in the square, and the fire was sending black sheets of smoke down the street. Some of the men had gone across the pasture and into the foothills to search for Dariša's camp, to find his wagon and belongings, which they half-expected to have vanished, just like Dariša himself. A few of the men had paused by the butcher's house and gone no farther; Jovo had found courage enough to run up and peer through the window, but had seen nothing.

My grandfather stood with his wet boots on the porch of the apothecary's shop, watching the icicles above the door twist into drops that rapped a quiet rhythm on the railings and the trees. When the apothecary opened the door, my grandfather just said 'Please.' And then he said it over and over again, until the apothecary pulled him inside and knelt down beside him with a warm glass of water and made him drink it very, very slowly.

Then the apothecary brushed the hair out of my grandfather's eyes, and said: 'What has happened?'

*   *   *

The steps of her house were powdered with snow, and the apothecary went up and stood on the porch. In his hand he carried the bottle in which he mixed the drink for expectant mothers, a drink he had often made of chalk and sugar and water. He tapped on the door with his fingers, lightly at first,

358

so that the sound would not carry across the pasture; when she did not answer, he banged harder until he remembered that she was deaf, and then he stood there, feeling stupid. Then he tried the door, and it gave. He paused, for a moment, remembering the gun, the blacksmith's gun, which had not surfaced in the village since Luka had brought it back down, wondering if the girl still had it, and how he might announce himself. He pushed the door open and looked around, and then he opened it farther and stepped into the doorway.

The tiger's wife was sitting on the floor by the fireplace, drawing something in the hearth with her finger. The fire was bright on her face, and her hair had settled around her eyes so that he couldn't see her properly, and she did not look up when he went in and shut the door behind him. She was sitting wrapped in her Turkish silks, purples and golds and reds draped around her shoulders like water, and her legs, which were folded under the bulge of her stomach, were bare and thin. What struck him most was the sparseness of the room; there was a table, a few pots and bowls over the tabletop. There was no trace of the gun.

She had not seen him yet, and he did not want to surprise her, but there was nothing he could do about that now. He took a step forward, and then another, and then she turned abruptly and saw him, and he held up his hands to show her that he was harmless and unarmed.

'Don't be afraid,' he said. Then he bowed a little and touched his fingers to his lips and forehead. It had been almost forty years since he had made the gesture.

She got up in one swift motion, rolled to her

feet, and the cloth slid down her shoulders when she did it, and she stood there, her face tight and furious, and the apothecary continued to hold his half bow and didn't move. She was very small, the tiger's wife, with thin shoulders and a long thin neck, which a river of sweat had caked with salt. Her belly was enormous and tight and round, unbalancing in the way it overpowered her frame and pulled her hips forward.

'The baby,' he said, pointing at her. He grabbed his stomach under his coat and shook it a little, and then held up the bottle. 'For the baby.'

But she had placed him, he could see that— remembered him, remembered his house, remembered that he had given her back to Luka— and the look coming over her now was one of intense revulsion. Her whole body was shaking.

The apothecary tried to explain. He shook the bottle again, smiling, holding it high so she could see it. The water was cloudy inside.

'For the baby,' he said again, and pointed again at her belly. He made a cradling gesture with his arms, pointed to himself. But her face did not change until he took a step toward her.

He expected something to shift between them, then. In such a short time, she had successfully frightened the villagers into reverential awe. He envied her that, admired it despite himself. He wondered if she could see it. She had done it without effort or intention; and even now, he suspected she didn't know she had done it at all.

The tiger's wife must have seen the hesitation in his face, because at that moment, her upper lip lifted and her teeth flashed out, and she hissed at him with the ridge of her nose folded up against her eyes. The sound—the only sound he ever heard her make, when she had made no sound over broken bones and bruises that spread like continents over her body—went through him like a rifle report and left him there, left him paralyzed. She was naked, furious, and he knew suddenly that she had learned to make that sound mimicking a face that wasn't human. He left with the bottle, without turning his back to her, reaching behind him to feel for the door, and when he opened it he couldn't even feel the cold air coming in. The heat of the house stayed with him like a mark as he walked back.

*   *   *

A little way down the pasture, where the creek had begun to come back in black flashes through the ice, the apothecary could see Jovo waiting for him. 'Go back to your house,' the apothecary said.

'She in there?' Jovo said, moving forward a little.

The apothecary stopped, turned. 'Go home,' he said, and waited until Jovo vanished.

My grandfather had been waiting with the ibis for the apothecary's return.

'Is she well?' my grandfather said.

The apothecary looked at my grandfather wordlessly for a long moment. Before he had gone out—after my grandfather had told him everything, after the apothecary had promised to help her—my grandfather had watched him light the lamp at his counter and bring jars and spoons and an empty glass down from the shelf. My grandfather had stood with his nose running and

361

watched the big, round hands of the apothecary working the mortar and pestle. Wiping out the inside of the glass. Bringing out the golden scales. Measuring the powders. He had watched the apothecary pour the warm water into a bottle and put in the sugar and chalk powder and mint leaves. He had watched the white clouding of the glass as the apothecary capped the glass with his palm, shook it, then wiped it down with a cloth. Rinsed his hands.

Now the apothecary had come back with that same bottle still full, and he said to my grandfather: 'She doesn't know me.' He held the bottle out. 'So, here, you must run and give her this yourself. She needs it.'

'Everyone will see me,' my grandfather said.

'Everyone has gone.'

So it was my grandfather who crossed the square, carrying the clouded glass, looking over his shoulder at the empty square; my grandfather who went into the butcher's house, smiling; my grandfather who held the hand of the tiger's wife when she propped the glass against her lips, my grandfather who wiped her chin.

It didn't take very long after that.

*   *   *

There is a huge tree just outside my grandfather's village on the bank of the stream that leads down from the Galinica River. In winter, the red boughs arch up from the trunk, bare as hip bones, curving like hands clasped in prayer. The tree stands near the fence where the braided cornfields begin, and Marko Parović tells me the people of Galina avoid

362

it at all costs; its branches, he says, cast a net in which souls are caught as they rise to heaven, and the ravens that roost there pick the souls out of the bark like worms.

It was here that Marko Parović witnessed the death of the apothecary of Galina, more than sixty years ago. Marko takes me down to the edge of the village to show me, to tap the trunk with his cane, stand back and point to the tree so that I will understand: picture the hangman, a green-eyed youth from a village to the south, recruited by the invading troops moving through the lowlands, and asked—not forced—to carry out the executions as they went from town to town. They dispatched headmen, the instigators of rebellion and resistance, or just men with a loyal following—the kind of following the apothecary had once again, now that everyone knew, without having to talk about it, that he had saved them from her, that he had been the cause of her death.

The apothecary—'such an ugly man,' Marko says to me, drawing his hand across his face, 'ugly, but great'—stood on the cornfield fence with the noose around his neck, wondering why they hadn't shot him instead, and still hoping they would. Of the sixty men who had come to the village, Marko tells me, the Germans numbered twelve, and these twelve did not come to the hanging. They were in the tavern, drinking, putting their cigarettes out in the patches of soil laid bare by the melt that had brought them there. The men who stood by the tree that afternoon were men whose language Marko Parović understood, and whose hatred the apothecary understood even more, and they had brought the entire village out to see the apothecary

363

writhe on the rope like a gutted animal, the first of many pointless examples.

Marko does not remember seeing my grandfather among the spectators at the hanging, though he was probably there, wide-eyed and hopeless, the victim of a betrayal he had already put together, barely speaking at all since the morning after his last visit, when they had found her dead on her own porch. That day, he wailed for hours, and when he looked for help, for absolution, the face he saw was kind but firm. Mother Vera said, 'Now it is done, so leave it to God.' After the war, she swore to him, and it kept him going. After the war, they would leave the village, go elsewhere, start anew. The summer Mother Vera died, my grandfather was already a doctor, already the man he would become.

But Marko does remember the intense stillness of the apothecary before the recruit kicked his legs off the fence, the apothecary's eyes steady and resigned, all the fight pulled out of him by something no one present completely understood, but everyone would later relegate to responsibility, to the grace of self-sacrifice.

'They didn't even bury him in the graveyard,' Marko says, bracing himself against his cane, waving his free hand toward the church. 'We had to put him there ourselves, after the war.'

'Where is the girl buried?' it suddenly occurs to me to ask him.

'What girl?' he says.

'The girl,' I say. 'The tiger's wife.'

'What has that got to do with anything?' he says.

THE RIVER

Halfway up the hill, the figure stopped to rest, and
I stopped too, in the cover of a low, wind-strangled
tree that was leaning over the road, the smell of
the lavender and sage straining my nostrils. He was
standing in the middle of the road, swaying on his
feet as he looked around, and I had the distinct
feeling that he was looking back at me, that he
knew I was there, and was trying to decide what to
do with me. I had not planned out what I intended
to do if he turned and came to confront me, and
for the first time I regretted the white coat I was
still wearing, and the backpack rustling against my
shoulders. I stood still while the man turned from
one side to the other, a slow, ponderous kind of
dance, shifting from one foot to the next, shoulders
hunched forward, ribs twisted up in the shadows,
so that I found myself thinking *mora,* and laughing
at myself in my head.

Then the moon came out, and threw the whole
plane of the hill into sharp relief, the shadows of
the trees and the humped rocks along the side of
the road, and I saw that the man was moving again.
Slowly, slowly, rolling on, he went up the hill. I
waited for him to disappear around a bend, and
then I set off after him. For a long time, now, I had
felt a sense of being tipped back, the steep thrust
of the mountain tilting forward over me the closer
I got to it, and now, as I came around the bend in
the road, the path turned right, and became what

felt and sounded like a shallow, almost empty riverbed, which led away from town across the flat, wind-washed side of the hill. Below me lay the iridescent outline of the beach, lit up with ice cream signs and restaurant terraces, harbor lights smeared in the water, the square of darkness around the monastery where Fra Antun's garden stood empty.

The man was moving steadily up the riverbed, through the thin channel of water, toward a timbered rise that was widening fast on the hill before us, and I walked behind in the open, hoping he would not turn to look for me again, because now that we were moving sideways across the hill I couldn't hide any longer. The wind had stopped, and, it seemed, the cicadas, too, and there was no sound except the slight cracking of the riverbed under my feet, and the chiming of my backpack clasps, and the occasional rustle of something that ran through the grass.

Far ahead, the figure walked unevenly, pushing himself forward through the water. He made a strange silhouette from behind, leaning forward, big feet padding along quietly on the earth, the head rolling over the shoulder. There was nothing encouraging about the man, nothing that indicated it was a good idea to keep following him. I stopped once, for a few minutes, my shoes soaked through, and I watched his advance as he moved away from me, and thought hard about turning back.

Up ahead, the man dropped suddenly, a swinging movement that brought him low, and then he straightened up again and moved on. I gave him more distance, straining to see ahead in the dark. Something was there, something that had

366

intercepted the man's forward momentum, and as I came closer it came out of the darkness at me slowly. It was a chain, I realized, a rusted metal chain that spanned the riverbed, slung between two trees on either bank. It was creaking a little, and as I came up to it, I saw, hanging between the two strands of the chain, the familiar red triangle: MINES. And any doubt I'd had—in my grandfather's stories, in my own sanity, in the wild darkness of the walk—fell away, and I was certain, certain that I was following the deathless man, certain of the madness that came with meeting him, the kind of madness that could make my grandfather tie a person to a cinder block and throw him in a pond, the kind of madness that was forcing me to throw my backpack over the chain and go down on my hands and knees and crawl into a minefield and stand up and keep going.

Then the man entered the trees, and I hung back for a little while, not knowing whether to follow him in. He could hide, I realized, behind some tree and watch me groping around in the dark, then collect me at the crossroads when I stepped on something I thought was innocuous and went up in a shower of blood. Or I could lose my way in the wood and be stuck there until morning. But I had come this far, so I went in, into the complete loss of light, the dead silence of the pines, thick-trunked, scissor-needled, ranged close together. I was breathing hard, I realized, because the slope had been steeper for some time, and the water weighed down my movements. I tried to quiet myself so that the man would not hear me behind him while we were in the wood. The riverbed wavered up through the pines, and my

367

feet were slipping on the wet rocks and needles that lay piled in it, and the cracking pinecones that kept getting caught in the fronts of my shoes were making too much noise. I kept expecting to look up from trying to see where I was going to find that I had come up on the man suddenly, or that he had stopped and was waiting for me. I couldn't see anything in that darkness, but I could picture him clearly, standing with his hat and the little jar, impatient, looking at me with a slanted face that had a sharp nose and big, unforgiving eyes and that persistent smile my grandfather had told me about.

When I came out of the forest, I had lost him. The riverbed had become a dry, empty path ringed with grass, rising sharply with the hill, and I forced myself up with my hands out for balance. At the top, the ground leveled off into some kind of field, and there stood a low stone bridge that rose over the stream, and I went up the bank and crossed it. From the arch, I could see houses, the outlines of abandoned houses rising on both sides of the dried-up riverbed, blocked here and there by the thick, rustling crowns of trees that were very different from the trees in the wood I had just come through. It occurred to me that this must be the old village that Fra Antun had mentioned, the one people had abandoned in favor of living closer to the sea after the Second World War. The first house I reached was on my left, and it stood apart from the others. It had a rounded façade with what looked like a small slit of a window on the now-unroofed upper level, glassless windows that had been smashed in, the grass from the field reaching up, high enough to touch the three or four shutters that were still hinged to their frames. The man I had followed here could have gone inside the house, could have been looking at me through the darkness of the empty windows. I couldn't see inside at all, and I passed by this first house slowly, looking over my shoulder as I went. Part of the wall around the house was broken, and there was a paved area inside that led off somewhere into what looked like a garden. The deathless man could be there, too, I thought, but if he was, I didn't want to find him.

The next house was on my right, shaded by one of the big trees, and I realized that it had once been a two-story inn. A wide stone staircase zigzagged across the front of the building, and empty flower boxes now hung from the staircase railing. The long balcony on the second floor had once supported a lattice with vines, but now it was just a couple of uneven rusted rods that stuck straight up, before fading into the partly collapsed roof.

The rest of the houses were clustered together along the streambed, yawning with shadows, and I walked sideways, first facing one bank and then the other, past crumbling archways and stacks of broken shutters, past piles of pallets, deserted courtyards scattered with buckets and gardening tools that lay heavy with disuse and rust with the grasses growing up around them. I passed what looked like the open veranda of a restaurant nestled between the corners of two buildings; there were a few tables and chairs scattered around the stone floor, and, to my surprise, a single plastic chair, on which an enormous cat was asleep, silent and unmoving, fur gray in the moonlight.

I was trying to remember—as though I needed

that kind of thought at the time—the particulars of those stories about mountain spirits, the ones that lived in fields and woodlands and existed for the sole pleasure of misleading idiot travelers. My grandma had once told me about some man from Sarobor who had gone up into the hills after his sheep and found himself eating with a house full of the dead, to which he had found his way by following a little girl with a white bonnet who turned out not to be a little girl at all, but something malicious and impossible to forget, something that changed him, preoccupied him until his own death.

Ahead of me, the streambed dipped down into a steep incline and beat a wavering trail into the valley below. There were a few final houses clustered around that bend in the road before the wilderness grew up again in clumps, and among them, coming down the trail sideways so I wouldn't slip, I saw a very small stone house with a raised threshold and a low, low green door, the only door that still hung in its frame in the entire empty village, and between the door and the ground I could see light.

On any other night, I would have turned and gone back the way I had come. But on any other night, I wouldn't have come at all. The man I was following, I said to myself, had gone into this house, unless he was already standing directly behind me, unless he had been watching me since I had come into the village. That thought alone was enough to make me climb the cracked stone staircase. It took me a little longer to open the door, but in the end I did open it, and I did go inside.

You're Gavran Gailé, I was going to say. And then whatever happened next would happen.

* * *

'Hello, Doctor.'

'It's you.'

'Of course. Come in, Doctor. Come in. What are you doing here? Come—shut the door. Take a seat, Doctor. This is a very bad business. You could have been hurt, gotten lost. I didn't realize you were following me.'

'I saw you in the vineyard.'

'Well, now, I didn't notice. I didn't realize—I would have stopped and made you turn around. Come to the fire. Come sit, I'll make room.'

'That's all right, I'll stand.'

'You must be tired. Please, sit down—here, sit just here. I'll move these aside. I've meant to get the place ordered, but there's never time. It's always so late. Come sit down. Don't mind the flowers, just push them all this way, and sit down.'

'I don't want to intrude.'

'You can move the flowers closer, Doctor, closer to the fire. The fire dries them faster.'

'I'm sorry.'

'The faster they dry, the less they smell. As you see, I do not throw them away. Are you cold, Doctor?'

'I should go back.'

'That is out of the question. You must wait. We must finish here.'

'I've made a mistake.'

'But it is all right now, and will be. You are here, and safe. We'll walk back together. Come—put these coins in the barrel for me.'

'My God. How much is this?'

'There was more, before.'

'I don't even recognize some of this currency.'

'Some of it is from before the war. Some of it is even older.'

'What's this?'

'That's Roman bronze—the hills are full of coins like that. It may not mean much to you, but it's still payment for the dead.'

'What will you do with it all?'

'Give it away. It's a bad business, giving the money of the dead to the living. But it's shameful to leave it sitting here when it could do some good.'

'You may have to expand.'

'Your feet are on the drawings, Doctor—let me move them.'

'I'm sorry.'

'I must find somewhere else to put them, somewhere away from the hearth. It wouldn't do for them to catch. Some are quite old. This one— see—the man who left this painting is himself dead now. I have been bringing coins from his grave here since last year.'

'You're the *mora*.'

'Not always. There's been a *mora* over a hundred years. Then the war came and they believed nothing. My wife believed nothing, she couldn't believe after what happened to my son. She would come home from his grave and say, *the drawings people are putting there get wet and the colors run everywhere, and the flowers get old and dirty and they smell, and all for what? For me to feel better? There is a hole in the ground and my son is buried in it.* Water, Doctor.'

'I'm sorry?'

'The water, behind you. Please. For my hands. One night, I clear the grave and bring the flowers and drawings here. No one comes here. Most of the mines are gone, but they say it is still dangerous. I cannot throw away the things from my son's grave—maybe even I believe. When my wife comes home the next night, it is as if someone has breathed a secret to her. She asks me if I've seen the grave—it is clear and clean, and she stands beside it and feels our son at peace. Human hands, she says, haven't cleared the grave. It's the *mora*. She knows this in her bones. Then she goes back and puts coins out, and what can I do? Besides bring them here.'

'But this isn't all from one grave.'

'No. Pretty soon people are putting coins on the graves of all their loved ones. Leaving more flowers. Clothes, sometimes food. They keep the dead safe and well fed, they comfort themselves. Sometimes I climb up here with bagfuls, and the walk is hard. Sacred earth, they say. Leave something for your dead here and it will reach them. The *mora* will take it.'

'And no one knows?'

'Someone always knows, Doctor. But I would be happy if it were only you, if only you are the one who knows.'

'No one from the village? Not your son?'

'If there are people who know, they are always the ones who do not say what they know, so it is difficult to tell them from the ones who merely think they know. Someone must know by now. Not that it's me, perhaps—but they must know. And

373

still they keep setting things down. So I keep bringing them here. You'll not tell my wife, Doctor? You won't, will you?'

But he had no need to ask. I had been taught long ago that there are some stories you keep to yourself.

People who talk about my grandfather's death now talk about the boys from Zdrevkov, the land mine that ripped into their legs and shredded their bodies. At the doctors' luncheon, I'm told, aging men pay their respects, admire how my grandfather, gaunt and gray-skinned, undeterred by an illness he hid like shame, abandoned everything and traveled four hundred miles to save the boys' lives. As I've pointed out to Zóra, whenever she calls me from the Neurology Institute in Zurich in a panic at all hours of the night—more and more often now that her son has reached that age where he understands objects best by hiding them up his nose—the fact that the boys themselves did not survive does not figure in the telling.

The doctors' knowledge does not extend to my grandfather's bag of belongings, or how I brought it home to my grandma two days after the funeral, or how it sat on the hall table for thirty days, as if part of my grandfather were still living with us, sitting quietly on the hallway table, all but demanding sunflower seeds. Leaving room for whatever miscalculations we'd made about his death, on the fortieth day my grandma opened the hospital bag—before taking his silk pajamas out from under the pillow beside her head, before putting away his clogs. When I came home from the hospital that night, I saw her as a widow for the first time, my grandfather's widow, sitting quietly in his green armchair with his belongings arranged in a cookie tin on her lap.

I sat on a footstool beside her and watched her

go through them. My mother was already there. For a long time, no one said anything, and there were only my grandma's hands with their smooth knuckles and big rings, and then my grandma said, 'Let's have some coffee,' and my mother got up to brew it, leaving my grandma room to disagree with her, to correct her technique, point out the obvious: 'Don't put that pot there—use the board, for God's sake.'

* * *

Of course I never told anyone about the firelit room in the abandoned village, the broken table and barrel brimming with coins, the carpet of dead flowers, rows of jars and bottles—clay and porcelain, glass and stone, wax-lipped lids and corks and caps broken or missing—empty offerings, cobwebs clinging to the lips of the bottles and the lids of the jars. The fire putting round shadows between their sides and edges, and all the jars and the bottles singing, and the paintings of Bis stacked like papyrus scrolls against the wall, and me, promising not to tell and demanding an equal promise in return, kneeling to open the bag in secret, absolved by a room which, for the rest of the world, did not exist.

In the bag I found his wallet and his hat, his gloves. I found his doctor's coat, folded neatly in half. But I did not find *The Jungle Book*, for which I searched, mourned in that hot little room above Brejevina. It took me a long time to accept that it was gone, gone entirely, gone from his coat and from our house, gone from the drawers in his office and the shelves in our living room.

When I think of my grandfather's last meeting with the deathless man, I picture the two of them in casual conversation, sitting together on the porch of that bar in Zdrevkov, *The Jungle Book*, the terms of the wager, closed on the tabletop between them. My grandfather is in his best suit, and the deathless man has taken him out, not for a cup of coffee, but for a beer, a long laugh before they take their journey to the crossroads together. For once in the long history of their acquaintance, they are not alone, and they go by unnoticed, two men you could pass on the street without a second glance. They have the comfortable demeanor of old friends, of two people between whom a lifetime has passed. For the deathless man, it is more than one lifetime, but you would never know it from looking at him. According to my grandfather's descriptions, he is a young man at ninety-five, and he will still be a young man long after my grandfather's forty days, and probably long after mine.

The few doctors who might have chuckled over the book my grandfather always carried in his pocket would probably guess that it had been lost, or stolen at Zdrevkov, misplaced somewhere on a dying man's journey. But the book is gone—not lost, not stolen, gone—and to me this means that my grandfather did not die as he had once told me men die—in fear—but in hope, like a child: knowing he would meet the deathless man again, certain he would pay his debt. Knowing, above all, that I would come looking, and find what he had left for me, all that remained of *The Jungle Book* in the pocket of his doctor's coat, that folded-up, yellowed page torn from the back of the book, with

377

a bristle of thick, coarse hairs clenched inside. *Galina,* says my grandfather's handwriting, above and below a child's drawing of the tiger, who is curved like the blade of a scimitar across the page. *Galina,* it says, and that is how I know how to find him again, in Galina, in the story he hadn't told me but perhaps wished he had.

*　　*　　*

Eventually, I will know enough to tell myself the story of my grandfather's childhood. But I will not explain what happened between the tiger and his wife. I think it's probably possible to explain it. It would be simple enough to reason away the tiger's attachment: he was only half-wild, and in his partial tameness he missed, without being able to articulate it, the companionship and predictability of life at the citadel. However expertly he learned to fend for himself, his life as a tiger had been tainted since birth—maybe that great, deadly Shere Khan light my grandfather believed in had already been extinguished. He had been dulled at the edges by circumstances, and it was simply easier for him to succumb to being hand-fed. It's possible to reduce the tiger's attachment to some predictable accident of nature, to make him as mysterious as a bear rummaging through a pile of overturned trash cans—but that is not my grandfather's tiger; that is not the tiger on whose account my grandfather carried *The Jungle Book* in his pocket every day for the rest of his life, the tiger my grandfather kept at his side during the war, and the long years he and Mother Vera struggled in the City, and during his studies; the tiger who was with

378

him when he met my grandma, and taught at the University, and met the deathless man; the tiger he carried with him to Zdrevkov.

One could also say that the girl was young, and foolish, and for a time, incredibly, incredibly lucky. That it was her great fortune, despite the odds against her, to encounter a tiger who was not all tiger, to see him face-to-face when she saw him first, to somehow carry the same scent as an old keeper of his, to awaken some lost memory. But that, too, would be oversimplifying it.

Maybe it's enough to say he enjoyed the sensation of her hand between his eyes. She liked the way his flank smelled when she curled up against it to sleep.

*   *   *

In the end, I cannot tell you who or what she was. I cannot even say for certain what happened to Luka, though I tend to side with those in Galina who say that he awoke, after leaving the girl tied in the smokehouse for the tiger, to find her kneeling at the foot of his bed, her wrists skinned raw, holding the blacksmith's gun against his mouth.

If the situation had been different—if the people of Galina had been more aware of their own ephemeral isolation, more conscious that it was only a matter of time before war tightened around them—their regard for the tiger and his wife might have been more cursory. *Isn't it strange,* they might have said, *here is a kind of love story,* and then moved on to some other point of gossip. But they attached their anxious grief to the girl so they could avoid looking past her to what was

379

coming. After her death, their time with her became the unifying memory that carried them into the spring, through the arrival of the Germans with their trucks, and later their railroad, which the villagers were made to build; and finally the train, the rattle and cough of the tracks that pulled them awake at night (every time they thought *don't stop here, don't stop*), and even further than that.

When you ask the people of Galina today: 'Why don't you let your children out after dark?' their answers are vague and uncomfortable. They say, *what's the point of being out after dark? You can't see anything—there is nothing but trouble. Why would we let them hang around at the corners, smoking cigarettes, playing dice, when there's work to do in the morning?* But the truth is, whether they think about him or not, the tiger is always there, in their movements, in their speech, in the preventive gestures that have become a part of their everyday lives. He is there when the red deer scatter down the mountainside, and the whole valley smells of fear; he is there when they find the carcasses of the stags split open and devoured, red ribs standing clear of the skins, and they refuse to talk to one another about it. They are aware, all the time, that the tiger has never been found, that he has never been killed. Men don't go to cut timber alone; there is a strong stipulation against virgins crossing the pasture on a full-moon night, even though no one is really sure of the consequences.

The tiger has died up there, they reason to themselves, starving on its own loneliness, on walking the ridge, on waiting for her. He has shriveled, rumpled up like skin, lain down somewhere, watching the crows wait on him to die.

Still, most summers, young boys take the sheep up to the ridge, hoping the sound of their bells might lure the tiger out of hiding. When they get to a clearing, someplace that looks like it might be what they're looking for, they cover their ears with the palms of their hands and call for him, trying to make a noise that sounds more like an animal than a human voice, but the sound that comes out of them sounds like itself, and nothing else.

There is, however, and always has been, a place on Galina where the trees are thin, a wide space where the saplings have twisted away and light falls broken and dappled on the snow. There is a cave here, a large flat slab of stone where the sun is always cast. My grandfather's tiger lives there, in a glade where the winter does not go away. He is the hunter of stag and boar, a fighter of bears, a great source of confusion for the lynx, a rapt admirer of the colors of birds. He has forgotten the citadel, the nights of fire, his long and difficult journey to the mountain. Everything lies dead in his memory, except for the tiger's wife, for whom, on certain nights, he goes calling, making that tight note that falls and falls. The sound is lonely, and low, and no one hears it anymore.

ACKNOWLEDGMENTS

I am forever indebted to:

my parents, Maja and Jovan, whose faith is boundless and unfaltering; my baby brother, Alex, the best illustrator ever; my grandmother, Zahida, who is a rock.

Dr. Maša Kovacević—my traveling companion, diapers to dentures—whose tolerance of late-night phone calls was indispensable to the completion of this book, and whose wit and wisdom have reconnected me to my roots.

Alexi Zentner, who is a force of nature in every life he touches. We've traveled so far, we two.

Parini Shroff, for giving me the birthday present that set me back on the right path again, and whose love keeps lifting me higher.

my teachers: Patty Seyburn, whose faith kept me going; Alison Lurie, for her kindness; Stephanie Vaughn and Michael Koch, for their generosity; J. Robert Lennon, for his enthusiasm.

Ernesto Quiñonez, for insisting that it was 'not a question of if, but when,' and for seizures of laughter, and for *Cosmos*.

my agent, Seth Fishman, for taking a chance on me, and for having all the answers, and for being my friend.

my editor, Noah Eaker, whose voice has been the guiding light for the past two years, and who puts up with my belief that just five more minutes will make a difference; Arzu Tahsin, who is amazing; Susan Kamil and Jynne Martin, for making me feel at home at Random House.

Branden Jacobs-Jenkins, Deborah Treisman, Rafil Kroll-Zaidi, and C. Michael Curtis, whose support and kindness continue to overwhelm me; Judy Barringer and everyone at the Constance Saltonstall Foundation for the Arts.

Tricia, who is family, for reading my work since I was ten.

friends and loved ones, from California to New York: Jared, whom I still might grow up to be someday; David, who always knows what I'm talking about, no matter how obscure the reference; Danielle, who bends reality; Colleen, for knowing what to say, every time; Christine, still the most generous person I know; Jay, who is always with me; Yael and the Incredible Zentner Family—Laurie, Zoey and Sabine—who aren't actually a rock band, though they sound like one here.

None of this would have been possible without you.